BY THE LETTER

JULIA WOLF

MORE BOOKS BY JULIA

THE HARDER THEY FALL (Billionaire office romance)

Dear Grumpy Boss

Sincerely, Your Inconvenient Wife

P.S. You're Intolerable

Not So Truly Yours

The Seasons Change (Rock star romance)

Falling In Reverse

Stone Cold Notes

Faded in Bloom

Where Waves Break

Savage U (college romance)

Soft Like Thunder

Bright Like Midnight

Sweet Like Poison

Real Like Daydreams

Savage Academy (academy romance)
   Save One Thing
   These Two Wrongs
   Jump On Three

Blue is the Color (Rock star romance)
   Times Like These
   Watch Me Unravel
   Such Great Heights
   Under the Bridge

Unrequited (Rock star romance)
   Unrequited
   Misconception
   Dissonance

Never Blue Duet (Angsty rock star romance)
   Never Lasting
   Never Again

PLAYLIST

"Deep End" Holly Humberstone

"The Joke" Brandi Carlile

"Falling Down" Lil' Pee, XXXTENTACION

"Day After Tomorrow" Phoebe Bridgers

"Souvenir" boygenius, Julien Baker, Phoebe Bridgers

"Dear August" PJ Harding, Noah Cyrus

"July" Noah Cyrus

"Kiss Me" Dermot Kennedy

"Power Over Me" Dermot Kennedy

"Nothing Compares 2 U" Chris Cornell

"Like Gold" Vance Joy

"Please Notice" Christian Leave

"Where's My Love" SYML

"I Found" Amber Run

"Carry You" Novo Amor

"Sleep On The Floor" The Lumineers

https://open.spotify.com/playlist/3ekO9fdv4GUgG1RfRiqOAd?si=a2116f226bb24b76

CHAPTER ONE
Shira

I was nervous, but that wasn't anything new. My system was so used to it I barely noticed it anymore, and my body simply didn't react. My brain might've screamed, *"Danger, danger!"* while my body said, *"Meh. If I die, I die."* Which I was grateful for. If my heart started galloping every time my anxiety went haywire, I was fairly certain it would have shut down a decade ago.

Tonight, though, my palms were sweating, and there was a knot in my throat the size of a fist. Nerves and trepidation met with excitement and a smidge of arousal...which made sense, considering I was in a sex club.

A sex club.

This was Bea's doing. My fearless, live-out-loud friend knew countless secret corners of Denver and had contacts in every walk of life. She was the one who had told me about the app I'd joined strictly out of curiosity, and she'd pushed me to explore.

I hadn't told her about my...conversations with WhenIn-Rome—or Wim, as I called him. He knew me as Goldie. Wholly uncreative on my part since it was a shortening of my last name, Goldman, but the first time Wim typed "Heeyyy, Goldie," I'd decided I liked the nickname.

I'd arrived early, just in time to see the Shibari show on the intimate stage in the center of the lounge. A raven-haired woman in nothing but sheer black panties was being wrapped in red rope by two shirtless men. I hadn't intended to watch, but I'd found myself tucked in a dark corner, entranced by what I was seeing.

If asked later, I might not have been able to describe exactly what the woman looked like, but I would be able to recount in fine detail her expression of pure euphoria. And the men? Oh, the men... Their devotion to their task and the woman between them sent shivers across my skin.

Idly, I wondered if I could do something like that. Give up all control to one or two men and let them move me around and do with me what they wanted.

Not in front of others. Never that. But maybe...

From nowhere, a tall blonde appeared next to me, her elbow bumping my arm. She was watching the show, solely focused on what was happening in front of us.

"Do you like it?" she whispered after a few breathless minutes.

The fist in my throat flexed as my jitters skyrocketed. Unexpected conversations were difficult for me. The comfort of the shadows cloaking us was the only reason I was able to push out a reply.

"I've never seen anything like it."

She turned to me, and I forced myself to face her, tipping my head back. I barely scraped five feet, though my heels were helping tonight. She blinked down at me, her eyes big and guileless.

"Is this your first time here?"

I nodded. "Yes. Do you...come here often?"

She snickered, and when it dawned on me she was laughing at my cheesy pickup line and not *me*, I smiled back at her.

"Every night, actually," she replied. "I work here."

"Oh? Do you do"—I nodded toward the stage—"that sort of thing?"

"Unfortunately, no. I'm more of a paper pusher. But right now, I'm on a mission, and I think you're exactly who I'm looking for."

"Oh." I tucked my hair behind my ear. I'd worn it down like Wim had requested. "I really doubt that. I'm just here to meet—"

"You're Goldie, aren't you?"

My lips parted in surprise. "How did you know that?"

She gestured toward my outfit and hair. "I was told to find a woman in a red dress with long black hair. You fit that description, my darling."

I nodded, retucking the hair I'd just tucked. This was why I always wore it up. I fidgeted otherwise, and that drew more attention than I liked.

Wim must have told this woman how to find me. Wim, who, before this moment, had been a faceless man on the other side of my computer. A picture of a headless body I'd drooled over for the past few weeks. A promise of fantasies fulfilled.

Wim was real, and this was happening.

Tonight, we'd meet, and he'd take me.

Oh god.

My thighs pressed together as arousal surged to my core.

"That's me." If she heard the quiver in my response, she didn't react. Trembles rolled through my limbs, forcing me to press my hand to the wall beside me for support. How was I going to go through with this when just the barest mention of Wim made my knees weak?

Because I need this.

One night, when it didn't matter what I looked like or who I was. Where I didn't have to talk or think or wonder if I was doing the right thing. A few hours of human touch, pleasure, a physical connection. Oh, how I needed this.

"I knew it. I'm Samantha. You are going to have so much fun." She took my hand and squeezed it. "Room ten is ready for you. Are you ready for it?"

"No." I closed my eyes and swallowed hard. I'd come here for this. I *needed* it. "I mean, yes. I think so."

"Then come with me."

She kept my hand in hers, leading me through the club. The lounge was dimly lit and luxuriously appointed. Couples and groups were scattered around. No one was having sex, but there was an overt erotic flavor to the atmosphere as if everyone was on edge but dragging out the anticipation until it reached its peak.

"You're going to love this, Goldie. I haven't been in room ten, but I've heard stories. It sounds delightful."

I breathed a laugh. "Delightful?"

"Mmhmm." We turned down a hallway with padded leather walls and several closed doors. "To be freely used...usually, I'm more of a participant, but I wouldn't mind someone bending me over and taking what they want every once in a while."

Before I could come up with an appropriate response—*was* there an appropriate response?—we came to a stop in front of a black door emblazoned with a large, white ten.

Samantha unlocked the door and pushed it open. "Your evening awaits, Goldie." Her brows waggled. "Have the time of your life, darling."

When I didn't move, she laughed, shoved me hard enough to get me going, then closed the door behind me.

I was all alone, with sweaty palms and wet panties.

Room ten looked like a studio apartment decked in mood lighting. Flickering electric candles flanked a king-size bed with a grand iron headboard. The other half of the room was a living area with even more electric candles on every hard surface surrounding a couch, armchair, and coffee table. There was even a small, sturdy dining table that hooked my attention. Well, not the table, but what was on top of it.

A gold mask and a slip of paper.

Trailing a finger over the smooth surface of the mask, I picked up the note.

Goldie,

I can't wait to see you.

Put the mask on and relax on the couch. I'll be there soon.

* *Wim*

A quiver vibrated my belly. He'd touched this paper. This was his handwriting. Without thinking, I rubbed it against my cheek and down my chest.

Wim and I had talked about how tonight would go over the app. Consent was important to him, and in a situation like this, we both needed to be on the same wavelength before we even met.

WhenInRome: *We won't talk. I'll do what I want with you.*

Goldie: *Will you hurt me?*

WhenInRome: *Never. But I won't ask permission. You're going to give it to me now, but you have the power to revoke it. All you have to do is tell me to stop.*

Goldie: I won't want you to stop.

WhenInRome: *Believe me, Goldie, I won't want to either. But I will. Know that.*

Goldie: I know it. You have my permission to take me, Wim. I want it so badly.

WhenInRome: *I guarantee I want it even more. I'm going to use you up until you're nothing but a panting, satisfied heap. Then I might use you again.*

Goldie: As many times as you want. It's okay if I'm nothing but ether by the time you're finished with me.

WhenInRome: *That kind of carte blanche is dangerous to a man like me. I have a thing for excess.*

Goldie: As long as that means making me come an excessive number of times before I become incorporeal…

WhenInRome: *Goldie…only you could make me laugh like a lunatic while I'm hard as* *steel. Fuck, I can't wait to get my hands on you.*

Wim knew exactly what I wanted. To be used, like Samantha had said. To be taken without discussion. Anonymously. In room ten, we were Goldie and Wim, not Shira and...well, whoever he was outside these walls.

He'd seen my pictures, just as I'd seen his. Anonymous, no faces, just bodies. I knew he wanted me, at least the parts he'd seen, and that was more than enough for me. This wasn't a grand romance. Wim would give me what I needed without having to go through the song and dance of courting or hoping to get picked up at a bar. Not that I would ever, *ever* do that. The thought alone made me want to run and hide.

This, though, I could do. I could be Goldie behind my mask, where nothing was expected of me except giving as good as I got. I could do that. I was *desperate* to do that.

Slipping off my heels, I curled up on the couch and pulled the mask over my face. There, I waited for my Wim.

CHAPTER TWO
Shira

He didn't keep me waiting long. The door swung open, and an imposing figure in a black balaclava filled the space. A rush of heat instantly flooded my core, and it was all I could do not to squirm.

He leaned one shoulder against the frame. "Heeyyy, Goldie." I could almost hear his smile muffled behind his mask.

I made myself stand and turn to him, letting him drink in his fill of me in the dress I'd bought for tonight—one I would have never worn other than to meet a man for sex.

Kicking the door shut behind him, he closed the distance between us, reaching for me without hesitation. The second his massive hands touched my bare arms, my eyes rolled back. He was so much bigger than I'd expected. For a moment, I wished I had left my shoes on to lessen our height difference, but Wim didn't allow me to get lost in my head about it.

He spun me and tugged the zipper of my dress down in one smooth motion, sliding the straps off my shoulders and over my arms.

"Pretty," he uttered, trailing his blunt fingertip along my spine. "Talk to me, Goldie."

I tipped my head back until it hit his chest and looked up at him through the narrow holes of my mask. The mask made me brave, allowing the knot in my throat to unfurl and a husky, sexy version of my voice released.

"Hi, Wim."

"Mmm," he hummed as he removed my dress, leaving me in nothing but sheer lace hipsters that revealed more than they covered. I'd bought them for Wim too. He shoved his hands down the back of them to cup my bottom, letting loose an appreciative growl, and warmth filled my belly, pleased at my decision.

He took me by the waist and turned me again, this time to face him. Head dipping, more low hums vibrated his chest as he looked me over. Under his perusal, my breasts grew heavy, and my nipples pebbled tight.

"Pretty," he repeated.

I hooked my thumbs in the elastic of my panties and tugged them off. Taking them from my hand, Wim brought them to his mask and inhaled through the fabric. He released a frustrated groan and tossed my panties aside, then he grazed his knuckles along my abdomen, stopping to palm my core.

Reaching behind his head, he yanked his black T-shirt off and dropped it to the ground. Then, with one arm under my butt, he lifted me, putting us mask to mask, and carried me to the table, lowering me to sit on the edge.

We were barely more than strangers, yet he didn't hesitate to step between my spread legs and put his hands on me. All over. From my breasts to my ribs, then lower, squeezing my waist and hips before returning to my breasts. He wasn't tentative about it either, kneading my flesh and rolling my nipples between his calloused fingers.

I wasn't as confident. At first, my hands were limp at my sides, and all I could do was stare up at his hulking frame. His shoulders were astonishingly broad, and I feasted my eyes on the muscle definition I'd never seen up close in real life. This man looked like he could carry redwoods without breaking a sweat. I dragged my eyes lower, and saliva pooled in my mouth. I was lucky I didn't drool.

I didn't experience big, exciting attractions. My life was quiet, as were my emotions, by both design and necessity. But I was Goldie tonight, and stepping outside myself had opened a gate I'd locked down tight.

My attraction to Wim was shockingly visceral. My hands moved on their own, following the trail of hair starting at his chest and going all the way down his slightly soft abdomen until it disappeared beneath his tented pants.

"Touch me," he urged. "Hands on me, Goldie."

This was new. I didn't know if what I was doing was right, but I palmed his length through his pants while scratching along his sides and back with my other hand, letting my instinct guide me.

His deep groan and thrust of his hips told me I couldn't have been entirely wrong, so I continued my exploration while he did the same.

We didn't speak, and that was perfect. I got to play with this stranger's body while he toyed with mine, and, god, I had never been so turned on in my life. Since I'd divorced myself from these feelings until very recently, that wasn't saying much, but now I was connected to my inner well of desire, feeding it with every stroke of Wim's skin and each groan I pulled from him.

He cupped between my legs again, his long middle finger pressing firmly on my sensitive flesh, and I froze, my mouth falling open behind my mask as he connected with my clit, tapping and rolling it in no discernible pattern.

And I forgot who I was, all my baggage set to the side. No longer was I a lonely, twenty-nine-year-old widow or the CEO of a failing company. With Wim, I became a wanton ball of lust and urgency. Scrambling with the button on his pants, I managed to pop it open in spite of his very distracting fingers sliding through my folds. When he plunged one inside me, I lost track of my hands, my balance—everything but the inches he was now claiming.

"Wet, Goldie. So, so wet."

Gripping my waist, he flipped me around and pressed me face down on the table. My breath was lost then found moments later when his hands spread my cheeks and his wet tongue made contact with my soaked flesh. He must have lifted his mask. The possibility of turning around to see what he looked like flitted through the back of my mind, but it didn't matter. Inside this room, what he did to me and how he made me feel were all I cared about.

I gasped, arched, cried, clawed at the table. Wim lapped at me from behind, taking something that had never been given. He knew it was his. All of me was. It was why we were here, in room ten. For tonight, he could take me, use me, have me any way he wanted, and I would love it.

Holding on to the edges of the table, I squeezed my eyes shut, feeling like I was outside my body yet more connected than ever before. Wim relentlessly licked and sucked long-neglected parts, awakening nerve endings that had atrophied. He did it with ease, tirelessly going at me.

And humming. I'd learned Wim hummed when he was pleased. Since he'd put his mouth on me, he hadn't stopped. The vibrations were...oh god, they were going to make me come. It couldn't have been more than a few minutes since he'd started, but I was barreling toward the edge. Pressure ballooned within me until my skin was too tight and my voice clawed at my throat with the need to scream.

I had *never* screamed. Not even once. But I didn't think I'd be able to stop myself.

"Wim," I cried. "Wim, please..."

His lips latched onto my ache and pulled it from me. My head flew back, and my mouth opened wide, ragged sounds breaking loose from somewhere foreign inside me.

It was...exquisite. Painfully beautiful. I crumbled, fell apart beneath his ministrations. Not just the orgasm but his hands on me. They'd never left, and they were purposeful. Stroking and caressing. Spreading and kneading. I'd been touched more by this stranger in the last ten minutes than I had in...I didn't want to think how long.

Tears welled in my eyes and spilled over, making me grateful for my mask. He didn't need to deal with the intensity of my emotions. They weren't sexy, and that was all I wanted to be for him.

"Christ, Goldie." He kissed the back of one thigh then the other. "In different circumstances, I'd have you sitting on my face for the rest of the night."

Oh, what I wouldn't give to live in the alternate universe where that was happening...

I felt him move only a beat or two before he grabbed me again and carried my boneless body to the couch. He placed me on my knees, my chest against the back cushion, and arranged me just so. Then he was there, curving around me, enveloping me in his arms. He put his face next to mine, and I didn't have to see to know he'd replaced his mask.

"Goldie, Goldie, Goldie," he murmured. "You didn't warn me about that sweet pussy."

He rocked his hips into me, the ridge of his erection prodding my lower back. With our height difference, he wasn't hitting where he needed to be—where I wanted him—but I liked feeling how hard he was and knowing it was all for me.

Rustling fabric and the sound of a zipper grabbed my attention. I turned my head to see him taking his pants off, wishing the eyeholes of my mask were a little bigger and the lights in the room brighter so I could see this man in fine detail. As it was, my memories of tonight would be candlelit and hazy, which I already regretted. I couldn't fathom I'd gather the courage to do this again with someone else. Wim was my one and only.

He was a beautiful one and only too. His cock stood out from his hips, long and proud, as he rolled a condom over it. I wished he'd flip me around and feed it into my mouth, but he had other ideas—ideas I was equally supportive of.

His hands were on me again, raising my hips higher until my back was dramatically arched and my knees were barely on the cushions.

The blunt head of his cock brushed my opening, and I clenched, suddenly frightened I wouldn't be able to take all of him.

"Shhh, Goldie," he soothed, stroking his cock against my clit. "Relax and let me in. It's gonna be a tight fit, but you can take it. All you have to do is let it happen."

"Okay," I whispered, willing my muscles to loosen.

To my surprise, he didn't plunge inside me. Wim eased in, coaxing me open for his intrusion. My body stretched to accommodate him, little by little. Every inch I took, I grew more slick. I was trusting my safety to a stranger who could do anything to me he chose. The edge of danger set me alight. As a woman who never took chances, this entire experience was one big head trip.

After forever, Wim sank into me completely, his pelvis flush with my backside, fingers anchored around my hip bones. He stayed there, still as night, the puff of his breath through his mask the only sound for a solid minute or two.

When he moved, it was treacherously slow. A thrust, then still, controlled, easy, while his hands roamed with abandon. One circled my throat as he wedged the other between my front and the couch to play with my breasts. Then he caressed my ass, squeezing and lightly slapping it before sliding around to my front to palm my stomach and ribs. His hands were so big they spanned my torso, and he managed to touch every inch of me in a few long strokes. There was something familiar in his exploration, as if we'd been lovers for a long time and this wasn't a random hookup at all.

I didn't let myself get caught up in that thought. Wim was good in bed, and he obviously liked the feel of me—that was all it was. I shut my brain off and lost myself in this moment, this man. Tonight was all we would ever have, and I intended to savor every single second.

Sweat coated my skin, and my throat was hoarse from panting, crying, screaming. Wim wasn't done. He'd taken me in every position I could have imagined and some I couldn't. We'd gone through three condoms and were on our fourth.

Time had lost meaning in room ten. Refractory periods seemed to be a foreign concept to the man above me. My breasts were in his hands, my legs over his shoulders. He was powering into me, his control lost somewhere between round two and three. I couldn't say how many times I'd come. After nearly blacking out while riding his face, I hadn't bothered keeping track.

"This is it, Goldie," he grunted, his hips slapping my backside. "One last time."

"One last time," I echoed.

He'd said that when he took me the second time, and it had sounded like he was convincing himself that was all it was. One more time for the road. Except that hadn't been it. From the moment he'd put his hands on me, we hadn't stopped. If we weren't fucking, he was eating me out or lifting the bottom of his balaclava to suck on my nipples.

I knew I'd be sore when we were done and sitting at my desk at work tomorrow was going to be a difficult proposition, but I was too tangled up in this man to care about those things.

Wrapping my fingers around his arms, I held onto him the only way I could while he drove into me, finding his pleasure in my body. In this position, I was helpless to him, and I loved it. He'd shut my mind off, numbing all thoughts and worries, whittling me down to my base. For once in my life, I wasn't nervous or anxious. I was nothing but desire and feeling, and it was so beautiful.

With a roar, Wim threw his head back, his hips jerking so hard he took my breath away. My inner walls clasped around him as warmth seeped into me.

Panting hard, his head fell forward, and not for the first time, I wished the lights were brighter so I could determine the color of his eyes as they gazed down at me.

"Goldie," he groaned, lowering my legs to the mattress, "you took it all out of me."

With nothing left to say, I slid my hands up his vibrating arms and squeezed his shoulders. He'd wrung everything out of me too, and I'd loved every second of it.

Pulling out of me, he fell to the side, and I sighed, knowing it was over.

"Oh shit," he uttered. "Goldie…"

I turned my head, the alarm in his voice dragging me out of my stupor.

"What is it?"

"I'm sorry." He dug the heel of his hand into his eye. "The condom is broken. I didn't notice…"

The warmth he'd left behind suddenly made sense. I clamped my legs together, my breath caught in my throat.

Moving to his side, he propped himself up on his elbow and ran a hand over my stomach. "I've been tested recently. I'm clean. You?"

I shook my head. "No…I mean, yes, I don't have anything."

"Are you on birth control?"

I had never had a reason. Maybe I should have thought about it before meeting up with Wim, but it simply hadn't occurred to me as a necessity.

"I'm not, but I'm sure it's fine."

Groaning, he swiveled around to sit up, his back facing me. "Okay. It's all right. The chances of anything—look, I'll leave my information with management. If the worst happens and you need to get in touch…"

"I'm sure it's fine," I repeated.

He gave me his masked profile. "I had a good time with you. Did you?"

"Yes," I whispered, my throat raw and aches blooming everywhere else on my body. "It was everything I wanted."

"Me too." He moved to run his hand over his face but stopped when he hit his mask. "Do you need anything before I go?"

"I don't." Sitting up, I pulled the sheet over me, not wanting to be naked anymore. "Thank you for tonight."

He rose to stand and turned toward me. Though I couldn't see his eyes, I felt them raking over me. "Best night I've had in a long time. Wish it hadn't ended that way."

I shook my head. "Please don't worry."

Circling the bed, he pulled on his pants, then stopped next to me, dragging his knuckles along my bare throat.

"Glad I met you."

"Me too." I allowed myself to lean into his hand for one beat of my heart before straightening. "Bright side?"

He huffed a laugh. I'd asked him the same thing online at the end of each conversation we'd shared. It was something I'd started with my late husband and still carried with me.

"Bright side was you." He gave my shoulder a squeeze. "Goodnight, sweet Goldie."

"Goodbye," I whispered, but he was already gone, gathering his shirt and heading for the door. He left without looking back, the lock clicking behind him.

Alone, I slipped my mask off and wiped my sweaty face with the sheet. Then I got up, pulled on my clothes, and slipped my feet into my shoes. Once I was back to myself again, the ache between my legs was the only evidence the last few hours had happened.

With one last look around room ten, I left too, putting a close to the hottest, most carnal night of my life.

Bright side: I now know a night like that is possible for me.

CHAPTER THREE
Shira

THE SOFT FUZZINESS OF my night in room ten stayed with me for a little more than a week. Eight days of going into GoldMed's office, trying my hardest to keep my late husband's company afloat when it was sinking so steadily, I couldn't bail fast enough. Eight days of trying my damnedest to be the confident, fearless leader my employees needed at the helm when that wasn't me in any way. Eight days of Roman Wells walking the halls, being friendly and amiable with every person but me.

Roman had a reputation in Denver as a shark. He swooped down on companies in need of capital or restructuring and bought up their debt or shares at a rock-bottom price. He often made aggressive moves within the companies he invested in, which ruffled feathers, but on the flip side, he rarely failed to turn those businesses around.

I'd been looking forward to meeting Roman in person, and eight days ago, it happened unexpectedly. My assistant and right-hand woman, Terry, had been out to lunch, so the knock on my office door had surprised me. Roman hadn't even given me a chance to say "come in" before entering.

From behind my desk, I looked up...and up...and up. Of course, I knew what Roman Wells looked like from photographs, but seeing him in person took me aback. He was tall, six and a half feet if I had to guess, but his grin softened the intimidation factor in the rest of his rugged features.

Well, for most people, it would have. My tongue was stuck to the roof of my suddenly dry mouth, and I seemed to have forgotten what to do with my hands. I didn't like surprises. Being put on the spot made me freeze and lose track of my brain.

"Hey, sorry to show up unannounced, but I was in the area and thought it would be nice to meet before all the formal introductions at the board meeting." He strode into my office, still smiling. "I'm Roman."

"I didn't expect you until tomorrow." I looked at my computer, at the calendar that held my appointments. There weren't many—I handled most things through email—and the few I had had been scheduled well in advance. "Tomorrow at nine. It's right here."

He pulled up short. "Right. Like I said, I was in the area—"

I typed his name in today's slot on my calendar as my heart thudded. What was this reaction? Why was this man's presence making me feel on the verge of a panic attack? My palms were so sweaty my hand practically slid off my mouse.

"You look busy," he stated dryly, clearly unimpressed. "Too busy to even tell me your name so I can confirm I'm in the right office."

Flustered, I looked up from my computer, finding this huge man studying me like a specimen under a microscope. I would have liked to do the same, but not when he was staring back at me.

Averting my gaze, I answered him. "Shira. I'm Shira."

"Hmmm. Okay, Shira."

"Okay, Roman," I echoed, sounding sarcastic even to my ears, which I hadn't meant. Dear god, why couldn't my mouth cooperate? I was a disaster.

In my periphery, Roman folded his arms over his broad chest. "I thought we might be able to build a rapport despite what I've heard about you. It seems I was mistaken."

I forced myself to look at him again, my brow raised. I wanted to ask what he'd heard, though, in truth, I wasn't certain I could handle hearing it. Being called things like "ice queen," "cold," "boring," and "void of personality" even once was enough for a lifetime. After ten or twenty times, it was impossible not to take to heart.

I took so long to think of how to reply, Roman shifted on his feet, exhaling heavily through his nose. If only I could explain I didn't do well with surprises. I needed time to prepare for conversations with new people—especially six-and-a-half-foot men with hands that could crush a small sedan and faces so roughly hewn they could have been carved from a boulder. This man was so outrageously handsome, I would have needed even more time than usual to prepare.

"If you'll schedule a meeting with Terry, we can speak then."

Oh no. That sounded much more formal than I meant it to. From the way Roman chuffed, he felt the same way.

"That's how it's going to be, Mrs. Goldman?"

I flinched at the bite in his tone. "It's just Shira," I murmured, flicking my gaze back to his, hoping he'd see the plea for understanding there. "My schedule...it's—"

He raised his hand, halting me. "I heard you loud and clear, Shira. If I need to speak to you again, I'll talk to Terry." Backing toward the exit, he slowly shook his head. Once he reached the doorway, he tapped on the frame. "I knew Frank a long time ago. He played a pivotal role in the direction of my life so I have a soft spot for GoldMed. Do you even care about this company?"

It was Frank's legacy. I had to care about it. For him. He'd turned my life around when I was spiraling. Offered me shelter and companionship when I'd been all alone in the world. Married me so I'd always have the security I'd lacked during the first part of my life.

I could have said all those things, but all that came out was: "I do."

He brought his hand to his jaw, which was heavy and squared off in the corners. "We'll see, Shira. We'll see."

Our first meeting had set the tone of my relationship with Roman Wells. Over the last week, every time we spoke, I'd put my worst foot forward. I just couldn't seem to stop doing it, and it drove me to the brink. Even worse, all my warm fuzziness had evaporated, and room ten was becoming nothing more than a distant memory.

Terry poked her head in my office, knocking me out of my thoughts. "Conference room in five. Do you need anything before the meeting?"

I shook my head. "No. I have my notes prepared. I think I'm good."

My assistant leaned against the doorjamb, one hand on her hip as she surveyed me. "He would understand if you didn't do this."

I shook my head. "I made a promise."

Terry sighed. "A promise he shouldn't have extracted from you. I could throttle that man..."

Terry had been Frank's assistant for twenty-five years. She'd known me since I came into his life ten years ago and was the only person who understood what our marriage had been from the beginning. Frank had trusted her with everything, and now, I did too. In her sixties, she should have retired a few years ago, but she was sticking around for me. I should have told her to go, but there was no way I'd get through a day at GoldMed without her.

"You couldn't," I said.

She cocked her head. "Couldn't what?"

"Throttle him. No body, after the cremation…"

She stared at me for a beat then slapped her thigh and snickered. "That's highly irreverent, Mrs. Goldman."

Grinning, I pushed up from my seat and snagged my tablet. "What's the use of being a widow if I can't make dead-husband jokes?"

She put her arm around my shoulders when I reached her. "You have a point. That man claimed most of your twenties. It's only fair *you* get some laughs out of it."

"Frank was your friend," I reminded her.

"He was. That doesn't mean I agreed with everything he did. I'm no yes-woman. That's why he kept me around for so long."

I leaned into her. "That, and you know every one of his secrets. Can't fire someone with all that blackmail material."

She huffed. "Please. As if anyone would ever fire me."

"I wouldn't, I know that."

One more squeeze, and she let me go. "I know that too. Let's go conquer this meeting."

The meeting with the executive team had gone as well as it could have, considering the circumstances. I'd prepared what I'd wanted to say, but Roman had managed to cut me off several times, disrupting my train of thought, and when he'd asked me questions, I'd either answered him curtly or allowed Terry to take over.

So...yes, it had gone as well as it could have, further cementing Roman's ill opinion of me.

In my hurry to vacate the conference room, I'd left my phone behind. Terry was busy when I made the discovery a few minutes later, so I ventured back on my own, certain the room would be empty by now.

As I approached, Mike Dietrich, GoldMed's CFO, emerged, halting me in my tracks. I pressed myself into the nearby alcove, allowing him to pass without having to make polite small talk—something I'd gleaned he disliked as much as I did. Mike was all business and numbers. People weren't his thing. He only dealt with us because he was required to. I would have explained he didn't have to engage in niceties with me, but I thought it was easier for both of us to simply hide away until he passed.

When I came out of the shadows, Roman was standing in the doorway of the conference room, staring straight at me, a bold line carved between his brows and a disapproving scowl pulling at his mouth.

Sucking in a deep breath, I started toward him. If I hadn't needed my phone, I would have abandoned it rather than go near him, but I had no choice.

"Excuse me." I went to tuck my hair behind my ear then remembered it was pulled back in a bun, as it always was at work. Instead, I smoothed my hand over the side and checked my earring was still in place. "I seem to have left my phone behind."

"I noticed." He unfolded his arms, revealing my phone clutched in his massive mitt. "You were in such a rush to get away from everyone you forgot it."

I shook my head. "I wasn't rushing to get away from everyone. It's that—"

"You ducked into the shadows, so you didn't have to speak to Mike. What kind of environment do you think that behavior fosters, Mrs. Goldman—when the CEO won't even wave hello to her CFO as she passes him?"

"It isn't that, and please, call me Shira."

I'd never been Mrs. Goldman. Officially, yes, but only because Frank had wanted me to have the protection his last name offered. The name had felt like a piece of ill-fitting clothing, never settling on me like it should have. If not for GoldMed, I would have gone back to my maiden name, just as my mother had when she left my father. I'd always thought Shira Saltzman had a ring to it.

Roman shook his head and heaved a sigh. "I can't figure you out."

I swallowed hard, wishing he'd give me my phone so I could go. "I understand."

"Do you? From what I've seen, you give maybe three or four people the time of day, and everyone else might as well not exist. A lot of work needs to be done to pull GoldMed out of the hole it's in, and I don't know if you see that."

I forced myself to meet his gaze. He had his chin tipped down, giving me his full attention. It was weighty. Filled with judgment and something more...something that felt a lot like ire. This man really didn't like me. Frank might've dug the hole GoldMed was in, but where Roman was concerned, I was fully responsible for the one I was in. The thing was, I couldn't figure out how to claw myself out.

"Of course I see it." I straightened, hoping to appear more confident than I was. "More than anyone else."

He chuffed, his eyes rolling to the side. They were brown, choco-laty. I'd seen how warm they could be when he was laughing with others, joking with Terry, greeting Rita, the floor's receptionist, but I'd never once gotten that. Roman had come to GoldMed with an opinion of me, and I'd only helped cement it with each passing day.

"Considering you won't even have a conversation with your CFO, I doubt that," he stated.

"Mike and I speak often. We both find it more efficient to email and text through the interoffi—"

"Efficiency is important to you, isn't it? You and your efficient calendar." He refolded his arms, tucking my phone underneath again. "Do you know, after my father died, Frank wrote me several letters over the years?"

A knot sprung from my belly to my throat, making it impossible to reply with words. Of course I knew. I was well-acquainted with those letters.

I simply nodded, and Roman went on. "There was a time I was floundering, and Frank offered me advice on the direction I took my life and business. One of the many things he told me to never forget was the human element behind the bottom line. The thing is, hu-man connection isn't always efficient, but it can lead to exponential growth. If the people who work for you feel connected to the person in charge of them, they will do a better job to please them. From what I've seen, Shira, you don't have that."

Roman had been in this office for two weeks and thought he knew the entire picture. In truth, he'd come in with a preconceived notion about what he would find and had let that color everything he'd observed. He didn't see my friendly chats with Mike through interoffice texting. He hadn't been in the room during my weekly lunches with Annabelle from HR. And he definitely didn't know when Gabriela from marketing had come to work with a poorly covered black eye. I'd held her hand while she filed a police report against her boyfriend and had hired a bulldog lawyer to keep her safe.

None of those things meant I was perfect. I was drowning in my position and absolutely miserable. But my promise to Frank superseded my discomfort. I would see our agreement through by the letter until it became impossible.

"I'm sorry you feel that way," I replied, my tongue too tangled to say anything in my own defense. "If there's nothing else, I'd like my phone back, please."

With a deep sigh, Roman scanned me as if he were trying to see inside me. If only he could see the panic his intrusive studying initiated in my limbic system, but I knew from experience I looked cool as a cucumber. My eyes hardened, and my expression vanished. Like a deer caught in headlights, my brain had decided on the path of least resistance—allowing the oncoming traffic to plow into me. Fight or flight wasn't an option for me. I was a frozen little cube of ice.

And all Roman could see was the ice.

With a look of derision, he unfolded his arms and held out my phone. Before I could bring my arm up to take it from him, he brought it back into him, clutching it against his chest. "Did Frank ever mean anything to you? Anything at all?"

With that blindingly awful question, the tethers of my panic snapped, sending a rush of blood and heat to my cheeks. I stepped close enough to snatch my phone from him and skittered back out of his reach.

"What a horrific thing to ask me," I whispered.

For once, my body did what I needed it to do. I fled from the scene of the crime in a hurry. Roman uttered my name followed by a curse, but I didn't turn back or stop until I made it to my office. There, I leaned against my door, swallowing back the bile rising in my throat and nausea swirling in my gut.

I'd thought Roman Wells would be the savior GoldMed desperately needed, and maybe he would be. At this point, he was our only hope of coming back from the brink of disaster. But after that conversation, my eyes were open. In the process of saving GoldMed, Roman might willingly destroy me.

CHAPTER FOUR
Roman

I'd held my brother off for a month, which had been a miracle in itself. Ben was a dog with a bone. When he wanted something, he didn't give it up, and he'd been vying for a look at our new investment, specifically the CEO, but I'd managed to keep him away. GoldMed was going through enough changes without Ben showing up to create chaos.

"Don't talk to anyone," I reminded him.

Ben held up his hands as if anyone would buy his innocence. Certainly not me. I knew him too well. He'd been up to no good all thirty-two years of his life. "Oh, believe me, I'll be on my best behavior," he claimed.

I sucked in a sharp breath through my nose. "Tell me why that doesn't reassure me in any way."

He chuckled, leaning forward to hit the button for the tenth floor even though the elevator was already ascending toward it.

"That's because you know me, Romeo." He bounced on his toes, hands tucked in his pockets. "I'm only messing with you. I just want to see what all the fuss is about. I'll keep my mouth shut."

I didn't bother reminding him not to call me Romeo, the nickname I'd been dubbed in my rugby-playing days. Ben had heard it once and he'd run with it despite the fact it'd been six years since I'd been on a team. Fortunately, he was the only person who still called me that, but dear god, did it rankle me. He was well aware of it too, and that was exactly why I refused to react.

Ben followed me when we arrived on the tenth floor of the Levy building. I greeted the floor's receptionist, Rita, who'd been with GoldMed since its inception, and introduced her to Ben.

"Did you have a nice lunch, Mr. Wells?" she asked.

"I did. Unfortunately, I picked up a straggler on my way back." Her fiery red eyebrows popped as she glanced from Ben to me. I put my hand on his shoulder, grinning. "This is Ben Wells, my brother."

Ben held up a finger. "His younger, more handsome brother."

Her eyes darted back and forth between us. Rita was sharp as a tack. She didn't fall for Ben's joke. Given the fact we shared a face, it'd be hard for anyone to fall for it.

"By how many minutes?" she asked.

"Four," I answered. Four minutes might not have seemed like a huge age gap to most, but Ben took his role as the younger twin seriously.

He slung his arm over my shoulders and winked at Rita. "You didn't say anything about me being the more handsome one."

She sat up straight, a glimmer in her eye. "I wouldn't want to insult you. We've only just met."

Laughing, I thanked her and steered Ben away from her desk. "Remember when you said you were going to keep your mouth shut?"

"I'm not allowed to greet our employees?"

"They're not 'our' employees," I reminded him.

"Not yet, right?"

I didn't reply, but he didn't need it. Swiveling his head, he took in the bland cubicles and hush of the employees. My first day here a month ago, the quiet had been what I'd noticed first. Not that it had been hard to miss. With my three brothers as partners, I'd invested in many companies the last few years, and I'd yet to come across an office without a constant din of conversation.

GoldMed, a medical supply company started by Frank Goldman nearly four decades ago, was now run by his young widow, Shira. From the research I'd done, the company had been on the decline for the last decade but took a sharp plunge when Frank passed just over a year ago.

I'd bought GoldMed's debt with the intent of turning the company around or selling it for parts if the situation was more hopeless than I thought. For the last month, I'd been working out of GoldMed's offices, fully immersing myself in the company to get a handle on exactly what was going wrong.

My presence wasn't welcomed by everyone, but in my line of work, I was used to chilly receptions. Blustering men who couldn't bear admitting they needed help didn't like the man who strode in from the outside, acquiring their debt and a controlling interest in their companies. Shifting that kind of attitude was my forte. The ones who refused to change were out the door.

With GoldMed, I'd pinpointed the biggest problem before walking through the entrance. It was only a matter of time before I could do what I needed to.

We neared my office, and the door next to it opened. Two women emerged. Terry Burns, a Black woman in her sixties who'd been Frank Goldman's PA for two decades, and Shira Goldman, the current CEO. Terry was now Shira's assistant and, as far as I could tell, the only person Shira deigned to speak to on any sort of regular basis. In fact, they were so attached, I rarely saw Shira without Terry.

Their heads were tipped toward each other, Shira's mouth moving while Terry nodded and laughed. Seeing Shira's face so animated was disconcerting, especially since it normally was locked in a tight line.

"That has to be her," Ben murmured. "Funny, she doesn't look like a trophy wife."

I wasn't a man who discussed a woman's appearance with other guys. I found it boring and not worth my time. Ben had a point, though. When I'd heard Frank had married a woman thirty years his junior, I'd pictured someone lavishly attractive. Lips made puffy by a few rounds of filler. Dangerous, eye-catching curves.

There was nothing eye-catching about Shira.

She dressed in monochrome, either black on black or gray on gray, modest to a fault. Her dark hair was always raked away from her face and wrapped in a neat bun at the base of her skull. Her face was the kind of plain that was easy to forget once she was out of sight. The only thing remarkable about her was her eyes, but I wouldn't say they were beautiful. A shade of green so pale there was something ghostly about them. Still, I'd caught myself staring at them several times. Maybe they were what had turned Frank's head.

Ignoring Ben, I raised a hand, catching their attention. "Good afternoon, Terry, Shira. Are you headed to lunch?"

Terry laid a hand on Shira's arm, and they stopped in front of us. Shira's expression slid back to her normal impassiveness—a direct contrast to Terry's warm smile. If I thought it would have made a difference, I would have danced a jig just to see Shira react. But I knew better. Since the day we met last month, Shira had blanked me out. I would have thought it was personal, but as far as I could tell, this was how she reacted to everyone. I didn't know why she insisted on staying on as the CEO if it caused her such abject misery.

"We just returned from my favorite ramen joint. Now we're on our way to talk to Mike." Terry looked from me to Ben. "This has to be the twin."

"Guilty as charged. Ben Wells." They shook hands, and he directed his focus on Shira. "Nice to meet you too, Shira. I've heard a lot about you."

Shira's eerie eyes flitted over my brother before settling on his shoulder. "It's nice to meet you, Ben," she responded, but there was no meaning behind the words. Flat, cold, emotionless—just like her.

I cleared my throat. "You'll have to email me the name of the ramen place, Terry. Unless it's a state secret."

She grinned, her fingers squeezing Shira's arm. "If you promise not to spread it around."

I held up a hand. "Scout's honor. You share the ramen joint, I'll give you the name of the Greek restaurant where we just had lunch. If you like lamb, theirs is so tender it basically melts in your mouth."

Shira made a sound somewhere between a cough and a whimper. Then, out of nowhere, she walked off. No word. Not even a salute. The woman just...left.

Ben whipped around to watch her go, and I caught Terry's concerned gaze following Shira down the hall.

Scrubbing my jaw, I frowned. "Guess she doesn't like Greek."

Terry tried to laugh, but there was no amusement behind it. "I don't think she's feeling well. I'm going to check on her. Excuse me, gentlemen."

I'd met a lot of people in my life, both in sports and business, and no one perplexed me the way Shira Goldman did. She'd been married to a man I'd once admired, but I was unable to understand what qualities Frank had seen in her that had made him throw away most of his relationships and give her full control of the company he'd built from the ground up.

"Huh." Ben rubbed his stomach, swiveling back to me. "That was...off-putting."

I took him by the shoulder, leading him into my office. It was sparse, but I was only here temporarily, so I hadn't bothered decorating. The view out the floor-to-ceiling windows was all I needed anyway. Elliot Levy owned this building. All his properties were well positioned and smartly designed, so even the most simple lines were pleasing to the eye.

My brother flung himself into one of two leather chairs facing my desk and let out a sigh. "So, that's Frank's young bride?"

I settled in my chair, half facing Ben, half turned toward the window. "That's her."

"Hmmm. I expected to meet her and find out Frannie had been exaggerating. Turns out, she'd grossly undersold her wicked stepmother."

I pressed my fingers together in a bridge. "Don't let her hear you calling her Frannie."

He winged a brow. "Is she in the office today?"

"I have no idea. Francesca doesn't keep me abreast of her schedule, but she's away more often than she's here."

We'd gone to high school with Francesca Goldman. Her father had been friends with ours. We'd never existed in the same social circles, but when Frank died last year, we'd started talking, and she'd spilled every dirty detail about her father's wife, who was nearly the same age as her. I took a lot of what Francesca said with a grain of salt since she thrived on drama, but if even a quarter of what she'd said was true, Shira was an even worse person than I'd already imagined.

Ben chuffed. "I don't blame Frannie. This place is like a tomb. Maybe you should play some music to pick up the vibe. Bring in some entertainers. Oh—a popcorn machine! Yeah, do that."

"What kind of entertainers? Were you thinking jugglers or strippers?"

"Neither." He twirled his hand in front of himself. "I was thinking those party facilitators who come with the DJ at bar mitzvahs."

I cocked my head, staring at my brother. "Do you even understand what goes on in an office?"

"I do not, and I never want to. Keep that to yourself, Romeo."

While my rugby career had been cut short by a shoulder injury, Ben's was going strong. He had two Olympics under his belt and didn't seem to be running out of steam. I didn't try to deny my jealousy that he still got to play the game we both loved, but I wasn't unhappy with where I'd ended up either. Life wasn't always fair, but I'd bought a stake in Denver's pro rugby team, the Mountain Lions, keeping my foot in the game in the only way it could be.

As for my brother, he had never worked an office job, and he had no intention of ever being strapped to a desk. The idea of Ben sitting still, working at a computer for eight or nine hours, was preposterous. We might've been identical in a lot of ways, but we diverged in our ability to hunker down and focus. We'd become business partners years ago, but that consisted of Ben giving me money to invest and me returning it tenfold. It worked for us both.

I rubbed the spot between my brows and sighed. "When are you leaving for New Zealand?"

Ben's team was headed overseas for training for a month, and I was dreading his absence as much as I was looking forward to the quiet. Not only was he my brother, but he'd decided to move in with me when he'd broken up with his girlfriend—the same time I'd split from mine a few months ago. He'd made himself comfortable and didn't seem to be going anywhere, and I wasn't in a hurry to get rid of him.

"Tuesday. Are you going to miss me?"

"Maybe." I shrugged. "Eating dinner alone will be strange. No one stealing the food off my plate, you know?"

He cackled. "I'm saving you from all those calories. Now that you're behind a desk all day, you're going to get a gut."

I patted my abdomen, which admittedly wasn't in the same shape it had been but was nowhere near becoming a gut. "I'm doing all right. I can still take my shirt off without shame."

Without warning, my office door swung open, and Francesca Goldman let herself in. With a smirk, she slinked up behind Ben and bent down, covering his eyes with her hands.

"Guess who?" she cooed next to his ear.

"Hmmm...you smell expensive, and your hands feel like they've never worked an honest day in your whole life. Gotta be Frannie."

With a yelp, she straightened and gave his shoulder a less-than-playful whack. "God, Benjamin, I've told you not to call me that. When will it sink into your thick skull?"

Ben climbed to his feet and gave her a bear hug, squeezing a squeal out of her. "I dunno, Frannie. My thick skull has taken a lot of hits.

Might be a while before I remember. Wait, what was I supposed to remember?"

I had to hide my laugh behind my hands. When Ben found someone's button, he pushed the hell out of it. I would have told him to cut it out, but Francesca deserved some razzing. With looks, money, and status, she'd been skating through life since birth. She was used to people kissing her thousand-dollar heels, even when acting like an entitled bitch. After a month of observing her lack of professionalism and work ethic, I'd come to the conclusion that was pretty much all the time.

I didn't bother talking to her about it. Things would be changing around here—and soon.

Francesca stomped her expensive high heels and circled Ben, her hands on her hips. Ben leaned back in his chair, his legs stretched out in front of him, a crooked grin on his face.

"I thought you'd be happy to see me," Francesca whined. "Must you be such a tease?"

"Yes, I must." Ben raised an eyebrow at me. "Rome and I were just talking about you."

"You were?" Francesca whirled around to me, her shiny pink lips pursing. "All good things, I hope."

"Ben was trying to ascertain your work schedule," I informed her. "I couldn't give him an answer since I'm not really sure what it is."

She waved me off like I was a big joker. "You know I work from home most of the time. I can't stand being here with *her*. Her presence upsets me so very much."

"Interesting." I steepled my fingers beneath my chin. "I never see you online when you're not in the office."

Her brow arched. "Have you been looking for me, Roman?"

Ben grunted before rising to his feet. "On that note, I'm going to get going. Nice seeing you, Fran." He winked at me. "Have fun, bro."

With a sigh, I nodded toward his vacated seat. "I've been meaning to schedule an appointment with you. No time like the present, right?"

"An appointment? This should be interesting." She perched on the edge of the chair, leaning forward to give me a view down the *V* of her dress. I turned away, and she made a little chirp of disgruntlement.

Given the admiration I held for her father, I almost felt bad for how strongly I'd come to dislike Francesca Goldman. Getting to know her over the last month had been enlightening in a way going to school with her hadn't. Francesca was thirty years old and still behaved like a spoiled princess who dodged work like that was her actual job. But there was nothing I could do about the mistakes Frank had made in raising his daughter.

GoldMed was my sole focus, and luckily for everyone, soon, Francesca would have no reason to pretend she worked here.

A couple more weeks, my plans would be in motion.

CHAPTER FIVE
Shira

I WALKED OUT OF the restroom, hollow and longing for a nap, and ran smack into a brick wall, nearly losing my footing as I bounced off.

A massive hand caught my elbow and righted me. I looked up, surprised to see bouncing brown eyes and lively, fluffy curls.

Ben.

Not Roman.

The twins were identical in features, but their personalities made them easily identifiable. Even to me, a veritable stranger.

"Excuse me, Ben," I murmured. "I didn't expect you to be waiting directly outside the door of the ladies' room."

One beat of silence, another, then Ben Wells tossed his head back and released the most melodious, happy laugh. Dimples dented both his cheeks, and crinkles bracketed his eyes, which were shiny and alight.

"Sorry." He shook his head, still grinning. "You took me by surprise. I didn't expect *you* to have a sense of humor."

"Then we've both taken each other by surprise."

He nodded, his chin lowering as he took me in. I didn't sense any interest behind his slow perusal. Nothing sexual or romantic anyway. Since men didn't look at me that way in general, it wasn't unusual. His study of me seemed more scientific, like he was curious about me.

"I guess we have," he said.

I cocked my head. Ben's hand was still on my elbow, but it didn't make me uncomfortable.

"Was there a reason you were stalking the restroom?" I asked.

I didn't have an explanation as to why I had no trouble meeting Ben's gaze and giving his face the same perusal he'd given me. It was almost like I was looking at Roman, getting to know the features I'd only allowed myself brief glances of without the intimidation factor. Sure, Ben was massive like his brother, and his jaw looked well suited to masticate animal bones, but I wasn't scared of him. He gave off an innate gentleness, whereas Roman was just...gah. There were no words for him other than he *wasn't* gentle.

"Sure there was. I'm checking on you. Your PA mentioned you were sick, and since I'm just as invested in GoldMed as my brother, I thought it would look bad if the CEO dropped dead on the floor of the bathroom and no one noticed." Ben bounced on his toes, his eyebrows rolling in waves, which was sort of a cool trick.

I smiled, though the queasiness hadn't abated. An awareness that the noodles I'd eaten for lunch might've not been the reason for this rested in the back of my mind, but I wasn't quite ready to face that possibility. "Not dead. Thanks for checking. I think the ramen rocked my stomach, but I'll live."

His nose crinkled. "Yeah, I'm going to have to tell my brother not to get the name of that joint. I don't have time to pray to the porcelain god."

Laughing, I tried to inch by him, but he moved with me. It was strange how at ease I was with him. This was how it had been with my best friends, Clara and Bea. Automatic soul sisters. But I'd never felt that way around a man. Usually, it was quite the opposite.

I guessed Wim had been a very big exception, but that had been an entirely different circumstance.

"I don't really either, but sometimes, sacrifices have to be made," I said.

Ben chuckled. "You're funny. Why doesn't Roman know you're funny?"

"Because I have a tendency to panic in his presence."

"Ah." He nodded, like he understood completely. "Yeah, I see that. Rome can be really intense if he wants to be. Add on his size..." He gestured to himself. "I try to make myself less disarming since I'm such a big dude. My brother doesn't share my concern. He's just out there charging through life, scaring women and children."

"It isn't that I'm scared..." Glancing to the side, I dug my teeth into my bottom lip.

"I hope not." He dipped his head. "Little secret: Rome's a nice guy. He wants GoldMed to succeed. Maybe you two can find common ground. I'd cheer for that."

I touched my hair, finding it still in place. "That would be wonderful if it were true."

Ben patted my shoulder, surprisingly gentle for a giant. "Give it a try. You could pretend you're talking to me—your favorite Wells brother."

I sucked in a little breath. "There are two more of you. I suppose I'll have to meet them to truly come to that conclusion."

"Nah, you're good. Nate and Adrian are sticks in the mud. Worse than Rome. I guarantee I'm always gonna be your favorite."

I swallowed down a wave of nausea that had nothing to do with the Wells brothers and forced out a smile.

"I doubt I'll have the opportunity to meet them anyway. I'll take your word for it." I nodded toward the hall. "I should probably get back to work."

"Yep. Glad we got to have this talk. Remember what I said about Roman. He's a good man under the bluster. Give him another try."

I offered a small smile. "I will. And...thank you for checking on me. That was really kind."

Leaving Ben to flirt with Rita, who was at least thirty years his senior, I headed back to my office. I had to pass Roman's on the way, and he'd sent me an email earlier I hadn't replied to yet. Taking Ben's advice, I decided to stop by and answer his questions in person as an olive branch.

His door was cracked, but I wasn't one to barge in. I lifted my hand to knock, freezing when I heard Francesca's distinct, sultry voice. Frank's daughter—technically my stepdaughter, though I'd never thought of her that way—disliked me more than Roman. Or anyone else, really.

"...it drives me crazy that she's still here. Why haven't you done anything about it?" Francesca whined.

"It's not that simple. Shira owns a controlling interest in GoldMed," Roman replied, and blood rushed to my face. If I could have forced my feet to move, I would have. The last thing I wanted to hear was their unfiltered opinion of me.

"It should be simple. You know how she treated me. Do you like her or something? Has she gotten under your skin like she did Daddy's?"

He grunted. "Absolutely not. I don't understand what Frank saw in that woman, but I can guarantee my caution with GoldMed has nothing to do with me liking Shira. She's the cause of GoldMed's situation and the stifling environment in this office. As far as I've seen, there is nothing redeemable about the gold-digging little—"

Bile rose so quickly up my throat, it was all I could do to rush to the nearest wastebasket before losing the little bit of water I'd sipped after my last bout of nausea. Once I was able, I ran for the restroom, all too aware of the eyes on me.

I wasn't surprised by what Roman had said. It didn't feel good, but I'd heard and endured far worse. It was just humiliating. The man I'd looked so forward to meeting and getting to know was bad-mouthing me to a woman who'd caused me boatloads of misery since Frank passed. Francesca didn't know the meaning of discretion. I had a feeling she'd be repeating everything Roman said as soon as she left his office.

Sinking to the tile floor, I covered my face with my hands.

I was determined to keep my promise to Frank, but how much longer could I do this? Had it even been fair of him to ask all this of me?

Probably not, but he'd given me so much...

Blowing out a heavy breath, I climbed to my feet.

I'd be okay.

I always was.

CHAPTER SIX

Shira

TWICE A MONTH, I met Clara and Bea for pedicures. The two of them had no trouble spilling their latest news, no matter how salacious, in front of our nail techs and whoever else in the salon, but I was a little—no, a lot—more circumspect.

I wasn't sure a picnic table at the farmers' market was the *best* place to have the "*I had an anonymous hookup at a sex club and now I'm pretty sure I'm pregnant but too scared to take the test*" conversation, but we had far more privacy than the salon, and after biting my tongue for the last month, I couldn't keep it in any longer.

Fortunately, Clara's three-year-old, Nellie, had passed out in her stroller while we'd been walking around the market, so I didn't have to spell the words out. Instead, I blurted them in one fell swoop.

"I think I'm pregnant."

Bea paused, a honey stick halfway to her mouth. Clara's eyes went comically round.

"Repeat that," Bea instructed.

"I think I'm pregnant. I've been allowing myself to be in denial and haven't taken a test, but the signs are all there—"

Clara, the COO of Rossi Motors and most levelheaded woman I knew, stopped me with a slice of her hand through the air.

"Let's back up a step. Are you sleeping with someone?"

I shook my head. "I *slept* with someone...almost two months ago."

"Who was it?" Bea put her hand on mine, leaning forward with keen interest. "And was it good?"

Patches of heat landed on my cheeks. "It was amazing, and...I don't know. I used the app you told me about, the one connected to the club—"

"The club?" Clara's brow furrowed. "Which club?"

Bea and I exchanged glances.

The three of us were quite different. Clara was thirty-seven, divorced, a mom, and an executive at a Fortune 500 company. Bea, an ultra-curvy, blue-haired goth babe, was a decade younger and ran her own small catering company. And I was...well, me. The quiet one with such extreme social anxiety, I was astonished I'd made and kept these two gorgeous friends.

As close as we were, Clara was now in a serious relationship with her boyfriend, Jake, and Bea and I were as single as humanly possible. Sometimes, there were things we talked about apart from Clara, namely our lack of sex lives and the dating scene. Although, Bea was the only one actually going on dates. From how skeevy the men she went out with were, it would remain that way.

That and the bean very possibly growing inside me.

Bea took over for me. "The Mile High Club. It's a sex club with a corresponding app. You can talk to people with common...interests and meet them at the club. I told Shira about it a few months ago. I never thought the little minx would actually go through with it." She squeezed my hand. "I have to say, I'm getting a little choked up here. I'd say I was a proud mama, but you know how I feel about kids—with the exception of Nell-belle and the little gummy bear growing in your belly."

Clara pressed a hand to her forehead. "Slow down, please. There's a sex club in Denver? And, Shira, you went to it? And had sex with someone?"

Bea wagged her honey stick. "Honestly, there are probably a few sex clubs in the city. MHC is the only one I personally know about, but even *I* haven't been to it."

Clara tried to school her expression, but the little line between her brows couldn't be smoothed. "You met a man...and didn't use a condom?" she whispered.

"Of course we used condoms," I rushed out.

"Oh, *multiple*?" Bea grinned. "Good for you."

"It *was* good for me." I sighed, the ghost of Wim still present if I moved my legs just right. "The last time, the condom broke. I know I should have taken Plan B, and I can't even tell you why I didn't, but it was dumb. Now, I've been nauseous for weeks, my breasts ache, and my period has gone on hiatus."

Clara took my other hand. "That sounds an awful lot like you're pregnant."

I nodded. "I think I am."

"Okay." Clara straightened, her eyes going cloudy for a moment, then she launched into executive mode. "You've told us now, so there's no more denial. First things first, you're going to take a test. Once we have a definite answer, we'll make a plan."

There were a million questions still up in the air, but having Bea and Clara on my side made me feel so much better.

I wanted to kick myself for waiting so long to tell them.

We ended up at Bea's house after dropping Nellie off with her grandparents. I'd taken three tests, and now we were standing in Bea's bathroom, watching each of them change.

Pregnant.

Pregnant.

Pregnant.

"Wow," I breathed, a bubble of panic working its way up my chest, escaping in the form of a maniacal giggle. "This is real."

Bea wrapped her arm around my shoulders, and Clara stroked my back.

"It'll be okay," Clara murmured. "Whatever you decide, we'll be with you."

"Mmhmm. And you don't have to decide anything today," Bea added. "Now that you have the information, you can really think about it."

I walked out of the bathroom and sank down on Bea's bed, where her dog, Benjamin, was curled up. He lifted his head, raised one brow, then dropped it back to his paws, unthreatened by my presence.

My friends followed, sitting on either side of me. For once, I wasn't nauseous. My thoughts were a jumbled mess, but I didn't feel sick.

"I don't know who the father is."

It sounded awful when I said it like that, but neither of my friends seemed to be judging me. I mean, I hadn't expected Bea to even blink when I told her, but Clara was more conservative and had been married for a long time before Jake. I should have known she would have been staunchly by my side, though. It was who she was.

"That's okay," Clara said. "We can find that out if we need to."

"Do we need to?" Bea asked softly.

I lifted my head, glancing between her and Clara, and nodded. If Frank were alive, this wouldn't have been a possibility. At nineteen, too young to really comprehend the impact of the decision, I'd accepted I'd most likely not have children. But Frank had been gone for over a year, and here I was, on the brink of having something I'd denied myself. The circumstances weren't perfect by any means. A partner to share this with would have been ideal, but since the idea of dating sent shivers down my spine, that wasn't going to happen.

So, here I was, pregnant, with more money in the bank than I ever could have dreamed and a support system I was confident wouldn't let me down. No partner, but life wasn't perfect, and if I didn't embrace this now, later might be too late.

"I've always wanted to be a mom, and I don't know if I'll have another chance. This seems...well, I don't believe in fate, but this situation feels like it was meant to be." I pressed a hand to my abdomen and sighed. "This is my baby."

Clara kissed the side of my head. "You're going to be an incredible mother, Shir. I don't know anyone with a bigger heart than you."

Bea nodded. "If I could pick my mom, I'd pick you."

I laughed. "Thanks. That makes me feel really good. I think I'll do an all right job. My mom was the best a kid could have asked for. I wish she were here, but she taught me well."

That last part, I had to whisper around the knot in my throat. It had been a long time since I'd lost my mom, but right about now, I wanted nothing more than to curl up in her arms and fall asleep to her stroking my hair like she used to.

As if reading my mind, Clara's fingers slid through the back of my hair, dragging from my scalp to the ends. The slow, steady movement relaxed me. I leaned into her, my head on her shoulder.

"So...can I ask if he was hot?"

I snickered. Leave it to Bea to ask the pertinent questions.

"I don't know," I admitted. "His body was out of this world, but he kept his face covered, and so did I. It was really, *really* anonymous."

"Whoa." Her brows popped. "You could pass this man on the street and have no idea."

"Right." I rubbed my lips together. "He said he would leave his information with management so I could contact him if, and I quote, 'the worst happened.'"

"Are you going to?" Clara smoothed her hand down my back. "Realistically, you don't have to tell him. He'd never know, and you'd never have to worry about potentially sharing custody with a stranger."

Another shot of panic hit me square in the chest. I'd just accepted this pregnancy, so the thought of giving up any part of this bean made my stomach lurch. Except I didn't have any family to speak of, and it wouldn't be fair to deny this child the chance to have as many people to love them as possible.

Bea bumped my shoulder. "It'll be okay if you tell him. If he turns out to be a dickhead, I know people..."

I snorted a laugh. "I can't become a mother and a murderer in one year. It's too much."

Bea patted my head. "I wouldn't even tell you it was happening. One day, he'd be here, and the next, he'd simply be gone. Poof."

"How do you know hitmen?" Clara asked, her lips curled in amusement.

"I like to talk to people. Sometimes they're hitmen. It's a crapshoot." Bea batted her long lashes. The crazy thing was I couldn't tell if she was serious or making a joke. With Bea, both were equally possible.

I took a deep breath and released it. "I'll tell him. We talked, you know, before, and he seemed decent. Anyway, it's only fair. I am choosing to go through with this pregnancy, so he should be allowed to choose if he wants to parent or not." I looked at my friends, unsure despite my conviction. I wasn't even certain I *could* tell him since he'd deleted his account after our night together. But I had to try... "Right?"

"If that's what you want, honey," Clara said. "It's your decision. I'm here, no matter what."

"Me too. I need to be Aunt Bea, though, okay? Nellie just laughed when I told her to call me that. Your sweetheart is my last hope."

Tears pricked my eyes, and my nose stung. "Oh no."

Bea's eyes went wide. "I don't have to be Aunt Bea if it upsets you. Oh god, Clara, what did I do?"

I shook my head as the first tear fell. "No, I love Aunt Bea." I fanned my face, trying to dry up the silly, unnecessary tears. "I think it's the hormones. You two are being so incredible. I've been so scared and feeling like crap all by myself. I just got a little overwhelmed with relief and gratitude."

Bea huffed like she was annoyed then wrapped me in the tightest hug. "God, you're sweet, Shir. You aren't by yourself. Not anymore."

"No, you aren't, and you won't be." Clara hugged me from the other side.

A heavy weight landed on my legs, and I looked down, finding Benjamin's big, gray head on my legs, his watery eyes watching our hugfest.

"Hi, Benjamin," I cooed. "I met a man named Ben recently. I bet you'd like each other."

Bea scratched behind her dog's ear, but he stayed firmly planted on my lap as if he sensed I needed the extra snuggles. And I really did. My cat, Mary, wasn't going to appreciate a dog's scent all over me, but she'd live.

"Who's Ben?" she asked.

"Roman's twin brother," I said.

"Hmm." Clara folded her arms. "Is Ben as rude as Roman?"

"Roman's not rude." I bit down on my lip, no clue why I'd rushed to defend the man who had been determined to dislike me since day one. Clara and Bea had been ready to storm GoldMed when I told them what I'd overheard Roman saying to Francesca. They weren't fans. "But from what I saw, they're not really alike."

"Good. I don't want to add another member of that family to my shit list," Bea stated.

Laughing, I assured her she didn't have to. Roman seemed to be the only Wells who had ill feelings toward me. It was a shame, but I had other things to think about now. Much more important things.

As soon as I got in my car, I gathered up all my courage and called the Mile High Club.

"You've reached MHC. This is Samantha."

"Oh. Hi," I stammered.

"Hi," she chirped, as cheerful as the night I met her. "How can I help you?"

"Well, I was there a few weeks ago. In room ten. I was hoping I could pass a message along to the club member I was with that night."

I told her the date and heard her typing on her computer. "Ah, is this Goldie?"

"Yes. You remember me?" I asked.

"Of course. I saw you leaving...many hours later. You had fun, huh?"

"I did."

"And you want to do it again? With the same mystery man?"

I licked my dry lips, nausea nearly overtaking me. But I could vomit later. I had to get this over with.

"Can you get a message to him? Is that possible?"

"I can't tell you any personal information, or vice versa, but I can certainly pass a message along. What do you want to say?"

"Please tell him..." I pressed the heel of my hand to my forehead. What could I say? I wasn't ready for a perfect stranger to know I got pregnant at a sex club, even though I had a feeling Samantha wouldn't judge. "Please say, 'The worst happened, and I'm happy with the result. Call me if you want to talk about it.' And please give him my phone number. And my real name—Shira."

"Shira," she repeated. "What a pretty name, although Goldie is cute as a button too."

"Thank you." I heaved a breath, battling my roiling stomach. "It was good to talk to you again."

"You too, Shira. I'll pass your message along ASAP. Hopefully I'll see you at MHC again soon."

We said our goodbyes, and I sat there for a minute, willing my insides to settle. I'd done the first series of hard things—taking the test, telling my friends, contacting Wim. There were plenty of hardships ahead of me, but for tonight, I could breathe a sigh of relief.

I touched my stomach again, and a twinge of excitement fluttered instead of the panic I'd been drowning in. I was going to do this. With or without Wim, I wouldn't be alone.

CHAPTER SEVEN

Roman

GOLDMED WASN'T THE ONLY pot I had my hand in, and as a result, my inbox held a dizzying amount of messages. My assistant sorted through my emails, starring the ones of highest priority. I clicked on an email sent last night from Shira. She'd replied to my questions about a manufacturer Frank had contracted six years ago.

She was certainly more talkative through email, but I still had several more questions and didn't have time to send them and wait for a response. Pushing back from my desk, I headed toward her office. Terry looked up from her computer as I approached.

"Hey, Terry."

"Roman." Her greeting was warm but wary. I hadn't quite won her over. "Is there something I can help you with?"

"Don't think so. I need to talk to the boss." I jerked my thumb toward the door. "Is Shira available?"

Terry stacked her hands over a pile of papers, the corners of her eyes pinched behind gold-framed glasses. "She's not in her office."

"Really? Hmmm. It seems that's been happening a lot lately."

Not only had she been late for several meetings the last couple weeks, yesterday, I'd gone to speak with her and found her sound asleep at her desk. I'd left her there. If I'd woken her, I would've unloaded about how little she cared for this company. Frank had left

GoldMed in her hands, and she repaid him by making a mockery of her position. It pissed me off. I was tired too, dammit, but I couldn't fathom what it would take for me to nap at work.

Terry's shoulders bunched, and she raised her chin. Despite everything, she was loyal to Shira Goldman. It bewildered me. She'd been Frank's right-hand woman and, presumably, just as loyal to him. She had to see or know something I didn't. I wished like hell someone would enlighten me.

"She's speaking with Francesa. I'm sure Shira will be back any minute. If you'd like to wait—"

"No, that's all right." I was already turning toward Francesca's office. "I'll find her. Thanks, Terry. And don't forget to send me the name of the ramen place. I'm jonesing for some noodles."

She sniffed, muttering as I walked away, "We'll see about that."

Francesca occupied the far corner of the floor. She was rarely in the building, and I couldn't say I'd ever ventured into her office. Her door was half open. Francesca was behind her desk, a wicked smirk on her painted red lips, while Shira had her back to me, both hands fisted at her sides.

"You can't do that again," Shira uttered.

Francesca lifted a shoulder. "Technically, it's my house. It isn't like I broke in."

Shira shook her head. "It isn't your house. It's mine—"

"Are you saying I can't come back to my father's home? My only connection to him, and you're taking that from me too? Haven't you done enough?"

"No, I'm not saying that. I just need you to—"

"I don't understand how you can be so cruel, Shira. I bet my father is rolling over in his grave right now."

Shira's shoulders bunched around her ears. "I don't think I'm being cruel. I'm sorry if you feel that way, but the things you took weren't for you. They were mine—"

Francesca had mentioned Shira not allowing her to have her father's things, but given the drama she liked to create, I hadn't truly believed her. There was no denying it now. Shira Goldman might've looked like a meek little mouse, but underneath her false timidity was a greedy snake.

I cleared my throat, and Shira whirled around. For a flash, I thought I saw Francesca's lips turn into a grin then her face crumpled.

"Oh, Roman. I didn't see you there," Francesca wobbled, jutting her bottom lip out. "I'm sorry, my former stepmother and I were having a personal conversation. We should have saved that for after work hours."

"It sounds like you two have a few things to work out." I shot a pointed look at Shira then addressed Francesca. "Maybe a third party would help. I don't know any inheritance lawyers, but I'm sure the firm I use could recommend one."

Shira's cheeks flamed bright red. "That won't be necessary. We've already worked it out." Then she marched past me, careful not to brush me.

I trailed her, incensed on Francesca's behalf. Determined to rein it in, I ground my molars into dust to stop the insults on the tip of my tongue from flying out.

Shira glanced back at me over her shoulder. "I don't know what you heard, but I—"

"I heard enough."

Her fists tightened, and she muttered, "No one will let me finish a flipping sentence. I might as well not even speak."

"Finish your sentence. Explain why you're mistreating Frank's daughter."

She kept walking, those little fists balling even tighter. At half my size, I could have easily overtaken her, but I allowed her to have the lead. She strode straight into her office, and I followed, closing the door behind me.

She slumped in her chair and started clicking away on her mouse, ignoring my presence. It was infuriating. I wanted to have an important discussion with this woman and she wouldn't even acknowledge I was standing in front of her.

"Shira."

"Was there something else?" Her voice was so soft I had to lean forward to hear her.

"There is, in fact. I read your email and have a few follow-up questions. Do you have the time to answer them?"

"Just a minute, please."

She tapped on her mouse, the corner of her jaw rippling with tension. Taking a sweep of the rest of her face, I noticed her pallor, a contrast to her usual golden tone, and the purple rings around her eyes. Shira was a fine-boned woman, but her cheekbones were more prominent than usual.

Uncomfortable, I shifted on my feet. "Are you sick?"

Her gaze flicked to mine. "Not with anything contagious. Don't worry."

I frowned. "You *are* sick. That's why you were sleeping at your desk yesterday."

She sucked in a sharp breath, her hand stilling. "I...I didn't mean to do that." Then she covered her face with both hands. "I'm so sorry you saw me like that. How embarrassing."

"Shira, if you can't stay awake, you shouldn't be at work. Go to the doctor, get some rest."

She moved her hands aside to look up at me. "I'm fine, honestly. As I said, I'm not contagious, and I can do my job. There's no sense in me staying home. I'll just worry about things here and won't rest." She let her hands fall to her desk and wove her fingers together, clenching hard enough to turn them white. "It won't happen again."

I took her in for a long beat. She really didn't look well. Wisps had escaped her normally tidy hair, framing her sallow, hollow-cheeked face.

"Are you eating?" I asked, immediately wishing I could take it back. What she ate or didn't eat wasn't my concern. Soon, nothing about Shira would be my concern. But I was who I was, and seeing a woman in distress, no matter my personal feelings, didn't sit well with me.

Shira pressed her lips together and looked away. "I'm fine, Roman. Thank you for asking. I won't fall asleep at my desk again, and I'll be sure to keep personal issues outside the office."

Dismissed. That was what I was. I hadn't gotten the answers I'd been seeking, but I wasn't going to keep standing here with my dick in my hand while Shira tapped away on her damnable keyboard. I'd figure things out on my own.

Once I moved forward with my plans for GoldMed, I'd be doing that anyway.

CHAPTER EIGHT
Shira

FOR THE LAST WEEK, Bea had been coddling me. Clara too, but Bea had gone above and beyond. I'd seen her every day, whether for a walk, lunch, or dinner, and she texted every few hours to check in with me. Tonight, I'd gone to her place after work for dinner. All too aware of my lack of culinary skills, Bea was trying to keep me fed. She was a great cook, but I'd brought most of my dinner home, too queasy to eat much.

When I arrived home, Mary greeted me at the door. I'd gotten her the week after Frank passed to keep me company in this big, quiet house, and she did a good job of it. When the rescue said her last owner had died unexpectedly, I knew she had to be mine. We grieved together and pulled each other through.

I'd never had a cat before, but I couldn't imagine a sweeter one than Mary. Delicate and small for her age, with tuxedo coloring, she wore a pink collar with a fluffy mini bow. She was a little love, always following me around or bringing her toys over to where I was sitting to bat around with her tiny paws. But Mary also did not suffer fools. Just as she did every time I visited Bea and pet Benjamin, she took a whiff of me and backed away with a look of utter betrayal.

"I'm sorry, Mary. I did pet a dog, but I was thinking about you the whole time."

"*Rrrreow,*" she replied, plopping on her butt to clean the filth I'd just dragged in off herself.

I looked around my stark living room. It used to be filled with antiques and trinkets, but Francesca had slowly removed most of them over the last year. I didn't mind her taking a lot of it, but she had a bad habit of letting herself into the house when I wasn't here, which made me uncomfortable. She'd also taken things that were mine—my dining room table and chairs, a few paintings, my favorite armchair.

"No one came in today, did they?" I asked my cat.

"*Rrrrowww,*" Mary informed me.

"I didn't think so."

Yesterday, I'd found Mary huddled on my front porch after one of Francesca's lootings. She'd claimed letting Mary out had been an accident, but my girl was an indoor cat, and I really doubted she wanted to be anywhere other than her comfy living room. Needless to say, Mary wasn't a fan of Francesca either.

I'd let most of the things Francesca had done and said during the time I'd known her go, but I couldn't allow my dislike of confrontation to risk the safety of my cat.

As always, Francesca had been flippant and dismissive.

And Roman had walked in on me looking like the bad guy, which would have been laughable if it weren't so terribly sad. Frank had made a lot of questionable decisions during the waning years of his life, setting up his daughter and I to be adversaries, being one of the worst. Now, Roman could be added to that list. He thought I was some treacherous floozy who'd taken Frank for a ride, and it couldn't have been farther from the truth.

I sighed, resting my hand on my abdomen. I wished things were different, but there wasn't anything I could do about it now.

I couldn't get Roman's look of concern out of my mind, though. Despite everything he thought he knew about me, he'd taken one look at me today and pressed about my health. Maybe he didn't want me getting him or anyone else sick, but my heart said it had been more than that—that Ben had been right about his brother, and beneath his inaccurate assumptions, he was a good guy.

Maybe I should have explained things to him so we could come to an understanding. I could tell him about the letters, how things had been with Frank, the promises I'd made him when he was sick...

Maybe.

That would have to come later. Concentrating on the bean growing in me was the most important thing right now.

*

Clara's ob-gyn wasn't taking new patients, but she'd pulled strings and gotten me in for an appointment two weeks after my positive pregnancy test. I had my own doctor, of course, but Clara's was the best in Denver. Since I only had lukewarm feelings about mine, I'd been more than happy to make the switch.

Bea and Clara crowded around me in the ultrasound room as Dr. Sharma slid the wand inside me. My friends had decided this pregnancy was a team effort. Both had accompanied me without question—something I was grateful for since I hadn't wanted to ask—and were excited to be there. Even Bea, who claimed to be allergic to all things baby and children.

With a couple clicks, the whoosh of a heartbeat filled the room, and my own heart stuttered.

"That's it," Clara whispered.

"Is that...the baby?" Bea leaned forward to get a better look at the screen. It was all fuzzy and gray, but the sound was unmistakable.

"It is. A nice, strong heartbeat," Dr. Sharma answered. "Let's take a look—see how the baby's doing."

She moved the wand inside me, and the scene on the screen changed. Amid all the gray was a dark circle, and within it, a bouncy, gummy-bear-shaped baby.

Big head, round body, little poky arms and legs. My baby. This was really happening. My body held a little life inside it, and soon—probably sooner than I imagined—I'd be holding that little life in my arms. Instead of feeling panic at the reality of the situation, a gentle sense of rightness settled over me as fresh, clean happiness bloomed in my chest.

Bea gasped. "Oh my god! It's so cute! It really is like a gummy bear."

I laughed, tears rolling freely down my cheeks. "I was just thinking that."

Dr. Sharma clicked a few things on her computer and took what felt like an excessive number of measurements. Then she printed off pictures, making copies for Clara and Bea as well.

"You're measuring right where you should be according to your last period. Eleven weeks and two days." Dr. Sharma removed the wand and helped me sit up, keeping the paper blanket covering my lap in place.

I turned to my friends, sitting side by side. Bea with a funny, dreamy expression, and Clara crying, I thought to myself I wasn't missing anything by not having Wim here with me. No one could possibly be as excited for me as my best friends were. Though a very small part of me wished Wim had at least replied to my message, even if it was just to say "good luck," this moment only cemented my decision to move forward with the pregnancy

Dr. Sharma wheeled her stool in front of me, a tablet resting on her crossed legs. "How are you feeling, my dear?"

"Happy," I rasped, my throat thick with emotion. "So happy."

She smiled warmly and let out a small chuckle. "That's always good. I was referring more to your health, though. You've been nauseous?"

"Oh." Laughing, I put my hand to my flushed cheek. Of course that was what she'd been asking. "Yes. I haven't been feeling the greatest, and eating a full meal is a real test. Most of the time, it doesn't stay down."

"Hmm. We'll keep an eye on that. If needed, I can prescribe you medication to help. For now, I advise you eat small meals throughout the day."

The doctor went over what to expect for my future appointments and answered my, Bea's, and Clara's questions with the patience of a saint. By the time we were leaving, I understood why she had been voted the best ob-gyn in Denver. I was more than pleased Clara had used her influence to get me in with her.

On our elevator ride down to the lobby, my stomach went haywire. As soon as the doors slid open, I ran to the restroom. Clara and Bea were hot on my heels, taking care of me as I knelt on the bathroom floor, heaving uncontrollably. The tears rolling down my cheeks now were for an entirely different reason.

As happy as I was to be having this baby, I'd never felt so depleted and weak. I had high hopes my nausea would settle once I hit the second trimester, but dealing with this for another day, let alone two or three more weeks, made me want to curl up in my bed and not leave it.

There was nothing left in me, but I couldn't stop choking and sputtering. Clara rubbed my back, and Bea tried to soothe me, telling me I'd be okay. It didn't *feel* like I would. My body was entirely outside my control, revolting against the changes happening inside it. The baby was snug and happy, nestled within me, but I was crumbling.

Eventually, the heaving stopped, and Bea and Clara pulled me to my feet and got me cleaned up. Clara got out her emergency kit, adding blush to my sallow cheeks and highlighter to my brows. Bea swiped some of her pink gloss on my lips, and I smoothed my hair back, putting it in a fresh bun.

"You poor thing," Clara murmured. "You're really going through it, aren't you?"

"You should get the medicine Dr. Sharma mentioned." Bea paced back and forth in front of me, her arms crossed over her chest. "It's not right for you to be so sick. Someone should fix it."

I nodded. "I'll call for the prescription when I have a chance. I really have to get to the office. There's a meeting on my calendar I shouldn't miss. As it is, I'm going to be late and give Roman another reason to dislike me."

Bea stopped pacing to scowl pointedly. "I don't like that man. I think I need to show up at the office and have a little chat with that ass."

"I appreciate the support, Beatrice, but it's fine—*I'm* fine," I assured her, though I didn't feel fine. It was mind-boggling how I could be filled with so much joy while simultaneously feeling like death warmed over, but here I was.

"Call for the prescription ASAP." Clara looked me over, concern evident in her caring gaze. "I'm really worried about you. You downplayed how sick you've been to the doctor."

"I didn't mean to. I've just been feeling so bad for weeks it's sort of become my normal," I explained, receiving startled glares from them both. "I'll call as soon as the meeting's over. I promise."

My friends walked me to my car and hugged me tight before sending me on my way. I really was running late, and I hated that. It wasn't professional in the least. Even worse, I hadn't been able to prepare for this meeting since Roman hadn't informed me what it was for. Hopefully, he'd do all the talking, and I could surreptitiously nibble crackers while I listened.

Traffic was dismal on the way to the Levy building, making me even later. By the time I'd parked and rode the elevator to the tenth floor, I was worried it would be over. I walked down the quiet corridors as quickly as my stomach would allow, which wasn't very fast, to be honest.

When I finally made it to the conference room, I wasn't certain I should enter. My forehead was covered in a cold sweat, and I was swaying on my feet. I probably needed to eat something, but I was afraid I'd be back on my knees again if I did.

I just had to get through this meeting, then I'd call Dr. Sharma and head home.

Sucking in a deep breath, I pushed through the door and nearly fell backward. I'd thought this meeting would be with Roman and a few of GoldMed's executives. Instead, the entire board was sitting around the table, grim expressions on each of their faces. Francesca was in the room too, but she was the farthest thing from grim. A smirk curved her perfect lips as our eyes met.

A powerful sense of foreboding nearly knocked me on my ass, but I pushed past it. I'd handled much worse than a surprise board meeting. Steeling my spine, I raised my chin. This would be no problem.

CHAPTER NINE
Roman

SHIRA GOLDMAN WALKED THROUGH the door of the conference room thirty minutes late. I would have been insulted if her absence hadn't made conducting this meeting far easier for me and less awkward for the board.

She raised her chin proudly, though I couldn't help but notice the beads of sweat on her forehead and the greenish tinge to her skin. Something wasn't right. If I could have delayed today's event until she was well, I would have, but the wheel had already been set in motion. It was happening.

"Excuse me. I apologize for my lateness. I wasn't aware the board would be here," she stated woodenly.

I rose from my seat, noting the men and women around me conveniently making themselves busy by studying the contract I'd presented to them. Cowards.

"You're right on time, Shira. Don't bother sitting down. This won't take long."

She gripped the back of the chair near her, her knuckles going white. "Okay. Will you tell me what I missed?"

"I will." Circling the table, I brought her the contract Francesca and I had signed earlier in the week. She took it from me, her brow crinkling as she read it. "As you can see, Francesca sold her shares of GoldMed to me, giving me controlling interest in the company."

Shira sucked in a sharp breath, her head jerking back. "Oh," she whispered.

"Since coming to GoldMed two months ago, it's become clear you and I don't see eye to eye on the direction it should be going," I continued, though without the sense of victory I'd expected as reality dawned on Shira. "As the primary owner, I called the board here to vote."

She swallowed. "Please, just tell me..." she murmured for only me to hear.

"The board came to a unanimous vote. As of today, you are no longer CEO of GoldMed. I'll be taking over until we can find a permanent replacement."

I'd bought GoldMed's debt in order to bring the company back to life to honor Frank Goldman and removing Shira had been my first goal. This was supposed to feel good. Vindication for the way she manipulated herself into this position. For the way she had treated Francesca. For isolating Frank at the end of his life. For driving Frank's company into the ground.

Instead, it all rang hollow. I wasn't sure doing it this way had been the right decision. Not when Shira looked like she'd been beaten and dragged through the streets for weeks on end. Not when she finally raised her eerie eyes to mine and something deep within me recognized her grief and despair.

"Okay." Shira looked around me and nodded to the board, men and women who'd known both Frank and her for many years. When it came down to lining their pockets, they'd been all too willing to oust her. "Thank you, everyone. I guess...I guess I'll go now."

Swiveling on her toes, her head raised, she marched to the door. Her fine-boned hand wrapped around the knob, pulling it open, and without a glance back, she walked out.

Murmurs started as soon as the door clicked shut, but I didn't move. Dread pooled in the pit of my stomach. Should she have looked so devastated? Her reaction didn't sit right with me. Sure, the moves had been made behind the scenes and without her knowledge, but Shira hadn't been angry. She'd seemed moments away from falling to her knees and crumbling to pieces.

Francesca's heavy perfume arrived before she did. She sidled up beside me, her fingers curling around my forearm.

"Ding-dong, the wicked witch is dead. Great job, Roman."

I peered at the woman next to me, uneasy she thought we were on the same team. I might not have agreed with the treatment she'd received from her father's wife, but I'd never mistake Francesca Goldman for a good person.

"That isn't necessary," I bit out.

"Don't tell me you feel sorry for her. She's sitting on a pot of my father's gold. I'm sure she'll be fine. And she doesn't have to pretend to work now."

I looked down at her, a raised brow. "Neither do you, Francesca. You're free to go clear out your office."

She huffed. "Just because I sold my shares to you doesn't mean I don't want to work here."

"No, but the fact that you don't actually do anything means there's no reason for you to take up space anymore."

She folded her arms across her chest, her expression sardonic. "Oh, are you feeling a pang of guilt for getting rid of my wicked stepmother the way you did and taking it out on me? Too bad there isn't a bike big enough for you to backpedal, Roman. You well and truly humiliated little Shira. If you feel bad about that…well, it's not my problem." She flicked her hair behind her shoulders. "You know, I think you're right. I'm done with GoldMed. You can go down with this ship all on your own."

She yanked open the door as two people ran by and commotion sounded from down the hall. Terry's urgent voice rose above everyone else, directing someone to grab water and paper towels.

Moving Francesca aside, I strode toward the small crowd. Terry was nowhere in sight, but I heard her, speaking softer now, saying it would be okay, an ambulance was coming, everything was okay.

Finally, the crowd parted, and I stopped dead. Terry was kneeling on the floor with two other women I recognized, but for the life of me could not conjure their names. Between them was Shira, pale as a sheet and unconscious.

"What happened?" I demanded.

No one responded to me. Those who weren't actively helping Shira were watching. Terry had Shira's head cradled in her lap, a cloth on her forehead.

"Terry—" I started but clamped my mouth shut when her eyes shot to mine, filled with venom and ire.

"Don't," she snapped. "I don't have time for you."

Minutes crawled by before EMTs showed up with a stretcher. By then, Shira had roused, but her head was lolling on her neck like it was barely attached. My hands twitched at my sides. I felt more helpless than I had in a long, long time.

The EMTs carefully placed Shira on a stretcher, and Terry stood with her, holding her hand.

"Bright side, baby: you can rest up now. No more stress—none of that," Terry cooed.

"Bright side," Shira repeated. "It's you."

A strong sense of déjà vu struck me right in the center of my chest. But I didn't have a chance to examine it—not when the EMTs whisked Shira past me, her eyes fluttering closed.

The crowd slowly dispersed, and I followed Terry to her desk. "What happened?" I barked more harshly than I intended.

She glared at me, her eyes dark and stormy. "That isn't any of your business, young man." Plopping her purse on her desk, she squared her shoulders. "Now, if you don't mind, I'm taking the rest of the day off. My friend needs seeing to, and to be quite frank, I'm pissed as hell at you for how you conducted yourself today."

I nodded. "Of course. I understand. We need to meet tomorrow to discuss what your new role at GoldMed will be."

Her lip curled into a small snarl. I had known she wouldn't be pleased, but she'd been with GoldMed for a long time. Once she had some time and saw my vision, she would come around.

The following morning, Terry came to see me first thing. She marched right into my office, a paper clutched in her hand, looking like she was ready to read me my rights.

"Good morning," I greeted. "I'm aware it's not my business, but I have to ask how Shira is."

She stopped in front of me, her mouth curved in a frown. I thought she'd ignore my question or refuse to answer it, but after a beat, she sighed.

"She'll be fine. She's home and resting. Her friends are taking care of her."

"Good." I nodded a few times. Since Shira was taken away yesterday, I'd picked up my phone more times than I cared to admit to call her and check in. I'd almost called Terry too. I'd even been on the verge of phoning the hospital, knowing they wouldn't tell me anything.

"That's good. I hope she recovers quickly. She hasn't looked well for a while—"

Terry's forehead crinkled, and her nostrils flared like a bull seeing red. "Oh, you noticed she hasn't been well but still went through with the bullshit you pulled yesterday?"

I jerked back, shocked she'd used that language in the office, given she'd never been anything but staunchly professional. I should have known she'd be angry. Despite everything, she and Shira were close, and I hadn't treated her well. I'd just have to work to bring myself back around to Terry's good side.

"Look, in hindsight, I should have handled things more delicately. I realize that now, but what's done is done. I'd like to move forward and build a healthy relationship with you. We can talk about a new title, but I need your insight as I move GoldMed forward—"

Terry slapped her paper on my desk. "Absolutely not, young man. I am sixty-five years old and should have retired years ago. The only reason I stayed was for Shira Goldman. Not Frank, Shira. If you think I'll work for the man who usurped that woman, you must've been born yesterday. As of today, I'm officially retired, and you're shit out of luck."

She punctuated her statement with her middle finger. "Oh, and that's effective immediately."

She marched out of my office before I could protest or even begin to wrap my head around my next course of action. Terry was part of the backbone of GoldMed. She would have been able to give me guidance on decisions that had to be made—

Another woman unceremoniously walked into my office. I recognized her from staff meetings but couldn't bring her name forward with all the thoughts bouncing around my brain. What I did know was she looked just as pissed off as Terry.

"Good morning." I braced for what I had a feeling was coming. "How can I help you?"

She wasn't as brazen as Terry had been. She took a seat on the edge of the chair across from mine while holding a piece of paper in her trembling hands.

"Good morning, Mr. Wells. In case you've forgotten my name, I'm Gabriela Watson. I'm head of marketing...well, I was. I let HR know, but wanted you to know too. I'm turning in my two weeks' notice. I'd rather leave today, but I'll work my two weeks because I'm a woman of my word."

Shit. Fuck. Shit. Shit. Shit. Fuck.

Inside, I was screaming, but I kept my composure.

"I'm very sorry to hear that. Would you like to tell me why you're leaving so suddenly, Gabriela?" Tension rode me like a demon. My shoulders were so tight it was all I could do to sit still and not react.

Gabriela, who struck me as somewhat timid, lifted her chin in a decidedly Shira style.

"Yes, I would. I won't work for men who mistreat women—especially not one as good as Shira. You might think the way you handled removing her as CEO was a business decision, but to me, it was personal."

I shook my head. "I have to disagree with you, Gabriela. I would have done the same thing if Shira had been a man. My actions had nothing to do with her gender, and I strongly disagree that I mistreat women."

Her eyes narrowed. "That's what my ex said after he punched me so hard my orbital bone was fractured. Do you know who helped me? Shira. She paid for my lawyer, so I didn't have to worry about anything except getting out of a situation that would have killed me. Then she helped with that too. That woman held my hand, literally and figuratively, all the way through. So, no, I will not work for the man who treated her poorly and made a humiliating power play. I'm done with men like you, Roman Wells." Scooting forward, she placed her letter of resignation in front of me. "For the sake of my coworkers, I wish you and GoldMed good luck."

She walked out, leaving me stunned. When I'd started working in GoldMed's offices two months ago, I'd spoken to several employees about their opinions of the work environment and Shira. Now, considering *who* I'd spoken to, it gave me pause. I'd had lunches with executive team members who'd been around since the early days. All members of the old boys' club, along with Frank. None of them fans of Frank's "child bride," as they called her, being in charge of the business. Why hadn't I talked to someone like Gabriela?

Before I could answer my own question, the door to my office opened, and Annabelle Ortiz, head of HR, marched in. My stomach dropped.

"I hope you're here to address the two resignations we've had this morning and not adding your own to the stack."

She slapped her letter of resignation on my desk. "Sorry to inconvenience you, but I refuse to stay at this company any longer. This is my four weeks' notice—and I'm only giving you four weeks because my role is critical to the rest of the employees. It's not a favor to you in any way."

I nodded to the chair behind her. "I understand. Would you have a seat and talk to me for a minute?"

She hesitated but finally decided to sit down. Like Gabriela, she perched on the edge of the chair, poised to take off at a moment's notice.

"You disagree with my decision to let Shira go," I started.

She scoffed. "Let her go? Is that what you call the ambush you orchestrated? When you came to GoldMed, you told us it was to rebuild the company, but your intentions have been clear since day one. From what I've observed, no changes have been made and you've barely spoken with any team leaders who are women or below the age of fifty. I know everything I need to know about you, Roman Wells, and I won't be a party to it."

Sitting forward, I clasped my hands to keep from pounding the hell out of my desk. She wasn't wrong. Not at all. How could I have been so blinded by my agenda I'd made such a massive misstep?

"You're right, Annabelle. I messed up. When I started here, my game plan was to consult the people who'd been here during GoldMed's most profitable years to find out where things had turned south. The consensus was that things had changed when Frank married Shira, and the decline had continued steadily over the last five years. But I should have been talking to newer employees too. That had been a grave oversight. Since we're being blunt with each other, can I ask you a few questions now?"

She did the Shira chin raise, and for a moment, I thought she'd turn me down, but then she nodded. "All right."

I had a hundred questions but went with the thing that had been bothering me the most since I'd first walked through the offices.

"Why is it so damn quiet?"

"That's simple." She flicked her long, manicured nails. "Frank began having chronic migraines triggered by sound. He didn't want anyone to know, so Shira asked me to instill a rule several years ago that all employees had to use headphones to listen to music. Meetings—even small ones—were to be held in conference rooms, and everyone was given new, silent keyboards. She also had panels installed on the walls that soak up sound, and she did all this under the radar to help Frank."

I narrowed my eyes at her pretty story. "It's like a graveyard out there."

She crossed her legs and leaned forward. "What a biased point of view, Mr. Wells. I've had multiple employees email me to thank me for the changes. Those are documented, and I will send them to you if you need to see them. So, while you might see a graveyard, many find the quiet peaceful, and it has upped their productivity."

"Okay. I'll give you that I was biased, and I would love for you to forward those emails to me." I flattened my palms on my desk. "What has made you so loyal to Shira? I ask this because all my encounters with her have been extremely icy."

She rolled her eyes. "Are you kidding me? You admit to being biased and came to GoldMed with an agenda—which was to get rid of her. Your dislike of her has been clear from the jump. If a warm reception is what you expected, I'm honestly shocked you've gotten as far as you have in business without the ability to read people."

"What do you mean, Ms. Ortiz?"

"I mean, Shira isn't icy. Even a moron can see she's just shy." Annabelle puffed out her cheeks, expelling a heavy breath. "Honestly, I don't have time to sit here and answer your silly questions. If you'd like to email me, I'll respond when I have a moment to spare."

And once again, another woman marched out of my office, leaving me speechless.

Shy?

Was I a moron?

No. Shira might have been shy, but that didn't change other things I knew about her. It didn't negate the damage that had been done to GoldMed since she'd taken over. Though I could admit I should have gone about it differently, getting rid of her had been the right thing. I wasn't proud of that board meeting yesterday, but there was nothing I could do to take it back.

I pulled up the first letter Frank had sent me after my father had died. I'd been twenty-two, bitter with grief, filled with self-doubt, and had written to my dad's friend to let him know he was gone. I hadn't expected a reply, but a few days later, he'd written back, and his words had pulled me through.

ROMAN,

I'M SORRY TO HEAR ABOUT MY OLD FRIEND, MARCUS, PASSING AWAY. HE WAS A FINE MAN WHO WILL BE SORELY MISSED BY ALL WHO KNEW HIM. WE HAVEN'T SEEN EACH OTHER IN SOME TIME, BUT WE'VE EXCHANGED EMAILS IN RECENT YEARS, AND HIS WERE ALWAYS BRIMMING WITH PRIDE FOR HIS BOYS. YOU, BEN, NATHANIEL, AND ADRIAN WERE THE MOST IMPORTANT THINGS TO HIM. I HOPE YOU KNOW THAT.

I UNDERSTAND YOU MIGHT BE FEELING LOST RIGHT NOW. THINGS THAT WERE ONCE VITAL DON'T SEEM AS IMPORTANT,

LIKE FINISHING YOUR DEGREE WHEN YOU COULD GO PRO WITH RUGBY AND LEAVE EVERYTHING BEHIND. IF YOU WANT TO DROP OUT OF SCHOOL TO GIVE YOURSELF DISTANCE FROM YOUR LOSS, TAKE IT FROM SOMEONE WHO KNOWS, THERE'S NOWHERE YOU CAN RUN THAT IT WON'T FOLLOW. HOWEVER, IF RUGBY IS YOUR PASSION AND YOU'RE JUST TREADING WATER IN SCHOOL, GO FOR IT. A DEGREE ISN'T THE BE-ALL AND END-ALL.

KNOW THAT WHATEVER YOU DECIDE, YOUR FATHER WOULD BE PROUD. HE ALWAYS TOLD ME, OF ALL HIS SONS, YOU WERE THE ONE HE WORRIED ABOUT LEAST. HE KNEW YOU HAD A SOLID HEAD ON YOUR SHOULDERS AND GREAT INSTINCTS. FOLLOW THEM, ROMAN.

THE DECISION YOU MAKE WILL BE THE RIGHT ONE. IF IT'S NOT, THERE'S NO RULE THAT SAYS YOU CAN'T ADMIT YOUR MISTAKE AND START OVER. YOU CAN WALK A HUNDRED PATHS IN YOUR LIFETIME. YOU AREN'T OBLIGATED TO STAY ON ONE ALL THE WAY TO YOUR GRAVE.

BE BRAVE.

• FRANK GOLDMAN

His letter hadn't been anything groundbreaking, but it had been a lighthouse when I'd been lost in a sea of anger. His advice had led me to playing professional rugby, which turned out to be some of the best years of my life. And when I became too injured to continue playing, with his words ringing in my head, I got up and started down a new path, which was to save GoldMed.

However, the three letters of resignation on my desk told me I'd screwed up. I'd begun in the wrong direction, too myopic to see the big picture, but that didn't mean I had to keep going that way.

Tomorrow, I'd start over on a new path—one that included speaking with every single employee.

CHAPTER TEN
Roman

Leave it to Adrian to keep me waiting for the dinner he invited me to. It was supposed to be a celebratory meal, but with two more employees resigning by the end of the day, I wasn't in the mood to party. Still, it had been a while since I'd sat down for a meal with my youngest brother.

So, I'd shown up—just to sit at his desk while he dealt with an issue out on the floor of his club, MHC. It had been over two months since I'd been here, and that hadn't been to meet my brother.

I shook my head before I got lost in the memories of *that* night. It had been my first time using Adrian's app, and the experience had blown all my expectations out of the water.

Goldie...

Jesus.

It would be some time before I could partake in anything like that again, and I really fucking doubted anyone else would live up to *her*. By the time I could come up for air and have a little fun again, Goldie would be long gone. I'd deleted my profile so I wouldn't be tempted to talk to her again, but she was never far from the back of my mind.

"Knock, knock." Adrian's assistant, Samantha, leaned her shoulder on the doorway of his office. "Fancy seeing you here."

Tall, blonde, gorgeous—Samantha was what men probably imagined when they fantasized about the things that went on in a high-end sex club. But my brothers and I had known her most of our lives. She and Adrian had always been best friends. None of us saw her as anything other than a goofy, bubbly girl who'd been taller than us our entire childhoods. We'd finally surpassed her in height in our teens, but she was still just as goofy and bubbly. How she put up with Adrian's serious, downright black moods was beyond me. But she was the only one, outside of his brothers, who could.

"Does my brother ever give you time off?" I asked.

She scratched the side of her head. "Time off? What does that mean?"

Laughing, I got up and crossed to her, giving her a hug and a peck on her temple. "It's been a while, Sammie. Are you going to dinner with us?"

"Not tonight. I have plans." She poked my chest. "You never replied to my email, you know. I wanted to see your reaction to that little message."

I cocked my head. "Email? I didn't get an email from you."

"Two weeks ago, my guy. I sent it to your Wells Brothers address."

"Ah." I shoved my fingers through my hair, giving it a hard tug. "My assistant sorts those out for me. She might've put it in the slush pile."

Samantha gasped and clutched her chest. "You mean emails from me aren't top priority? I'm shocked, Ro." Then she gave me another poke. "Hope those emails don't get automatically deleted. I don't think you'll want to miss this one."

Curious, I took out my phone and opened my email app. "Give me a hint. What was the topic?"

She gave me a cat-that-caught-the-canary smirk. "Goldie."

My breath hitched. "Goldie? From room ten?"

"Mmmhmm. She called for you. I emailed you her message and phone number. You should really do a better job sorting your emails—"

I blanked out on everything else she said, falling backward until I landed in a chair out of sheer luck.

I found the email, every single word glaring at me on my small screen.

To: <u>romanwells@wellsbrothersinvestments.com</u>

From: <u>samantha@mhc.com</u>

Hey, you!

I'm passing along a message from your sweet little Goldie you met in room ten. She wants me to tell you:

The worst happened, and I'm happy with the result. Call me if you want to talk about it.

Her phone number is: 555-235-6662

Good luck, Ro-go!

xoxo,

Sammie

P.S. Goldie's real name is Shira!

Black dotted my vision.

Fuck. Shit. Fuck. Fuck. Fuck.

It couldn't be. There was no way Shira was Goldie from room ten. Goldie...Goldman...Christ was I stupid.

Just to be sure, I checked Shira's contact information on my phone, confirming what I already knew I'd find. That was her phone number. There was no question my Goldie was Shira Goldman.

Goldie: It's been a really long time for me.

WhenInRome: I won't take it easy on you.

Goldie: I don't want you to. I want you to do anything you want to me.

WhenInRome: Are you a dirty girl, Goldie?

Goldie: I think I am, but I'm too shy to ask for what I want. I just want someone—you—to take it—take me.

WhenInRome: Oh, I can do that. Send me a picture. Show me what I'm getting.

Goldie: No faces, right?

WhenInRome: No faces, no names. The anonymity makes it all the more fun, shy girl.

Her headline had said, *"Shy, but I want you to use me,"* and I'd been too intrigued to resist messaging her even though I was only supposed to be checking out the app for curiosity's sake. Then she'd sent me pictures of her body, all petite and delicate with the most luscious curves, and...wow, that had been Shira. The best night of my life, bar none, had been with Shira Goldman.

Samantha kicked my foot. "Hey. Why do you look like you've seen a ghost?" She leaned over me, running her sharp nail along the message still on my screen. "What does 'the worst happened' mean?"

"If the worst happens and you need to get in touch..."

"I'm sure it's fine."

"I had a good time with you. Did you?"

"Yes," she whispered so sweetly, a foreign pang twinged inside my chest. *"It was everything I wanted."*

"Me too."

Flashes of the past few weeks played out in my head. Shira, pale, dark bruises rimming her eyes. Racing to the bathroom when I mentioned Greek food. Falling asleep at her desk. Her clammy forehead. Running late for meetings—for the board meeting where I'd ambushed her. Passing out in the hallway.

She was pregnant. With my baby? All signs pointed to yes. Holy hell.

I looked at Samantha, though she barely registered. "I have to go."

"Okay." She straightened, giving me room to stand on shaky legs. "What should I tell your brother?"

I rubbed my forehead, trying to clear out my mess of thoughts. "Tell Ade I had an emergency. I'll call him later."

❧

I found Shira's address in GoldMed's files and was at her door in less than thirty minutes. I had no game plan other than to find out if it was true—if she was really pregnant with my baby. Once I knew for sure, I'd begin to unravel the layers of fucked-upness I was dealing with.

I took a deep breath before I pounded on her door, forcing myself to stay calm. Going in guns blazing wasn't the move here. This woman had just been hospitalized yesterday. The last thing she needed was the man she couldn't possibly like very much throwing a fit on her porch.

Shira wasn't the one who swung the door open, though. A blue-haired woman who looked like a goth Marilyn Monroe with soft curls and a fluffy black dress stood in the doorway, her hands on her rounded hips.

"Yes?"

I cleared my throat and tried to peer around her. She wasn't especially tall or wide but managed to block everything out behind her.

"Is Shira here? I'm Roman W—"

"Oh, I know who you are, and I can't even begin to fathom what you're doing on my friend's doorstep. Did you come to take something else from her? Humiliate her some more? Sorry, but you'll have to wait at least forty-eight hours after her last hospitalization."

"I'm not here to antagonize her, but I do need to speak to her."

She arched a brow. "About what?"

"Look, I get you need to protect your friend, but what I need to talk to her about is personal."

"Not gonna happen, buddy." She stared me down, folding her arms over her chest. If I'd wanted to, I could have picked her up and set her aside, but the chances of coming away with both hands were undoubtedly low. "Move along."

I decided to try a different tactic. "If you won't let me see her, can you pass along a message for me? Then Shira can decide what she wants to do. Tell her Wim is here."

Her eyes narrowed, and for a moment, I thought she would slam the door in my face. In the end, that was exactly what she did, but first, she told me to wait while she spoke to Shira.

My head was a riot of thoughts and a tangle of emotions, none of which I could firmly latch onto. The blue-haired woman kept me hanging on Shira's porch for so long I was on the verge of giving up and forming a new game plan when the door swung open again.

This time, it was Shira in the doorway.

With her ribbons of ebony hair spilling around her shoulders, bare except for the thin straps of her tank top, I recognized her immediately, not as Shira but as my Goldie. I felt like an utter idiot. In all the time we'd worked down the hall from one another, how had I not seen it?

I said the first thing that popped into my head. "Heeyyy, Goldie."

Eyes rounding in panic, her hands flew to her mouth as she gagged, then she spun and ran away.

Guess I know how she feels about the news.

Chapter Eleven

Roman

With the door hanging open and no blue-haired woman around to stop me, I stepped inside, carefully closing the door behind me. The sounds of Shira retching traveled through the house as if she were in the same room. The reason for the insane acoustics became apparent as I entered the living room. The walls were barren, and a couch was the only furniture. The dining area was equally empty—no table at all. Was she moving?

A minute later, the blue-haired woman emerged from a hallway, her brows angry strikes of lightning over stormy eyes.

"Shira will be out after she cleans up. Your presence made her vomit. She hasn't done that since her doctor gave her the good meds yesterday. Take that news however you'd like. Personally, I hope." She jerked her hand toward the lone couch. "Sit down. No use in looming like that."

"I'm not looming." I shook my head, wondering why the hell I was defending myself to a stranger, then I took a seat, as ordered.

She exhaled, glancing toward the hallway. Somewhere back there, water was running. At least my presence was no longer making Shira throw up.

Hands on her hips, Shira's friend addressed me. "I'm Bea Novak, Shira's best friend. She doesn't owe you anything, but for some reason, she's agreed to talk to you. She's told me all about you, and I will not stand for you being a dick to her one more time."

"Fair enough. I don't intend on being a dick."

"Sure you don't." There was nowhere else for Bea to sit, so she perched on the arm of the couch opposite me.

I rubbed my sweaty palms on my legs, glancing around again. There was *nothing* here.

"Why is this house so empty?" I asked, unable to contain my curiosity.

Bea scoffed, her hands balling into fists. "You should ask Shira's sweet little stepdaughter."

I cocked my head. "Francesca?" Usually, I was more on the ball, but damn, a lot of information had been dumped on me at once. My brain was struggling to wrap around what was going on. "She told me Shira wouldn't let her in the house or allow her to have any of her father's things..."

Bea rolled her eyes. "Okay, Einstein. That's plausible. I know you've met Francesca. Do you really think she could be kept out of this house? Bitch doesn't have to be let in. She has a key and has been taking advantage of that fact over the last year—and Shira's kindness. Shira would never even consider locking Frank's daughter out of this house. If I had known the extent of her pillaging, I would have called the cops on her myself."

My mouth was open to ask questions, to press her for more information, but I was interrupted by a dulcet, "Bea. Don't."

Shira came into the living room, a tiny black-and-white cat cradled in her arms. Her hair was tied back, and she'd thrown a sweater over her tank. Not that it mattered. I couldn't unsee her as Goldie if I tried.

Bea hopped up, concern and worry etched on her face. "Sorry, Shir. This guy pisses me off. I'm going to chill. Promise."

Shira's tired, eerie eyes were soft on her friend. "I love you, Beatrice, but can you give us a little privacy? We have some things to talk about."

She hesitated but eventually agreed. "I'll be upstairs. Call me if you need me to toss him out."

"No violence," Shira murmured. "He can sue the pants off us, and I can't go pantless everywhere now that I'm going to be a mother."

Bea walked away laughing while I stared at this new version of Shira, who made jokes, cuddled a tiny cat, and apparently fucked like a little demon. It still didn't make sense to me.

Once we were alone, I shot to my feet and held my arm out toward the couch. "Please, sit. I can stand or sit on the floor if that makes you more comfortable."

Shira sat down with her back against the arm and her legs tucked under her. Her cat, who was as dainty as its owner, curled up in her lap, watching me with wary green eyes. I'd never been a cat person, but this one was pretty, even if mistrustful. I wondered what Shira had been telling her about me.

"There's enough room for us both," she said softly. "You don't need to sit on the floor, and I'll get a crick in my neck if you stand."

I sat back down on the opposite side of the couch, keeping a cushion between us to give her space.

"For the record, I wouldn't sue you, even if your friend tossed me out on my ear."

She sniffed, almost a laugh. "Good to know."

I spread my hands out on my legs. "We should get our facts straight before going any further. You're Goldie?"

She nodded then nibbled her bottom lip. "And somehow...you're really Wim?"

I winced at how fucking surreal it was to hear that name from her lips. "WhenInRome. Neither of us was too clever with our names, were we?"

She shrugged. "We weren't, yet we didn't figure it out."

The cat in her lap purred loudly as Shira carved her fingers through its fur. She wasn't giving me her eyes or even much of her attention. A week ago, I would have called this behavior cold and indifferent, but I was seeing her in a new light. Did my presence make her uncomfortable? Was meeting my gaze difficult for her? Did she not want me looking at her the way I was?

I shifted so I wasn't facing her head-on. Since there was nowhere else for me to go and not having this conversation was out of the question, it was all I could do to make her feel better about the situation.

"I read your email. I want you to know I wasn't ignoring it. I didn't see it until this evening, and I came straight here for answers. Are you pregnant, Shira?"

She nodded. "I am."

"Is it mine?"

Another nod.

"You're sure?" I had to ask.

A sharp inhale. "There's been no one else." Finally, her eyes lifted. "It's Wim's. If you're really Wim, then yes, it's yours."

Blowing out a heavy breath, I sunk back into the cushion, bewildered by how this was happening...how it was even possible. I wasn't a kid who played it fast and loose with contraceptives. I'd had plenty of sex in my life. I was always safe, had never had a pregnancy scare, and now this...*fuck*. How the hell did I get here?

Shira went on, shaky and so quiet I had to lean in to hear her. "It's my choice to continue this pregnancy. I don't expect anything from you. If you want to bow out, I understand. I have support, so I don't need—"

"Me? You don't need me?" I dragged a hand over my face before dropping it into my lap and squaring off with her. "I might need a minute to adjust, but there's no way in hell I'm going to have a kid walking around in this world and not be a part of their life. No way."

Based on the way Shira jerked back and her cat meowed, I might've been too harsh, but the idea of not knowing my child struck a deep nerve. She wasn't threatening me. Logically, I knew that. But it felt like she was, so my hackles were up.

"Okay," she whispered.

"*Fuck*," I gritted out, pissed I was going about this all wrong. "Look, I'm sorry. This is a lot, and I'm not in my best form. I need to wrap my head around this, but I'm in, Shira. That isn't a question at all."

"That's good. I understand it's a shock. I still can't believe it and my body hasn't felt like my own for weeks."

She wasn't as green as she'd been the last time I'd seen her, but she was still far too pale, her cheeks disturbingly gaunt. I hadn't liked it before I knew she was carrying my baby. Now, it made me furious. With no one to aim my anger at, I got up to pace the length of her empty living room.

"How are you?" I flexed my hands at my sides. "I know you're not well, but are you doing better? Your friend Bea mentioned medication? Is it helping?"

"I'm doing better, yes. I've only thrown up once today, which is incredible for me lately."

I halted my steps, my eyes lasering in on her. "Because of me?"

Her mouth twitched, but her eyes only lifted to my chin. "It was pretty shocking to find out the man who hates me is the father of my baby."

"I don't hate you, Shira. That's not—"

"It's fine." She sucked in a breath, her shoulders rising around her ears. "We can talk about what coparenting will look like later. I'm not up for that right now."

"That's a good idea. You need to rest, and I need to let all this sink in."

I cupped the back of my neck, my gaze sweeping over her. She was so damn delicate, even more so than she'd been in room ten. I didn't like knowing something I'd done to her was making her as sick as she was. Was it even good for the kid if their mother was throwing up all the time? I had no idea. As soon as I got home, I was going to be looking it up.

"Oh..." Shira climbed to her feet, her cat still tucked against her chest, "I have something for you if you want it."

I tracked her path into the kitchen, listened to her opening and closing a drawer, and watched her walk back to me. She stopped a good three feet away and extended her hand.

"This is from yesterday," she said softly. "That's why I was late."

I took the printout from her, my brow furrowing as I studied it. The image was grainy, and I was no expert, but I made out a round head, torso, and four limbs.

"Holy hell," I hissed. "It already looks like a baby."

"Bea downloaded an app. She said the baby's the size of a strawberry this week."

I lifted my gaze to look at Shira again. She'd let her cat down and was standing with one foot on top of the other, her sweater twisted around her fist. I made her nervous. How had I not seen that before? But I knew. I'd been blinded by my agenda. I'd gone into GoldMed with a narrative of how things would play out and refused to see anything that didn't fit that.

"A strawberry?" Using my thumb and index finger, I made a circle about that size, and my heart slammed against my chest. "With legs and arms...I need to download that app. Need to do a lot."

I held the ultrasound up, unsurprised to find my hand shaking. "Thank you for this. Is it all right if I show it to my brothers?"

"Oh, um..." She tucked a loose strand of hair behind her ear. "Yeah, if you want to. I've shown it to Bea and Clara—well, they were with me, so they saw it live and in person, but you know what I mean."

"Right. I'm glad they were there with you." I took a step back. "I'm going to let you rest. I will text you my phone number so you can let me know when your next appointment is. If you're comfortable with it, I'd like to be there. And if you need anything else, get in touch with me. Please."

"Thank you, Roman."

Her agreement felt more cursory than true, but I couldn't blame her. Up until an hour ago, I hadn't once treated her with kindness.

Luckily, I had six months to turn that ship around. She was the mother of my child, and I refused to bring our baby into the world in the midst of dissonance.

Once I let this new settle in, I'd make a plan to become the best friend Shira Goldman ever had.

First, I had a baby fruit app to download.

CHAPTER TWELVE

Shira

IT TOOK ANOTHER DAY to convince Bea I could be on my own. As much as I loved her company, she had a business to run, and I didn't need to be babysat from sunup to sundown. The medicine was helping with my nausea, but if I was honest, the reduction in my stress levels from no longer bearing the burden of keeping my late husband's company afloat had made the biggest impact. I could finally take a breath without worrying about what I should have been doing, who I should have been talking to, or what literal or figurative fire I should have been putting out.

With my newfound freedom, I'd spent two days in loungewear, snuggling Mary until she got tired of me, and catching up on TV I hadn't been able to pay attention to with all the moving parts going on in my life.

A strong sense of peacefulness had been uncovered when the rug was ripped out from under me, and I was taking my time to bask in it. I couldn't remember a time when I hadn't felt like a guillotine was hanging over me, waiting for the rope to snap. Maybe in my early days with Frank, when he'd been well...but I'd been too wrapped in the grief of losing my mother to really notice.

Mary trotted over, a stuffed mouse clutched in her teeth, and dropped it in front of me. Her green eyes flicked from me to the mouse, making certain I saw what she'd brought me.

"Look at that mouse," I cooed. "It never stood a chance in the face of my big, brave warrior princess, Mary."

"*Rrrroowwww.*" She pounced on the stuffed mouse, batting it between her little paws, both delicate and fierce, as she attempted to eviscerate it.

"Is this what you do all day when I'm gone, darling? Kill your toys?" I'd often returned from the office to Mary presenting me with a pile of her toys. Now, I understood she'd been showing off her hunting skills. "You're the best girl, Mary. I'm going to take some lessons from you on how to be tough. You do it with style."

She nosed the fully dead stuffed mouse toward me, sat on her fluffy bottom, and waited for praise. "Rrreoww."

I rubbed her head and back while her tail swished. "Good girl, Mary. You really killed that mouse dead. I don't think any other cat has ever killed a mouse so thoroughly."

Raising her paw, she placed it on my wrist and tilted her head. "Rrreooowwww." She butted her head into my palm one more time, then trotted away, probably off to find a spot of sun to nap in after all that hunting.

Alone in my barren living room, I took in the depressingly stark walls and state of my furnishings. The house had been Frank's before I moved in with him. He'd bought it after his divorce from his first wife, and Francesca had already been away at college by then. Why he'd decided he needed five thousand square feet all on his own was beyond me. I was drowning in this empty space.

I'd been thinking about moving for a while but hadn't been able to bring myself to add one more thing to my plate. Now that my plate had been scraped clean...

I cupped my belly. "No time like the present, is there, Beanie?"

It just so happened Bea had mentioned the house next to hers was for sale. This morning, I'd looked at the listing pictures with her and had fallen hard. I just needed to summon the energy to see it in person and put this place on the market.

Maybe I'd start on that...after a little nap.

Two things woke me at once: Mary nuzzling my face and my doorbell ringing insistently.

"If that's Bea not using her key, I'm going to be grumpy," I mumbled, moving Mary off me so I could get up.

But it wasn't Bea standing on my porch. Not Bea at all.

I opened my door to Roman holding a big box with several bags scattered around his feet. All it took was one look at him for me to remember I was only wearing a camisole and cashmere lounge pants that had a habit of hanging *low* on my hips.

My body was fine. Even good by some standards—breasts too big for my small frame, narrow waist, round hips and butt. The thing was, I was incurably allergic to attention—especially of the male variety. Roman had seen everything once, but that was when he'd been Wim and I'd been Goldie. Now that we were us, the last thing I wanted to be was exposed in front of him, but here I was.

Maybe he'd leave quickly.

"Hi."

"You have a cat," he stated.

"I do." Frowning, I glanced at the box. "Why do you have a robot litter box?"

"The last thirty-six hours, I've done nothing but read about pregnancy." That was...unexpected. I would have even thought it was nice had he not sounded so angry. At least he didn't seem to be paying any attention to my nipples poking through the thin fabric of my cami.

"Okay..." I whispered, unsure where this was going.

"Do you know what I discovered, Shira? Pregnant women aren't allowed to clean litter boxes. Have you been cleaning Mary's?"

Blood rushed to my cheeks. "Bea helped when she was here, but Mary's my responsibility, and I used gloves—"

"That means yes." He moved me aside—gently—and put the box down in my foyer. Then he went back to the porch for the bags and carried them into my living room. "I figured that would be your answer, so I bought this automatic litter cleaner. I've never owned a cat, but the man at the store said this one is the top of the line. When it needs to be manually emptied, I'll do that, but the robot will clean it on a daily basis."

"You'll do that?" I echoed.

He looked at me directly, not quite angry anymore, but stern for sure. "You're not to have anything to do with the litter. This is about keeping the baby safe, and that concerns me too. You don't want our baby to be exposed to something that could be harmful, do you?"

My heart leaped into my throat, and my eyes burned. I'd only come around to accepting I was having a baby. I'd yet to fully digest Roman was the father. If Wim had been some random man with no connection to me, it would have been a thousand times easier, but that wasn't the case. I was having a baby with a man who thought very little of me, who'd damaged me without provocation and had decided who I was based on others' opinions and not my actions. Now, he was standing in front of me, accusing me of being careless with our baby's health. It was the cherry on top of the sundae. Of course he would think that.

I paused, thinking it through. Had I been careless? God, maybe I had.

I blinked at him, my nose twitching, the burn in my eyes overpowering. "I don't want that. Thank you for looking out for Beanie."

I was an expert at locking down my emotions, but my little passenger must've held the skeleton key. Suddenly, my floodgates were wide open. A torrent of tears and a raspy sob broke free. I covered my face with my hands, but not fast enough to hide what was happening from Roman.

"*Shit,*" he bit out. Then he was there, taking me in his arms, gathering me against him. My head only came to the center of his chest, but it was a pretty fine place to be. Broad and warm, his heart beat rapidly beneath my cheek as he palmed the back of my head, holding me there. "I'm sorry for coming in so hot, Shira. I panicked when I read about toxoplasmosis this afternoon. Who the hell would have thought that was a thing?"

"Okay," I whispered.

His other hand rested on the middle of my back, his fingers spread wide. One reached the top of my camisole, gently stroking the bare spine between my shoulder blades. It was too intimate but familiar. Those huge hands had once been all over me.

"No, it's not okay. You don't need me storming in here, making you cry. We have to figure out a way to coparent this...Beanie."

Another sob broke loose. That was *my* nickname. I'd only started to say it out loud today. But my hormone-addled emotions liked hearing him say it, sharing that with him. How screwed up was that?

"You don't have to hug me," I said, though I wasn't trying to move away from him.

"I know, but I made you cry. The least I can do is comfort you."

That was what it took to finally snap me out of it. I slipped out of his embrace as memories of sitting on the bathroom floor after overhearing the things he said about me to Francesa came flooding in. He'd made me cry then too, and he certainly hadn't comforted me. Maybe it wasn't his fault he'd formed such a negative opinion of me, but that didn't mean how he had treated me was okay. I'd watched my mother make excuses for a man who hurt her until she couldn't do it any longer. I knew better than to follow that path.

"Thanks." I wiped my tears with the back of my hand then wrapped my arms around myself. "I'm fine now. Don't worry about me."

A deep crevice formed between his brows as he frowned down at me. He seemed like he wanted to fight me on that but clamped his jaw tight and shook his head instead.

"All right. Show me where Mary's litter box is and I'll set this thing up."

I led him to the utility room, pointing out the box and supplies on a shelf above it. He got to work on putting the massive robot machine together while I stood in the doorway, becoming increasingly doubtful this was a good idea. Mary was sweet, but she could be contrary. Like any girlie girl, she liked things just so.

"I'm not sure Mary will like this," I stated softly.

Roman looked up from where he was crouched by the giant cat bathroom. "What's not to like? The guy said this one has the best reviews. I looked, and it has the most features out of all the other brands. You can't find anything nicer."

"Mary's a simple girl," I said. "But she can be snobby about certain things. I tried to replace her old bed with an ultra-soft, luxurious one, and she clawed out all the stuffing."

He scratched his head. "Is that normal?"

I shrugged. "It's Mary. She's very sweet, but she has a temper."

"Is she going to be okay around the baby? If she's violent, I can't have her—"

"Don't you dare." My hand shot up between us, bringing him to a halt. "Mary is nonnegotiable. She may tear apart beds she doesn't like, but she would never, *ever* hurt a fly, much less a baby."

For once, I made direct eye contact. My cat was *that* important. If this man thought he was going to come in and throw his substantial weight around, he had something to learn. I'd ship him off to Siberia before I got rid of Mary.

Something in Roman's stance shifted. He exhaled as his brown eyes searched me, from my eyes down to my chest, which I felt flush from my indignation. He was giving me attention I didn't want or like because I'd reacted to him. My skin prickled with awareness and unease. I didn't think Roman would hurt me physically, but I certainly didn't trust him. He'd taught me not to.

"Okay, Shira. I hear you. Mary stays." He spoke to me carefully, like I was an injured animal. For my part, I wasn't doing anything to alleviate that treatment. I backed out of the utility room, keeping a wary eye on him.

"You don't have any say in that," I managed to push out once I had some distance from him.

His eyelids lowered, and he exhaled. "I know that."

"Good." Swiveling, I returned to the living room. It may have been barren, but at least it was a wide-open space where I could be far away from Roman and his judgment.

Roman followed me after a moment, staying several feet away as he gazed at the blank walls. His brow pinched and mouth puckered like he'd tasted something bitter, then he smoothed his expression and turned to me.

"Like I said, I've never had a cat and don't know how they work. If you trust Mary, I believe you." He blew out a heavy breath and shoved his fingers through his hair. "The last couple days have been a lot, and I've done nothing but ingest information about pregnancy. I think I'm overloaded now...and quite possibly freaking out."

I couldn't stop the laugh from bubbling out. "I can't imagine anything freaks you out."

The corner of his mouth hitched. "Some things do. You're right, though. It takes a lot to rile me." He nodded toward me—toward my belly, to be precise. "This did it. Something huge is happening, and it's completely out of my control. I'm not used to letting go of the reins, but I have to. It's...more difficult than I expected."

I nodded. "That's understandable."

And it was. I didn't know Roman well, but his reputation preced-ed him. He'd grown up with a well-known family name behind him. Wealth had given him an innate power and the ability to control his world in many ways. For the next six months, his child would be living in my body, and he had to trust the woman he'd hated and mistreated to take care of his baby. If the roles were reversed, I wouldn't trust him. Then again, he'd given me reason not to.

He glanced at the door then back to me. "I think I've done enough damage for the day. Do you need anything before I go? I can have groceries delivered or dinner..."

I shook my head. "I'm fine. Eating is still hit or miss, but Bea made me soup that Beanie seems to love, so I'm sticking with that for now." Remembering something, I raised a finger. "Before I forget..."

I grabbed the packet of papers my ob-gyn had sent to me and handed them to him. "These are instructions for the paternity test. You go to this lab—"

"Paternity test?" Roman echoed.

"Yes. It's a simple blood draw. You can go—"

"You want me to take a paternity test?"

Frowning in confusion, I answered, "Yes...don't you?"

"Is there a question of paternity?" he pressed, his rough tone shooting alarm up my spine.

"No. Not for me. But I assumed you'd want to be sure. You know, since we barely know each other, and...well—" I cut myself off, biting down on my lip.

"Well, what?" he gruffed. "Just say it, Shira."

I peeked at him from beneath my lashes then looked away. It seemed he wasn't leaving until I replied, and since I really did want him to go, I acquiesced.

"Considering your low opinion of me, I didn't think you'd take my word that this is your baby."

Roman's exhale was harsh and sharp as the papers crinkled in his hand. "I earned that." He lowered his hand, clutching the papers at his side. "I was there. I saw the broken condom. I know the baby's mine. We'll do the test to make things official, but I don't doubt you."

"Okay."

"Okay," he echoed. "Text or call if you need anything at all. Big or small, whatever it is, I'll make sure you have it."

It was nice he believed me, but it would take a lot more than lovely words for me to trust Roman Wells. I guessed it was good we had six months before we had to coparent. By then, hopefully he'd figure out I wasn't the conniving gold digger he'd made me out to be, and I would be able to be in the same room as him without flinching.

Chapter Thirteen
Roman

I'D DECIDED I'D MESSED things up enough on my own over the last forty-eight hours. It was time to bring in more people to be on my side. My brothers weren't experts on women, pregnancy, or babies, but they could be a sounding board for my choices, so I didn't barrel into Shira's house and make her cry again.

I sent the ultrasound to our group chat with the caption: "Mine."

It took less than thirty seconds to get a response.

Ben: *WTF?*

Adrian: *Not funny.*

Nate didn't bother texting. Perks of living in the condo next to mine, my older brother let himself in and stalked up to me, bending down so we were almost nose to nose.

"Are you fucking with us?" he growled.

I shook my head. "Nope." Then I handed him the ultrasound picture so he could look at it up close.

Ben: *You're going to drop a bomb like that and leave us hanging?*

> **Me:** *Nate stormed in, sorry. And I'm not trying to be funny, Ade. This is real.*

Nate sat next to me on my sofa, his elbows on his knees as he tapped on his phone.

> **Nate:** *He's not fucking with us. Looked him square in the eye.*

My and Nate's phones both went off simultaneously with a video chat request, and he moved closer to me so we could share my screen.

Ben was grinning, and Adrian seemed perplexed. They spoke at once, asking two starkly different questions.

"Who's the mama?" Ben asked, seemingly excited by this news.

"Are you sure it's yours?" Adrian, the most pessimistic of our quad, asked.

Nate poked at the numbers at the top of the printout. "This says eleven weeks, two days—and that was three days ago. This woman is almost twelve weeks. How many weeks are a pregnancy?"

"I don't know." Ben started counting on his hands. "There are fifty-two weeks in a year, but ladies aren't pregnant that long. It's nine months, right? Four weeks in a month...what's nine times four?"

"Thirty-six," Nate supplied. "She's already a quarter of the way pregnant?"

"Not how it works," Adrian sighed. "A quick web search says a typical pregnancy is forty weeks. The first trimester is thirteen weeks."

Ben scratched his head, frowning. "It's not divided in quarters? That'd make a lot more sense."

"It's trimesters," I replied. "She's almost through her first trimester."

"You didn't say whether you're sure it's yours," Adrian reminded me.

"It is." Like I told Shira, I'd seen the faulty condom. She could have been with someone else before or after me, but I truly didn't believe that. "I'm taking a paternity test to alleviate any doubt, but I know it's mine."

Ben clucked his tongue. "I thought you always wrapped it. I'm aghast at your recklessness."

He sounded more amused than anything. It took a lot to shock my twin. I'd thought my impending fatherhood might've done it, but it seemed he was rolling with it.

"Broken condom," I replied.

Nate studied my profile. "You don't seem upset."

"I've had two days to process it." I lifted a shoulder. "It still doesn't feel real, but no, I'm not upset about becoming a father. I think I'm capable and have the resources I need to give my kid a good life."

Adrian leaned in toward the camera. "I wasn't aware you were seeing anyone. Who's the baby's mother?"

Nate brought the ultrasound up to his face. "It says it right here. Goldman comma Shira. Wait...what?"

Ben's eyes bugged. "Shira? *Shira* Shira? Like, the woman you trounced all over?"

"I didn't trounce all over her," I protested. "But that's the one. Do you know any others?"

"I mean, I don't know *her*." Ben puffed up his cheeks and blew out a heavy breath. "How the hell did that happen? Don't you hate each other?"

"Wait. Slow down. Shira Goldman is carrying your baby?" Adrian pressed. "What the fuck, Roman?"

It was on the tip of my tongue to explain room ten, but I stopped myself. I couldn't really articulate why since my brothers and I were open books. We were so close in age, we were stairsteps—with Ben and I sharing a step. At only a grade apart, we'd shared friend groups, played the same sports, and had taken care of each other at home when our mother had been disinterested in parenting and our father had been wrapped up in work.

This felt different, though. Something I wanted to hold sacred. Probably because we'd made a child out of it. It made what had come before it a hell of a lot more important than any ol' fuck. If I was honest, even before I knew about the pregnancy, I had kept that night in room ten close to my vest.

"It happened before I came to GoldMed. We didn't know who the other was, and the condom broke," I explained. "It's complicated with how everything went down, but we're going to make it work."

"How?" Adrian asked bluntly. "You don't even like the woman. Didn't you just recently refer to her as 'the gold digger'?"

Ben shook his head. "I knew she was cool. I tried to tell Rome, but he was all wrapped up in his mission..."

"Should've wrapped up his dick better," Nate muttered.

Without turning my head, I backhanded him in the gut. "Shut the hell up."

He rolled away, chuckling. "You gotta laugh, man. This situation is so beyond ridiculous. You sent that woman to the hospital—oh, wait, she passed out because of the pregnancy?"

Remorse struck me hard and fast, leaving me winded. "Yeah."

Ben tsked. "Wow. You have a lot to make up for, man."

"He doesn't have anything to make up for," Adrian intoned. "He was working with the information he had when he made his decisions. Now he'll move forward with the current state of things."

Ben's eyebrow winged. "Okay, sure, IceMan. Ro, I'm gonna suggest you not take advice from the man who has the emotional capacity of a corpse."

"I wasn't planning on it." I dragged my hand along the scruff on my jaw. "I've discovered I was wrong about a few things. It makes me wonder what else I could have misjudged."

"Like what?" Nate had retaken his seat beside me so he could share my screen.

"Like Francesca lying through her teeth about being allowed in the house. She cleaned the place out. It's like...a tomb in there. Nothing on the walls, barely any furniture." My fingers curled into my palm as anger rose in my gut. "I can't figure Shira out. She's got it all locked down—"

"Like Adrian," Ben chimed in.

I chuffed. "Sort of, but not really, unless Ade's hiding a debilitating shyness."

Adrian rolled his eyes. "I'm the owner of a sex club. There's no room for shyness. And I'm not hiding a thing. This is who I am."

"Cool, cool." Ben made jazz hands. "I, for one, am excited as hell to be an uncle. If I weren't in New Zealand, I'd be on my way over there to give you the biggest hug you've ever been given."

Adrian grimaced. "Do you actually believe this woman will allow us to be part of the baby's life?"

"Will she?" Nate asked.

"She will," I replied. "Shira didn't have to tell me about the baby. She chose to. I don't know what coparenting will look like yet, but it'll happen. Which means you three are going to have to figure out how to be uncles to this kid."

"I'm in." Nate clapped me on the shoulder. "Anything you need, Ro."

Adrian did not look convinced, but he inclined his chin. "Of course."

Ben fist-pumped. "*Yes*. I'm all about it. I cannot wait to confuse the hell out of your baby with my sparkling personality while having its boring dad's face."

"It's a human, not a toy," Adrian reminded him.

As they bickered back and forth, Nate squeezed my shoulder. "You okay?"

I thought about it for a beat before nodding. "I think I will be."

As long as I didn't keep making Shira cry.

⁂

The next morning, I woke up to a picture of cat shit.

Shira: *I'm going to go back to the regular litter box.*

Me: *Don't do anything. I'll be right there.*

Lucky for me, Shira's place wasn't far. Even luckier, it was Saturday, so I didn't have to go into the office. Though, I probably would. Work didn't stop just because it was the weekend.

I drove as fast as I dared to Shira's neighborhood. She said she wouldn't touch the litter, but a knot of panic had lodged in my gut. She struck me as a person who didn't like to bother anyone, so I was relieved and happy she'd texted me this morning, even if it meant seeing a picture of shit before I'd cleared the sleep from my eyes. But she probably didn't like having to wait for me to show up to fix the problem I'd created. All I could do was drive faster and hope she had patience.

I parked and ran up to her porch, my phone dinging just as I rang her bell. Another picture came in. This time, it was from Ben.

A laugh burst out of me as my brother wearing a shirt that said, "Best Uncle Ever," filled the screen. I wasn't even surprised by how quickly he'd done this. It was very fucking Ben.

Shira opened the door as I was tapping out a reply. "What's so funny?"

I looked up, grinning. Her hair was down, flowing over her shoulders in raven waves, so dark it was almost blue, and her eerie eyes were lively and curious. "Hey, Goldie. My brother just sent me something incredible."

She covered it quickly, but I took note of her flinch at me calling her Goldie. I hadn't even meant to say it; it had just slipped out. I wasn't going to point it out and make her uncomfortable, though. Instead, I showed her my phone.

Her eyes lit and danced over the picture. Then a miracle happened: a slow, easy smile curved her lips as she lifted her head and met my gaze.

"I guess you told at least one of your brothers."

"I told all of them." I held my thumb and index finger a half inch apart. "Ben's a little excited. If you give him an in, he'll be all over this pregnancy. It's a good thing he's in New Zealand training."

She blinked a few times before stepping back to let me in. "You told them...it's me?"

"They know."

"And they're still excited?"

"Ben is. Nate and Adrian will take longer. Not because of you, though I can't say they weren't surprised. Adrian is fairly unexcitable in general, and Nate is more of a skeptic. Ben's our resident golden retriever. It doesn't take much to work him up."

"Did you tell them you signed up to clean a cat bathroom?"

I huffed a laugh. "Failed to mention it."

I found it cute that she called the litter box a bathroom and refused to say shit or poop. I didn't even know why, but it was charming and sweet.

"Mary's been talking to me all morning about the robot. I caught her staring it down a little bit ago. She really hates it."

I glanced around but didn't see her. "Where is she?"

"After her terrible morning, she's napping in a strip of sun on my bed."

"I guess shitting on the ground takes a lot out of a girl."

Shira smirked and quietly murmured, "That's something I wouldn't know."

I chuckled. "Thank Christ for that." At the utility room door, I stopped in front of her, blocking her way. "You're not going in there. I'll clean it all up and get rid of the robot. Go relax."

Her lips curved gently. "I'm not going to argue with you."

Once she was far away, I tackled the mess Mary had left for me. Her displeasure was obvious, not just in the putrid pile but the litter scattered everywhere. I had a feeling she'd known I'd be the one cleaning it up, not her beloved Shira. I got through it, reminding myself this was for the good of the baby. I couldn't even fathom Shira doing this. I'd make sure, even after the baby came, someone else would do this for her. Never her again.

After washing my hands, I sought out Shira. I found her in the kitchen, sitting on the counter, nibbling on a cracker.

"Back to normal. Your cat hates me, by the way."

"It's not hate, Roman. She has to express her unhappiness somehow since she can't speak."

"Agree to disagree." Leaning a hip against the counter, we fell into silence as she munched on her cracker. Slow, delicate bites followed by careful chewing. She'd be eating that cracker all day at the rate she was going. "How did you get up there?"

One brow quirked. "I'm more spry than I look."

"How will you get down?"

"I was thinking I'd fly." Her cheeks flushed a rosy pink. "But most likely, I'll end up hopping down."

I eyed the distance from her swinging feet to the tile floor and instantly took a disliking to it. Jumping that far didn't seem like a good idea on a normal basis—even worse when nauseous and pregnant.

I also didn't think she'd take kindly to me saying that, so I let it go. For now.

"I need a key to your house."

Her mouth fell open. "Um...why?"

"So I can let myself in to clean the litter in the morning. Stopping in on my way to the office will be easiest, and I'd rather not wake you."

"Hmmm." Her teeth dug into her bottom lip as she thought it through. "Since I no longer have a job, sleeping in would be nice."

"Shira—"

She waved her half-eaten cracker. "No, it's done. I don't want to talk about it. I'll give you a key, but if it's too big of a burden, let me know and I'll figure something else out."

"It won't be a burden. If there happens to be a day I can't make it, *I'll* make alternative arrangements. This isn't something you need to worry about anymore."

"Thank you. And I'm sorry I woke you up this morning."

"Don't worry about it. I have work to do." I folded my arms across my chest. "Are you aware of the resignations that came in after you left?"

"I—" Her hand dropped to her lap. "Yes. It was Terry's time. After everything she'd done, she needs rest. The others, though...I told them they didn't have to do that. I told them to stay. They did what they thought was right."

"It's put me in quite a spot."

Her eyes flicked to me then away. She looked like she was going to say something but clamped her mouth shut.

"Shira, you obviously have an opinion. Just say it."

She sucked in a breath. "I would say you put yourself in this spot, Roman."

I let that settle for a moment before nodding. "Fair enough. But tell me one thing, do you believe you were the best person for the position you held?"

Her answer came without hesitation. "No."

"No?"

"No. I was there because Frank wanted me to be, but I was drowning. I wish you and I could have worked together to find a solution that helped GoldMed. That's what I'd been hoping for when you came aboard."

"You could have said that to me."

She tilted her head, her eyes finding mine. The sun streaming through a nearby window dappled them in amber and gray, like a clear lake on a warm afternoon.

"Would you have listened?"

It was me who looked away this time. Heaving a sigh, I shoved my fingers through my hair. "I honestly don't know."

"It's done now. I hope you'll be able to save GoldMed or, at the very least, take care of the employees left. I can't give it any more of me. I have to focus on staying healthy for Beanie."

"You can rest easy. Take care of yourself and Beanie, knowing I'm doing my damnedest, Shira. If it can be saved, I will."

"Thank you," she whispered.

It was astounding to hear her thank me after everything. Now that I was beginning to see the truth of who she was, my treatment of her shamed me. There was no rewriting history, though. I could only push forward with my friendship campaign and hope one day the animosity I'd created between us could be left in the rearview.

"Yes, well…" I straightened, brushing my hands off on my pants. "I should leave you to your weekend."

"Oh, all right." Before I could stop her, she leaped down from the counter. Her landing was featherlight, but my heart dropped straight to my feet like it weighed a thousand pounds. "I'll get your spare key."

She moved around the kitchen with grace while I stood there like a buffoon with my mouth hanging open. When she came to me, a key in her upturned palm, I hadn't yet gotten control of my jaw.

"Here you go." Her head tipped back as she offered me the key.

I looked down at her, suddenly viscerally aware of her delicate stature. This small woman was carrying my child in a rough, vicious world. How was that safe? How was I supposed to function when she was hopping off counters and walking down sidewalks where anyone could jostle her or…Christ, much worse things.

"No more climbing on counters," I groused, unable to keep the anger out of my tone. I wasn't angry at Shira. It was the loss of control.

She, however, didn't know that, and her flinch told me so. "Oh, okay," she whispered. "I'm sorry."

"Shira," I growled. "There's nothing for you to be sorry about. I just want you to be safe."

"Okay. I won't do it again." Chewing on her bottom lip, she shoved the key toward me. "Your key."

I slid it out of her hand, wishing I'd kept my mouth shut. Snapping at this woman wasn't going to earn me her friendship or trust. I couldn't treat her like one of my rugby teammates or brothers.

"I'll be back in the morning, but text or call if you need anything else before then, all right?"

All I got was a nod.

With a brief goodbye, I got out of there as quickly as I could so I didn't do any more damage to the minuscule progress I'd made.

CHAPTER FOURTEEN

Shira

OVER THE NEXT THREE weeks, I only caught brief glimpses of Roman. As promised, he came every morning to clean Mary's litter box, and I was often woken to my girl meowing her head off at him and Roman responding gruffly about picking up her shit. My cat giving him a hard time made me irrationally pleased since I didn't have it in me to do so.

I'd sort of expected him to drop his promise as the days dragged on, but he showed up every morning. After that first day, he'd begun to leave me gifts and notes. Always juice or a smoothie, and often some kind of pastry too. Since I was no longer throwing up after every bite I took, I left him a note strongly encouraging him to keep the pastries coming.

The next day, he'd brought me two.

```
Shira,

I'll feed you anything you want. Tell me
your favorite food, and I'll make sure you
have it.

BTW - Mary still hates me.

   • Roman
```

I'd left a little letter on the counter for him to find when he returned in the morning.

Roman,

Everything is starting to taste really, really good. Especially that mango tart you brought me. And the blueberry Danish. I like the smoothies too. None of the food you've brought me has gone to waste.

Mary doesn't hate you, but she is known to hold a grudge. Here's a helpful hint: she loves to be praised, and she adores toys—especially stuffed mice.

Thank you for everything you're doing for me and Beanie.

Yours,

Shira

And so began the daily ritual: Roman leaving food and short notes, me replying with my thanks and answering his questions.

Shira,

They were out of your favorite mango tarts this morning, but I spoke with the manager. You now have a daily standing order. Please let me know if you get tired of them.

Mary laid in wait for me today. As soon as I entered the utility room, she jumped off a stack of towels. My heart stopped. It's by sheer luck you didn't wake up to my corpse on your floor this morning. Your cat definitely hates me.

• Roman

I scolded Mary for scaring Roman. Very lightly. First, I wasn't much of a scolder. Second, my girl was only protecting me and herself. I really couldn't blame her. Besides, it wasn't like she'd *hurt* Roman. She was making him work for acceptance.

Roman,

I don't think I'll ever be tired of mango tarts. Please keep them coming!

I'm sure Mary just wanted to play with you. She's a sweet angel kitty. She would never purposely scare anyone.

Yours,

Shira

Shira,

Did you like the lemon bar? I noticed it disappeared and no crumbs were left behind.

I've promoted Angelina Chin to head of marketing. What do you think about that decision? She seems solid, but I've misjudged character in the past.

This morning, I told Mary she's a good girl—a drastic stretch of the truth, in my opinion—and she headbutted my shin. I don't know if this is a good thing.

• Roman

Mary purred in my lap as I read Roman's note out loud. "Did you headbutt Roman?"

"Rrrreoowwww," she replied.

"I'll take that as a yes."

She gave me the side-eye then started to clean herself.

Roman,

Lemon bars are now a close second to mango tarts. I think Beanie likes citrus. The last week, I've been craving oranges every day.

Angelina is whip-smart and knows the marketing department like the back of her hand. I think offering her the position was a great decision.

Mary told me it was a friendly headbutt. Keep the "good girls" coming, and you'll have her wrapped around your finger.

Yours,

Shira

That evening, I received a delivery of navel oranges and clementines. The note on the receipt said, "For Beanie, who's already making a stand against scurvy." I read that one to Bea and Clara, who were still pretty anti-Roman despite the efforts he'd been making. I couldn't say I was comfortable with him or trusted him, but he was chipping away at me.

Shira,

The results are back, and as we both knew, the baby is mine. I passed that news to my brothers, and Ben's reaction was nothing if not predictable. Can you guess what he said?

I noticed quite a few orange peels in the trash. Looks like Beanie is still going strong in their fight against scurvy. Do let me know if that changes. I'll gladly load you up on cookies or movie theater popcorn if that's what the bean demands.

Mary still hates me, and she's becoming more wily. Today, she presented herself for pets. When I answered her demands, she turned around, swatted at me, and hissed. Did you know she hisses? For a small creature, she scares me.

• Roman

He'd left the paternity test results for me, though I'd received a copy already. I smiled when I noticed he'd underlined the results three times.

Roman,

~~I'm happy you're the father and it's not the delivery driver.~~ There was never a doubt in my mind Beanie is half yours.

As for Ben...I think I can guess he said something about your identical DNA and throwing his hat in the ring as a possible father. Unless it was really him behind that mask, he's going to have to live with being Uncle Ben.

I'm still loving anything citrus, but I have to admit, Beanie perked up at the mention of popcorn. I haven't been to a movie in a long time. Maybe I'll have to go.

Mary has never hissed a day in her life. I'm sure she was simply trying to communicate.

Yours,

Shira

The following day, a massive bucket of popcorn was delivered to my door. The best part—aside from the intense thoughtfulness that made my nose sting? It was still warm.

⚘

The prospect of seeing Roman for the first time in weeks was on my mind when I walked up to the building that held Dr. Sharma's practice, which was why I didn't notice the couple approaching the doors until we were almost on top of each other. I stopped, backing up a step to let them through.

"Shira!"

My gaze jerked up to the very pregnant, auburn-haired woman in front of me, and a smile stretched across my face. "Kit! Oh my gosh, I wasn't paying attention. How are you?"

She patted her round bump and grinned. "I'm good. Feeling large and in charge, but—"

"You aren't large, sweetheart," her husband, Elliot Levy, admonished as gently as he was capable. "You're carrying and nourishing our daughter. You're the exact right size you should be."

She melted against his imposing form. "Thank you for the reminder."

I had known Kit in passing for several years. First as Elliot Levy's assistant, then as his wife. Elliot owned many of the high-rises in Denver, including the Levy building, which housed GoldMed's headquarters as well as Levy Development.

When Kit and Elliot got married almost four years ago, she'd started a nonprofit that provided rehabbed homes to needy families, and I'd gotten to know her better through that since I shared the passion. Frank and I had donated heavily to Building Dignity, and I'd continued after he passed.

I didn't know Elliot as well. For one, he was one of the most intimidating men I had ever met, but also, he seemed fairly closed off with everyone but Kit. With her, their daughter, Joey, and their son, Theo, he was openly adoring.

"You look beautiful," I said.

Kit's cheeks flushed a pretty rose. "Thank you, Shira. Are you going to see Dr. Sharma?"

Without thought, my hand went to my barely-there bump. It wasn't visible in clothing yet, but when I looked at myself in the mirror, I could see the soft curve in my lower abdomen—probably more so thanks to my steady diet of pastries and smoothies.

But maybe it was a little bit the baby too.

"I am," I confirmed.

Kit gasped. "You're expecting?"

"Yes. I'm fifteen and a half weeks along."

"Wow. That's amazing news. We can be pregnant together. Well...for the next ten weeks, but you know what I mean."

I laughed. "I do know."

Elliot reached out and pulled the door open. "Since we're all going to the same place, let's continue this conversation on the way there."

Kit sniffed. "Bossy."

"That's right, Catherine. I am," Elliot murmured as he guided her into the building. He held the door for me too, ushering me in after.

As we waited for the elevator, Kit turned to me. "How have you been feeling?"

"The first trimester was terrible. I had hyperemesis and had to be hospitalized for a night." I shuddered at the memories of constant nausea. I still had bouts, but it was now once a day instead of once an hour. "Fortunately, since I left GoldMed and have had time to rest, I'm feeling much better."

She winced. "I heard some of what happened. Roman Wells is a bastard. I told Elliot he should cancel his lease for what he did to you."

"And I told you I would if you truly meant it," he intoned, never taking his eyes off his wife.

She huffed. "I don't know if I do. What do you think?"

I grinned. "I'm pleased you want to stick up for me, but Roman's a small part of GoldMed. I'd rather not hurt the rest of the employees just to spite him."

Her brow winged. "Fine, okay. What *would* you do to spite him?"

"Don't they say living well is the best revenge?"

"Maybe." She accepted my response but didn't seem satisfied with it. Pregnancy had made her bloodthirsty.

The elevator arrived, and Kit and I stepped in. Once again, Elliot made sure we were both inside before he joined us. He pressed the button for the twelfth floor and moved to the back of the elevator, giving us room to continue our conversation.

Kit rested her hand on top of her bump and studied me thoughtfully. "I've been considering bringing on a partner at Building Dignity."

"Not considering," Elliot mumbled. "You will be doing it."

She crinkled her nose at me. "With the imminent arrival of Baby Levy number three, my husband is insisting I take on less work, which is impossible since I'm essentially a one-woman show. I have an assistant and someone who runs the numbers, but everything else is on me. Now, my gears are turning, and I'm wondering if you would be interested in partnering with me. I know Building Dignity is just as important to you—"

"As a volunteer?" I asked, trying to keep myself from becoming too excited. But my toes were curling in my shoes, so it was too late.

"A *partner*, Shira. I think we'd work really well together. And look, I'm slowing things down in preparation for my maternity leave, so if you come on board now, it won't be a heavy load like it has been for me."

"Too heavy," Elliot groused.

The elevator doors opened, and Elliot put his arm out to allow us through, then quietly followed.

"What do you think?" Kit pressed.

"I think I am really interested and would love to come into the office to talk to you about it."

"Perfect." Her smile lit up her pretty face. "I'm so glad we ran into each other. This was fate, don't you think?"

I couldn't help smiling back at her. "I guess it was."

She continued chatting down the hallway to Dr. Sharma's office then abruptly cut herself off.

"Holy hell, what is he doing here?" she hissed.

I glanced from her toward where she was glaring, knowing who I'd see. Roman was waiting for me by the office door, tapping on his phone and pacing, therefore not noticing our approach. He, however, was impossible to miss, taking up more than his fair share of space in all directions. I often forgot how large he was until I was in his presence again.

"He's here for me," I whispered.

"What?" She frowned. "For you...? Oh, Shira, is he—?"

I touched my stomach once more. "He is. But don't worry about calling him a bastard. He deserved it. Since then, he's been making it up to me in pastries and cleaning my cat's litter every day."

"Oh." Her shoulders slumped. "Okay, wow, I have to reframe everything."

Elliot moved ahead of us, extending his hand. "Roman."

They shook, and Roman greeted him, though his attention kept bouncing to me. It had been three weeks since we'd been face to face. During that time, we'd passed messages back and forth daily and texts on top of that, but seeing him in person after all the words we'd shared was somewhat disconcerting. He was suddenly more familiar yet still a stranger. I supposed that could have been said for the entirety of our relationship. This man had bent me over backward, and I was carrying his child, but I didn't know his middle name or even where he lived.

"This is your doctor too?" Roman asked Elliot.

"Of course. She's the best in Denver," Elliot replied matter-of-factly. I guessed, to him, it *was* a fact that he'd only bring his wife to the best ob-gyn in town.

"Ah, that's good to know," Roman replied.

Kit hooked her arm with mine and jutted her chin. "Are you surprised Shira picked a good doctor all on her own?"

Roman's eyes widened, somewhat panicked, his gaze bouncing between us. "No. Of course not. It's nice to see you again, Kit."

She chuffed. "Sure it is." Then she turned to me and gave me a warm hug, promising to call me later. Since Roman and I were early, we lingered in the hall after Kit and Elliot went in for their appointment.

He lowered his chin, giving me a long once-over. "How are you?"

"Really good. I haven't been nauseous today. I'm really hoping this means I'm turning a corner."

He rapped his big fist against the trim of the door. "Knock on wood. Let's not test our luck. I can't have you getting as sick as you were a few weeks ago."

Something soft and fuzzy coated my skin at his vehemence. "Unfortunately, I don't think you have a say in that."

"That *is* unfortunate. If I did, you wouldn't have been sick for even an hour. It's utter bullshit you had to go through that."

"That's a nice thought."

I tried to temper my reaction, but it was difficult when he was constantly examining me and openly displaying how angry my being so sick made him. I reminded myself Roman would have never spoken to me again if I weren't carrying his baby. Our last interaction would have been him ripping GoldMed away from me. With that cold reality, most of my fuzziness evaporated.

Roman was here for Beanie—not me.

"Yeah." He cleared his throat. "I didn't know you were friends with the Levys."

"Elliot, not so much, but Kit, yes. We're friendly." I blinked up at him. "Why would you know that? You don't know very much about me."

His flinch was subtle but unmistakable. I hadn't meant any harm, but it was true. We were diving into the deep end together and neither of us knew whether the other could swim.

"You're right. I don't." He cupped his nape and shifted his feet. "We should probably remedy that, don't you think?"

"Probably. We have time, though."

"We'll make it a priority, Shira," he declared decisively, frowning at me. It wasn't quite an angry expression, but he didn't seem especially happy. Then again, as we'd just covered, I barely knew this man and couldn't presume to read him.

So, I agreed, even though I didn't quite understand what I was agreeing to.

CHAPTER FIFTEEN

Roman

It was no wonder Dr. Sharma had been voted the best in the city. She had a calm, self-assuredness that immediately put me at ease. Even better, Shira appeared comfortable with her, smiling and answering questions willingly.

I'd done a lot of reading and had come into this appointment with an idea of what to expect. For the most part, there were no surprises, yet all of it took me off guard. There was a vast difference between reading about a pregnancy in theory and being a part of the reality.

From my chair in the corner, I listened to Shira and Dr. Sharma talk about how she was feeling. Then Shira laid down and the doctor measured the height of her uterus, assuring us both everything was moving along as it should. All normal and expected, but with each passing moment, my blood heated to an intense level, becoming loud inside my ears, pumping through my body like raging rapids. My fingers flexed on my knees, and it took a concerted effort not to grind my molars.

I had accepted this was happening about a minute after I became aware of it, but the realness was slamming into me hard and fast. In a few short months, I would have a child. I'd be a dad. That was a massive mindfuck, and I had no one to talk to about it with. My brothers were my closest friends, but none were anywhere near parenthood and wouldn't come close to understanding.

In a perfect world, I'd discuss these things with the person going through them with me, but I doubted Shira wanted to hear about my momentary panic after my treatment of her. Not to mention, she was the one carrying my child and had been sick as a dog for months. I doubted she'd feel too sympathetic toward me. Rightly so.

Dr. Sharma wheeled her stool to the side to catch my eye. "Normally, at this appointment, we use the Doppler to check the heartbeat, but since you missed out on seeing the ultrasound last time, I thought we could take a quick peek. Are you up for it, Dad?"

Holy hell.

My fingertips dug hard into my thighs as I nodded. "That would be incredible."

I pushed up on shaky legs to stand beside Shira. She shot me a smile before biting into her bottom lip. Was she nervous about the ultrasound, or was I making her feel that way?

If Ben were here, he would have asked her, but I had more respect for people's private thoughts. That wasn't to say I would have objected too much if he'd charmed an answer from her.

When Dr. Sharma brought the small wand to Shira's stomach, I followed it with my eyes, taking in the shape of her abdomen. An outsider wouldn't have known she was pregnant, but I saw the faintest curve below her belly button that hadn't been there before.

Then the surrealness of this situation multiplied by a thousand. Dr. Sharma showed us our bouncing, wiggling, kicking baby. It had grown so much since Shira's last scan, now less gummy bear and more human-shaped.

The doctor did some measurements and clicked her tongue. "You're measuring a little bit ahead, but nothing to be alarmed about." She flicked her gaze to me then smiled at Shira. "Now that I've seen the father, I can see why that might be the case."

"Maybe this baby will have a chance at being average height thanks to Roman's DNA," Shira joked.

"I suspect above average." Dr. Sharma moved the wand to the side of Shira's abdomen and paused. "Were you planning on finding out the sex?"

Shira turned to me. "I was thinking yes. What about you?"

"Whatever you want," I replied. And I meant it. There were only two options, and I didn't have a preference.

"We'll be finding out," Shira told her doctor. "It might take us the rest of my pregnancy to agree on a name."

The doctor chuckled and clicked a few things on the machine. "I don't typically make sex pronouncements at this gestational age, but you have a little exhibitionist on your hands. I can tell you if you're ready."

My heart stopped beating. Just like that, it had forgotten it was required to do its job in order for me to survive. Speaking was out of the question, but I managed to force my head to loll in an obscene semblance of a nod.

"Yes, please," Shira whispered.

On instinct, my hand moved to wrap around hers. After a beat, her fingers curled into mine. The way we got here might've been nontraditional, but holding her hand while finding this out felt right.

The doctor zoomed in on the still image and pointed out a darker area with a smirk. "That is, undoubtedly, a penis. Congrats, parents, you're having a boy."

A breath burst out of Shira, followed by a soft giggle. "A boy. Whoa." She looked up at me. Her eyes were the opposite of haunted now, shining with life and light. "A boy, Roman."

A boy. I hope he has his mother's eyes. He'd be lucky if he did.

I shook my head and squeezed her hand. "I want to say I'm surprised, but I don't think the Wells family makes anything other than boys."

That got another laugh from her. "You might be right."

❧

The elevator ride downstairs was quiet, but as we headed toward the exit of the building, Shira touched my arm.

"By the way, I'm moving tomorrow. I'll be next door to Bea. She's promised to help me with Mary's litter, so you're off the hook."

"Wait. Slow down. You're moving?" Taking her by the elbow, I drew her to the side of the glass doors. "You're moving tomorrow? Is this...this is sudden."

"It's not that sudden. The house is too big for me, and I'm far from my friends. They're my only support system, so when Bea told me the house next to hers had been put on the market, I snatched it up."

"Where?" My question came out more gruff than intended. Shira's flinch proved that, but I felt like I'd been given a pop quiz everyone else in my class knew was coming. Behind and confused, I was doing my damnedest to catch up. "Where are you moving?"

"It's a row home right on the edge of RiNo. Three bedrooms, everything's been updated, and there's the cutest little picket fence in the front yard."

"River North?" A vein pulsed in my temple. "I'm not sure that's the safest—"

"Bea's lived there for two years and loves it." Shira's interruption was soft yet inarguably firm. "It's the first place I'll truly be able to call my own. I have a feeling Beanie, Mary, and I are going to love living there."

I mulled this news over, not at all happy about it, though I couldn't pinpoint why. I'd have to read crime reports for the area, though I doubted it would change Shira's decision.

"They're not your only support system," I stated.

Her brow furrowed in confusion. "I don't have family, Roman, so, yes, they are."

"Shira," I sighed, "I'm talking about me. *I'm* your support system. And you're moving across the city from me."

"Oh." She looked down at her feet, her hair spilling over her shoulders in ebony waves. I didn't know why she'd always worn it up in the office, but I was relieved she'd stopped. Hair like hers deserved to freely flow, catching the light when she moved, caressing her skin when—

"Roman—" I jerked back to awareness. Christ, had I really gotten lost in thoughts of Shira's hair? "—I've known Bea and Clara for years, and I'm comfortable counting on them. I appreciate you helping me the past few weeks, but that doesn't mean I expect it to continue. I'm not sick anymore, and I can feed myself, you know. It's okay."

"It's not a hardship at all." I tucked my hands in my trouser pockets so she wouldn't see them balling into fists. Something was being taken from me—something I hadn't realized was important until I'd felt the loss. I didn't like it, but there wasn't much I could do. This was Shira's show right now. I was just a spectator. It was a bitter pill to swallow, but I had to choke it down.

"I'll let you know if I need your help with anything." Her fingers grazed my arm. "I promise."

"What about moving? I'm assuming you have movers doing the lifting, but do you need help unpacking, putting furniture together, hanging pictures—the kinds of things you absolutely shouldn't be doing?"

Her smile was almost dreamlike and so soft it blurred at the edges. "Clara's boyfriend, Jake, and his brother are pitching in. If I know my friends, they won't allow me to lift a finger."

"As it should be." I rocked back on my heels, supremely dissatisfied but out of hands to play. "Well, if there's no other news, I have to get back to the office."

"There's nothing else." Shira was doing her best to look me in the eye, and I was doing my worst to make it easy on her. Not on purpose. Never that. But I'd lost control of my frown, and it had carved itself onto my face of its own volition. "I guess I'll see you at my next appointment."

"Yes." My jaw was so rigid it was in danger of snapping. "I'll see you then."

That hadn't gone how I'd expected. I should have been pleased not to have to fight a feral cat in a pink bow every day, but I wasn't. Truthfully, Mary had been starting to soften toward me, and I'd thought I'd made inroads with her mother too.

Obviously, I'd been wrong.

⁂

Ben and Nate had made themselves at home in my living room, stuffing their faces with Peruvian chicken while a rugby game blasted from the TV. Technically, this *was* Ben's home since he'd moved in one day without asking and didn't seem inclined to go anywhere.

I sagged onto the sectional, grabbing the remote to turn the volume down so I could hear the thoughts in my head.

"Did you save anything for me?" I asked.

Nate nudged a box sitting on the coffee table toward me with his toe. "Get on that before Benny makes it disappear."

I sifted through the chicken, but I didn't have much of an appetite. Since leaving the doctor's office hours earlier, my gut had been churning, and something felt incredibly off.

When I sat back without taking any chicken, Ben raised a brow. "Not hungry?"

"Not really." I crossed my arms over my chest. "I went to Shira's appointment today. Got to see the baby."

Ben paused, chicken poised beside his mouth. "Oh yeah? Did you get any new pics?"

I slipped the images from my shirt pocket and passed them to my brothers. They both studied the images, though I wasn't sure they knew what they were seeing in most of them.

"Huh." Nate studied the image that looked like a little baby being cradled, his brow puckered in concentration. "This is cool as hell. Our niece or nephew is just kicked back and relaxed in there."

Ben took it from Nate, giving it equal attention. "I doubt any relative of ours is chilling. Kid's probably taking a rest after bouncing off the walls."

I stole the ultrasound picture from Ben and carefully tucked it away. "He has Shira as a mother. As far as I can tell, she's as low-key as they come, so there's a chance."

"You said 'he,'" Nate pointed out. "Something you want to tell us?"

"We found out it's a boy."

Ben shot to his feet, his hands on his hips. "Holy shit. Are you kidding me? We're having a boy?" He threw his hands up. "We're having a *boy*! How fucking cool is that?"

I laughed, warmth swelling inside me. There hadn't been a moment for me to really soak in this news. I'd gone from Shira's whirlwind announcement back to the office, which was a battlefield these days. But with my brothers grinning like crazy, I felt it click into place. I was having a son. Another Wells boy to add to our pack. That thought filled me with anticipation for the future and a moment of pure, unadulterated joy.

"It's really fucking cool," I said.

Nate leaned over, giving my shoulder a squeeze. "Congrats, Ro. That's awesome. We actually know how to deal with boys, so we've got you covered."

Ben's head tipped back as he laughed. "Of course you're having a boy. The Wells only make boys."

"That's what I said." The knot in my gut unfurled. No matter what else had happened, this had been a good day. "The doc says the baby is measuring big. Said it's my fault."

Ben slammed down beside me, slinging his arm around my shoulders. "Again, that's no surprise."

"You're a behemoth. How could you not have behemoth children?" Nate poked.

"He's half Shira's, and she's tiny. I'd be surprised if she was even five feet tall." I scrubbed at my jaw, suddenly worried. "Shit, what if this kid's too big for her?"

"I wouldn't worry about it." Ben gave me a shake. "Our mother managed to carry the two of us, and she wasn't exactly made of hardy stock."

"Mom is almost six feet," Nate reminded him.

"I don't mean physically," Ben replied. "Our mom doesn't like challenges. When the going got tough in our family, she skedaddled. Makes me think her pregnancies couldn't have been too much of a hardship since she kept doing it."

"Shira isn't anything like our mom." That woman got bored of parenting when our cuteness began to fade. From the time the first of us hit puberty, she became a dragonfly in our lives, fluttering around over us and occasionally landing, but never for long. I didn't know Shira well, but I was certain she would never be that kind of mother. Or friend. Or person in general.

"Exactly." Ben got up again, grabbing a piece of chicken. "That's what I'm saying. She'll be fine."

"This is a happy occasion. Why are we talking about our mother?" Nate groused. "If I never think about her again, it'll be too soon."

"Thank you. I'd like to think of anything but her." I leaned forward, my fingers steepled between my knees. "Shira told me she's moving across town and doesn't need me to do the litter box thing anymore."

"Did you tell her you didn't mind doing it?" Ben asked.

I turned to him. "What makes you think I don't mind?"

Nate chuffed. "Please. You're constantly looking up food to bring to her and buying toys for her psycho cat."

"Mary isn't psycho." From the shocked looks on my brothers' faces, I'd defended her a little too effusively. "Okay, she's sort of crazy, but we were developing an understanding. I don't mind not being the one to clean up her shit, though."

Ben lowered his chin and raised his brows. "Really? Do you even believe what you just said?"

I let out a humorless laugh. "You think I like cleaning up after a cat who wants to eat my face?"

Nate laughed. "Yeah, sounds like you're developing a real deep understanding."

Ben got serious—a rarity for him. "I don't think you are especially into that aspect, but I know you, Ro. You're a caretaker. The last few weeks, you've been in your element coming up with ways to take care of Shira. I know you as well as I know myself. You can't be happy at having that taken away."

I let out a heavy sigh. This was the reason my gut had been so damn unsettled today. I'd been relegated to the outside, and that wasn't where I wanted to be. I wasn't carrying the baby, but I needed to be an active participant, and going to doctor appointments every few weeks wasn't enough.

"You're right." I squeezed my eyes shut, pressing the heel of my hand into my socket to relieve some tension. "She doesn't need my help, though. And now she'll be on the other side of the city, making it harder than it should be to stop by. Naturally, that has my mind spinning to when he's here and having to figure out how to carve out time to be with my son. Christ—" I gnashed my molars to keep myself from spinning out. I wasn't much of an anxious person, but control was important to me, and I had less than none in this situation.

"No need to get your panties in a bunch," Ben pronounced. "Move closer to her."

I dropped my hand and stared at him. "That's ludicrous."

"Not really," Nate stated, giving me pause. He was the most practical of my brothers. "It makes sense, honestly."

I swiveled my head between them, stopping on Ben. "I sense ulterior motives. Do you want me out of this place so you can live here on your own?"

He raised both hands. "Nah, not me. Chances are, I'll follow you wherever you go. You know I don't like living alone."

My eyes narrowed. "And if you're not invited?"

He chuckled. "Have I ever needed an invitation?"

I shook my head. "This is crazy. I can't just move. I don't know why we're talking about it. I have a life here. I'm close to my offices...no. Out of the question."

Nate tsked. "Never say never, Ro."

Moving wouldn't be happening. As for the rest? I'd have to figure it out. Sitting on my hands, however, wasn't an option for me. Shira would be getting my help, whether she liked it or not.

CHAPTER SIXTEEN

Shira

I WAVED GOODBYE TO the couple who lived in the house next door as they made their way down my porch steps. Bev and Donnie had been in their place since the seventies. They were grandparents now and had told me all about their grandkids over the plate of cookies they'd brought over to welcome me to the neighborhood. They'd also offered their babysitting services when I'd told them about Beanie.

"Wow. Those two haven't said more than a handful of words to me since I moved in," Bea said dryly.

Clara bumped her with her shoulder. "Think that could have anything to do with your resting murder face?"

Bea put her hands on her hips like she was going to object, then she took a breath and nodded. "You know, you're probably right. And as much as I like cookies, they're not worth having to listen to the story of Billy's first day of kindergarten in slo-mo."

I crinkled my nose at her. "They were sweet."

"Maybe. But even you can admit they talked *sooo slow*."

Clara snorted. "They did take their time getting to the point, didn't they?"

The three of us took seats around the mid-century modern table Bea and I had found at an antique store, which looked stunning in my new dining room. Clara's boyfriend, Jake, and his brother, Jeremy, were putting together my bed upstairs. Nellie, Clara's daughter, was up there with them *assisting*. From the sound of it, she was spending most of the time running circles in the two empty bedrooms. Everyone had forbidden me from even attempting to help, which was fine with me. I wasn't handy in any way, and moving had taken it all out of me.

"I should buy a toolbox," I mused.

My new home had been built in the late 1800s, and I loved every bit of the creaking wood floors and exposed brick walls. I'd never dared to conjure up what my dream house would look like, but now that I was here, I decided this was it. It wasn't overly large, but that suited me. I didn't need space or ostentatious fixtures and furniture. Cozy comfort was more my style I was learning.

"If you need help with anything, Jake will be glad to do it," Clara offered. "He hasn't met something he's been unable to fix yet."

Bea fluffed her blue waves. "As a woman who's fully independent of the male race, I have a fully stocked toolbox and would be happy to lend you what you need. I learned how to use it all from a class I took at the hardware store."

Clara laughed. "I'm happy to be dependent on Jake to figure out plumbing and electrical issues. I have plenty of talents and skills—none of which lie in that department."

"I want to know how to do all those things." I straightened my shoulders. "I was too complacent with Frank, letting him take care of me, and here I am, almost thirty and can barely change a light bulb or cook an edible dinner."

Bea tipped her chin. "You deserved everything Frank gave you, and let's be real, babe: you took care of that man more than he took care of you."

I waved her off. "I don't want to talk about him now. What's done is done. This is a fresh start. I think I'll look into taking the class you took."

Bea looked like she had more to say—she always did—but she nodded and promised to send me the information for the class.

Jake and Jeremy finished soon after that. I tried to convince everyone to stay for dinner to thank them for all their help today, but Nellie had exhausted herself with all the running around, so she was a little cranky. Jeremy had to get home to his wife, and Bea had a waitressing shift. That left me alone in my new house.

I walked the creaky floors, envisioning the art I'd hang on the walls and what furniture I needed to buy to make it feel like it was truly mine. With Bea on one side of me and Bev and Donnie on the other, I already felt safe and comfortable here. I'd made this choice quickly, but my gut told me it had been the right one.

I nearly jumped out of my skin when my doorbell rang. Bea must've forgotten something. Or maybe Bev was coming back for her plate.

I checked the camera app on my phone, and it wasn't Bea or Bev. Taking up more room than he had the right, Roman Wells was pacing back and forth in front of my door. His wide palm cupped the back of his neck, and though I couldn't tell, I had a feeling his square jaw was rippling and tight the way it had been when I'd left him at Dr. Sharma's office the day before.

With a slightly shaky hand, I pulled the door open. "Roman...hi."

Even after all this time and what we'd shared, he still made me nervous. One day, I'd be comfortable with him, but I wasn't close to there yet. If he were a little smaller, a smidge less handsome, I might've been able to behave like the grown woman I was and not a stuttering tween.

"Shira." His gaze swept over me from the tips of my toes to my hair piled on the top of my head. He had developed a habit of doing this, and it always made me feel naked, even wearing loose pajama pants, a tank, and a cardigan. "The house next door is black."

I stuck my head out to peer at Bea's house. Someone had painted the brick black a long time ago, and Bea had rolled with it, installing a matching swing on the porch and a gothic-looking fountain in the tiny, fenced-in front yard. It was the perfect house for her.

"That's where Bea lives."

He huffed, his hands stuffed deep in his pockets. "It suits her."

"It does," I agreed. "A little scary on the outside and cute and sweet on the inside—just like her."

He turned his attention back to me and cocked his head to look beyond me into my house. "Think I could come in?"

"Oh, sure." I backed up to open the door and stumbled over my own feet. Luckily, I was holding onto the knob, so I didn't go tumbling. "There's not much to see yet. I just moved in today."

"I don't need to be entertained. I'd like to see the house." His lips rolled over his teeth, then he pushed out, "The neighborhood isn't as horrible as I'd pictured. I do have misgivings about the mission being four blocks away, though."

"There's a sweet park only a block away," I retorted.

I didn't look at unhoused people the same way a lot of people did. Once upon a time, my mother and I had lived in her car then a shelter. I understood being unhoused wasn't a character deficit. Sure, some people living on the streets could be violent, but there were violent billionaires too. I refused to judge someone I didn't know because of their housing situation. Besides, Bea knew this neighborhood well, and I trusted her judgment. If she felt safe here, so did I.

"Hmmm." Roman stuffed his hands in his pockets, but not before I saw his fingers curling into his palms. "Have you met your neighbors on the other side?"

"I have. They're a nice older couple. They brought me cookies." I padded to the dining room where I'd left the plate and grabbed a cookie. Whirling around, I waved it at Roman. "Would you like one?"

One beat of hesitation, and he accepted it. The bite he took was as big as he was, demolishing half the cookie at once then putting away the other half seconds later. Something about watching him eat with such vigor made my stomach swoopy and warm. My toes dug into the thick rug under my feet.

"Good cookie." Roman wiped his mouth with the back of his hand. "Have you eaten dinner yet?"

"No. I was considering ordering a pizza."

"I could go for a pizza." He took out his phone and started tapping. "Any toppings you don't like?"

I frowned at him, not that he noticed since he was intent on his screen. I understood why he might have wanted to check out where his child would be living, but I couldn't comprehend why we would be having dinner together.

"You're having pizza with me?"

"Toppings, Shira. What do you like or dislike on your pizza?"

"Oh...um, I don't eat pork. I like lots of vegetables."

His brow furrowed. "Okay, we'll get a veggie pizza. Done." He looked up once his phone was back in his pocket. "Want to give me a tour while we wait?"

"There isn't much to see yet, but...um, okay." The first floor was pretty open. It took no time for me to point to the kitchen and living room, then we started for the stairs. A flash of black-and-white fur darted from nowhere, heading straight for Roman's ankles. "Watch out, Mary's coming," I cried out in warning, but there was no need.

Without missing a beat, Roman bent, scooped up my cat, and cradled her against his chest. Mary mewed and squirmed but quickly got comfortable on her new perch. Her paws curled over his forearms as she blinked at me, her tail swishing lazily.

"It doesn't look like she hates you so much," I said.

Roman gave her head a scratch. "Her claws are digging into my arm. But sure, she doesn't hate me."

"Don't be a baby."

His mouth fell open, but his surprise quickly morphed into a grin. "Have you ever felt her claws? They're razors."

"I haven't." I folded my arms. "Mary would never hurt me."

His eyes narrowed. "That's because she doesn't hate you, Shira."

With a laugh, I spun toward the stairs. I didn't have to look back to know Roman was on my tail. His footsteps were like thunder on my old floors. They didn't make men as big as him back in the nineteenth century.

Upstairs, I showed him the full bath, two empty bedrooms, and the primary bathroom. So far, all I had was a king-size bed and two nightstands—all new. I'd brought some things from the old house but wanted my bedroom here to be only mine.

"That's a big bed," Roman remarked.

I sat on the end of it, spreading my hand over the dusty-pink comforter. "It's a bit ridiculous, but I have plans of starfishing right in the middle." I patted my slightly rounded stomach. "And if this guy is anything like I was as a kid, I bet he'll be creeping in here for snuggles most mornings and some middle of the nights."

Roman's jaw did that rippling thing again as he averted his gaze from me to sweep over the room. His arms must've been just as tight. Mary yowled at him before leaping onto the bed next to me, immediately getting to work on bathing herself.

"You're okay, honey," I cooed, stroking her back. "That was a big jump, my brave girl."

Roman cleared his throat. "It's a nice house, Shira. I'm still unsure about the neighborhood, but at least the house seems solid. Will you use the bedroom next door as the nursery?"

"That was my plan, but I'll probably keep a bassinet next to my bed the first few months."

He nodded. "That makes sense. Your plan for the third bedroom?"

I lifted my shoulders. "Logically, it should be a guest room, but I don't have any family to stay there, so it might be an office or playroom. I haven't decided."

"A guest room would be smart. Then I can stay over once he's here. Otherwise, I'll crash on the couch downstairs."

My couch wasn't Roman size. He'd have to sleep curled up in a ball to fit himself.

"You think you'll be staying here?" I asked in surprise.

"Of course." He lowered his chin to stare down at me. "Do you have a problem with that?"

I thought about it, and I couldn't come up with any objections, so I shook my head. "We just haven't talked about how it will be."

"We will. Just know I intend to take leave from work when he's born, and I would like to be as hands-on as possible."

My throat tightened, making it difficult to swallow, let alone speak. I hadn't let my mind wander too far or imagine what it would be like to share a child with Roman. Up to this point, he had kept every promise he'd made, but it was the early days, and I'd been let down plenty of times before. Even now, I wouldn't let myself believe he would follow through on his intentions. It was just too good to be true.

"I-I'll buy a bed for the third bedroom," I said softly.

"Thank you." He turned his head toward the door. "But let me buy it."

"You don't need to do that. Money isn't a problem for me—"

His gaze swung back to me. "I'm glad money's not a problem, but I'd still like to buy the bed. Let me, all right?"

I nodded in agreement to avoid arguing. I'd simply order a bed tomorrow and tell Roman via text I had it covered. It was much easier for me to be assertive when he wasn't looming over me and I didn't have to see his carved-from-granite frown.

The pizza came soon after that. The two of us settled in my dining room, and Roman served me two slices before taking two for himself. He also made me sit down while he got us glasses of ice water.

"First dinner at my new house."

"Congrats. Shira." Roman raised his glass and tipped it toward mine. I picked mine up and clinked it against his.

"Cheers."

"Cheers to new beginnings." He put his glass down carefully and peered at me, a thoughtful furrow to his brow. "Hopefully we can start anew too. Today, I realized I never really apologized to you for how I treated you when we were working together."

"It's all right. It was just business." I shouldn't have been excusing his behavior. It hadn't been all right in the least. But I had this knee-jerk reflex to smooth over conflict, even to my detriment. *Often* to my detriment. Years of therapy hadn't cured me of it. I didn't know what would—if anything.

"No, it isn't." He leaned forward, watching me carefully. "This afternoon, I passed Mike Dietrich on my way to my office. I had some quick budgetary things to discuss with him, so naturally, I stopped him."

I ripped the crust off my pizza to keep from cringing. Mike did *not* like making chitchat in the halls.

Roman went on. "When I returned to my desk a few minutes later, Mike sent me a message. Do you know what it said?" I shook my head, though I had an idea. "He said, and I quote, 'I would like to go back to the way Shira handled things. From now on, please confine your questions to scheduled meetings or chats through the messaging app.' I saw you hide from him and decided it was because you didn't want to talk to him, but you did it for him, didn't you?"

I nodded, still tearing at my crust. "Mike is a genius at numbers, but he's not a people person."

"You couldn't have told me that?" he asked as gently as he was capable—which wasn't very gentle and lined with gruffness, but the effort set me at ease.

"No, Roman. After you lectured me on ignoring everyone in the office and having no connection to the employees, I didn't feel like I could tell you anything."

His nod was heavy and slow. "I did say that. Then I asked you if Frank had ever meant anything to you. What a bastard I was." He hung his head in his hands and groaned. "I screwed this all up. I'm sorry, Shira. I really am."

"Okay."

My pizza was in a pile, nothing left to shred, but with my stomach a mess of nerves, it wasn't like I'd be eating it anyway.

He looked up, and I was shocked to see how ruddy his cheeks were. "Since I understand what it means to be born into wealth and privilege, I have tried my best not to be an asshole. But I really failed here, huh?"

I worried my bottom lip with my teeth, only nodding slightly in response.

"Yeah," he breathed. "Those letters Frank had sent me meant a lot. I'd convinced myself I was doing right by him, but holy hell was I blind."

My stomach bottomed out. The damn letters. It always came back to them. Letting this go on for another second longer didn't feel right. Roman was being honest and laying it all on the line, so it was time I did too.

"Roman, since we're starting fresh—"

He pinned his gaze on me as he leaned in halfway over the table. I had to look down at the napkin in my lap in order to free my confession from the confines of the vault in the back of my throat.

"—Frank didn't write those letters. I did."

CHAPTER SEVENTEEN

Roman

WHAT?

What?

WHAT?!

Five letters. All at pivotal times in my life. Frank Goldman and I hadn't been pen pals, but we'd exchanged important words—words I'd taken and used to guide me on my next steps. And now...*what?*

"I'm sorry," Shira rushed out. "The first time you wrote to him, I showed him the letter, but he was busy and asked me to reply for him. He just wanted me to send his condolences, but I felt...I couldn't leave it at that. You seemed lost, and so was I, I guess. My mother had died a few months before, and Frank had been there for me, so I decided to channel him a little and be there for you."

...take it from someone who knows, there's nowhere you can run that it won't follow.

"You wrote to me?" A heavy exhale fled my lungs as I fell back in my chair. "I should've known. You sent flowers when I got injured. The letter you wrote..."

Roman,

I'm sorry to hear about your injury and the possible end to your rugby career. From what I read, you were dynamite on the field, and the game will be worse for your absence.

Do you remember what I told you the first time I wrote you? You can walk a hundred paths in your lifetime. If this one is coming to an end, that doesn't mean it's the end of your dreams. You'll get up, walk down a new path, and find the next dream.

Take time to heal and grieve if you need to. This isn't what you planned, and that is a painful reality. It's all right to be down, but don't stay down. Feel this in full then put it away. Don't let your grief keep you under.

You will have a beautiful life. Lean on those brothers of yours. Your relationships with them are your true wealth. Most people don't have that. You may not feel lucky now, but in many ways you are.

I look forward to your next move.

Frank Goldman

"I'm really sorry for deceiving you. I just couldn't let your letters go unanswered, and I didn't think you'd want to hear from a random girl you didn't know." Shira pinched her bottom lip hard, her clear eyes imploring and back to being haunted.

I stared at her for a long time, her delicate fingers dancing on her lips, the subtle flush in her cheeks, her dark brows dipping with anxiety over her light eyes, and wondered how I ever could have been mean to her. No matter what I thought of her marriage to Frank, a man I now knew was little more than a stranger to me, Shira was exactly who she presented herself to be. Soft-spoken and kind, shy and flutteringly nervous. She might've been deceptive, but it had been out of kindness and compassion.

I should have been angry. I'd charged in to save GoldMed when Frank Goldman hadn't actually given a single shit about me. That would sting once it settled in. I knew that. But when it came down to it, I couldn't find it in me to be bothered that it had been Shira who'd cared. In fact, I was going to leave here tonight and reread those letters with her velvety soft voice in my head.

The tremble in her bottom lip brought me to a stop. My insides froze as her eyes welled until sheer panic took over my muscles, shooting me out of my seat. I was around the table in two steps and had her out of her chair in one tug. Then my arms went around her, tucking her against my chest.

"You can't cry," I barked, too sharply for the situation, but damn if her tears didn't make me feel like a madman. If I could have taken them one by one in my fist and shattered them into vapor, I would have. Instead, I hugged her. She'd liked it the last time.

"I was trying hard not to," she mumbled into my shirt. "It's just...the hormones...and the way you were looking at me—I'm really sorry, Roman."

"You're forgiven." I cupped the back of her head, keeping her in place. "Just don't cry, okay? I can't stand it—especially not when I'm the one who made you do it."

Sniffling, she pushed against me. I was of the mind to resist, but in the end, I let her go. She stepped away, wiping the few tears that had slipped free with the back of her hand.

"I can't promise that's the last time I'll do it." She patted her stomach, which was frustratingly hidden behind her loose sweater. "I'm not a crier, but this guy seems to have turned me into one."

I pulled her chair out and nodded toward it. "I made you cry, but I'm not going to let you go hungry. Sit, eat the slice of pizza you didn't ruin, and I'll get you another one."

She complied, and I stood over her until she took a big bite, satisfaction sliding through me. Nate had been accurate in his assessment of me. I *was* a caretaker. I could admit it. Ensuring Shira was fed and taken care of was as much for me as it was for her.

"My father's death was sudden." Shira looked up from her pizza, her brows raised. I continued. "He worked himself to death. He wasn't a terrible father, but he didn't really know what to do with four boys on his own, so he became an absent one. Once I got older and had a mind for business, he related to me. We'd been starting to get close when he died. It had been a massive blow. I'd been reeling, wondering what the hell the point was to following in his footsteps if he wasn't there to be proud of me. I don't know why I wrote to Frank...except I'd needed *something* and had been reaching out blindly."

"And you found me," she said softly.

"I guess I did." I crumbled my napkin in my fist. "What about your mom—was it sudden?"

She shook her head. "She was sick for a couple years but refused to go to the doctor until it became unavoidable. The cancer had spread everywhere. We'd known it was coming, but I think death is always sudden. One moment, your person is here, and the next, they're gone and you're alone in the world. That's how it was for me anyway."

"Until Frank."

Her mouth curved into a slight smile. "I guess I reached out blindly too, and found him."

I had thoughts about Shira being a twenty-year-old bride, but I kept them to myself. She wouldn't appreciate me talking about her late husband, and I wasn't in any position to ruffle her feathers.

We finished our dinner, and I sent her into the living room while I cleaned up. She tried to tell me I didn't know where everything went, but I ignored her, stacking the dishwasher while she retreated to the couch. Since the first floor was open, I felt her watching me, but I'd done dishes more than a few times in my life. I wasn't too worried I was doing it wrong.

Once everything was put away, I joined her on her alarmingly small couch. It looked like it had been made in a different era when people were smaller. I wasn't sure it would hold me up.

"Did you pick this out?" I asked as the sofa creaked under me.

"I did. It didn't make that sound when I sat on it."

Raising my brows, I looked her up and down. "I'm more than double your size. My brothers are too. Put two of us on this thing and we'll make matchsticks out of it. We're going to have to upgrade to something sturdier."

"Your brothers are going to be sitting on my couch?"

"You don't know them yet, but we're tight, and they're going to be excited to be uncles. So, yes, they will be sitting on your couch when Beanie's here because they'll want to be with him too."

Her eyes widened with alarm as she glanced at her doll-size furniture. "I didn't think of that. I don't have family. It didn't occur to me that your family...okay...well, I guess I'll find something to accommodate a crew of giants."

I huffed a laugh. "Good idea. I'd offer to buy it, but I don't think you'll accept."

"You're right. I won't."

I grinned. "Glad we understand each other." However, I had every intention of leaving here tonight and buying a bed for the guest room as well as a replacement sofa suitable for full-size people. She'd just have to accept it was what I needed to do.

"Now, we're going to play a getting-to-know-you game. Where's your wallet?"

Her brow crinkled. "Um...in my purse, which is in the closet."

I hopped up as gingerly as possible and grabbed her purse out of the hall closet. Returning, I set it on the cushion between us and withdrew my wallet from my back pocket.

"I looked up icebreaker ideas last night," I explained. "One was trading wallets. You look through mine. I look through yours. What do you think?"

Her nose twitched. "I think you came prepared for this game while I'm being blindsided."

"True, but I swear I didn't remove or add anything to my wallet. And you can blindside me next time. Trade?"

One beat of hesitation, then she fished her wallet from her purse and tossed it into my lap. I handed her mine. This wasn't the most exciting game, but I thought it might be the easiest for Shira.

I waited until she unfolded my wallet and peered inside before turning my attention to hers. It was a bifold, mustard-yellow leather, which already surprised me. Shira's clothes were normally so muted while her wallet was bright. Maybe this was her true story.

Inside, there were two credit cards and a bank card. Membership cards to a gym, grocery store, and the library. The picture on her license gave me pause.

The motor vehicle worker must've liked Shira. I had never seen lighting that looked like it belonged on a photo shoot. Her dark hair tumbled over her shoulders and framed her face in soft waves. Her glossed lips were tipped in a smile that looked genuine. Her eyes were dancing with mirth.

I held out her license. "What were you laughing at?"

Shira looked up from my wallet. "Oh, um...Connie was hyping me up. She made me take my hair down and was telling me I should have been in a shampoo commercial. It was very sweet."

"Connie? You remember her name?" She'd been issued the license two years ago.

"Of course," she replied simply, holding out my license. "Why do you look like you're about to bite off the head of the next person who speaks to you?"

"That's what most people look like after spending any amount of time in the Department of Motor Vehicles. Most of us don't have our own personal hype woman."

Her cheeks flamed bright pink as she returned to sifting through the contents of my wallet. I let the subject be, curious what else I'd find.

She had thirty dollars in cash plus coins. A receipt from a convenience store where she bought a chocolate bar and a Sprite. I made a mental note of that. Then I landed on a worn, square photo of a man I didn't recognize. Definitely not her late husband.

"Who's this?" I asked.

"I don't know," she replied.

"You don't know? He's not an old boyfriend?"

Her laughter was a rebuke in itself. "Not even close. It's silly."

"I doubt it. Tell me about it."

She rubbed her lips together then sighed. "I found that picture on the floor of a post office when I was nine or ten. My mom told me it was a passport photo. I thought the guy was cute, so I kept it. Then I started making up stories about where he might've been going with his new passport. I've carried it with me ever since. I like to think of all the adventures he's been on over the last twenty years. I hope he's had a nice life."

"That's..." I was at a loss for words.

"I told you, it's silly. It's sort of become a hobby of mine. I pick up things people drop, like receipts, business cards, invitations, that kind of thing, and make up stories in my head about them. This picture is the only thing I've saved, though."

Her fingers were fast, but I didn't miss her shoving back the condom I kept in my wallet as habit.

"It's probably expired."

Her eyes shot up to mine. "For a man who recently had a condom mishap, you're living on the edge."

I chuckled, enjoying how easily Shira surprised me. "I've carried one in my wallet since I was a teenager. Most expired before they were used."

"Okay," she murmured, slapping my wallet shut. "I'm done snooping."

"All right. Think I am too."

She yawned so big her eyes squeezed closed. I took that as my cue. Tucking her wallet back in her purse, I returned it to the closet. By the time I came back to the living room, Shira was on her feet, hands hidden in the sleeves of her sweater.

"I'm going to head out." I reached out, tugging a loose tendril of her hair. "You look like you're dead on your feet. Get some rest."

"I will. Thanks for the pizza, Roman."

I looked down at her, my gut souring at the idea of this delicate woman sleeping in this house all on her own. Since she'd been alone in her last house, it was completely irrational, but I'd been less than five minutes away then. Now, we had a whole city between us, and it didn't sit well with me. Not at all.

"If you need anything at any time, call me," I ordered gruffly.

Shira shrank slightly but nodded. "Okay."

"I need a key."

"*What?*"

"I don't want off the hook, Shira. You moved, but nothing's changed. I'm going to be here every morning to deal with the litter and bring you breakfast."

Her eyes flared, and her hands twisted her sleeves. "That's not necessary. Truly. I have Bea, and it's too far for you to come every day."

"Let me be concerned with the distance. I need to do this."

"Need?"

I nodded. "Need."

She worried her lip for several seconds before spinning away to fetch me a key. I slipped it in my pocket and headed for the door. My arms started to lift to give her another hug, but she wasn't crying so I didn't think she'd welcome it.

Not yet.

Giving her hair another gentle tug, I walked out the door. The moment I heard the lock click into place, I found the nearest trash can, took out my wallet, and tossed the unneeded condom into it.

It took exactly one minute to hear from Shira after I ordered her new furniture. I found myself grinning when her name popped up on my phone.

> **Shira:** *Why did you just send me a receipt for a bed and couch?*

> **Me:** *So you know to expect a delivery.*

> **Shira:** *ROMAN…why?*

I could almost hear her soft, exasperated voice.

> **Me:** *They're more for me than you. It only makes sense for me to be the one to buy them. If they're not to your taste, you can exchange them. I won't be offended.*

Shira: *Well, I'm offended you paid for my furniture!*

Me: *Are you really?*

Shira: *I'm huffing right now.*

I could almost hear that too. My grin widened.

Ben swatted the back of my head as he passed me in the kitchen. "What are you smiling about?"

I held up my phone. "Shira."

His brow winged. "Oh yeah?"

Ignoring him, I tapped out a text.

Me: *But are you offended?*

Shira: *Fine. No, I'm not. Thank you for being so generous.*

Me: *No need to thank me, Goldie. I like making sure you have everything you need.*

Ben cracked open a can of sparkling water and leaned against the counter. "Must be some conversation."

"She's funny." I left it at that because that was all it was.

"Don't wanna say I told you so…"

"Then don't."

Shira: *You can't stop me from thanking you.*

Me: *Okay, I accept. You're welcome. Give Mary a scratch and tell her it's from me.*

Shira: *She says, "Rrrreeeoooow."*

That cat was definitely going to be the death of me. And sooner rather than later.

Me: *I'm suspicious. What is she planning?*

Shira: *You'll have to wait and see. Good-night, Roman.*

Me: *Night, Goldie.*

The smile stayed on my face long after our conversation ended.

Chapter Eighteen

Shira

I strode up to the Levy building, smiling and waving at Kit as she approached from the opposite direction with Elliot. He was taking small, slow steps to keep pace with his very pregnant wife, which I found unbearably sweet and considerate. They were a prime example of "opposites attract," and the more I saw them together, the easier it was for me to see why they worked.

Elliot still made me a little nervous, but since his attention was almost always focused on Kit, it wasn't difficult to be around him.

"Good morning," Kit chirped.

"Good morning!" I replied.

This was my second week working with Kit. Last week, she'd taken me through everything she was doing at Building Dignity and showed me the systems she had put in place. We'd divided up tasks and brainstormed ideas for the future. Before she'd asked me to work with her, I couldn't have said what my dream job would be. But this was it. There couldn't possibly be anything better than providing safe, quality housing to families in need.

Kit hooked her arm around mine as we strode through the lobby. Elliot stayed on her other side, hovering but giving us the chance to chat. Our offices were on the same floor as his, so he and Kit saw each other throughout the day—and he found every opportunity to stop in and check on her.

"Were the new stools delivered yesterday?" she asked.

"Yes. They fit perfectly at the island. Thanks for the suggestion."

"I hope you're planning on inviting me over so I can see all the decorating you're doing in person."

"This weekend?" I asked.

She turned to Elliot. "Am I free this weekend?"

"We have brunch Sunday, but no plans otherwise," he replied. "I'll be on Joey and Theo duty if you want to go out."

She kissed his bicep then grinned at me. "I'll be there for some adult time. We should probably do some shopping."

I nodded. Kit's taste was much more colorful than mine. I needed that kind of influence or risked ending up with a beige house. "It's a plan."

Moving had been the best decision. I'd been in my new house for almost three weeks, and with each passing day, it felt more right. I slept better than I had in years, at peace in my cozy bedroom, knowing my best friend was right next door. Mary was happy too. The house had tall windows, allowing long slashes of sunlight to spill through. She'd found new favorite spots to bathe in the warmth, and when I came home, she always pranced around merrily, talking up a storm.

We stepped into the elevator together, and a voice called for us to hold it as the doors started to slide shut. Elliot's arm shot out, and the doors opened, revealing a slightly rumpled Roman.

Our eyes latched immediately.

We hadn't seen each other since that night we shared a pizza. He'd been by every morning, just like he promised, but if I was awake, I stayed in my room. We still passed little notes back and forth, but I needed physical space from him before the warm feelings I'd begun to have possibly bloomed into something more. That, I couldn't have. The last thing our co-parenting relationship needed was an unrequited crush. Keeping our meetings to doctor appointments and the in-between remaining friendly but distant was simpler.

"Are you getting on?" Elliot intoned.

Roman jerked as if he'd been in a daze, then moved into the elevator beside me. "Thanks for waiting for me. It's been a rough morning."

He turned to sweep his gaze over me again, stopping on my abdomen. In the three weeks since we'd been in each other's presence, my belly had gotten rounder, and my jersey dress molded over it.

"Did Mary give you trouble?" I asked.

He blew out a heavy breath. "She pounced on my feet as soon as I took my shoes off and made me spill half of your smoothie all over my shirt."

I scrunched my nose. Mary had never attacked my toes. That didn't sound like her. But half of my smoothie *had* been missing. "I thought you drank some of it."

"Who's Mary, and why is she attacking you?" Elliot asked.

"Shira's cat." Roman's eyes remained on me as he answered. "She hates me."

Elliot sniffed. "Shira or the cat?"

Roman's brow winged. "The cat. Though, the woman is questionable."

"I don't hate you. And I don't think I have to remind you that you volunteered for Mary duty."

"No, you don't have to remind me." His mouth hitched in a crooked grin.

"He brings you smoothies?" Kit asked.

I turned away from Roman, but I was all too aware of him studying me. From the side, my belly was even more pronounced.

"He sees it as his duty to keep me fed," I explained.

Elliot put his hand on Kit's shoulder. "He's right. It's his duty to take care of your every need," he stated like it was an inarguable fact. Since I would never argue with Elliot Levy, it sort of was.

We arrived on the tenth floor, and Roman started to step out. When I didn't follow, he stopped between the doors and frowned.

"Aren't you visiting GoldMed?"

"Oh, no." I pointed to the ceiling. "I'm going up to Building Dignity."

His frown deepened. "Why?"

"Well...I work there."

Elliot huffed with impatience. "In or out. Choose one."

Roman's brow puckered with indecision, then he checked his watch and sighed. "We have a lot to talk about, but I have a meeting I'm running late for." He pinned me with a hard stare. "Later."

"Later," I whispered.

On the top floor, Kit followed me into my office, and I fell into the chair behind my desk, which was more like a throne. All the chairs on this floor were inexplicably plush. If I'd had this during my first trimester, Roman would have caught me sleeping in my office more than once.

"Okay—what was *that*?" she asked.

My eyes rounded at her excitement. "What?"

"How Roman was looking at you. It was like he was angry yet enthralled. I'm deeply familiar with that expression."

I shook my head. "No, that's not—he's not enthralled with me. Maybe the bump, but not me. Getting pregnant by him was a fluke, and we're trying to be friends, but it's not more than that. And I'm not sure why he would be angry."

Her hands rested on her belly as she hummed serenely. "I could be wrong." She wagged a finger. "I don't think I am, but I could be."

I snorted a laugh. "You are. Now, sit down so we can talk about the charity auction."

Building Dignity's annual fundraising event was coming up in three weeks. Elliot had insisted it be pared down this year to keep super-pregnant Kit from being too stressed, so we were throwing a luncheon with a silent auction instead of the three-thousand-dollar-a-plate gala she'd put on in the past. The next hour, we went over details and brainstormed ways to fill in a few available spots for auction items. A knock on my office door came while we were wrapping up.

"Shira Goldman?"

I waved at the young man I thought I recognized from the mailroom. "Hi, that's me."

He walked in and placed a plastic bag on my desk. "This is for you."

"Really?" I peeked inside. A Sprite and a chocolate bar along with a note.

Shira,

Three weeks and our son has made his presence known. You look great. Here's a

little treat to congratulate you on the good
work you're doing. If my boy is anything
like me, he's got a big appetite, so I'm
going to have to do a better job of keeping
you fed. Convenient now that I'm aware
you're in the same building every day.
Would have been nice to know sooner, though.
What's that about?

X,

Roman

"It's from Roman," I whispered.

Kit hummed. "Totally enthralled."

I waved her off. "He's keeping his baby fed." The messenger was
still standing there so I scribbled a note.

Roman,

I do have a nice little bump, don't I?

Thanks for the treat. How did you know
this is exactly what I wanted?

I'm working with Kit at BD. I'll keep you
apprised of all my jobs in the future.

Yours,

Shira

"Can you bring this to Roman?"

The messenger took the folded piece of paper and jogged out with
a backward wave. I wondered if this was part of his job description
or if Roman had commandeered him for the task.

Kit smirked. "That's cute."

I tapped my lips. "Shhh. We're not doing this."

"Pay me in chocolate, and I'll keep quiet."

I swept the candy bar off my desk, clutching it to my chest. "This was a gift."

Her eyes narrowed. "You won't share? Really?"

Laughing, I ripped open the wrapper and snapped off a few squares. "This is for the baby, not you."

She snagged the chocolate, grinning as she bit off a corner. "The baby says thank you."

We chatted a couple minutes longer before she got up to leave. As she did, the same messenger appeared, his forehead slightly sweaty.

"Hi, Ms. Goldman. Mr. Wells has another message for you," he panted, placing a piece of paper on my desk.

```
Shira,

I paid attention during our wallet-snoop-
ing game. You had a receipt for candy and a
Sprite.

I sense smartassery, but I wouldn't mind
being kept apprised of all your big news.

We'll talk tonight. I'll be at your place
after work.

X,

Roman
```

I bit down on my bottom lip to stop from grinning, fully aware Kit was watching me. The last thing I wanted to do was add fuel to the fire she'd conjured up in her mind. It wasn't her fault. Being madly in love and pregnant, she couldn't help seeing love stories everywhere. That would never be Roman and me. If I weren't having his child, he wouldn't have given me a second thought. We were stuck with each other—nothing more.

Even if I wanted it to be—and I didn't—Roman was a six-and-a-half-foot former pro athlete with pretty eyes and a smile that stopped people in their tracks. And I was me, short, plain, nothing special at all. We only worked as a faceless, anonymous hookup. Any smiles he caused were strictly friendship-related.

I sent the messenger on his way without another note. His sigh of relief answered whether passing notes was part of his job description.

Kit smirked, and I shushed her again. "None of that."

CHAPTER NINETEEN

Shira

I'D JUST PULLED MY first-ever lasagna from the oven when Roman let himself into my place.

"Heeyyy, Goldie," he called, and my stomach swooped. Hearing him say that nickname reminded me too much of our night in room ten. He really had to stop calling me that, but I couldn't bring myself to ask him not to. Then again, I'd never been good at asking for what I wanted.

"In the kitchen," I returned, grateful there was no tremble in my voice.

A moment later, he strode in, placing a bag of oranges on my island. "What's cooking?"

"Lasagna." I peered at my creation. The cheese was bubbly, but this pregnancy had caused my sense of taste and smell to be more than a little off, so I wasn't sure if the aroma was mouth-watering or tear-inducing. "I'm teaching myself to cook. Well...trying. I'm not sure it's going well. I didn't have a chance to learn to cook from my mother, and Frank had a chef, so I never got around to learning."

"Are you learning for our boy?" he asked.

I nodded. "It feels like a skill I should have before he's here. I can't feed him grilled cheese for every meal, and that's the extent of my culinary skills at the moment."

My nerves went haywire as Roman picked up one of the cranberry gingerbread muffins I'd made the day before. "Did you make this?"

"I did."

I bit down on my bottom lip as he peeled the wrapper off and popped a piece into his mouth. He chewed slowly, his eyes flaring. I couldn't quite decipher his expression, but my breath caught in my throat as I waited for his verdict.

Finally, he swallowed. "Wow, that was gingery."

"Oh no," I whispered, tears pricking my eyes. "Was it that bad?"

His mouth fell open, his eyes rounding, stricken with panic. He really didn't like it when I cried. Neither did I, for that matter. What kind of mother would I be if I couldn't even make a simple muffin?

"Absolutely not." He stuffed another piece of muffin in his mouth, chewing and swallowing faster this time. "Delicious, Shira. It's like a taste of Christmas."

My cheeks flamed. I thought I might've messed up royally when I'd accidentally tripled the amount of ginger, but if he thought my muffins were delicious, I couldn't have screwed up that badly.

"Thank you. You'll have to try my lasagna. I hope you haven't eaten dinner yet."

"I came straight here from the office. Feed me."

He cleared his throat a few times as he took a glass from my cupboard and filled it with water from the refrigerator. I almost got distracted by the way his throat bobbed with each deep pull but forced myself to turn away and plate lasagna and salad for us both.

I dug into my salad first, watching Roman as he took a bite of the lasagna. He was a careful chewer, but once he got started eating, he really shoveled it in. Curious if it was as good as he was making it seem, I tried a piece and immediately grimaced. I'd spilled a little—okay, a *lot*—extra from my jar of minced garlic, but I'd thought it would probably cook off. Plus, I loved garlic. There was no such thing as too much. Except maybe there was. And the pepper I'd added to even it out hadn't exactly done the job.

Roman seemed to be enjoying it immensely, though. It had to be my screwy taste buds lying to me. I wished I could enjoy it as much as he obviously was. He'd barely taken a breath in between bites, scarfing it down like he was starving.

I ate my salad with the same gusto and broke off pieces of the fluffy French bread I'd bought on the way home. Apparently, my palate wanted bland and simple. I'd make the lasagna again after I had the baby so I could enjoy it.

Roman was almost finished with his meal, but I couldn't imagine he was full. A man his size surely always had seconds. Probably thirds. He might not ask for more, thinking he should leave it for me, but I couldn't possibly eat another bite. If I did, it wouldn't stay down.

"Turns out I'm not in the mood for pasta tonight." I picked up my plate and held it out to him. "Here, you seem like you're starving. Eat mine."

Roman looked up from his plate, which he'd just scraped clean. The protest registered in his eyes and open mouth, but he clamped it shut and accepted, transferring my lasagna to his plate.

Once he'd cleaned his plate a second time, and I'd eaten half a loaf of bread along with my salad, he insisted on cleaning up. Since I knew he wouldn't allow me to help, and I was tired, I settled on my new couch.

Roman had bought me a pale-gray sectional that felt like angels had filled it with clouds. It had arrived three weeks ago, and I'd fallen asleep on it more times than I cared to admit.

He strode into the living room a few minutes later, his jaw working as he chewed a piece of gum and settled on a cushion beside me.

"You were right," I said.

"Oh, yeah? About what?"

"The couch. I love this one."

The corners of his eyes crinkled as his face split into a wide grin. "I'm glad. I have a larger version at my place. It's been tested by all my brothers and withstands us."

"I'm sure the other one would have been fine, but...I like this one better. Thank you."

His knee nudged mine. "What'd I tell you about thanking me? Not necessary."

"And didn't I tell you there was no way for you to stop me?"

His chuckle was like a marble on wood, rolling through the room and over my chest.

After a beat, he grew serious. "So, you have a new job?"

"I do. I've been working at Building Dignity for two weeks. It's not going to be full time, which is perfect for right now. I love Kit, and BD is doing really incredible work. In fact, I was going to ask you for a favor."

"Anything," he replied.

"A lung?" I joked.

"Do you need a lung?" He was nothing but serious.

"No, I don't." I bit down on my bottom lip, formulating how to ask him for what I truly did need. It would have been easier to email him my request, but since he was here, watching me expectantly, this would have to happen now. "Building Dignity is hosting a silent auction next weekend—"

"Wells Investments bought a table. We'll be there."

"Oh, good. That's really good." I tucked a stray tendril behind my ear. "We're still seeking a few more auction items, and I thought, since you are part owner of the Mountain Lions, perhaps you would be willing to donate a—"

"I'll donate fully-catered box seating for ten people. How does that sound?"

I wrinkled my nose. "It sounds lovely. Thank you. Kit and I really appreciate your generosity."

"Then why the face?"

I touched my nose. "Oh. I didn't mean to make a face. Sometimes it just happens."

"Okay, but why did you?"

This was difficult. With Bea and Clara, speaking my mind had become second nature. It was becoming like that with Kit as well. But I wasn't there with Roman. I doubted I ever would be. His presence was too overpowering, and my cowering instinct, leftover from a childhood where becoming invisible had been the only thing to protect me, came out all too often around him.

"Shira?" he pressed as gently as he was capable.

My hand went to my stomach, and so did his eyes. Not having them on my face made it easier to tell the truth.

"You interrupted me twice," I pushed out in little more than a whisper. "That's why I made that expression."

His eyes shot back to mine. I braced for anger but didn't find it. "I did?" He rubbed the back of his neck. "You're right, I did. I didn't mean to barrel over you. I'm sorry about that, Goldie. Do you want to finish what you were going to ask me?"

"Well...no."

"No?"

The corners of my mouth twitched. "I was going to ask you for regular seats. In this case, I'm sort of glad you barreled over me."

"Ah. It worked out for the best, but I won't make a habit of it. Thanks for pointing it out." He nodded toward my stomach. "Now that that's settled, let's talk about the other reason I'm here. Can I see?"

"My stomach?"

His brow crinkled. "Is that too much to ask? You can tell me if it is. I won't be mad. I'm just...curious. Fascinated."

I rubbed my lips together nervously. This man had seen every inch of me, yet I was internally balking at showing him this—a small part of me that was home to his son.

With a deep breath, I opened my sweater. The tank I wore beneath molded over my curves like a second skin. My stomach was still pretty small but distinctly round and firm.

Roman grunted, his hand gravitating toward me. At the last second, before he made contact, his eyes lifted to mine. "Can I?"

Speechless, I nodded, and his huge hand engulfed my belly. His palm was almost bigger than my bump, and the warmth of it seeped through my shirt.

"I thought it would be soft," he murmured. "I remember you being soft here."

I didn't know what to say to that. Before now, we hadn't done much talking about what we'd done in room ten.

"He's the size of a mango." Roman's gaze trailed up my body to meet mine. "Have you felt him move yet?"

I shook my head. "Sometimes I think I might feel a flutter, but I'm not sure."

"I bet you'll feel him soon. Will you let me know?"

His hand hadn't left my belly. He was moving it in small, slow circles, his fingers occasionally pressing into me. And I liked it. If he'd asked, I would have let him pull up my shirt so he could be skin to skin with me. But he didn't, and I would never, *ever* offer.

"I'll tell you," I promised.

"Thank you." He exhaled and settled back on his cushion, his hand still on me. "I'm not mentally prepared to drive across town yet. Mind if I hang out for a while?"

"I don't mind." It would be nice to have some company for a change. "Should we watch a movie?"

Roman's head was back, his feet were kicked up on the ottoman in front of him, and his breathing had slowed, more relaxed than I'd ever seen him.

"Anything you want, Shira." His fingers drummed on my stomach. "I'm good here."

He stayed just like that through an entire movie. I got up once to use the bathroom, and when I returned, so did his hand to my belly. When he got up to leave, it was late, and Mary was meowing for me to come to bed. He stopped at my front door, locking eyes with me.

"Set the alarm after you lock up."

"I always do," I assured him.

With a deep sigh, he hooked an arm around my shoulders and pulled me in for a hug. My cheek hit his chest, settling into the spot that alarmingly felt like mine. "Thanks for having me over. And for everything else. It was a good night."

"Anytime."

He let me go and grinned down at me. "I'll hold you to that, Goldie. See you soon."

The next week went by in a flash. Kit and I had been working like madwomen to get ready for the silent auction. I'd had my anatomy scan—Beanie was still big and his organs were developing just like they were supposed to—and I'd continued my foray into learning to cook. Roman had dinner with me several evenings, scarfing down my experiments just as enthusiastically as he had the lasagna. When I knew he was coming, I made sure to add extra garlic and pepper to the dishes. It didn't taste good to me, but judging by his continued scraped-clean plates, he seemed to love it.

The first hitch in the week came when I got home from work Wednesday afternoon to discover a moving truck in front of Bev and Donnie's house.

"We had no plans of moving, my dear, but we got an offer we simply couldn't refuse," Bev explained.

"I'll miss you." My heart plummeted, and my brain whirred. I wasn't the best with change, and I'd just gotten used to having Bev and Donnie living next door. "I hope my new neighbor is as nice as you."

She patted my shoulder. "There won't ever be another Bev, but I'm sure you and Beatrice will be just fine without me."

So much for her promises to babysit.

The following day, things went even more haywire. Bea and I had gone out to dinner with Clara, and when we returned, there was another moving truck in front of Bev and Donnie's former home.

"Someone's moving in," Bea remarked as we stopped on the sidewalk to watch the movers going in and out of the house. "They better be as cool as my girl Bev, or they might wake up to their house TP'd."

"You can't toilet paper someone's house just because they're uncool." I held up a finger. "Actually, you can't do it because you're not a teenager and it would be sad."

Bea folded her arms and hmphed. "Fine. Eggs it is."

Bea had to get ready for her waitressing job, so she left me sitting on the swing on my front porch. If the new neighbors saw me, hopefully they'd be convinced I was an innocent pregnant woman enjoying an evening swing and not the Nosy Nellie I was.

The movers left the house one final time, closed their truck, and drove off. A massive, silver SUV pulled up to the curb in their place, and two men got out. My breath caught in my throat when I spotted the wild, curly hair, followed by an even wilder smile. The second man wasn't as big in stature or smile, but their resemblance was undeniable.

"Ben?"

His name escaped my mouth without thought. It couldn't have been loud, but his head swiveled in my direction, and when he found me, his entire being lit up.

"Shira!" he called. "Get over here."

Confused, I rose from my swing and made my way down my porch steps. Ben had my gate open for me by the time I made it across my small front yard.

"Long time, no see." He alighted on my bump and gasped. "Holy shit, look at you. I was half convinced Roman had made this baby thing up. Seeing is believing." He looked over his shoulder. "Nate, get over here and meet Shira."

The second man, who shared Roman and Ben's dark curls and square jaws, was almost as tall as the twins but nowhere near as broad. He was more sleek than rugged, and if I had to guess, I would say the eldest of the Wells brothers.

He offered me his hand. "Shira. It's nice to meet you after hearing so much about you."

His hand engulfed mine in warmth, his shake neither weak nor overly powerful. Often, men barely gripped my fingers. I appreciated Nate giving me a real handshake.

Still, I was confused about why they were here.

"Did Roman send you to check on me?" I asked.

Ben rocked back on his heels. "No, he did not. Boy, do I have a surprise for you."

"Ben..." Nate groaned.

"Will you come next door with us?" Ben asked.

I glanced at Bev and Donnie's former home. "Are you my new neighbor?"

He waggled his brows. "Not me." He put a big hand on my shoulder. "Come on, let me show you."

The brothers surrounded me, and seeing the two together, I understood why Roman had been worried about my first couch. Add two more of these guys, it probably wouldn't have survived.

I walked next door with them, a million thoughts whirling around my head. One kept trying to make its way to the forefront, but I refused to believe it.

Until Roman stood in the doorway, his arms crossed, amusement tipping his lips.

"Heeyyy, Goldie. Aren't you gonna welcome me to the neighborhood?"

CHAPTER TWENTY

Roman

NATE TOLD ME I was crazy.

Adrian was convinced I'd lost my mind.

Ben was all for the idea.

That should have given me pause, but once I'd made the decision, it had been full steam ahead.

The idea of moving to be near Shira had seemed ludicrous when it was first suggested, but that day on the elevator, after three weeks of not seeing her and all the changes that had happened, had filled me with a great sense of loss.

I didn't like it. I'd missed the first trimester; I'd be damned if I didn't have front-row seats to my son continuing to grow inside his mother. I'd do anything to have that. Including eating Shira's barely edible dinner experiments so loaded with garlic and pepper I was liable to develop an ulcer. And grossly overpaying for a house in a neighborhood I was dubious about.

I'd pulled Shira into my new place, and Ben and Nate had followed. She'd been quiet while I'd shown them what I'd planned to do with the kitchen when I gutted it. She'd chewed on her bottom lip when I'd walked them around upstairs so they could see the bedrooms. When I'd dished out the dinner I'd cooked—no garlic in sight—she'd sat on her hands and rolled her lips over her teeth.

She only spoke once Ben and Nate had disappeared into the living room with their plates and we were alone in the kitchen.

"You bought Bev and Donnie's house?"

"I did."

"Besides Bea, they were my favorite neighbors."

There was no emotion or inflection in her words. If anything, she appeared shell-shocked, which wasn't exactly surprising. To her, my actions might have seemed extreme, but they were well in line with my typical way of conducting life. I thought about my next move for as long as I needed to, then acted. After spending a month traveling across the city to take care of Shira and her damn cat, I'd decided that had been enough.

"If it's any consolation, I looked into buying the building across the street, but it was recently bought by a tech billionaire who wouldn't sell no matter how high I went with my offer. Bev and Donnie were much more amenable."

I grazed my palm over her belly. It was like second nature now. She never stopped me, and I'd found I couldn't stop myself either.

"What made them such good neighbors?" I asked affably, sensing she needed me to take it down a notch. I wasn't a particularly gentle man, but around Shira, I seemed to attempt to match her more mellow, careful nature.

"They made me cookies and offered to babysit when Beanie arrives. They were quiet and always waved when we passed." She lifted a shoulder. "They didn't do anything out of this world, but they were nice and made me feel welcome."

"No problem. I can do all those things. You'll forget Bev and Donnie ever existed."

Her nose crinkled. "Are you sure living next door to each other is a good idea?"

"I am. For now, there's no place I'd rather be living than next to the mother of my son. Since you've decided to settle in this questionable neighborhood, this is where I'll be."

She swatted my arm, and I wondered if this was the first time she'd initiated contact with me. I thought it might've been and took it as a good sign. She was getting comfortable with me. My plan to become her best friend was well underway.

"The neighborhood is great." Her eyes roamed over the tall ceilings and cabinets. "The house is beautiful too. I didn't realize it was so much bigger than mine."

It was twice the size of Shira's and had a small yard out back—a boon for city living. I'd been in a condo for a long time. I thought I'd enjoy having the outdoor space. Plus, if my son was anything like me, he'd need it to run himself ragged. Wells boys didn't do well confined to the indoors.

"I like it too." I spread my fingers over her bump. "Is our boy hungry?"

"I ate dinner with Bea and Clara."

I lowered my chin to catch her wandering gaze, asking again, "Is our boy hungry?"

She sucked in a breath then told the truth. "Yes. He always is lately."

"Don't be afraid to tell me if you need something. I'm always going to provide it for you."

"I'll try." She tucked her hair behind her ear. "I still think this is crazy, you know."

"Maybe the way I went about it was a little extreme, but I don't see how me moving in next to you can be called crazy."

Her head canted, a little smile playing on her mouth. "You can't?"

I shook my head. "Nope. Now, let's get you and the boy fed." I grabbed our plates and nodded toward the living room. "Come on."

Nate and Ben had turned on a basketball game and were well on their way to finishing their plates by the time we settled on the sectional. Shira was surrounded by me and my brothers, and by the increased rise and fall of her chest, it made her nervous. Ben didn't allow her to sink into those feelings, though. He chattered away, telling her about his trip to New Zealand, and peppered her with questions too personal for people who'd only met twice.

"Are you prepared for how huge you're going to get?" he asked.

Nate threw a napkin at him, and Shira flushed a violent red.

I squeezed her knee. "There's no need to answer him."

"Ignore him like we all do," Nate added.

"I don't think I am," Shira replied quietly. "I don't do the best with unexpected attention, and I've already had several old ladies ask me when I'm due. By the end, with me being so short and Roman being a giant, I can only imagine my bump will have its own gravitational pull. I might have to stay inside so no one looks at me."

"Did you hear that, Ben? She doesn't like a lot of attention," Nate intoned. "Take a hint."

Ben patted his chest. "That doesn't include me, right? We're basically family now."

Shira's cheeks were almost glowing, and it was...striking. Sweet. If she didn't like attention, she'd need to stop being so adorable.

"You're fine," she replied. "I expect it from you, so I'm prepared."

Ben elbowed Nate. "See? I'm fine. Shira and I are already friends."

Nate leaned around Ben, leveling Shira with a soft look. "You can ignore him. He doesn't mind."

"Thanks, Nate." She offered him a small, timid smile. "I guess I have to get used to you guys since Roman says you'll be around a lot once Beanie's here."

Nate chuckled. "We're around a lot in general. Don't know if it's healthy or not, but that's us. Before this big move, Rome and Ben lived together, and I was next door. It's going to take some adjusting now that he's on this side of town."

"We might move too," Ben added. I wouldn't be surprised if they did, nor would I object.

I raised a brow. "You're not living with me."

"What about your other brother...Adrian?" she asked.

"Adrian's job keeps him busy at night. He's harder to track down," Nate said.

"Oh? What does he do?"

"He owns a club," I told her, leaving out the minor detail of which club. I didn't want her to feel embarrassed about my brother's connection to where we met.

Leave it to Ben to blow it by snickering. "A club? Be specific, man. Sooner or later, Shira's going to find out Adrian owns a sex club."

Her body went solid beside mine, but she kept her reaction off her face. "Oh. Okay. I guess a place like that wouldn't exactly be a brunch spot. Working nights makes sense."

That made my brothers laugh, and I breathed a sigh of relief. I couldn't tell how she was feeling, but she was smart enough to connect the dots and figure out MHC was Adrian's club. If she was bothered, she didn't show it as she tucked into her dinner, scrunching her nose at the game she watched with Nate and Ben.

When her plate was empty, I took it to the kitchen. She tried to claim it was time for her to go home, but all three of us insisted she stay. So, she settled beneath the fuzzy blanket Nate had draped over her, and before long, her eyes fluttered closed, and she fell asleep.

Hard to believe it was possible with Ben shouting at the TV and Nate leaping to his feet then slamming back down when his guy missed a shot, but her face remained placid, and her breathing was slow and steady. Again, I was hit with a deep sense of satisfaction. Shira felt secure enough to fall asleep next to me and my brothers. There wasn't much more I could have asked for.

"Is she asleep?" Nate whispered.

"She is." I swept hair off her forehead. "Growing a kid is tiring work."

When Shira still hadn't stirred a little while later, Nate looked from her to me, his brow furrowed in thought.

"How could you have gotten her so wrong?" he asked.

I knew exactly what he meant. How could I have spent any time around this woman and thought badly of her? I believed everything I'd heard about her, and what I hadn't heard, I'd formed assumptions based on observations. I'd been wrong. Deeply, undeniably wrong.

"I'm an idiot."

Ben nodded enthusiastically. "Glad you said it."

"She's closed off and shy. When I met her, I misread her as icy and arrogant."

Ben chuffed. "Because you believed the bullshit Frannie said about her."

I couldn't deny it. "That and the letters." I rubbed the space between my brows and exhaled. "She wrote them. It wasn't Frank at all. Every time I sent him a letter, it was Shira writing back to me."

It took a lot to catch Nate off guard, but he jerked like he'd been shocked with electricity.

"What the fuck?" he hissed. "That's...interesting. How do you feel about that?"

I shook my head. "I don't know. Much less attached to GoldMed, for one. Frank Goldman instantly went from something like a mentor to a lecherous creep for going after her when she was nineteen years old."

Ben flipped his hand over, his palm up. "To be fair, he was always that. You just looked past it because of your daddy issues."

"Fuck off," I said without any venom. He wasn't wrong. I'd gone to therapy for my insatiable need to make my dead father proud and still ended up in this position. Obviously, I had more work to do, but I'd taken the first step of removing my head out of my own ass. Hopefully, it would remain that way.

"For what it's worth, I'd say she's forgiven you." Nate nodded toward the peacefully sleeping Shira. "I like her. Quite a lot, actually. She doesn't strike me as conniving or opportunistic. I'd say she's pretty down to earth."

"I agree, and I like her too." I brushed my fingers over her forehead again. "She'll be a really good mom."

Ben waggled his brows. "Sure, sure, but do you *like* her? I'm getting vibes..."

"She's the mother of my child," I stated.

"Leave it," Nate snapped. "Not everything's a joke."

Ben raised his hands. "All right, I'll drop it. I was just saying what we were all thinking."

Shira woke later in the evening, soon after my brothers left. Her eyes sprung open, and she sucked in a breath, her head whipping left and right.

"Have a nice nap, Goldie?"

Her wide eyes landed on me, still seated beside her. "I fell asleep?"

"You did. Looked like you needed that nap."

"I guess I did." She rubbed her eyes and yawned. "Nate and Ben are gone?"

"Just left. Ben's never been quiet a day in his life. Him slamming the door on his way out was probably what woke you."

"He managed to be quiet enough for me to nap for over an hour."

"Miracles happen once in a blue moon."

Straightening, she arched her back, her waves cascading along the curve of her spine like a waterfall. I tried not to be captivated, but it was impossible. It was just as well she usually wore her hair tied up when she went out. The general public didn't deserve to see her this way.

Not that I did, but I wasn't going to look a gift horse in the mouth.

"Shira, I need to assure you Adrian doesn't know about room ten. But even if he did, he'd keep it to himself. Discretion is of utmost importance in his line of work."

Her soft mouth opened then closed. Finally, after moments of what looked like indecision, she whispered, "Okay."

"I thought it would be better to keep it between us. If it were just me, I'd tell my brothers all about that night, but I'd rather them not know that about you. I assumed you would prefer that too."

She nodded. "Thank you. I still can't believe that night happened." She smoothed her hand over her belly. "If not for this, I might think I dreamed it."

"I take it that was your first time at MHC?"

She snorted softly. "Oh, yes. Bea told me about the app. I don't know why I downloaded it, but once I did, I was curious, so I looked at profiles."

"And that intrigued you?"

"You know me, Roman. Going to a bar to be picked up is out of the question. I wanted...an experience—to feel good about myself and not be alone for one night. Then I talked to Wim—to *you*—well, I still didn't think I'd go through with our plan. Then I was there, and it happened, and...well, what about you?"

"Curiosity on my part too."

Her brow arched. "I would think, since your brother owns the club, you have sated your curiosity quite a bit."

"You'd think that, but that was my first time doing something like that as well. I went through a breakup a few months back, and I'm not one for picking women up in bars. Ade told me about his new app, and I skimmed through it just to see who was on there. When I came across a shy woman who wanted to be used, I was too intrigued to pass that up."

Her shudder was subtle, but I didn't miss it. Nor did I miss her pink tongue darting out to wet her lips. "Have you been back many times since?"

"I haven't even thought about it."

She pushed out a humorless laugh. "The first time was so bad you didn't it want to try it again?"

"Shira," I leaned closer, capturing her gaze, "I think you know there was nothing bad about what happened that night. Not between you and me, and not what came from it."

My hand was already on her belly, where it perpetually rested these days, and I moved it in slow circles.

"Was it bad for you?" I asked though I knew the answer. Her cries of pleasure would be emblazoned on my brain until the end of time, which was troublesome considering we were supposed to be friends and co-parents. Anything more would be complicated.

"No, Rome. It wasn't bad at all." She rubbed her lips together. "If I did that again, I'd—"

I went still. "If you did it again?"

"Obviously not now. But one day, a year or two from now, I might want to again. I don't know."

"What did you like about it?"

"I didn't have to ask for what I wanted. That's one of my downfalls in regular life. And in that setting? Well...I just can't. I liked that you gave me what I needed."

I bit back a groan, curling my fingers into my palms to stop myself from pressing against my half-hard dick.

"I liked giving you that." I kept my voice as steady as possible, which wasn't all that steady.

Tossing the blanket on her lap aside, she scooted forward. "I should go home. Mary's probably angry at me for being gone so long."

If it had been up to me, we would have continued our conversation, but Shira was clearly done and pushing her further was out of the question. I needed her to feel at ease with me—talking about the out-of-this-world anonymous sex we had wasn't going to get her there.

"Don't tell her I'm the cause of your absence. She hates me enough as it is."

Shira offered me a smile so soft, it could have been made of velvet. I'd noticed the slight overlap of her two front teeth, but this was the first time I'd wanted her to keep smiling so I could study it.

When we'd first met—and I was being an uncharitable bastard—I'd been surprised Frank hadn't paid to have her teeth fixed. Now, I was eternally grateful he hadn't seen this slight imperfection as something that needed fixing. Her smile, when she brought it out, was sweet and real.

Standing, I offered Shira a hand. She slipped her palm against mine, and I tugged her to her feet. Underestimating my strength and how light she was, I pulled too hard, resulting in her colliding with me. Her small belly hit my hip, and on instinct, my arm snaked around her, keeping her there.

"Oh!" Her hands flew to my upper abdomen, steadying herself. "You sent me flying."

I chuckled, my fingers spreading on her lower back. "I did. Sorry about that. Glad I was able to catch you."

Her mouth opened to reply, but instead of words, she expelled a gasp. "Whoa, I think—" Heading tipping back, her wide eyes landed on mine. "I just felt him move. It's like a little butterfly in my stomach. You sent him flying too."

"You feel him?" I stepped back, both hands cupping her belly. "Right now?"

"I do. The flutters are right below my belly button. It's like he's swimming laps back and forth." Her hand slid between mine as we both stared at her middle in wonder. "I can't feel it like this."

"No. He's still too small. The app says it'll probably be a few more weeks before we can feel him from the outside." Keeping one hand on her abdomen, I grazed my knuckles along her smooth cheek. "I'm so damn glad I was with you for this."

She raised her eyes to mine, giving me that uneven smile of hers in full beam. "Me too. Even though you can't feel him yet, I'm glad we shared this."

Because it seemed right, and my elated head was in the clouds, I dipped down and covered her mouth with mine. My hand dropped from her cheek to her nape, pulling her into me. She whimpered beneath my lips, then softened, parting slightly to slot our mouths together.

I took us there but no further.

"So damn glad," I murmured against her lips. Then I slid my fingers into the sides of her hair and touched my lips to her forehead. "You're doing incredible, Goldie. Just incredible."

Her "thanks" was little more than a whisper. Then she slipped away from me, making a beeline to my door. I followed, stopping right behind her. With her hand on the knob, she turned, giving me her profile.

"Kit and I are going to be working longer hours over the next week to get everything ready for the auction, so I won't be around as much."

My stomach tightened. "Don't work too hard. Neither of you should."

Her lips tilted a little. "I won't. Between you and Elliot, I don't think either of us could get away with overworking ourselves."

"That's right." I touched her shoulder, ignoring the small jolt that went through her. "If you need help, let me know."

"Okay." Her gaze swept over mine but didn't linger. "Thanks for dinner. Welcome to the neighborhood."

She twisted the knob, but before she could leave, I bent over her, used my fingertip to tilt her head back, and kissed her softly.

"Goodnight, Shira."

"Goodnight, Roman."

She dashed over to her house, and I watched until she disappeared inside.

I'd flustered her, but the god's honest truth was I was right there with her. I couldn't say kissing Shira hadn't ever crossed my mind, not when she was as sweet as she was and how astonishingly sexy it was seeing her slowly bloom with my baby, but choosing to follow through hadn't been planned. Instinct had led my lips to hers—a reaction to sharing something wonderful and happy.

At least the first kiss could be explained that way.

The second? Not so much. That was for me, to test whether her lips had really tasted as good as I'd thought.

I should have been kicking myself. I always avoided unnecessary complications, and kissing Shira certainly added complications to the web we'd already tangled ourselves in.

Instead, I found myself grinning as I closed the door. I may have been the one to kiss her first, but there was no question Shira Goldman hadn't hesitated to kiss me back.

CHAPTER TWENTY-ONE
Shira

WHEN I'D BEEN MARRIED to Frank, I'd attended more galas and charity functions than I could've counted. My lifestyle with him had been so drastically different from how I'd grown up. I never could have fathomed all the moving parts that went into throwing an event like that.

Now, I knew, and I was exhausted.

Kit was only a few weeks from her due date and much to Elliot's chagrin, she was running around the venue like a hyperactive bunny. He stayed right behind her, constantly offering her chairs, water, food, and I imagine a chariot too. Meanwhile, I was fifteen weeks behind her, and I was dreaming about crawling into my bed when this thing was over, and it hadn't even begun.

For an introvert with social anxiety, weeks of phone calls and in-person meetings had drained me. That was why I was currently in the kitchen with Bea, ostensibly to help her set up her charcuterie trays, but we both knew I was hiding.

Bea was in full concentration mode, creating roses out of meat, folding cheese artistically, arranging it all on large wooden trays that would be placed around the room for guests to graze from.

My mouth was watering as I watched her. Somehow, she noticed, passing me a small cup of nuts, crackers, and dried apricots without even looking up.

"So...I had a run-in," she stated, her movements smooth and efficient.

"A run-in?"

"With the billionaire."

My Beatrice was a menace. There was something about her that caused men to walk into brick walls trying to get a look at her. Not only that, but she seemed to constantly find herself in the center of minor disasters. For the last two years, this often happened in the presence of her mysterious billionaire. She'd only seen him from behind and through the window of his limo, but she knew his driver's name was Igor.

"Oh? Did you incite a riot? Cause a forest fire?"

She smirked as she worked. "Nothing so mundane. Benjamin and I were out for a walk in the park near our houses, and he found a puddle."

"Oh no." While Bea was frequently the center of disasters, Benjamin was even more frequently the cause of them.

"A muddy puddle. He managed to plant himself in it and soak every inch of his fur. Then he saw a squirrel."

I cringed. "Oh *no*."

"Oh *yes*. Naturally, I was distracted by the puddle, so when he darted after the squirrel, I wasn't holding on to his leash as firmly as I should have been, and he escaped. Of course, the squirrel was headed straight for the road."

"Then what?"

"Two men walking by heard me scream and dove for Benjamin—the worst thing they could've done. He hates men, and he really doesn't like them diving at him."

"Who does?" I quipped.

"Some people, I'm sure, but not me or Benjamin. Anyway, he dodged them, but one had such momentum *he* ended up on the road at the same time a delivery guy on a moped was driving by. Luckily, the delivery guy stopped in time, but pizza went flying everywhere."

"Benjamin loves pizza."

She nodded. "He loves it more than squirrels. He took a sharp turn and pounced on an entire pie that landed right next to...can you guess?"

"The limo."

"Mmmhmm. I almost made it to him when he remembered he was soaked in puddle water. Naturally, he had to shake it off before he could eat."

I pressed my fingers to my mouth. "Were the windows open?"

She finally turned to me, one brow arched. "Of course they were.

"Of course they were," I repeated.

"By the time I contained my bad, bad dog, the windows were up, but I felt him looking at me. One day, I'm going to find out who that creep is and let Benjamin commit chaos all over him."

"He'd probably enjoy that."

"I know he would."

The kitchen door swung open, and Kit marched in, Elliot hot on her heels.

"Everything's ready out there. Guests will be arriving imminently." Kit surveyed Bea's creations. "These look delicious. Are you almost ready?"

Bea placed a final meat flower and made jazz hands. "I'm finished." She snapped her fingers over her head, and four waiters appeared out of nowhere, ready to be ordered around.

Kit grinned at me as Bea led the guys carrying her trays out of the kitchen. "I like her. Men are scared of her, huh?"

"Scared, enthralled, confused." I shrugged. "I'm sorry I was hiding."

"No worries." She hooked her arm through mine. "But no more hiding until later. I need you out there with me."

I sucked in a deep breath and nodded decisively. "I'm here. Let's go."

The room filled with the one percent of Denver mingling, placing bids for yacht weekends, rugby boxes, jewelry, luxury vacations. Clara and Jake were checking out the auction items, along with her brother and sister-in-law, Luca and Saoirse Rossi. Rossi Motors had donated a gorgeous motorcycle to the cause. In another life, where I was wild and brave, I would have bid on it.

I stopped by the sheet for the rugby box, checking out the bids. It was getting some action but not enough for my liking, so I scribbled my identification number and a bid on the sheet.

"Are you allowed to do that?"

I spun around and looked up, already smiling before I laid eyes on Roman's face. He grinned back at me, his eyes bouncing and lively. He'd been that way since the night I fell asleep on his couch, in a perpetual good mood. If I didn't know any better, I would have mistaken him for Ben.

We'd shared a couple dinners over the last week, but what we hadn't done was talk about the kiss. I'd figured them out on my own, though. We'd had a powerful, emotional moment, and Roman kissing me was a result of that.

Nothing more.

And we *really* weren't talking about the second kiss.

"Well, hello." I smoothed my dress down my sides. "I didn't know you'd be here today."

"I hear this is the place to be." He pointed to the bid sheet. "You didn't answer. Are you breaking the rules?"

I tucked my hair behind my ear even though it was already pinned there, then dropped my hand to my side so I wouldn't fidget. "As far as I'm aware, my money spends the same as everyone else's. If there's a rule against it, I guess I'm breaking it."

"Yeah." He pumped his fist. "I'm into your rebellious side."

"I don't know about that."

"I do." His gaze swept over me, then he reached out to touch the silver barrette keeping my hair away from my face. "I like your hair like that. You look really pretty."

Despite myself, my cheeks heated. I had taken great care with my hair, which was in smooth waves down my back, and my subtle, glowing makeup. My dress was burnt orange, flowy and feminine, grazing over my newfound curves, leaving only my shoulders and collarbone exposed. I'd felt good about myself when I'd looked in the mirror, but really pretty? I didn't know about that.

"That's nice of you to say, Roman."

"I said it because it's true." His lightness evaporated as he frowned. "Do you not like how you look pregnant?"

"Oh, no." I laid my hand on my bump. "I love this part of me."

"As you should. The rest of you is just as sweet."

"Okay." I forced a smile and shifted the focus to him. In his dove-gray suit and light-blue tie, he looked like he belonged in an ad for the designer. "You look great too."

"Thanks, Goldie." He leaned in, dipping down. "Think between the two of us, we're going to make one cute kid."

I had no response to that, so I just smiled. "Have you bid on anything yet?"

"Not yet. I just got here. I was hoping I'd receive a personal escort to all the auction items. I hear there's a motorcycle up for grabs."

I grabbed his sleeve. "You're not riding a motorcycle. I need you whole for Beanie."

"Come on, Goldie." He slipped his arm around my shoulders and pulled me closer. "You can't see yourself on the back of my motorcycle?"

My nose scrunched. "Maybe if it wasn't moving."

He chuckled. "Isn't your friend Clara a biker?"

"She is, but I'm no Clara."

"No." His expression turned warm, as did his gaze as it bounced over me. "As lovely as she is, I'm glad you're you. I'm probably too big to ride a motorcycle anyway. And I've sustained enough head injuries to last a lifetime. I shouldn't take any chances."

My heart leaped into my throat. "Head injuries?" I didn't like the sound of that.

"Can't be a rugby player without getting a concussion or two." He rapped on his skull with his fist. "Lucky for me, I'm pretty hardheaded."

"You're in a good mood," I observed.

"Why wouldn't I be? I'm here with you, and once this thing's over, you won't be so busy all the time. I'll be able to lure you over for naps on my couch."

"I can take naps on my own couch."

"But I have the fuzzy blanket you like."

"I could get my own," I pointed out.

Roman stopped and turned to me, putting us almost face to face. "I hope you understand I'm trying to lure you over to spend time with you. Do you get that?"

His bluntness was a hard pill to swallow, making it too difficult to speak. All I could do was nod, and he tucked me into his side again.

"Good. We're getting to be friends, Shira. I want to continue that so we're rock solid once our boy's here. Don't you?"

Again, I nodded. That made more sense. This was all for the baby. Roman and I should definitely be friends. It would make everything easier in the long run.

"If that's what you want."

Again, he caught my gaze and locked it down. "Is that what you want?"

I was saved from responding when Clara and Jake approached. Roman and Jake were acquainted through his brother, Jeremy, so no introductions were necessary. Jake and Roman caught up with each other while Clara and I roamed the outskirts of the room to check out the auction items.

"Have you bid on anything yet?" I asked.

"Yes, but I'm not going to jinx it by telling you." She quickly changed the subject. "You and Roman looked like you've turned a corner in your relationship. It seemed we interrupted something."

"You didn't. He was just declaring what good friends we're going to be. It's great—exactly what should happen."

"That is absolutely ideal," Clara agreed. "Jake and Carly are the best co-parents because they're friends. It can work really well if you want it to."

"I do want it to."

We caught up to Bea and were chatting with her when I glanced to my side, catching sight of Roman standing by the bar, speaking to a tall, pretty brunette. Her hand was on his arm, and he was leaning toward her with familiarity. I didn't know who she was, but they looked nice together. She was neither plain nor icy. Her smile was wide, stunning, and Roman answered it with one just as beautiful.

"Who's that?" Bea asked.

"I don't know," I replied. "She's pretty, though."

"In an obvious sort of way," Bea replied.

Clara chuffed. "You say that like obvious beauty is a bad thing."

"I guess it's not, but she's not *my* type." Bea crossed her arms and glared at the woman who had done nothing wrong except be pretty and stand near Roman. "What's so funny? Why is he laughing?"

"You have no reason to be bitchy," I said.

Bea scoffed. "There's *always* a reason to be bitchy. In my opinion, it's tacky for Roman to be flirting openly in front of the mother of his child. Do that behind bars."

Clara laughed. "You mean behind closed doors."

Bea arched an eyebrow. "Do I?"

As if sensing we were talking about him, Roman straightened and scanned the room, his eyes landing on me in moments. He smiled, but I averted my gaze. It wasn't fair how off-balance he managed to make me.

One day, my heart wouldn't pitter-patter every time Roman looked at me.

Today wasn't that day.

CHAPTER
TWENTY-TWO
Roman

"I WANT TO MEET her." Rosalie put her hand on my arm, trying to tug me toward Shira.

"Some other time. She's working right now, and she's not one for surprise meetings. She needs a little time to prepare."

Rosalie was Nate's ex-girlfriend. They'd been broken up for nearly two years, but before that, she'd been part of the family. Them not working out meant I saw her a lot less these days, but I was always happy to run into her.

"Oh my goodness. Is she shy?"

"She is."

"Oh, that's so sweet. How does she handle four rowdy Wells boys?"

"Surprisingly well. Ben cracked her shell first."

Chuckling, I glanced at Shira with her friends halfway across the room, and my breath got stuck in my throat. It was incredible to think a few months ago, I'd thought her face was forgettable. *Nothing* about her was forgettable.

Her beauty was soft, subtle, but it was there if you took the time to look. I saw it when she was asleep on my couch, wrapped in a fuzzy blanket, but today, she was something else. Her hair, which I'd become somewhat obsessed with, had been curled and arranged away from her face, flowing down her back. Her dress was sweet, pretty, feminine, exposing her delicate collarbone and floating over the rest of her like a dream.

"Of course he did." Rosalie leaned closer, dropping her voice. "Though, I'd argue it was you who did the cracking since you're the one who got her pregnant."

"And you'd be wrong. I may have gotten in there, but I still don't think I'm *in* there."

She patted my shoulder. "You're no quitter, dude. Don't give up."

I laughed again. Rosalie was a gem. Nate had definitely fumbled the bag.

"I'll keep that in mind."

When lunch was served, Rosalie and I were seated with Jake Hayes, Clara Rossi, and Luca and Saoirse Rossi, along with a few other people I knew socially. We ate, made small talk, and listened to the presentations about everything Building Dignity had done and planned to do in the future. Shira was nowhere in sight, but I assumed she was running things from somewhere in the background, where she preferred to be.

I would have laughed at how utterly out of his gourd Elliot looked by the time Kit took the stage if I hadn't understood him on a deep level. Kit and Shira had been working day and night to get ready for today when they should have been resting, and there was nothing either of us could have done to stop them. I had a feeling it was doubly worse for Elliot since his wife was so close to her due date, but it hadn't been easy for me to watch Shira dragging ass every night when she got home.

I tuned in to Kit's speech when she mentioned Shira's name.

"As some of you might have noticed, I brought in a partner to run Building Dignity with me. I met Shira Goldman a few years ago. She and her late husband, Frank, have been our most steadfast, generous supporters, and I came to recognize how personal affordable, safe housing is to Shira. She and I think it's important to humanize those in need and understand how people might become unhoused. She gave me permission to tell you a little bit of her story."

I barely breathed as Kit continued, bracing myself to hear something I already knew would wreck me.

"Shira's father was successful in his high-paying career, while her mother stayed home with her. From the outside, they were a perfect little family, but as some of us know too well, things aren't always as they seem. Her father was a violent, controlling alcoholic who abused her mother and kept her pinned beneath the boot of his wealth and power. Over the years, Shira learned to be quiet. She only cried in her closet and never asked for anything. Her mother endured until her father turned his violence on Shira. As soon as her mother was able to get them out, they left, with only the clothes on their backs and the address of a shelter."

She learned to be quiet.

My fingers dug into my thighs hard enough to bruise, but it was my chest that hurt, cracking, splitting, splintering into sharp, jagged pieces.

"Her mother hadn't been allowed to work during her marriage, and with no skills, it was difficult to find a job. But she endured, and they survived. Years of kindness and charity led to them finally being approved for affordable housing. Shira didn't have a permanent home until she was in her teens."

Kit scanned the sea of faces, most of whom had never struggled, had never known any kind of hardship or strife, myself included.

"It shouldn't take years of surviving and enduring to give a child a home they can call their own. Every family should have a safe place to live. Shouldn't we all view that as a basic human need? At Building Dignity, our mission is to help as many Shiras as we can—to break down obstacles so no mother has to survive and endure while her daughter cries in her closet."

Kit paused to take a sip of water, and the entire room waited with bated breath for her to continue.

"While bidding on our wonderful auction items, think of that little girl. Think of all the children who are learning to be quiet, the families torn apart in shelters, the dignity you can help restore to hardworking people who just need a helping hand. Open your hearts and your bank accounts. We can't help everyone, but the ripples you can create with your generosity will go on and on. Our Shira is proof of that. She's here today, giving back because of the helping hands she met along her journey. Who could you help with your donation? Only time will tell. Thank you."

My gut had been emptied with a dull spoon. Every word Kit uttered had been a punch to the solar plexus. There was nothing I could do to change what had happened to Shira, and it destroyed me.

How could anyone hurt her?

She cried in her closet.

She'd disappeared so Kit could tell her story. There was no way she wanted anyone to look at her while those details were being shared, but she had sacrificed her privacy to loosen the wallets of the audience—for the cause. So one less child had to survive and endure.

Beside me, Jake asked Clara, "Did you know all that?"

"Yes," she murmured. "That was the bare-bones version."

Unbearable.

Hearing this, knowing I was the last in a line of men—a line that had started with her own father—to hurt and mistreat Shira was unbearable.

I shot to my feet, but there was nothing for me to do and nowhere for me to go. I sat back down. The last thing Shira would want was for me to create a spectacle, and goddamn did I feel like sweeping every plate and glass off this table, smashing them to smithereens on the floor.

But if little Shira could be quiet for years, I could hold my tongue and tamp down my reaction for a few hours.

I would not be another angry man storming through her life.

CHAPTER TWENTY-THREE
Roman

MARY TRIED TO MURDER my toes when I walked into Shira's house after the luncheon, but now that I'd been here for an hour, she'd settled herself in my lap, allowing me to pet her. Her purring was the only thing keeping me calm as I waited for Shira to come home.

I'd texted her I was here so when she walked in, she wasn't terrified to find me in her living room. I'd done her enough harm already.

"Hi." She dropped her keys and purse on her entry table and kicked off her shoes. There was nothing different about her. No change. It was a wonder to me. Then again, she'd been carrying the heaviness of her past all her life. I was the one who'd changed. "Mary looks comfy and not like she hates you at all."

At the sound of Shira's voice, Mary lifted her head, mewed at her, then settled back into her nap. Shira sat beside us, stroking the top of her cat's head.

"We're beginning to understand each other," I replied tightly. I was trying for normal, easy, but it wasn't happening. The barbed knot in my gut was clawing at me, too fucking violent to ignore.

Her lips curved. "You mean you're beginning to like her?"

"Maybe."

Eyes flicking to mine, she gave me a tired smile. "I'm going to change and wash my face. I'll be right back."

"Sure."

She was gone a minute or two when I decided I was done waiting. Mary didn't like me very much when she lost her napping spot on my lap, but that was nothing new for us. She swished her tail at me before settling in the corner of the couch, a strip of late afternoon sun shining on her.

I expected Shira to have gotten dressed in the loungewear she always wore at home by the time I made it upstairs, but when I entered her room, she padded out of her walk-in closet wearing only a snow-white bra and matching panties.

I'd come here after the luncheon to talk. To offer her another apology for how I'd treated her. To hug her if she let me. To ask questions I wasn't sure she'd answer.

Once I laid eyes on her like that, those intentions fled.

"Shira," I bit out harshly, falling onto the end of the bed. "Come here."

Her lips parted as she inhaled sharply. Her head lowered, but she came, stopping between my spread knees. I dropped my forehead to her chest and curled my arms around her, groaning against her skin. She was so warm, whole, unharmed.

"Shira, Goldie...*Jesus*." I rolled my forehead on her soft breasts, holding her tighter, mouthing her through her bra, breathing in her scent, trying to settle the vicious torment churning in my gut.

Her fingers threaded through my hair, stroking tentatively. It only set me more on edge. Her bra became wet the more my mouth roamed and sucked. I didn't know what I was doing. All I knew was I needed her to be close, to make her feel good and cared for.

"Rome," she whispered. "What—"

"Let me make you come." I slid my hands down her back to cup her ass. "I need to make you come, Shira."

"I—you need it?"

"God, baby, you don't understand how badly I need it." Gathering the waistband of her panties in my fists, I looked up at her. "I'm going to take these off unless you stop me."

Her fingers tightened in my hair, and her breath hitched, but she didn't object or try to take my hands away. I gave her a few seconds—it was all I had in me—then I tugged her panties down to her knees and had her bare ass in my hands and my mouth all over her.

"Shira," I gritted out as I fell to my knees, kissing down her body. Every place my lips touched, I swiped my hand over, checking her for marks or scars, ensuring she wasn't injured. The need didn't make sense, but it was visceral.

Taking her by the hips, I spun her around, dropping her to sit on the end of the bed. My palm cupping her nape, I spread her legs, sliding my other hand up her inner thigh to find her core already wet and silky. I remembered this. One look at her that night, and I'd needed my mouth on her. It was different now. She wasn't just a sensual body; she was someone I now cared for. Erotic to amorous, but my desire was the same, fiery in my gut, molten in my veins.

The pads of my fingers met her clit, and her breathing wavered, soft and sighing. I rubbed her and held her, kissing her neck and chest, sucking her puckered nipples through her damp bra. Her mouth was near my ear, and the sounds of her pleasure were velvet over the barbs lodged in my gut.

"Shira," I whispered. "Let me hear you."

Her fingers clenched my hair, but she remained quiet as ever, only panting faster and faster.

"This. Do you need this?" Twisting my hand, I slid a finger inside her—not deep, not hard—and curled it near her entrance, pressing up.

"Oh," she cried. "Oh, Wim, please."

I yanked her against me, giving her more of what made those sounds and words come from her. In return, she rewarded me with moans and sighs. My name, the one she'd first known me by, was a whisper into the air, a ghost of a thing, but I caught it, held it—held her while she shook. Her thighs quivered. Her inner walls fluttered. I opened my mouth over her throat to feel it when she came.

It was a gentle vibration on my tongue. Silky juices on my fingers. Shaking muscles beneath my palm. Shira came apart quietly, beautifully, but it wasn't enough.

Taking her in my arms, I shifted us up the bed. She let me move her, bring her over my face, and she squeezed her eyes closed. Instinctually, I knew this wasn't an easy position for her, but once I had her there, I couldn't let her go.

Giving her no time to spiral into self-consciousness, I took her thighs in my hands, pulled her down to my mouth, and fastened my lips over her hot, swollen flesh. The taste of her...dear god, the taste of her. It was better than I remembered, and I remembered it being the sweetest thing I'd ever had.

She fell forward, holding the top of her padded headboard. Her head was turned to the side, not watching me as I pleasured her, allowing me to look up at her and take everything in. Pink, parted lips, furrowed brow, almost pained. Breasts spilling over the top of her bra. The gentle swell of her abdomen and newly added roundness of her hips. All of her was intoxicating. If she had let me, I would have continued looking at her and looking at her.

But this wasn't for me. My focus was on making her feel good. Wringing pleasure from her with my tongue while I caressed her hips and ass with my hands. Keeping her firmly planted on my mouth. Letting her know without words she was exactly where I wanted her.

When she came again, some of the screaming in my head tempered, but I was no less determined to keep giving to her. I went slower, dragging my tongue along her sensitive folds. She'd soaked my lips and chin, but I wanted more—for her sake and mine.

I shifted her again, positioning us so we were lying face to face. Shira curled into me, her head buried under my chin as I held her and plunged two fingers in and out of her. Her hips moved with me, rolling waves of sensuality.

"Wim," she sighed, her lips brushing my shoulder, making me wish I was undressed so I could feel her skin on mine.

"Let me give you this. One more, Goldie."

I kissed her face and hair as I held her and fucked her with my fingers. She was safe here, tucked in my arms. She was cared for, my lips all over her. She was never going to be hurt again in my presence.

Hot breath on my throat, fingertips digging into my arm, Shira gave me what I asked for, her inner walls clutching my fingers deep inside her. I kissed her face and rubbed my nose along her temple and hair until she calmed then slowly slipped my hand free.

Shira pulled her face away first, then her hand left my arm. With a heavy sigh, she rolled to her other side but stayed close, her body in the cove of mine. I gave her that. Though it wasn't my first choice, if she needed that little bit of space, she could have it.

We lay like that for a while, silent as Shira's breathing returned to normal. Goosebumps pricked her skin, and I reached down to the bottom of the bed, grabbed the chenille blanket she had artfully arranged there, and pulled it over her shoulders.

Her fingers curled around the edges, and she twisted her neck to give me her profile. "Thank you."

"No problem." I grazed my finger over hers. "Are you okay?"

"I'm fine." She chewed on her bottom lip for a beat before rushing out, "I wish you hadn't heard that."

"Kit's speech? Why not?"

"I don't like you feeling sorry for me."

"That's not how I'm feeling."

"Then what are you doing in my bed, Roman?"

Pushing up on my elbow, I looked down at her. "If I'd heard that about a stranger, I'd have been upset. Hearing it about you...I'm devastated for the little girl who'd learned to be quiet. It kills me to think of what you must've gone through. But that's not why I'm here with you now."

"Then why?"

"I don't know if it can be put into words. I thought I was waiting here to talk to you, to apologize all over again for being so unforgivably shitty, maybe give you a hug...then I saw you looking so damn pretty and vulnerable, and all I wanted to do was give you something good." I smoothed her hair away from her face and lingered with a lock of it between my fingers. *Like silk.* "Are you okay with what just happened?"

Her nod was slight. Her mouth stayed silent. And I just had to trust she meant it and I hadn't screwed up in a massive way yet again.

"I'll give you that any time you need it, Shira. Will you ask me for it?"

She sucked in a breath, her shoulders bunching around her ears. Then she sighed. "Probably not."

"You won't ask?"

She shook her head, and I puzzled over what she meant, but only for a second. My shy Goldie didn't like to ask for what she wanted. She needed it to be freely given.

"Because you're too nervous?"

I finally got a nod.

"Would you want me to do that again?"

Another nod.

I kissed her head. "Then I will. And, Shira, your cunt is the sweetest thing I've ever tasted, so expect me to freely use it with my tongue." I gave her a squeeze and another kiss. "Get dressed. I'm going to go see to Mary and make you something to eat. Then we can talk."

***

"There were things she left out." Shira scooped up a nacho and popped it in her mouth.

We were on her couch, a basketball game on the TV. Mary had pranced away when she realized I wasn't leaving, so it was just the two of us, plates in our laps, talking about the auction. Shira was the one who'd brought up Kit's speech.

"We lived in my mom's car. Then my dad reported it stolen and had it impounded. That night was the only night we had to sleep outside. Well, I slept. My mother didn't even blink. We talked about it later—when I got older. She hadn't been afraid for herself. She'd stopped being afraid for herself after my dad had snapped her arm like a twig. She'd been petrified for me. After that, she got us into a shelter. It wasn't nice—there were waiting lists for the nice places—but we were together."

She ate another nacho, and I didn't even twitch. "I had to be quiet there too. I spent a lot of years being quiet. My mom always told me, 'When Daddy turns into a hurricane, you tiptoe, quiet as a mouse, to your closet. The storm will be over before you know it.'" She took a long pull from her water bottle. "Sometimes I wonder who I would be if I'd had a different start. Would I live out loud like Bea? Be a confident and free biker girl like Clara? I'll never know."

"I think you'd be who you are when you're with people who make you feel comfortable." I squeezed her knee. "You'd feel like that all the time and let everyone see how funny and thoughtful you are."

"Sweet of you, Rome."

"Just telling the truth." I rubbed my palm up and down her leg. "Where's your dad?"

She lifted a shoulder. "We lived in Cheyenne. I would bet he's still there. My beautiful mother died young, but the world is the way it is, so I'm sure my monstrous father will live to a hundred and two."

"I could probably arrange it so that doesn't happen."

Shira grinned, and it would have knocked me down if I hadn't already been sitting. "Again, sweet of you, but I need you around for Beanie—no murdering."

I looked for signs of distress but found nothing. She ate her nachos and talked about murder as if she hadn't just divulged the horrors she'd gone through—things I could never understand.

"You amaze me, Shira."

She blinked, her nose crinkling. "I do?"

"You do. Look where you are, how far you've come."

She gestured to her surroundings. "All this is from Frank's money."

"I don't mean where you live or what you have. I mean *you*. I spent a lot of years pissed off at my mother for dipping out when she got bored with having kids. Spent even longer doing everything I could to get my dad to pay attention to something besides his work. Playing rugby, excelling in college...nothing I did turned his head. After he died, I kept going, blinded by it."

I scoffed at the understatement of the year.

"Well, you know how blind I was. What I'm saying is you haven't used your trauma as an excuse. You're shy, yeah. Quiet, hell yes. Those are the results—not an excuse. You're still good, you care a hell of a lot, and you can laugh. You're telling me about sleeping on the street in one breath and laughing with your whole chest in another. So, yes, you're amazing. I know from experience how easy it is to let it beat you. You didn't."

"I'm not the saint you're making me out to be, Roman. I've worked on myself, but I'm almost thirty, and this is the first time I've genuinely felt like I'm living for myself. You screwed up, but I have too. Plenty."

My brow dropped. "What do you mean this is the first time you're living for yourself?"

"I think it's obvious. I married a powerful man at a very young age. As a girl who had nothing and no one, do you think I voiced my opinions if they opposed his?"

I did not like the sound of this. "Shira, did he—?"

She held her hand up. "Frank was wonderful in a lot of ways, but I knew why he married me. He didn't want to be challenged. I don't know if he would have divorced me if I'd gone against him, and I was never in a position to test that, so I lived for him. It's been a year and a half since he passed, and I spent most of that time attempting to run his company because it was what he wanted. Then you came along and set me free. Even if that wasn't your intention, it's what you did." She rested her hand on her bump and offered me one of her serene smiles. "I like where I'm headed now."

"Think I'm just going to follow you then."

Her laugh was a welcome balm. "All right. I won't call the cops if I see you lurking back there."

I grinned, thoroughly taken by her lightness. "See? Amazing."

"I don't know about that." Another nacho headed to her mouth. The hum of satisfaction she made as she ate it was even more of a balm. "What kind of food comes with the rugby box?"

"We're changing the subject?"

"Hopefully."

I swiped cheese from the corner of her mouth then sucked it off my thumb. "The food is incredible. There's wings, pasta—wait. Why are you asking? Did you win the auction?"

She nodded, beaming at me. "Will you go with me?"

"Hell yes. I'd love to share some rugby with you."

She leaned into me, her shoulder against my arm. Turning, I kissed the top of her head and rubbed my nose against her silky strands.

There was nothing I could do to rewrite Shira's past, but I would do all I could to make sure the days ahead were as easy and peaceful as she deserved.

Chapter Twenty-Four

Shira

I'D CONVINCED MYSELF EVERYTHING that happened after the auction had been a one-time event—that it had been Roman's overprotective streak going haywire, resulting in his drive to pleasure me over and over without thought for himself.

Well, I was wrong.

The next day, and the next, and the next, he walked into my house, picked me up in his arms, placed me where he wanted me, and buried his face between my thighs. I could have been cooking dinner, vacuuming...it didn't matter. Roman seemed to be on a mission to make me come, and he was immensely successful. Sometimes, he would do it once, we'd have dinner, and he'd do it again before going home.

Everything else stayed the same. He came in the mornings and left me notes and breakfast. Some nights, we hung out with his brothers and watched whichever sports game was on TV, often leading to me falling asleep.

We didn't have sex, and the kisses he gave me were on my forehead, hair, or light brushes on my lips.

If this was his version of being a good friend, I supposed it was nice, but it was also driving me mad. On the one hand, I had never come so regularly in my life. On the other, I wanted to be fucked, dammit.

I blushed at admitting it inside my head. Asking for it was out of the question. And if he rejected me? Well...nothing good would come of it.

So, time passed, the world kept spinning, we left notes for each other, we ate dinner together most nights, Roman and Mary warred, and we didn't fuck.

✽

Shira,

Mary brought me the mouse I gave her last week. She'd gutted it. No stuffing left in it at all. What do you think this means? Is it a threat?

I have a question for you: would you rather have rocking chair legs or slinky arms?

See you tonight for dinner.

X,

Rome

✽

Roman,

Being given a gutted mouse is the highest compliment you can receive from a cat. I'm starting to worry Mary loves you more than me.

My answer might have been different before Beanie, but I think rocking chair legs could come in handy soon, so that's my choice.

Would you rather always wear a mask or have a face everyone forgets within five minutes?

Sorry for falling asleep last night. Thanks for not letting Ben draw a mustache on me. You're always looking out for me.

Yours,
Shira

Shira,

Mary jumped out of a pile of towels again this morning. We're back to where we started. No worries about me usurping you in her affections. You've got her locked down. I'm just her unwitting victim.

I'd rather wear a mask. I seem to have really good luck wearing masks.

Come over to my place tonight. Ben's out of town with his team. No danger of mustaches. You can fall asleep without any worry.

See you then.
X,
Rome

A month flew by. In that time, Kit and Elliot welcomed their baby girl, Brooke, into the world. They weren't ready for visitors yet, but Kit and I talked often. She was adjusting well, going from two to three little ones, and proclaimed it had a lot to do with Elliot being a rock star dad.

I was beginning to believe I would have something like that with Roman too. His interest in our baby had been constant since he'd found out, and his caretaking was so steady, I didn't doubt it. It was like he couldn't help himself. Even though I'd promised I wouldn't, I'd let myself get used to it. When it came down to it, I simply couldn't see him leaving me high and dry. And if he did, I'd be able to take care of Beanie and me, so leaning on him wasn't as scary as it could have been.

Briefly, I wondered what Frank would have thought if he saw me now. Our marriage had never been meant to produce babies or be a fairy tale. We'd been companions who had understood what we'd been and what we'd never would have.

If I knew my late husband, he wouldn't have been overjoyed I was no longer at GoldMed, but I thought he'd be happy seeing me on the verge of motherhood. He'd always been contrite for taking most of my twenties, but I'd known what I'd signed up for, and that meant leaving behind my illusions of a conventional happily ever after.

Roman appeared in the doorway of my bedroom as I was slipping on the Denver Mountain Lions jersey he'd given me. He leaned against the jamb, folded his arms, and drawled, "Heeyyy, Goldie. I like seeing you wearing my team's colors."

I gave him a soft smile. "Hey, Wim. Do I look like a real rugby fan?"

"Don't know about that, but you are cute as a button."

Tonight was the night we put my auction win to use. We were headed to my first-ever rugby game, and we were doing it in style. His brothers would be in the box with us, as well as Clara, Jake, and Bea. I was looking forward to the game, but it was the food I'd truly been fantasizing about.

Straightening, Roman approached me, his head cocked. "You looked like you were deep in thought."

"I was." I pushed a small gold hoop into my lobe. "Just imagining what Frank would think about where my life is."

His fingers flexed on my belly. I flicked my eyes up to his face, and his jaw rippled. "Do you miss him?"

"Of course I do. He was my husband, Rome." I turned away from him to put on my other earring. "I know you think I was only with him for his money, but that isn't true. I cared for him deeply."

It hadn't been a love match, but I'd spent nine years with him. If I hadn't come to care for him, what kind of person would I have been?

"Sorry. That was a stupid thing to ask. Why wouldn't you miss him?" He dropped his hand from my belly and took a step back. "The car's waiting for us. Are you ready?"

"Just need to run to the restroom."

He nodded. "I'll wait outside for you."

A few minutes later, I climbed into the limo parked by the curb. Roman was sitting on the far side of the cushy bench, a can of beer in his hand resting on his thigh. Things seemed unsettled, and since conflict made me want to run and hide, I couldn't resist the urge to fix it.

"My mother worked for Frank. That was how we met." In my periphery, Roman went solid. He *really* didn't like hearing about Frank. "She cleaned his house and ran his errands. Then she got sick, and I had to quit college to take care of her. We needed money, and Frank had adored my mom, so he hired me in her place."

I picked at the hem of my jersey, wishing I was talking about anything other than this. I would have much rather told Roman about the good parts of my mom, but that wasn't for today.

"She went fast. So, *so* fast. Then I was alone, and I couldn't stay in our apartment without her. Frank paid for my mom's burial and asked me to move in with him. I was in no position to say no, and I didn't want to. I was adrift, and he offered me safe harbor."

Roman hummed, his fingers open and closing in his lap, but he didn't ask questions or interrupt.

"He asked me to marry him, promised me security and a home, and I accepted. I was twenty."

"He took advantage of you," he gritted out. "Don't you see that?"

"I know why you would think that."

I didn't blame him for believing that. Not one bit. But I hated how tense he was. Maybe that was why I spilled the secret I'd kept almost entirely to myself for a decade.

"We didn't have sex."

Roman's head whipped to the side, his brow furrowed deep. "What?"

I swallowed, then blurted out, "Frank and I didn't have a sexual relationship. Before I met him, he had advanced prostate cancer. The surgery and treatment were aggressive. They left him permanent-ly...unable."

He blinked three times as if trying to decipher whether I was real. "Did you know that before you were married?"

"I did, and I was okay with it. We were dear friends, and we loved each other very, very much, but not like that. The treatment had left him with permanent damage to his heart and a dim prognosis for his lifespan. He'd wanted a wife to be by his side and take care of him when he got sick again, and...well, you know why I was with him."

"Fuck." He drove his fingers through his hair. "All those years...nothing? He didn't take care of your needs?"

I shook my head. "No, Rome. It wasn't like that between us. When I tell you we were friends, I mean it in the truest form."

His eyes went cloudy as though he were lost. Clara and Bea had had a similar expression when I'd told them. It had been hard for them to understand why I would have agreed to something like that, and I'd been glad they'd never been so desperate and alone in the world to be able to put themselves in my shoes.

"Christ, Shira, I don't know what to say. This is messing with my mind."

"Frank was a prideful man, and he would hate for anyone to know this about him. Please keep this between us."

His eyes landed on me, hard and steady. "I would never tell any-one. It's no one's business."

I blew out a heavy breath. "Thank you. I don't even know why I told you. I guess so you might understand a little more about me."

Nostrils flaring, he inhaled sharply. "You hadn't been with anyone before the night we were together—after Frank...?"

I smiled at his incredulousness. "Not since my first and only boyfriend in college ten years ago."

"*Fuck*." He scrubbed his face hard with his hands. "You have so much lost time to make up for."

It took everything in me to whisper, "I'd like to."

He lowered his hands to stare at me, his eyes ablaze. "That's not happening."

My heart dropped along with my jaw. "Oh. Okay, I—"

Grabbing my thigh, he yanked me across the bench so I was flush with his side, then he took my chin between two fingers and tilted my head back, bringing us almost nose to nose.

"I mean, if you need to make up for lost time, it will be with me."

My nose crinkled. "You've been helping with that."

He touched my nose with his fingertip. "Then what's this about? When that nose gets wrinkly, I know there's something you're not saying."

My heart was a battering ram against my chest, and my chin had begun to quiver. Roman didn't make me so nervous anymore most of the time, but the way he was looking at me and the topic...it was difficult to breathe, let alone form a cognizant thought.

"Are you nervous, Shira?"

I nodded.

He shifted his body so he was half over me, pressing me into the back of the seat. His hand braced next to my head, caging me in. I should have felt intimidated, but I felt safe in the cave Roman had made for me with his body.

"You don't have to be nervous with me, Goldie," he uttered so gently my body responded. My heartbeat slowed, allowing me to take a full, deep breath. "There's my girl. Now, tell me what you want."

I closed my eyes. There was no way I could say this with my eyes open.

"You, inside me."

His exhale was a stuttering, messy thing. "I can give you that. I would fucking love to give you that."

My eyes fluttered open, unsurprised to find his burning into me. "Okay."

After a beat, his mouth stretched into a grin. "You had to bring this up before the game, didn't you? No way you want to skip it and head back home?"

I shook my head, smiling back. "No way."

"Christ." His forehead dropped to mine. "Well, I guess we're going to have to hope the anticipation doesn't kill me."

My toes curled in my sneakers. *Let's hope.*

CHAPTER TWENTY-FIVE
Shira

BEA WAS GLUED TO the game—and not because she was particularly a fan of the sport.

"Were you aware of the thighs on these men?" she asked no one in particular. Then she raised a brow at me. "Clearly, *you* were aware."

I bit into a breadstick instead of answering her. Not that she was waiting around for one. She'd already turned her attention back to the field. It wasn't a far stretch to look at Ben in his skimpy shorts and assume Roman must have looked exactly the same when he'd played.

The one time we'd been naked together, the room had been dim, and my mask had obscured my vision, so I hadn't been able to fully take in all he was.

Maybe I'd get to...perhaps even tonight.

My stomach dipped dangerously. Getting caught up in what might happen later would only make me too nervous to enjoy what was happening now.

The Mountain Lions' stadium was beautiful, the box luxurious. Roman had made sure the food and drink spread was extensive. There were waiters standing by to serve us, but he'd personally filled my plate and kicked Nate off the leather couch so I'd have the best seat.

Everyone is eating, chatting, mingling, and watching the game. The only hiccup had been Adrian. Tonight was our first time meeting, and he didn't seem overly thrilled about it, but I tried to reserve judgment. I knew what it was like to be seen as cold when I was shy, though I doubted Adrian was. He seemed to have no problem making conversation with Clara and Jake. Even Bea had almost made him smile. But me? He'd shown little interest beyond a few calculating stares.

Clara wandered over and sat down beside me. "Are you ready for your surprise?"

I put down my breadstick and wiped my mouth with my napkin. "I don't know. Am I?"

"It's a good surprise. I won the auction for the cabin in Breckinridge. You, me, and Bea are going next month for your babymoon. We'll eat, spa, and relax. What do you say?"

"A babymoon?" My eyes immediately started burning, which was unacceptable. If I cried at a rugby game, I'd probably be banned from the sport for life. "I don't know what to say. I love the idea. Are you sure you want to use your prize on me?"

"Absolutely. I bid on it with you in mind. The house is huge. If you want to invite more people, you can, or we can keep it a girls' weekend."

"Let's just keep it the three of us." I bumped my shoulder against hers. "Who knows how long it'll be before we can do something like that again, you know?"

"That's what I was thinking. Girls' weekend it is." She patted my belly. "The end of one era and beginning of another."

A shadow fell over us, then Roman's voice rumbled next to my ear. "You're going on a trip?"

I turned my head, my nose almost colliding with his. He was leaning over the back of the sofa, too close for me to decipher his expression.

"A weekend in Breck next month," Clara replied.

"She won it at the auction, and she's taking me and Bea with her. It's my babymoon."

"Isn't that something couples do?" he asked.

Clara shifted beside me so she could face Roman. "Are you implying Shira shouldn't have a babymoon because she's not in a relationship? Bea and I love her and want to treat her. That's a babymoon in my eyes."

Roman hesitated before nodding. "She should have whatever she wants, but I'm not certain Shira should be traveling."

I rolled my eyes, and he lasered in on the action, his mouth tightening.

"It's not far, and I'll still be fine to travel next month." To ease his worries, I reached up and brushed my hand over his clenched jaw. "But I'll double-check with Dr. Sharma to be sure."

His gaze stayed pinned on me for three rapid beats of my heart. "Thanks for humoring me, Goldie. Fair warning, I'm pretty sure I'm going to become more protective as the weeks go by."

I groaned. "I hope you know I'm fully capable of taking care of myself."

"I do know." He dipped down and kissed the top of my head. "But why should you have to when I'm here?"

With that, he strolled away to speak with Nate, Jake, and Adrian, and I picked up my breadstick but couldn't take a bite with Clara staring at me.

"What?" I asked.

Both brows popped. "He kissed you."

"Oh. Just my hair."

"Just your hair? Does he do that often?"

I could have told her everything, but I knew she would think it more than it was. I'd had this conversation enough times in my head; I didn't have the energy to have it out loud. We were friends, there was a mutual attraction and care, but it was all situational. If I weren't pregnant with his baby, Roman wouldn't be interested in me. If I explained that to Clara, she'd try to convince me how wrong I was, and it would be a waste of everyone's time and energy.

"Lately, yes. He's sweet, and we're friends."

She blew out a puff of air. "I don't kiss your hair."

The corner of my mouth hitched. "Maybe you're not that sweet."

Her elbow gently connected with my side. "That's Beatrice. *I'm* your sweet friend."

"Then I guess you should show it and start kissing my hair more."

She did just that, sending us both into a fit of laughter. A hush fell over the box, and I sat up straight, my eyes wide as I looked around. A few people were at the glass, but Roman and his brothers were crowded around the screen. Chills ran down my spine.

"He's not moving," Nate muttered.

"Goddammit, Benny. Get up," Adrian gritted out.

Roman was stiff as a board, his hands opening and closing at his sides.

"Shit, is Ben injured?" Clara whispered.

"Get the fuck up!" Adrian barked, startling me.

Clara jumped to her feet and held her hand out to me, pulling me off the couch. She slipped her arm around my back as we watched, neither of us breathing. It was impossible to tell what was going on with so many people crowded around Ben's prone form.

Minutes passed that felt like hours, no one knowing what was happening when a team finally ran onto the field with a stretcher. Roman's fist flew to his mouth as his twin was loaded onto the stretcher and wheeled off the field.

After that, things moved fast. Roman made some calls to find out where Ben was being taken, then he and his brothers gathered their things to head out. He stopped by me, cupping my face with a hand that was undeniably shaky.

"We need to get to the hospital," he rasped. Seeing this huge, steady man trembling, his eyes glassy, tore me apart.

I pressed my palm to his chest. "I'd like to come with you if that's okay."

He yanked me into him, his face falling to the top of my head. "I'd like that, Goldie."

"Then I'm there. Let's go."

Ben had suffered a head injury and lost consciousness for a worrisome amount of time. He was undergoing testing, so all we could do was wait. The Wells brothers did not do well sitting in the small waiting room. The three of them were taking turns wearing a path into the floor. When they weren't pacing, they were either staring blankly at their phones or the wall.

Hospitals were familiar to me in a way that filled me with dread. I'd spent hours and hours in one with my mother and months in another with Frank. I had to remind my brain that wasn't what this was. Ben was injured, but he'd walk out of here.

I hated to leave the room in case the doctor came back, but I couldn't ignore my bladder another second. As unobtrusively as possible, I started for the door.

"Shira," Roman called. "Are you leaving?"

I whirled around, alarmed by the panic in his voice. "I have to use the restroom. I'll be right back."

He exhaled harshly and bobbed his head. "Okay." Then he came to me and cupped my face, his tired eyes darting between mine before pulling me into a hug. He curled around me, engulfing me in his scent and warmth, and I circled my arms around his waist, embracing him as fiercely as I could.

"Shira. *Fucking Ben*. What the fuck?"

"It's okay," I whispered into his chest. "He's going to be okay."

The strangled sound he made broke my heart. "Gotta believe that."

"He's tough," I reminded him. "With a big, hard head—just like you."

"That's right." He stepped back, running his hands down my arms and over my belly. "Don't...you know, take too long."

"I won't," I promised.

I caught Adrian's eye before I turned toward the door. He sneered, then he shook his head and went back to looking at his phone.

If he were anyone else, I would have let his opinion of me roll off my back, but I didn't want Roman's brothers to dislike me. We'd be around each other for at least the next eighteen years. I wouldn't be able to bear snarls and headshakes for almost two decades. I'd have to find a way to fix this. If he wasn't willing to make an effort, I would just have to kill him with kindness.

Not tonight, though. I wasn't up for it, and it wasn't the time. If it made coping with what was happening with Ben easier, Adrian could hang onto his foul mood. I could handle it for one night.

CHAPTER TWENTY-SIX
Roman

I squeezed my brother's hand. The motherfucker. Where the hell did he get off giving us a scare like that? Unconscious for seven minutes...what was that about?

Ben winked at Shira, who had been huddled by the wall, trying to make herself as invisible as possible, until he'd insisted she come stand by his bed. "Sorry I cut your first rugby match short. I'll make it up to you."

She let out a mix between a sob and a laugh. "I think you've cured me of rugby, Ben."

"Nooo." He lifted his free hand to his chest. "Say it isn't so. I promise they don't all end in bloodshed."

"Your blood wasn't shed," Adrian intoned. "Your brain was scrambled."

Ben snapped. "That's right. My scrambled brain forgot why I was in this bed. Think they'll let me keep the snazzy gown?"

Ben was fucking terrible at reading the room. Nate, Ade, and I were beside ourselves, and good ol' Benny was cracking jokes. I knew it was his defense mechanism, his way of handling the situation. So he didn't have to worry about how bad of a hit he took or what that meant for his season, but he needed to give it a rest. Ade looked about two jokes away from exploding, and Nate and I weren't far behind.

His doctor came in, taking time to show us the images of Ben's brain and neck. He was concussed and his neck strained. Since it wasn't his first of the year, they'd have to do follow-up tests. But there were no immediate signs of bleeding or swelling, which made us all release a collective sigh of relief.

"He'll need to stay with someone for at least tonight, ideally two or three nights." The doctor scanned the room. "I see he has no shortage of family. I'll let you all decide who will be responsible for Mr. Wells once he leaves."

As soon as the doctor exited the room, I declared, "Ben'll come home with me."

Ben grinned at Shira. "I think he loves me."

"Shush, you," she admonished. "You worried us."

Adrian folded his arms and lowered his chin. "Where will he sleep? Have you gotten a guest bed yet?"

"I—" I opened and closed my mouth. He had me there. I racked my brain for another idea. "He can take my bed. I'll sleep on the couch."

"Nah, I'm not kicking you out of your bed," Ben declared. "One night on the couch will tweak the hell out of your shoulder."

He had a point, but I didn't want to admit it. He'd be fine staying with Nate or Ade, but I wanted him with me. It was irrational, but when it came to Ben, my literal other half, thinking straight when he was hurt was difficult.

"I have a guest bed," Shira said softly. "You both can stay with me."

"Okay, this I like the sound of. High five." Ben held up his hand, and Shira smacked it with great care.

"Sounds like a good plan to me," Nate said.

Adrian shook his head and growled under his breath. I hadn't missed the looks he'd been giving Shira all night. He wasn't convinced I'd been wrong about my first impression of her, and he was worried I'd end up screwed over. It came from a good place, but I seriously didn't like it. After I ensured Ben wasn't going to have a brain bleed and pass away overnight, Adrian and I were going to address his behavior. Not tonight, though.

"He needs to be with family," Adrian stated lowly.

"And he will be," I replied.

His eyes shifted, narrowing on Shira. "You know what I mean."

"I do. Like I said, everyone in this room is family." I folded my arms across my chest. "This discussion is over."

Adrian's jaw rippled. "You're making a mistake, Rome."

Adrian was the most distrusting of us, and he had his reasons to be, but he should have known my judgment was sound. He didn't have to love Shira, but he knew I was levelheaded enough to choose who I brought into our fold. Pregnant or not, I would never have invited Shira into our collective lives if I thought she would harm one of my brothers. That Adrian was questioning that pissed me off. That he was doing it right in front of Shira, who had done nothing to deserve it, really pissed me off.

"I'm staying at Shira's," Ben announced. "The rest of you can fuck off."

I shot Ade a smirk. "Looks like Benny had the last word."

Shira went home ahead of us to get things ready for Ben. When we arrived a couple hours later, she'd set up the guest bedroom with fresh flowers and a basket of water bottles, juice, and snacks on the nightstand. The bed was turned down, the pillows fluffed, and a bathrobe was draped across the corner.

Mary hopped up on the bed with Ben, padded up his abdomen, and nuzzled her head beneath his chin.

"Hey, princess," he cooed, stroking her silky fur. "Are you gonna take care of me tonight?"

Shira stood in the doorway, one foot on top of the other, chewing on her bottom lip. "I can take her out of here if you don't want her in bed with you."

Ben wrapped his arms around the cat and scowled at Shira. "Nope. No way. She chose me. I'm keeping her."

That made Shira smile. "If you're not careful, she'll purr you right to sleep."

Ben laid his head against the pile of pillows and sighed. "I don't have a problem with that." He scratched Mary's head, his eyes drooping. "Never been purred to sleep before."

I patted his shoulder, reluctant as hell to go. If I thought for a second he'd let me sleep beside him, I would have.

"I'm going to be just down the hall. Call if you need anything. Otherwise, I'll be back in a couple hours." I pinned him with a glare. "Don't die on me."

He shot me a lazy wink. "And leave you to have all the fun? Never." He waved at Shira. "Night, sweetheart."

"Goodnight, Benny," she said softly.

I followed her down the hall to her bedroom. She stopped at the foot of the bed and glanced up at me.

"If you're not comfortable sharing the bed, I can sleep on the couch. As you've seen, I have no trouble falling asleep there—"

"Absolutely not." Thunder rolled through me, and it took every ounce of grit not to let it out. "Shira, no, absolutely not. I wouldn't have said yes to staying here if I thought for a second you'd try to give up your bed."

Her eyes swept to the side, and a shuddering breath shook her shoulders. "I wanted to offer it and not presume anything."

I advanced on her, cupping her belly from below. I found I had the urge to do that more and more often, but tonight, it was a need I could not fight. "Don't offer me or *anyone* anything that would be to your detriment to give away. The mother of my child is not giving up her bed or any creature comforts. And if you thought I would mind sleeping in this bed with you, you haven't been paying attention."

Her fingers curled around the top of the footboard, her lashes lowering to brush her cheeks. "Okay, Roman."

"Okay, Shira."

Just as I was about to let her go, my right palm received a sharp, distinctive jab. Our eyes collided, both round and wide with surprise.

"Did you feel that?" she whispered, slipping her hand between mine.

"Hell yes, I did," I whispered in return.

Three more jabs followed—*bam, bam, bam.* Our boy was on the move and letting us know it.

"Holy shit." I stared at her, and she stared back. She'd been feeling him fluttering for a couple weeks, but this was the first time I got the privilege of experiencing it too, and dear god was it like magic. "That's our boy, Goldie."

She nodded, her lips pressed in a flat line, her eyes shiny. "There he is."

I couldn't stop myself from falling to my knees, arms around her, my head against her middle.

"You knew we needed that, huh? Reminding us of everything good and pure we have coming?" I kissed her belly again and again. "We had a rough night, little boy, but you just made it all better."

"Rome." Shira's fingers slid through my hair. "He settled. I think he likes the sound of your voice."

I looked up at her, closer to tears than I'd been all night. "You think?"

"Mmmhmm. I do."

"Christ." I laid my cheek on her belly and sighed. "This is the best thing I've ever experienced in my life."

She let out a little laugh. "Me too. Without contest."

I gave my boy another kiss, then climbed to my feet, wrapped my hand around her nape, and pressed my lips to hers. "Let's get ready for bed."

This wasn't how the night was supposed to end. What we'd started in the back of the limo wasn't going to happen, and while that was disappointing, slipping into bed with Shira wasn't anything to complain about. She rolled to her side, and I molded my front to her back, cradling her soft ass with my hips. It was easy to curl around her and fit her body in my arms.

It took a few minutes for Shira to relax and let her weight melt into me. When she did, I finally exhaled.

"Thanks for letting Ben and me stay here."

"I'm glad I could help. I mean, you bought the bed he's sleeping in. It's the least I could do."

With a grin, I tucked my face into her hair. "That's right. So, I should tell him he's welcome to stay anytime?"

Her hand slid over mine, where it rested on her belly, light as a feather. "I wouldn't mind, you know. I didn't have siblings, but I like yours."

"Hmm. Even Adrian?"

"I don't *dis*like Adrian. I think it's the other way around."

"He takes his time warming up. He'll get there." I moved my nose back and forth along her silky strands. "It's not something you need to worry about."

Her movement was subtle, but I didn't miss her ass wiggling closer. She might not have meant anything by it, but it was hard to ignore those plush cheeks rocking against my half-hard cock.

She yawned and snuggled back into me even deeper. "I'm not too worried."

Closing my eyes, I soaked in the feel of her, deciding I liked this. I wasn't fond of the circumstances that led me into her bed, but now that I was here, I couldn't think of anywhere else I'd rather be.

"Goodnight, Goldie girl."

"Goodnight, Wim."

CHAPTER TWENTY-SEVEN
Shira

LAST NIGHT HAD BEEN a blur. There had been no time to get nervous about sharing my bed with Roman. I'd been too worried about Ben and scurrying around to make things perfect for his stay.

That was twenty-four hours ago, and I'd spent most of it working myself into a lather. It was the weekend. I had no excuse to leave, and for some inexplicable reason, Roman and Ben had hung around my house all day. Ben spent most of it milking his injury and playing with Mary, who was in heaven from all the attention. Roman hovered over his brother and me, cooking all our meals and asking if we were comfortable every few minutes. And I got to witness Roman and Ben's deep, magical bond.

They seemed to live on the same wavelength and often didn't bother to finish sentences. Their unabashed love for each other made my chest feel too full and tragically hollow all at once.

Now, Ben was in the guest room with Mary again, Roman was closing up the house, and I was stalling in my en suite bathroom.

With Roman no longer on edge with fear of his twin dying during the night, I couldn't help thinking back to our conversation in the limo. As I washed my face in preparation for bed, it almost felt like I was back at MHC being escorted to room ten. My toes curled into the bath mat below my feet, and my heart jammed into my throat.

I put on the one nightgown I owned that still fit. A stretchy, black cotton number with spaghetti straps. The lace edge hit midthigh, and my breasts, which had always been big and had just gotten bigger the past few months, threatened to spill out of the bodice.

It might've been too obvious, but this was as brave as I got. Roman could take my message and run with it, or he could let me off the hook by pretending he didn't understand what I was offering.

I really hope he took me. My panties were wet from the anticipation of what might happen, and my sex was swollen and achy.

With a deep breath, I opened the door and slipped into the bedroom. The lights were dim, but I made out Roman's mountainous frame easily. He was sitting on the side of the bed, his feet planted on the floor, watching me as I made my way across the room.

As I came near, he held his hand out. "Come here, Goldie."

I let him tug me close until I was standing between his spread legs. With him sitting and me standing, we were face to face.

"Look at you," he murmured, dragging his gaze over me with undisguised appreciation. "All this for me."

He started at my hips, tracing the shape with his huge hands. Kneading and caressing, his hands moved to my ass, upper thighs, the line of my back, ending at my breasts. There, he took his time, weighing them in his palms, shaping his hands around them. Then he leaned forward and groaned as he buried his face in the valley of my cleavage, his breath hot on my already sizzling flesh.

One hand trailed down to cup me between my legs, and another deep, guttural groan traveled up his throat when he encountered the damp fabric sticking to my lower lips. Nudging it aside, his fingers parted my slit and slid from my beaded clit to my drenched opening.

"So wet, Shira." He opened his mouth over my nipple, drawing deep while he teased my sensitive flesh below. A quiver traveled up my legs, weakening my knees, so I grabbed onto his shoulders to steady myself. "Yes, baby. I want you to touch me while I make you come."

Slamming my eyes shut was the only way I could let myself explore him. I ran my hands down his back and gathered his T-shirt in my fists to touch his skin. Warm and smooth, I traced the lines of his lateral muscles. I'd never felt anything like this, the rippling and definition, his breadth, the strength his body housed. All of it under my fingertips, his kisses and caresses grew more fervent.

"Yeah. Like that," he drawled, his mouth next to my nipple. "Like your hands on me, Shir."

His mouth suddenly covering mine was a surprise. My lips parted in a gasp, allowing his tongue to plunge inside. I whimpered, leaning into him, and Roman cradled an arm beneath my ass, sweeping me off my feet. I spread my legs to straddle his lap and dug my fingers in his hair.

He positioned me over his bulge and pressed me down on him. Through thin layers of cotton, my clit hit the hard ridge of his cock, and I nearly doubled over from my nerve endings sparking to life. Our lips grazed as I gasped, and he exhaled, giving me the air my body desperately sought.

"Ride it, Shir. I feel you shaking." He formed those words with kisses to my mouth and chin. "Come on, baby."

I rocked and rocked, clinging to his neck, my legs spread so wide to accommodate his huge, muscular thighs. He had my hips and backside in his palms, moving me, grinding me down on him. It didn't take long. In fact, if I hadn't felt how rock hard he was and couldn't hear his heavy, needy breaths, I would have been embarrassed by how quickly I fell apart. But Roman was just as desperate. Everything was different now, but we both wanted more of each other—of what we'd had that night in room ten.

Roman shifted, freeing his cock from his sweats. He rubbed his bare flesh against mine, the wide head along my pulsing clit, making light explode behind my eyelids.

"Rome," I moaned. "That's…"

"So good," he filled in. "So damn good. Gonna get better now."

He lifted me enough to position himself at my entrance. He had complete control of me, moving me where he wanted, slowly impaling me on him. His fingers dug into my hips as he lowered me inch by inch. Once I was fully seated, I was struck by a sharp sense of relief at how perfectly this man filled me.

"Yes," I whispered.

"Yes," he echoed. "Oh god, yes, Shira. Ride me. Ride me hard."

My eyes were closed as tight as they could be, but I felt his gaze all over me. He'd flipped the bodice of my nightie down and had one breast in his hand while the other guided my movements, lifting me up and down by my ass.

This was what I'd been aching for: Roman splitting me apart, squeezing my soft spots, sucking on my hidden, tender areas. Taking everything he wanted, using my pussy for his pleasure, giving me almost too much in return. I was heavy between my thighs and so wet each stroke of his cock made obscene, erotic sounds, turning me on even more.

"On fire for me," he gritted out. "I feel that, Shir. Love that fire only I get to see. That's mine, isn't it?"

"Yes," I panted, not quite sure what I was agreeing to. I was close again. Blood roared in my veins as I rolled my hips over him.

"You're so fucking wet, baby. Do you know how much I like that?" He held my breast up to his mouth and drew my nipple in deep, suckling hungrily.

My head fell back, mouth opening to sigh my pleasure to the stars circling above my head.

"You make me so hard. These tits, your ass, your hair, the sounds you make…" He arched up as he shoved me down, thrusting so deep I lost my breath. "I can't last for you. Not with you bouncing in my lap, looking like a ripe peach I want to devour and lap up every last drop of the juices."

"You have a filthy mouth," I panted.

"You're filling my mind with filthy thoughts." He palmed my crown, drawing my face to his. "Give me your mouth, Shira. Need it right now."

Then he took it himself, not allowing me a chance to give it to him. With our lips sealed, Roman moved, taking me with him. Flipping us around, I was on my back, my legs locked around his waist, and he was standing, one knee on the mattress.

Holding my hips, he powered into me with purpose. Teeth clamping his bottom lip, he watched my breasts bounce from the force of his thrusts, and I watched him looking at me. His attraction was laid bare and raw. I tried to grasp it, keep it with me, but my mind was a slippery thing. And when his gaze snapped up to burn into mine, I arched my neck and slammed my eyes closed to avoid it.

Reaching down, he rolled my clit with this thumb. "I want to feel you coming around me. Give me that," he ordered.

I was a sucker for this man. He'd wound me up for the last month, had made me needy for his cock, and had learned the rhythm of my pleasure like it was his own. When he drove deep and touched me, it was done with expert precision. Roman wanted me to ignite for him, and I did. Gasping, panting, my legs pedaling next to his hips, I held my breasts, squeezing them and plucking at my nipples as I fell to pieces.

The shattered groan Roman made would forever be burned in my brain. It was the sound of a powerful man surrendering, accepting his fate. His grip was tight on my hips as he plunged into me a few more times then stilled, our pelvises flush, practically sealed together. Liquid heat coated my clenched channel, my internal muscles working to take everything he had.

Careening forward, he braced his fall with his hands on either side of my head. Hot breath on my lips, his nose sliding along mine, I forced my lids to open, and our eyes collided.

"That what you needed?" he asked.

I nodded. "Exactly."

His lips touched mine in a quick, firm kiss. "Good, baby. Then we both got it."

The next part wasn't my favorite, losing him from inside me and the awkward shuffle to the bathroom to clean up. But what followed made up for it.

Roman lifted the covers for me, and when I climbed into bed, he arranged his body around mine, tucking me against him—right where I'd been longing to be again.

"Was that okay?" he asked.

I laughed. "Okay?"

His chest rumbled through my back. "I'm asking if I hurt you, not if you came. That, I know the answer to."

I turned my head, which he'd fitted beneath his chin, and rubbed my cheek against his chest. "I feel really good. You didn't hurt me at all."

His hands splayed on the curve of my belly, and after a moment, I placed mine on top of his. Two of my fingers made up the width of one of his. I imagined these massive hands had been good for playing rugby. I wished I could have seen him on the field.

"Does your shoulder still hurt?" I asked.

"Hmm? From my injury?"

"Yes. You never mention it."

"I've grown accustomed to living with constant, low-level pain. If I didn't have to move, I wouldn't feel it, but—"

"Moving is sort of necessary."

"Yeah," he breathed, his palm gliding over my belly. "I had surgery and rehab. It is what it is now. I try not to do anything to exacerbate it, but living with pain is one of the downsides to being a pro athlete in a high-impact sport. I'd known that going in."

"Why rugby?"

He chuckled. "Why not?"

"Well, football is king in the US. I'm surprised you and Ben didn't get recruited to play in school."

"Oh, coaches tried. Ben played a few seasons. Not me, though. I had my eye on the prize, and that was to go pro in rugby." He dipped his face into my hair, inhaling. "You might've noticed this about me, but I'm single-minded in my goals. When I start something, I have no choice but to become the best I can at it. I chose rugby. Therefore, I devoted every waking minute to it."

"And when you lost it…?"

"I was torn up for a while. That letter you sent me? It helped. Everyone was telling me my life wasn't over, but that letter…you gave me the room to grieve. Every direction, people were saying, 'chin up,' 'it could be worse,' but you told me to feel it in full, and I did that. I dealt with the premature end of my goals, and once I'd accepted it, I was able to move on. I miss the game, but it doesn't hurt to watch Ben play. I can be proud of him without feeling jealous. And I've devoted myself to other pursuits."

"Like GoldMed."

He hummed again, and the vibration that ran through me was almost as soothing as Mary's purrs. "Yes. Sometimes my single-mindedness makes me myopic—a fact I'm coming to terms with. Once again, you've turned my eye inward, forcing me to examine my thinking and come up with a solution to change it." His lips pressed against my crown. "I don't think we'll be able to save GoldMed, Shira."

A chill ran through me, not from the inevitable fate of Frank's company but due to the palpable remorse in Roman's admission.

"Some things aren't meant to last forever," I whispered.

"No, times change. The world keeps moving. Nate and I are working on it, but I suspect the wisest option is to sell off the remaining assets. We'll have to make a decision soon."

I twisted my neck so I could look up at him. "I won't be angry if you decide that's the best course, Roman. Please don't worry about me when choosing how to move forward. I know you wanted it to work and did all you could. If this is the end, that's okay."

Our son decided to join the conversation, landing several kicks and jabs. Roman sucked in a breath, stilling. I found myself grinning wide as the baby used my belly as his own personal jungle gym, rolling and stretching.

"That's incredible," Roman whispered in awe.

"Isn't it? He's already amazing."

His forehead rested on the back of my head, and he stayed like that for a long time, feeling the movement inside my stomach.

"Thank you for allowing me to be close to you like this, to share this with you," he murmured. "Means the world to me not to miss any of it."

"You don't have to thank me."

"Means the world, Shira," he repeated, his arms holding me snugly against him.

I was setting myself up to fall. It would hurt like hell when I landed, but my silly brain, whose survival instincts swung back and forth between abject panic and grave acceptance, said, *"Meh...if I crash, I crash."* So, I snuggled closer to Roman, deciding to soak up every fleeting second I had in his arms.

CHAPTER TWENTY-EIGHT
Roman

BEN LIVED BY THE motto *Idle hands are the devil's playground*. He didn't do well when he wasn't busy, but he'd been forced to take a month off from training and playing rugby. We were two weeks into his forced sabbatical, and he had become everyone's problem.

I had seen my twin more in the last two weeks than I had all year. That I couldn't complain about. It was his running commentary on the most mundane activities that was driving me up the wall. He'd gone on daily strolls through my new neighborhood, exploring all the cafés and art galleries, and offered me a full, written report when I returned from work. He'd also cleaned my house from top to bottom and weeded my, Shira's, and Bea's lawns, documenting all of it through an alarming number of texts he sent throughout the day.

Today, I'd marked a couple hours out of my schedule to have lunch with him and Adrian. I was hoping Ade would be convinced to entertain Benny for a while. If he didn't, I suspected I'd go home to all my walls repainted and Ben climbing them.

The three of us were seated at a secluded table in our favorite pub, each nursing a pint. I had a burger in front of me, Ade had a steak salad, and Ben was plowing through a massive plate of fish and chips.

If Adrian wouldn't entertain Ben after this, I was aiming for him to get full and buzzed enough to go home and take a nice, long nap.

But the fact was, Adrian owed me. We'd spoken since he was an asshole in Ben's hospital room, but we hadn't addressed the root of his assholery. To be frank, I'd been dealing with one brother. This one could wait.

"...and then I stopped by the Sheridan Gallery. Tomahawk was working, and they let me have a sneak peek at the new exhibit debuting next week—bags of the artist's blood stapled to canvases. Tomahawk cried when they showed it to me." Ben balled up his napkin as he recounted his morning. "Honestly, I don't get it. If I was allowed to expand my brain, I'd do some reading on modern art, but Dr. Jack prohibited me from reading until next week."

Adrian wagged his fork over his salad. "You could have your computer read aloud to you."

Ben's brow pinched. "Not sure if that's kosher. I'm supposed to be on brain rest. Seriously, Dr. Jack told me no learning."

I swallowed my burger, feeling it go down my throat like a lump of coal. The seriousness of Ben's brain injury unsettled me. Fortunately, he was following the doctor's orders, but he planned to get back on the field as soon as he could. I understood that desire, but it wasn't going to be easy to step back and watch him do it.

"Are you planning on moving back to your place anytime soon?" Adrian asked.

Ben shrugged. "When I go back to work. It's more convenient to get to the stadium from the condo. For now, I'm digging Rome's house and the neighborhood. The neighbors are a pretty strong incentive too."

Adrian grimaced without saying a word. Not that he needed to. His expression said it all. Ben had caught it too.

"What's that look?" he asked.

Adrian sawed at his steak, avoiding looking at both of us. "Nothing. I wouldn't get too used to the neighborhood. I doubt Rome will stay there long term."

My brow dropped. "Why do you doubt it? My son is going to be living there."

"I understand that and why you're there now. But once he's no longer a newborn, it won't be imperative you live right beside him. You can get back to your real life once you have an ironclad custody agreement with his mother."

Cocking my head, I studied him, trying to figure him out. He'd been the youngest when our mother left and undoubtedly the most traumatized by it, though he'd never admit it. He'd also been jerked around by women in the past, vaulting him into this place where he very rarely trusted anyone outside our circle.

In my eyes, Shira was firmly in our circle. Adrian clearly didn't agree.

"Shira," Ben stated. "Her name is Shira, and her house smells like lavender and vanilla. Plus, she has a cool cat and great taste in snacks. She's a terrible cook, though. Avoid her cooking at all costs—if you can."

My foot found his shin beneath the table. "You'll never say that to her face. *Ever.*"

I'd taken up making dinner most nights to avoid Shira's attempts at cooking. I still ate her food when she served it. The thought of her eyes filling with tears if I told her she used an obscene amount of garlic and overcooked chicken until it was little more than leather was motivation enough for me to choke it down. If Ben wanted to see tomorrow, he'd do the same.

He raised his hands in innocence. "You saw me eating that muffin, didn't you? You know, people have died from eating that much cinnamon at once. I was in peril. Did you hear me complaining? Not once. I'm not gonna hurt her feelings. No way."

Ade blinked at him. "All right. Cooking aside, you liking her means next to nothing since you like everyone."

"I like her too," I intoned. "Does that mean something?"

He put down his fork. "It's not about liking or disliking. I don't know her, so I can't form that kind of opinion. I do know she married a man for money. Kept his daughter away when he was dying. And by some strange coincidence, which I cannot suspend disbelief far enough to accept as an actual coincidence, got knocked up by you weeks before you took over GoldMed. Excuse me if I—"

"No," I snapped.

He raised a brow. "No?"

"Yeah, no. I'm not excusing you. I will not go into the details of how Shira and I met, but unless you think she has the technical skills to hack MHC's app, it was a cosmic coincidence she and I met and hooked up. The other things have been explained to me in a way that I understand where she was coming from, but they aren't my story to tell. So, you can accept I have sound judgment and get on board, or you can be on the outside looking in when it comes to my life with my son and Shira."

Ben let out a guffaw muffled by his fist. "Shira—shy little Shira—was on MHC's app? You have shocked me through and through." He fanned his face with all the drama he possessed. "Oh, my, lordy be, I am flummoxed."

I snapped my napkin at him. "When did you turn into an old southern belle?"

"When you told me my pal Shira used the app," Ben quipped. "Where are my smelling salts? I feel faint."

Adrian calmly folded his hands on the table and stared at me. "The app hasn't been hacked." He tilted his head, searching my face. "I do think you make sound decisions, but I also believe you're letting your emotions lead you this time."

I leaned forward, making sure he heard me. "I moved into that house to be near my son, who is, for the time being, growing inside Shira. Those were my emotions then. Through time, gathering information, and being open to learning who Shira is, I've formed the intention to stay in that house because I want to be near her as well. If you see a problem with any of that, I suggest you work that out on your own. I won't have you behaving like you did in Ben's hospital room ever again. She doesn't deserve that from you. I want her to feel safe with my family and like she's a part of it."

"She isn't," Adrian insisted.

Ben swatted the back of his head. "Stop being a jackass. Our nephew is her kid. If that's not family, I don't know what is." He waggled his brows at me. "Plus, if I'm not mistaken, Romeo has the major hots for her."

I did not admit he was right, but I certainly didn't deny it. My attraction to Shira was profound, and my desire to be in her presence was almost overwhelming. I hadn't worked out how much of that had to do with the baby and what was all her yet. Luckily for me, she was willing to break bread with Ben and I most evenings, and when she'd fallen asleep on my couch a few nights, I'd convinced her to stay over in my bed after I'd carried her there. I had time to sort my feelings out *with* her.

Adrian groaned. "This is what I mean. You're clouded, Rome. On a normal basis, you'd never look twice at—"

I was a breath away from cutting him off, but Ben got there first, slamming his fist on the table. Silverware rattled, and water sloshed over the edges of glasses. Ade's eyes rounded, but he clamped his mouth shut as Ben leaned into him.

"I've had enough of you. If you say one fucking word about her looks, brain injury or not, we're throwing down," Ben hissed. "That is my friend you're talking about. That is the mother of our nephew. Put some respect on her name, Adrian."

Closing his eyes, he pulled in a deep breath. On a slow exhale, he opened them, looking back and forth between Ben and me.

"I'm sorry. Clearly, I'm in the wrong." He shoved his fingers through his hair. "This entire thing is a departure from anything I'm used to."

I blew out a puff of air. "It's new for all of us, but you're the only one who's being left behind."

He nodded once. "I see that. I'll get a handle on this."

"That'd be good. We only have a couple months until our boy is here, and I won't have you around him if you're going to bring any negativity."

Adrian's mouth dropped open, his eyes stricken. "I don't want that."

I didn't either. "Then, like you said, get a handle on it."

That night, I had Shira in my bed. She was sleepy by the time I'd deposited her on my mattress, but she lifted her arms by rote, allowing me to take her top off. I reached around her and unhooked her bra. She groaned as her breasts were freed from the cups and in my waiting palms.

"Stop wearing bras when you come over, baby." I kneaded them, hefting them in my palms. Shira's tits were gorgeous, big by any standard, but especially for her small frame, and had only grown during her pregnancy. Her nipples were bigger too, and darker. My mouth watered at the sight of them, and a mental image of them dripping milk brought my dick to full mast.

"Maybe if Ben wasn't here." She leaned her head against my arm as I caressed her. "I don't think your brother should see my nipples trying to poke a hole through my shirt like it's their job."

A green slash of jealousy hit me like a lightning bolt. "He absolutely should not. But you can throw a sweater on. He won't notice."

"I don't know, Rome. My nipples are powerful these days. They'd probably break through the strongest wool."

She was joking, and normally, I would have chuckled, but her pretty tits were in my hands. I was rolling one of those powerful nipples between my fingers, so I wasn't feeling very humorous.

I dropped down to my knees in front of her and opened my mouth to take as much of her breast in as I could. Her groan was immediate, and her fingers dug into my hair to cradle me there. She was addictively soft and so damn sweet I craved the taste of her skin when I didn't have it on my tongue.

Moving to the other breast, I drew deep, filling my mouth with nipple and her lush, round breast. As I sucked, I wrapped my arms around her, scooping her ass into my hands. She'd gotten a little bigger there too, and fuck, did I like it.

"Rome," she sighed. "That feels really good."

I raised my eyes to find hers, and when I did, she immediately slammed hers shut. It was a habit she had, and I didn't like it—her letting me have full access to her body but not her eyes. I had to guess that was her keeping a part of herself back from me. A form of self-preservation. I'd address it soon, but not now. Not when she was giving me so much already.

I broke from her breast to rid her of her pants and underwear, then I propped her on a pile of pillows and spread her legs. She was swollen and slick, too pretty for me to look at for long without putting my mouth on her. I let myself play with her for a minute, sinking two fingers inside and rolling her beaded clit under my thumb. Shira cupped her breasts while I moved my fingers in and out of her, curling to press on the spot that made her entire body shake.

Once I got her close, I laid down and covered her pretty cunt with my mouth, lapping up her arousal and bringing her over without any effort. Her moans of pleasure were dulcet, barely above a whisper. She kept her fingers in my hair and her feet on my back, sliding and digging in.

"Rome," she cried. "That's so good."

I had to rock my hips into the mattress to find a fraction of relief. Having my mouth on her and her taste on my tongue turned me on in an almost uncontrollable way. My need for her was too big to keep locked down, my urge to bring her pleasure the only thing stronger.

She fell apart like a house of cards. Utter destruction, which barely made a sound. Whole in one moment, fluttering to pieces in the next.

I would have kept going, but she gave my hair a tug, drawing me up her body. First, I got rid of my pajama pants, then I settled on my side behind her, nestling my cock between her slick lower lips.

I put my mouth to her ear. "Say it, Shir."

"What?"

"Tell me where you want me."

She slid her foot up the inside of her opposite leg, opening herself to me.

"Words," I demanded gently. "I want to hear them." She didn't have to give me her eyes, but I had to have her voice. It had turned me on to levels I didn't quite understand the first time she said it, and I'd been seeking out that same high ever since.

"Inside me, Wim." She reached between her legs to wrap her fingers around my cock, giving it slow, firm pumps. "I want to feel you inside me."

There it was. A shudder ran through me as the rush hit my veins. This woman had so much power over me, and she had no idea.

I pushed inside her, slow and easy, one arm hooked under her leg, the other wrapped around her so I could hold her close and play with her breasts.

"Turn your head and kiss me, Shira."

Complying, she twisted around, and her lips sought mine. Warm and giving, I let her peck and suck, responding but not taking charge. I liked when Shira took what she wanted. It didn't happen often enough, so when it did, I reveled in it.

"That's my girl," I drawled against her wet lips. "Give me that for a thousand more years. I could live off it."

She whimpered, and I closed in, kissing and fucking with all the built-up greed within me. Not hard. Steady, deep, gentle. I didn't have any need to be rough with this woman. My urges were centered around making her come until she was wrung out and limp then planting myself inside her as long as I could stay. There, we matched. She might've had trouble asking for what she wanted, but her non-verbal responses told me everything.

Her fingers grasped mine, following me over her curves as I caressed her. Breasts, hips, ass, belly, she let me touch it all, but when I tipped her face to mine, she closed her eyes like always. I growled, and she mewed, but those eyes stayed closed.

She was going to give them to me one of these days. I'd work for it until she felt comfortable enough to share that with me.

"Shira," I groaned, thrusting into her deep and stilling.

"Rome." Her inner walls clasped around me, pulling me in. "I'm close."

"I feel you, baby. Give me one more."

"Okay."

She gave me another and another until I gave up the ghost and followed her into writhing, moaning, gasping pleasure.

⚜

Cleaned up, lights out, we lay in bed, Shira's head on my chest, my arm around her, the other hand on her belly. Beanie was stretching and rolling, and I was grinning like an idiot in the dark. I didn't think I'd ever get over this. Not ever. Even when he was in my arms, I'd remember him making himself known to me from inside his mom's stomach.

Shira laughed softly. "He's wild tonight."

"Comes by it honestly."

"Benny," she whispered. "I can't believe he's having a sleepover with Mary."

My grin widened. While Shira was here, Ben insisted Mary couldn't be alone all night, so he was spending the night in her guest room with her cat.

"I can. Soon, you won't be surprised by anything Ben does."

She lifted her hand, hovering it over the center of my chest, and my breath hitched, waiting for impact, but it never came. Instead, she balled her hand and tucked it against herself. If she were less skittish, I would have taken it and placed it there for her, but I wasn't sure how she'd react. So, just like her eyes, I let her hold back.

For now.

"He seems to be doing better," she said.

"Yeah, but he could lose a limb, be gushing blood, and he'd never let on it bothered him. He doesn't like to be down and out. I'm not sure how he's really feeling, but I can tell you I'm worried about him taking another hit like that. And Adrian keeps sending me studies about the long-term side effects of multiple concussions. Like I'd be able to get Ben to retire even if I tried. That means I'm juggling Ben's recovery and Ade's neurosis. Luckily, Nate's pretty chill."

"You sound like their dad."

Sighing, I slid my fingers through the back of her hair and stared up at the shadows dancing on the ceiling.

"I've heard that from them more than once. Nate's the oldest. By rights, he should be the one in charge, but they always looked to me.

We kept those roles as we grew up. Ade might be pushing thirty, but he's still my baby brother."

It was quiet, but I didn't miss her huff.

"Shir, he's a good guy, but he was a dick to you at the hospital. You should've heard Benny letting him have it today at lunch. I had some words too. He won't treat you like that again."

She shook her head. "You guys don't have to defend me. I promise; I'm used to making a terrible first, second, third, etcetera impression."

"Well, that's bullshit."

"Your first impression of me was terrible, and not just because of what you thought you knew about me. It's okay, Roman. I know I come off as cold. It's up to me to either rectify that or accept when I'm disliked. Adrian's your brother and Beanie's uncle, so I'm not giving up. I have a game plan."

My throat was tight. I hated that she was so used to people misunderstanding who she was that she'd accepted it as fact. But I loved that she wasn't giving up on my asshole brother.

"What's the plan, baby?" I asked.

"Kill him with kindness. If he scowls at me, I'll just pretend it's a smile, smile back, and ask him how his day was. If that doesn't work, I'll bribe him with Beanie snuggles."

"Like that plan, but I hate that you think you have to do it." Kissing the top of her head, I inhaled her lavender scent. "He'll dig his head out of his ass."

And if he didn't, we'd have words—and they wouldn't be pleasant. If I had anything to say about it, the days of Shira accepting mistreatment were over.

CHAPTER TWENTY-NINE
Shira

THE TIME FOR MY babymoon girls' weekend had arrived before I knew it. Bea, Clara, and I were in Breckinridge, only a couple hours from Denver, but it felt like an entirely different world.

I wasn't a skier, and neither was Frank, so we'd never come here. As soon as Clara drove us down the main strip, I fell in love with the town. Even more when we wound our way up a mountain to our cabin. It was early spring, so it wasn't as busy as it probably was during the height of ski season, but less hustle and bustle was a nice change.

Our cabin was set back on a wooded lot. Huge picture windows overlooked ski ranges in the distance. The interior was modern rustic, with wood beams, vaulted ceilings and massive stone fireplaces which could be turned on with the flip of a switch.

As soon as I chose my bedroom, I took a picture and texted it to Roman.

to find something to eat before our first spa appointment.

Roman: Looks nice. Make sure the locks are secure.

Me: Locks? What are locks?

Me: The locks are fine, Rome. I'm fine, and so is Beanie. Dr. Sharma told you not to worry. I promise I'll keep you updated on my activities and how I'm feeling.

Roman: Not the time for jokes when you're thirty weeks pregnant and hours away from me.

Roman: Sorry, Goldie. I want you to have a really nice, relaxing weekend. Ignore me. It's hard for me not to hover.

Me: I don't mind reassuring you, so, no, I won't ignore you. But don't spend the entire time I'm away worrying. I would hate that.

Roman: I'll give it a whirl. ⊠ Be good. Say hi to your girls for me.

Me: Talk to you soon. XX

I tossed my phone down and smiled. It was cute how concerned Roman was about Beanie and me. He didn't even try to hide it. The man needed to be within touching distance of my bump as often as possible, or he got cranky. He possessed a fierce protective streak only a notch down from his need to caretake. I didn't try to deny him either.

Like when I complained about my hatred of my bras, he went out and bought me a pile of angel-soft nursing bras. He'd researched this for several days before making the purchase and had presented a list of backup options in case I hadn't liked them. There was no need, though. My boobs now felt like they were nestled in a cloud.

Doing this sort of thing was who he was.

I had a feeling by the time I got home Monday, he'd be pacing and tearing his hair out. Either that or driving his brothers crazy.

Clara stuck her head in my room. "Are you ready for lunch, or do you need to rest?"

I hopped up from my bed, pressing my hands together. "Lunch. These days, I'm never too tired to eat."

"Then let's go get you and that baby fed."

After a huge lunch, we headed over for our first round of spa treatments at the Sky View Resort. Pedicures came first, though it was hard to call the extensive massaging, masks, and scrubs the same as what we got at the little salon we regularly went to back home.

Once our feet were baby soft, we parted for facials.

My skin was brand new by the time I made it back to the locker room to get redressed. Bea and Clara were spending time in the sauna, so I planned to go sit in the resort's lobby next to the massive, crackling fireplace.

I was pulling on my leggings when someone gasped nearby. I turned and found myself face to face with Francesca in a robe matching the one I'd just discarded. She wasn't looking at me, though. At least, not my face. Her focus was on my belly, which was bare since I hadn't yet put on my shirt.

"You're pregnant."

My hand went to my bump instinctively. "Hi, Francesca."

"You're *really* pregnant," she repeated, then lowered herself to the bench behind her. Once she did, I grabbed my shirt, yanked it over my head, then sat down on the bench a few feet away.

"How are you?" I asked.

Finally, she tore her eyes from my belly to look at my face. "I'm...shocked. Are you remarried?"

"No. This was a surprise. A happy one, though."

"I expect so." She blinked a few times, bringing her hand to her chest. "My father didn't want more children."

"No." I swallowed the lump in my throat. "No, he didn't, and I was okay with that. Life changes, though."

She rubbed her lips together. "Is the father involved?"

"Yes. He's excited to have a child."

I'd let Francesca walk all over me, for Frank's sake. He had loved his daughter very much and made it his mission to shield her from strife and the world's capacity for ugliness. He did this out of guilt for putting her through her parents' volatile marriage and subsequent divorce but also because he simply felt it was his job to give her an easy-breezy life.

The days of doing that were over now. Francesca and I had no more reasons to exist in the same sphere. She didn't get to know about Roman and Beanie. They were mine, and I was keeping them to myself.

"Good. That's good." She waved her hand near her face and pushed out a humorless laugh. "Pardon me. I'm flustered. I didn't expect to see you here, let alone hugely pregnant."

I pretended to flinch. "No one wants to be called huge."

"Oh, right. I just meant you're really big."

I barked out a laugh. "That isn't better."

She gestured to my belly with both hands. "Well, you are. I mean, you're normally so tiny. It's disconcerting to see you with big boobs and round cheeks and that belly. It's not a bad thing, just..."

"Disconcerting." I laughed. "I understand. Sometimes I shock myself when I look in the mirror."

Huffing, she rolled her eyes. "My god, Shira. How can you be so nice?"

"I'm not being—"

She cut me off. "I always assumed it was fake, but since leaving GoldMed, I've had far too much time to think and came to realize I convinced myself of that because it made disliking you easier."

This wasn't what I expected to hear from her.

"Why did you need to dislike me?" I asked, out of curiosity more than anything.

"Because..." She rubbed her palms along her thighs. "Because my father married you when you were barely out of your teens. If I made you into this...this vixen who'd seduced him, then you were the bad guy and he was your victim, and I didn't have to think of my father as the kind of man who would do that."

I sighed, suddenly exhausted. "He was human. He made mistakes, but he wasn't a bad guy, Francesca. He can still be your hero in your memories if that's what you want."

She nodded, her lips rolled over her teeth. "He isn't my hero, just my dad." And then her shining eyes found mine. Francesca Goldman was a stunningly beautiful woman, and she was well aware of that fact. This was the first time I had seen her look real, and she was more lovely than ever. "I don't understand why he didn't tell me how sick he was."

"I don't either," I admitted. "Except he clung to his pride like it was his lifeline. He didn't want you seeing him that way."

"And he made you be the one to tell me I had to stay away."

"Yes." My shoulders rolled forward. "I should have fought him harder, but it happened faster than either of us had expected. There was no time. I'm sorry for that. I truly am."

That was the only apology she would get from me. She might've been contrite now, but she'd spent years hating me and, months after her father died, outright abusing and stealing from me. Not to mention, she'd put my cat outside—something I'd never forgive.

But I *should* have fought Frank when he wouldn't allow me to tell his daughter his heart was failing. I should have called her and explained the severity of his illness. But going along with his wishes had been easier, even when I knew they were wrong. I would always regret that they didn't have the time together they should have. Pride could be such an ugly thing, and Frank had been overflowing with it.

There was no going back. No changing things. All we could do was acknowledge what we'd done wrong and try not to make the same mistakes.

"Thanks." She tossed her hair behind her shoulder and straightened her spine. "I suppose I should apologize for being a bitch."

I waited, but an apology was not forthcoming. I guessed *I* was the only one acknowledging what I'd done wrong.

I almost snickered at how very Francesca that was, but I didn't think she'd take kindly to being laughed at, and I was hoping to escape this encounter unscathed.

She went on. "I was working with what I had, you know? My dad's dead, and I'm pissed about that. I think anyone would be. Yeah, I might've screwed you over with GoldMed, but it's not like you're not set for life. I know Daddy was generous with your inheritance. It's public record, after all."

"He *was* generous," I agreed. "I'm very lucky."

She lifted her chin, fully coming back to her classic Francesca haughtiness. "You are. I'm pleased you're aware of it."

I smiled wanly at her.

"It's good we had this talk. Now it can all be water under the bridge and we can move on." She nodded toward my bump. "Good luck with the baby. I'm glad you're getting a second chance at life. Hopefully the baby's father isn't old enough to be yours too. But...I don't know, maybe old is your type. Who am I to judge?"

I let myself laugh. "Thank you. Good luck to you too."

When Bea and Clara found me a little while later, curled up in an armchair by the fireplace in the lobby, I still had a smile on my face.

Bea circled her finger near my mouth. "What's this about?"

"I had a run-in with my former stepdaughter," I said.

Clara's brows shot up. "What? She's here?"

Bea put her hands on her hips. "I haven't been in a fight since high school, but I'm ready. Where is she?"

My shoulders shook from laughter. "No, Beatrice. You will not get into fisticuffs on my behalf. Besides, Fran and I came to an understanding. She was barely even a bitch."

Clara perched on the arm of my chair and peered down at me with a concerned frown. "What kind of understanding?"

"Basically, we wished each other well." I lifted a shoulder. "I wouldn't say it was a nice conversation, but I'm glad we had it. No matter how she's treated me, she deserved better from her father."

"Bitch deserves jack," Bea muttered.

"Maybe." I spread my fingers out on my belly. I hadn't realized I'd been carrying guilt over what had happened with Francesca at the end of Frank's life until my load had been lightened. "Maybe I deserved a chance to explain and apologize. Now, it's done, and we're moving on. That's how she and I left it, and I feel pretty great about that."

With a soft groan, Bea plopped down on the other arm of my chair and leaned over to kiss my head. "Fine. Be a much better person than I am."

Clara snorted. "Our girl couldn't hold a grudge to save her life."

I swiveled my head between them. "You know what I am going to hold a grudge about? If we don't immediately return to that bakery we passed on the way here so I can consume my weight in chocolate chip cookies, I'll be absolutely pissed until the end of time."

Luckily for us, the bakery was still open when we arrived. Even luckier, no one said a word when I bought every last cookie left in the case and didn't share a single one.

CHAPTER THIRTY
Shira

Roman: *You're not allowed to cry, Shira. I thought I made that a rule.*

Me: *Then don't be sweet, Roman.*

Roman: *I'm only stating facts.*

Me: *Sweet.*

My head lolled against the seat of Clara's car. I couldn't remember a time I'd been so utterly relaxed. We'd spent the day at the spa. Every part of me had been rubbed, masked, scrubbed, and pampered, and my muscles were jelly.

Bea twisted around from the front seat to look at me. "You can't fall asleep."

"Just for a minute," I mumbled.

"Nope. We have reservations. No time for napping. Besides, your hair looks too good to mess it up on a pillow."

I huffed but forced myself to sit up. She had a point. After all my spa treatments, I'd gotten my hair blown out and my makeup done for the fancy dinner Clara had arranged for us. We were on the way back to the house to get changed, then we'd be off again.

"Fine. I'll stay awake, but I won't like it."

Bea exchanged glances with Clara. "She's sassy when she's pregnant," Bea stated.

"Very sassy," Clara agreed. "I like it a lot."

"That goes without saying," Bea replied.

I waved at them. "Hello. I'm right here."

Clara giggled. "Sassy."

I wasn't sassy. What I was was happy. The last two days had been exactly what I needed. Solid time with my best friends with no responsibilities away from the outside world. To myself, I could admit I was relieved to have some time away from Roman too.

I liked him, and I'd gotten used to falling asleep with his arms around me. Once Beanie was here and things went back to normal, I would miss that terribly. So, space was good and very much needed in order for me to collect my feelings and tuck them away in a jar stored in a far corner of my heart.

When we arrived at the house, Bea and Clara corralled me in front of them, which was strange, but I shrugged it off and went inside.

I very nearly peed my pants when a cacophony of voices yelled, "Surprise!"

The living room was covered in blue streamers, balloons, presents, and a banner that said, "Happy Baby Shower!" Standing in the middle were my handful of friends, including Terry, Annabelle, Gabriela, a few other women from GoldMed, and even Kit, with her baby, Brooke, in a wrap on her chest.

Behind them all was Roman. His eyes locked on me as he mouthed, "Heeyyy, Goldie."

I burst into tears. Ugly, scrunched face, racking sobs. I cried so hard I couldn't see or speak or move.

Warm, strong arms wrapped me up and pulled me into an even warmer chest. I pressed my face against Roman's shirt, wetting it with the river flowing down my cheeks.

"Shhh. I know those are happy tears, but I can't even stand those, baby," he cooed. "Settle down. Settle and let your friends celebrate you."

"What are you doing here?" I cried softly.

"Someone has to lug all your gifts home." He chuckled, his arms holding me tighter. "Your girls told me this was happening, and I couldn't miss it. That okay?"

"Yeah," I quaked. "It's okay."

Bea's soft body molded to my back, and her lips pressed against my crown. "If you go into labor, Roman will have Clara and me thrown into jail."

I snorted a laugh and turned my face to see her. "I'm not going into labor. Everyone's lucky we're not standing in a puddle of pee, though."

She curled her lip. "Okay, maybe surprising you wasn't the most well-thought-out plan."

Sniffling, I wiped my cheeks and eyes with the back of my hand and turned in Roman's arms. He held me against him, his hands roaming over my belly before settling in the middle and cupping it possessively.

"What did you do, Beatrice?" I whispered, overwhelmed by the beauty of this gesture.

Clara crowded into our group, her hand on my shoulder. "We love you so much, Shira, and you and this baby deserve to be celebrated. I knew you'd never ask for this, so Bea and I decided to give it to you. Are you mad?"

I shook my head, biting on my lip to stop a fresh wave of sobs. "How could I be mad? This is the sweetest thing anyone's ever done for me."

"Then come on. Let's celebrate." Clara took my hand in hers. "There's cookies."

With that promise, my feet came unglued, and I followed her into the living room, where all my friends were waiting.

Kit and Elliot's first two children had her auburn hair. The newest one had thick, ebony hair, just like her father. She was tiny and adorable when strapped to Kit's chest, but in Roman's arms, she looked like a miniature baby doll.

He was holding her to give Kit a minute to eat, and I couldn't take my eyes off him. He didn't seem frightened by holding something so innately breakable. She was nestled in the crook of his arm, peaceful as he cooed at her.

Terry slid in next to where I was perched on a stool at the kitchen island. Retirement suited her. She'd cut her hair to little more than a buzz and had exchanged her power suits for athleisure. As shocked as I'd been by my departure from GoldMed, I was happy Terry finally got to relax after devoting so many years of her professional life to the company.

"I see it," she stated.

"You do?"

"Mmm." She rounded on me, stern and serious. "I was worried about you when you told me Roman Wells had gotten you pregnant. I truly thought you'd lost your mind. But now I see it."

"Bright side, he'll be a great dad," I told her, knowing in my gut it was true.

One eyebrow winged. "That's all?"

"That's all. Well, we've become good friends over the last few months, which I think is important—"

"Okay, honey. Just let me know when the wedding shower is. I'll be there with bells on too. That's my bright side. I'm retired now, so I never turn down an invitation to a party."

A laugh burst out of me. "Your bells are going to get rusty since that won't be happening." I squeezed her hand. "Thanks for coming all the way to Breck. It means a lot to me."

"Of course." She leaned closer, squeezing my hand in return. "I miss my friend, but seeing you move on like this makes his absence less hard to swallow. You need to make the most of this life you've got, Shira. Grab it with both hands."

"I'm trying."

She glanced over her shoulder at Roman then back to me. "Hope you don't miss out on all the good that's there for the taking." Then she straightened and picked up a cube of cheese from the charcuterie platter on the island. "Now I'm in the mood to watch you open presents. Let's get this party on the road."

❧

Presents were opened. Cheesy games were played. Everyone touched my bump when Beanie put on a wild rolling show. After Elliot appeared with Joey and Theo to collect his girls, a million hugs and kisses were given, loads of cookies and cake were eaten, and Roman and I closed ourselves in our bedroom.

We showered, laughed about the games, brushed our teeth together, and kissed in front of the mirror. He told me he'd missed me, and I shared my encounter with Francesca. We agreed Brooke was the sweetest little baby and neither of us could wait to hold our own boy in our arms.

Now, I was in his lap, his cock planted deep inside me, letting him rock me how he wanted. He'd already made me come twice, and I had become as malleable as clay. He had his mouth latched to my breast, my ass in his hands, guiding me up and down on his length.

"These are going to be full of milk soon." He trailed his tongue around my pebbled nipples. "Will you let me taste it when they start dripping?"

"If you want to."

He pulsed inside me. "Oh, I want to." He pulled my nipple between his lips, drawing it deep. Imagining him drinking from me made my inner walls clasp at his cock and a flood of heat slickened my channel. He groaned around my flesh, and the vibrations made my head fall back, a sigh of pleasure escaping my parted lips.

"Can't get enough of you, baby," he crooned. "I think about these tits and the rest of you all day when I'm trying to work. You're smart to keep them covered most of the time. Drives a man to distraction, knowing what's under your clothes."

"Roman," I panted. "Stop talking."

"Stop being so fucking gorgeous," he gritted out as he arched into me, taking my breath away. "Can't get enough. Can't do it."

When he brought his head up, I slammed my eyes closed. We were too close for it to feel safe to keep them open. He was looking at me, I knew that, but when my eyes were closed, I could pretend he wasn't. It was better this way. Easier for both of us.

His fingers tangled in the back of my head, and he brought his mouth to my ear. "One of these days, Shira, you're going to give that to me. Someday soon." Then he fitted his other hand between us to roll my clit under his finger. "Now, give me another orgasm, baby. Let me feel you coming with me."

Like always, when Roman took, I gave, and we fell together.

Once we caught our breath and cleaned up, Roman tucked me against him and stroked my hair. We'd spent a lot of time like this recently. Even as my belly grew, he managed to curve around me perfectly. It was nice to have this while I was pregnant. Going through it on my own would've been lonely. Mary snuggled, but not this well.

"We haven't talked about a name."

I started, jerking in his arms, and he chuckled.

"Was that a shocking statement?" he asked.

"Just lost in my thoughts." I let my hand drift away from me, spreading my fingers over his ribs. I wished I had the nerve to stretch my arm across his broad torso and hold him the way he held me, but I didn't know if he'd want that. "Do you have name ideas?"

"I think I'm a fan of the classics. Nothing newfangled."

I snickered. "Newfangled? Okay, Grandpa."

Laughing, he took my timid hand and stretched it across him like I'd wanted to do. "What about you? Do you have a list of names you like?" he asked.

"Not a list..." I'd sort of hoped we could skip this conversation and I'd just show him the birth certificate after I filled it out. Not that I didn't want Roman's input, it was just that once I'd thought of Beanie's name, my heart had become set on it. So...I kind of didn't want Roman's input unless he agreed with my choice wholeheartedly.

I realized I couldn't actually not involve him in this decision, though.

And that sucked.

He pushed up on his elbow, a line between his brows as he peered down at me. "No list? You have one name?"

"Yes. You can veto it if you like. I won't say it won't hurt my feelings, but we don't have to choose the name just because I like it."

"Shira." He cupped my cheek, halting my spiral. "Just tell me."

"Jonah. My mom's name was Joanne, and I thought it would be nice to name him something similar. Just a little piece of her. But like I said, we don't have to."

His eyes darted between mine, the line deepening. "Jonah," he whispered. "Jonah...yeah."

He knifed up, splaying his hand beneath my bump. Then he lowered his face so he was nose to belly button with me. "Hey, Jonah. Your mom and I picked out your name. I hope you like it, buddy. You're named after your grandma."

My nose tingled. I bit down on my bottom lip to stop from crying yet another time today.

"You like it?" I squeaked hopefully.

He turned his head to grin at me when the baby kicked the hell out of us right on cue. My sweet boy liked his daddy's voice already.

"I do. More importantly, it seems he does too. Jonah Wells." He took his place beside me, planting a hard kiss on my lips. "I fucking love it, baby. Giving him a piece of his grandma will be really meaningful. And not for nothing, but Jonah Lomu's one of the best rugby players of all time."

"Then it's perfect." Serendipitous, almost. "You can pick his middle name if you want. I haven't thought of that yet."

"Yeah?" He touched his lips to my cheek. "That's a big responsibility. I'm probably going to have to consult my council."

"Your brothers?"

"Absolutely."

I laughed. "I love the way you are with them."

"We're a mess." He rolled his forehead along mine. "Just wait. In a year or two, you'll be consulting the council for all your decisions too. You can be a mess with us."

My lonely, only-child heart fluttered at the idea, trying to lasso around it to keep it as my own.

"Wouldn't that be nice?" I murmured.

The thing about being lonely most of my life was it was difficult to believe that would ever change—even with this big, lovely man in my bed and a beautiful offer in front of me.

"Just wait, Shira. You'll see."

I closed my eyes, hearing Terry's voice. "*You need to make the most of this life you've got, Shira. Grab it with both hands.*" Instead of dismissing Roman, I spread my fingers on his ribs and snuggled closer, taking what I had for now.

"We'll see."

Chapter Thirty-One
Roman

Adrian scanned the piles of wood on the ground, scratching his head. "Can't you hire someone to put this together?"

I frowned at the instruction manual. "I can, but I won't. Doesn't sit right with me to hire out the construction of my son's crib."

"Oh, I see." My brother nodded. "This is some misguided display of caveman masculinity."

I chuffed. "How is it misguided to want to build my baby's crib? I've built other furniture. I'm capable."

He folded his arms over his chest. "I don't doubt that, but this is probably the most important piece of furniture you'll ever have. Seems hiring a professional would be the way to go."

I put the manual down and picked up a rail. "Ade, think about it. No one's going to care more than me that it's put together right." I nodded toward the other box in the room. "Put yourself to good use and get started on that changing table."

With a groan, Adrian discarded his jacket on the floor, took the Swiss Army knife he always carried out of his pocket, and sliced through the tape, keeping the box closed.

The last couple weeks since Shira's shower, we'd put together a few baby things at her house and had washed piles of impossibly small baby clothes. She hadn't bought a crib yet, since she planned to use a bassinet, but I needed the nursery at my place finished and ready, and I'd called Adrian over to help. Not because I needed it but because we'd been off for a while and I wanted it nipped in the bud.

My brothers and I weren't distant. That wasn't how we did things. My life was changing, and putting myself in Ade's shoes, I could see how that would be difficult to swallow. My plan was to bring him inside the change—to make him a part of it so it wasn't so jarring.

"We picked a name," I said.

His head jerked up. "Yeah?"

"Mmmhmm. He's going to be called Jonah after Shira's mom, Joanne."

His brow furrowed. "So, she picked it."

"She told me a name she liked, and I agreed. It's nice, classic, and him sharing a name with Jonah Lomu is not a downside." I frowned at him. "Why? You don't like my kid's name?"

He grunted and got back to work on the changing table. "It's a fine name. Nice to name him after someone."

"I thought so too. I have to come up with a middle name. Any ideas? We don't exactly have too many family members worthy of giving him their name."

"Hmmm. Let me think about it."

We did our own thing side by side in silence. When Adrian said he wanted to think, he meant it. I could practically hear his mind churning.

"Weren't you just telling me about Ryan Carson's new charity?"

"Yeah…"

I didn't know where he was going with this. Ryan Carson had been one of the stars of New Zealand's national team, the All Blacks. Since he retired, he'd been doing a lot of good for underprivileged kids and helping other players manage their lives after retirement. I didn't know the man personally, but I admired all he'd done, both on and off the field.

Adrian cocked his head. "Jonah Carson Wells has a ring to it, doesn't it?"

I let that rattle around in my brain then said it aloud. "Jonah Carson Wells. JCW. Good initials." I scrubbed my jaw, letting the name settle. "Huh. I think…yeah, I like it."

He grinned. "Now watch him hate rugby."

I chuckled. "That's all right. He can like what he wants. Being named after good people doesn't mean he has to go down the same path. I just want him to emulate the good."

"He doesn't need a name to do that. He's got you as a dad, steering him where he needs to go. He'll be good."

"And Shira as a mom," I added.

He grunted. "Right."

Before I could list all the ways Shira was good, kind, forgiving, incredible, she appeared in the doorway.

"Hey. I knocked, but I assumed you were hammering and didn't hear me—" She cut herself off when her eyes landed on Adrian. "Oh, I'm so sorry. I thought you were alone and wanted to bring you the cookies I just baked. I can come back."

She was already turning by the time I climbed to my feet and closed the distance between us. I caught her hand, pulling her right back around.

"You're not going anywhere, Goldie," I rumbled. "You need to come try out the glider that got delivered this morning."

She blinked up at me, giving me those fathomless eyes of hers I had to battle to keep on me.

"Are you sure?"

"I wouldn't have stopped you from leaving if I didn't want you here. Come supervise us. Make sure we don't miss any pieces."

I tugged her into the room with me. Adrian had stood, but he wasn't exactly jumping with joy to greet her.

"Hey, Shira." He tucked his hands in his jeans, his eyes locking in on her belly, which was hard to miss these days. "How are you feeling?"

Knowing what he was asking, she peered down at her bump then up at him. "Unwieldy, but otherwise really good." She tried to slip her hand from mine—I suspected to tuck her hair—but I wasn't letting her go. "Anything is better than the first trimester."

He nodded but didn't say another peep. Still, he kept looking at where my son was growing, the undeniable bloom of life springing forth from Shira's center.

I had a hard time not staring at her bump too, so I got it.

Taking the box of cookies from her, I guided her over to the glider, which was really a cushy armchair that moved. "Sit down and give this a whirl. I think you're going to like it, baby."

Her butt hit the plush seat, and Shira sighed, letting her head loll against the cushion. "Wow," she sighed. "If this doesn't put Beanie to sleep, he's superhuman. I'm almost ready to knock out, and I just sat down."

"Then knock out," I told her. "Ade and I are doing our manly duty and building things."

Her giggle was light as air. "I hope manly duty includes changing lots of diapers in a few weeks."

Adrian saluted her. "I am willing to pitch in for liquids but draw the line at solids."

She scrunched her nose and laughed. "Then what good are you?"

Bending down, I kissed the top of her head. She wouldn't say it, but she was nervous. I saw it in the tightness of her mouth and the slight tremble of her hands. She was good at hiding it, but now that I knew what to look for, I couldn't miss it. Despite that, she was trying, and watching her try to joke with Adrian made my chest feel like it'd been filled to overflowing with concrete—heavy and stuffed and difficult to take a full breath.

"I helped Rome with the...uh, baby's middle name," Adrian informed her. "So, there's that."

Shira's gaze flashed to me. "You picked a middle name?"

"Just before you showed up. But you have full veto power."

"Tell me."

"Jonah Carson Wells. Ade suggested it. Carson comes from Ryan Carson, a rugby player from New Zealand. On top of a stellar career, he runs a charity for underprivileged kids—"

She raised a hand. "Sold. I'm sold. Jonah Carson." Her smile grew wide as she mouthed the name. "I guess we have a theme, huh? I like themes. Elliot and Kit named their kids after characters from *Little Women*—ours will be rugby."

She didn't mean "ours" as in plural children, but as soon as she'd said it, I imagined getting her pregnant again—this time on purpose—and my dick jerked. I liked the sound of that way too fucking much. It'd make sense for us to have more kids together. She'd described herself as a "lonely only," and I wanted my boy to have siblings. We'd have to talk about it, but my skittish girl would run for the hills if I brought it up now. First, we'd have this baby, then we'd work on having more.

"Guess we have a theme," I agreed.

Adrian cleared his throat. "Glad you like it."

She smiled softly at him, but the tightness had reappeared around her mouth. "I do. Thank you, Adrian."

He offered her a small smile. "I'm honored I could be a part of choosing my nephew's name. It means a lot."

"One day, you'll have to tell him how you and his daddy came up with it," she replied.

"Yeah." He looked down at his feet. "Wild he's going to be here for me to tell him things like that."

"Wild," she agreed.

Ade and I exchanged a long glance. He was trying, and Shira was too. It made me optimistic this breach could be closed and they would become friends. If nothing else, Ade would learn not to be an asshole around her. That would never happen again.

It didn't take long for Shira to nod off. Seeing her sleeping in this nursery, my heart thumped in irregular beats. Maybe I'd convince her to stay here with the baby and rock him to sleep in that chair.

"What the hell is this?" Adrian hissed.

Jerking out of my thoughts, I whirled around to find my brother frantically wiping his tongue; one of Shira's cookies crumbled beside him. I'd put the box down without warning him not to eat them. Fatal error in judgment.

"You ate one of her cookies?" I asked.

His eyes went round with indignation. "Those aren't cookies. Those are an abomination."

I laughed as quietly as possible. "She's a shit cook, but she's learning. I think she's getting better."

He poked his finger at the cookie. "*This* is better? There's so much ginger it scalded my tongue. I'm not going to be able to taste anything else for days. You can't let her feed this to the baby. His taste buds are going to get all screwed up," he whispered.

"She mentioned food tastes weird to her because of the pregnancy. I'm counting on her getting back to normal after she has him. If worse comes to worse, I'll cook all our meals."

He stared at me for a drawn-out moment. "You would, wouldn't you?"

I glanced at Shira, curled up in my chair, cradling our son inside her with her arms around him, then back to my brother.

"For my son and her? Yeah, I would."

He nodded, taking that in at the same time I did. It was big, but it was true. There wasn't much I wouldn't do for the two of them. Shira and Jonah.

CHAPTER THIRTY-TWO
Shira

ROMAN HAD BEEN WATCHING me ever since I woke up from my accidental nap in his nursery. Adrian had gone home, most of my cookies had been eaten, and the crib and changing table were all put together.

He'd planted me on a stool at the island in his kitchen while he made us dinner then fed me his delicious cooking. While he cleaned up, he kept an eye on me, even though all I was doing was lapping up the luxurious treatment he was giving me.

"You know, there was a reason I came over today, and it wasn't just to give you cookies." I rested my chin on my fists. "Kit emailed me the pictures of two houses our builders just finished rehabbing. We're going to give them to two families next week. We'll get to be there when they do their first walk-through. Kit's done this several times, and she said it never gets old. I'm giddy. I don't think the day can come soon enough. The kids will be there too, Rome. They'll get to have their own rooms and their forever home."

He shut off the water at the sink and picked up a towel to dry his hands while circling to my side of the island. Once he reached me, he dropped the towel and hooked my nape with his palm.

"Your cheeks get pink when you're excited." He dragged a finger along my cheek, his mouth curving into a hint of a smile. "Wish I could be there with you to watch. That sounds like it's going to be an incredible experience all around."

"You could come if you want to. I'm sure it wouldn't be a problem."

He exhaled, his shoulders rolling forward. "I would love that, but Nate and I are flying out to Chicago on Sunday to meet with Vantage Health. We've been in talks with several companies for some time now, but they're the most serious about merging with GoldMed."

Disappointment settled over me heavily. "You're leaving town?"

"I am, but I'm going to try to make my time there as short as possible. Decisions need to be made about GoldMed, and I'd like it to be settled before you have the baby. Obviously, I won't be traveling for a while after this, so I have to make this trip worth it in every sense."

We'd avoided the topic of GoldMed for the most part, except for a few mentions here and there. I wasn't surprised Roman had sought out an interested buyer. He'd put months into turning GoldMed around, but I'd known, from my experience at the head of the company and spending years in the background before that, it might not have been possible. I believed Roman had done what he could and had to move in a different direction while looking out for his investment. So, I wasn't disappointed about a potential merger, but the ramifications of that were difficult to swallow.

"I hope you'll find a way to treat GoldMed's employees fairly," I said softly.

"That will be part of the discussion," he assured me. "I am aware most will not want to relocate to Chicago, but I would like to be able to offer that option."

His forehead fell to mine. "This is the hard part. I don't like seeing anyone out of a job, let alone the sheer number GoldMed employs. No matter what happens, we will work to give everyone decent severance packages. It's all going to be folded into the negotiations in Chicago."

"Good." I gingerly put my hands on his sides, though I'd rather have wrapped them all the way around him. Even after all the time we'd spent together and what we'd been through, I was still shy and unsure about what he wanted from me. "Take all the time you need in Chicago so you can get that. Beanie and I will be fine. I'm sure Bea can take over your litter duties."

He lifted his head, the corner of his mouth hitching. "I've already recruited Ben and Adrian. You'll be taken care of while I'm gone, but that doesn't mean I won't be in a rush to get back. We only have a few more weeks to enjoy your pregnancy. I'm not going to miss that."

While I searched for a response to that utterly lovely statement, Roman took the lead, pressing his lips to mine. Then he cleared my mind with the sweep of his tongue between my lips and his palm on my breast. His lips were hot, and his kiss deep and thorough, taking my breath away. This man had the key to working me up in five seconds flat. It was like magic.

I was whimpering by the time he pulled back, staring down at me with flames in his gaze.

"Do you want to play with me, Shira?" he asked.

"Play?" My head tilted in confusion. "What do you mean?"

He touched my hand, still loose at his side. "I mean, when we're together, I feel you hesitating to put your hands on me, and I would love nothing more than to feel you all over me. I want you to feel comfortable to explore. Do you want to let me help you get there? Do you want to play with me?"

Swallowing hard, I nodded once. "I do."

He took my hand in his and pulled me to my feet. "Let's go to my bedroom. I'll show you what I have in mind."

My pussy was so wet arousal had seeped to my inner thighs.

Roman was naked, lying in the center of his bed, wearing a blindfold. His body was simply astounding. Every part of him was massive, from his thighs to his thick trunk to his heavy cock resting swollen on his belly. The muscles he'd earned from years as a professional athlete were still present but softened now that he spent more time behind a desk. I liked that. I liked every inch of him.

He'd given me my own personal playground and the room to play on it without worrying about having his watchful eyes on me. He'd told me nothing was off limits. All he wanted was for me to *really* touch him. The problem was I didn't know where to start.

Kneeling on the mattress next to his feet, I dragged my finger along his shin. The moment I made contact, he jerked and groaned.

His reaction emboldened me. Crawling up his leg, I dipped to kiss different spots and rub my cheek against his dark hair.

Nerves fluttered through me. This was an endeavor I'd never let myself fantasize about. I had no map for how to move forward.

All I knew was I wanted to do this. My fingers tingled with the anticipation of getting to know every inch of Roman's flesh.

I moved, roving over the length of his legs, one then the other. I crawled past his cock, saving it for later, and dragged my nose along the ridge in the center of his abdomen.

"You smell like a meadow." I inhaled his scent and sighed. "I love how you smell."

His mouth tipped. "I'll be sure to stock up on this soap."

I splayed my palm on his chest, and the rat-tat-tat of his heart made me gasp. Was he nervous too? How could that be?

I moved my hand to kiss him there then up to the crook of his neck. "Even better here."

"Hmmm." His hum vibrated my lips, reminding me of room ten. I loved his hum even more than his scent.

I kissed him there again and nuzzled my lips against his pulse while my hands glided over his chest. My nails caught on his beaded nipples, eliciting a sharp inhale from him. I did it again and received the same reaction. That was a good spot for him. Retreating down his body, I used my mouth. I'd never done this before, but I flicked my tongue against his nipple the same way he did mine and watched his hands clench the sheets beneath them.

"Good?"

"Hell yes," he answered, so effusive, I believed him completely.

I continued my exploration, crawling over and around him. Burying my face in his armpit and licking a line down his flank. Suckling his hip, tugging on the nest of hair around his cock. I rubbed the tops of his thighs then kneeled between them. My belly made it harder to position myself how I wanted, but I worked around it.

I trailed my fingertip along the seam of his sac to the underside. Then lower.

"Is this okay?" I asked.

He moved his legs a little farther apart. "Anything you want to touch is yours, Shira."

"I want to touch everything," I whispered.

"Please do, baby."

I cupped his balls in my palm, caressing them while teasing him below with my other hand. His abs rippled, and bursts of breath escaped his lips. I wanted more from him, to see him writhe the same way he made me. Shifting on all fours, using his strong legs for balance, I lowered my mouth over him. I lapped at his sac and sucked as much of it as I could into my mouth.

When I moved lower still, licking the sensitive path to his valley and back up again, his fists jerked the sheets, and a feeling of power thrummed in my veins. Making this massive man shake was a feat, and I was doing it. The muscles in his thighs were trembling from his effort to force them to remain still.

To give him a small dose of relief, I reached up and circled my fingers around his length, slowly pumping as I continued my exploration.

"Jesus, Goldie. Fuck me, fuck me, fuck me, what are you doing to me?" he gritted out.

It was so good. He tasted fresh and hot on my tongue, his cock like silk in my palm. Impossibly hard, thick and pulsing. I longed for it, wanted it, but it would wait. I couldn't squander this opportunity, and I wasn't finished with him. Not yet.

I crawled up him, kissing him along the way until my breasts hung over his cock. The problem was, I couldn't figure out how to squeeze them around him and balance myself.

"I need your help, Rome. Give me your hands." He immediately complied, and I placed his huge hands on the sides of my breasts. "There. Perfect. Now push them together."

Once he did, burying his cock between them, I rocked back and forth, fucking him with my breasts. For a moment, I got lost in watching how beautiful it looked, my soft enveloping his hard. Plush against steel. It was like we belonged, carnal and sexy, a match in opposites.

"God, Shira. You have to do this again when I can see. I know it's the hottest thing."

"It is," I told him, emboldened by his praise. "Your cock is huge, but it's getting lost between my tits."

He practically whimpered. "Baby, I like when you give me filthy words with your sweet mouth. You're killing me."

I slid my hand over his torso until I reached his nipple, rolling it between my fingers. He groaned, his hips arching into me. I'd *never* seen him this way. Panting for me, squirming, wanting. I'd been holding back by not giving in to my desire to touch him the way he touched me, and this desperation was the result. Roman had been needing this from me, and I hadn't given it to him.

To make up for my poor neglect, I gave him more until the movement of his hips became consistent and my pussy was a messy, pulsing thing I could no longer ignore.

"Rome." I climbed astride him, holding his cock between my pussy lips and sliding back and forth. I was so incredibly slick it took no effort to move over him. "You can touch me too now. Put your hands on me, but keep the blindfold on."

This time, I wanted to watch him while we fucked, but I didn't think I was ready to have his eyes on me. Just once, I'd take this chance to let loose without my insecurities stopping me from enjoying every last second.

With a heaving breath, Roman vaulted toward me, knifing upright to surround me with his arms and latch onto my neck with his lips. His desire for me was unbound, and it spurred me on even more, rocking on the thick head of his cock over and over. So good on my clit. Just right. He made my limbs feel like they were unattached, shaking somewhere in the ether.

"Wim," I panted, pushing down harder, seeking that delicious friction. "Yes, baby, yes."

"You got it. Keep going," he urged.

I did. I ground my pussy on him until I exploded, my head falling back to cry to the rafters. I felt him shaking beneath me, arching into me urgently but not taking what I hadn't given yet. His restraint turned me on further, making me needy for him all over again. After I regained the use of my limbs, I took him inside in a smooth slide.

I pushed on his shoulders. "Lean back. Let me be the one to fuck you."

He fell against the headboard, handing complete control over to me. "Filthy mouth," he murmured. "Too sweet, baby. I'm not going to last long. Warning you now."

The new shape of my body was unwieldy, so it took some patience to find my rhythm, but when I did, I fell into it, riding his cock with sureness.

"You don't have to last long. Just long enough."

A burst of energy and confidence rocketed through me. Undoing this man turned me on in a way I hadn't expected. Making him mew and whimper sent me on a power trip. All I wanted was to elicit that response again and again.

I rode him, putting my mouth on the parts of him I could reach. I let my hands rove over the broad planes of his chest, soaking up the feel of his skin on mine. It was intoxicating to have free roam of such a huge, powerful man without any worry of doing the wrong thing. He was melting beneath me, making it potently clear everything I was doing was just right.

I brought his hands to my breasts, where I knew he'd want them. "You can move if you want to. You can touch me."

His groan was deep and pained as he leaned forward to take my nipple into his mouth. Opening wide, he wrapped his lips around my breast and suckled as much as he could fit. I loved how he did this, how he was a glutton for my tits, stuffing himself full and still wanting more. Watching him now, blindfolded, lapping and sucking with wild need...liquid heat spilled between my thighs, and my inner walls clasped his length, pulling him deeper.

We went on like that, touching, fucking, tasting, grappling. It became frantic, our hands and mouths greedy for more, until he was rutting into me from below and all I could do was hang on to his shoulders.

At the last moment, as we were tumbling faster and faster toward the edge, I wanted more. Not just this physical explosion but a connection that went beyond. Ripping his blindfold off, I held his startled eyes.

"Shira," he rasped. "Oh god, Shira."

"Yes." It took everything in me not to look away and sever this raw, visceral bond stretching from me to him and back again. "Yes, Rome."

His brown eyes went soft on me, never leaving mine. Not even when climax struck us like a lightning bolt, electricity passing back and forth between us. Holding my gaze, he cupped the back of my head, his fingers tangling in my hair, and filled me to the brim with his pleasure. My heart cracked, letting the feelings I'd successfully kept at bay flood in and drown me.

I would not put a name to them. If I did, they would bloom into something bigger than I could keep inside, and that wasn't a possibility. We were friends, and we did this, and that was good. More than good. Roman wanted to take care of me, and this, what we were doing here, was part of that. I couldn't lose what we had by turning it into something more in my mind.

I knew my limits, and they didn't include getting to keep this beautiful man as mine. He was my friend, the father of my baby, but he wasn't mine.

He pulled me down on his chest, pressing his lips to the top of my head. "That was incredible."

I let my eyes flutter closed. "Yeah, it was. Thank you for letting me play."

He chuckled. "I think I should be thanking you, baby. I got the most out of it."

"Yet I came twice."

"You did, but I got to have your mouth all over me." He palmed my ass and gave it a squeeze. "I'm gonna need some more of that now that I've had it."

I trailed my fingertips over the soft definition of his pecs, something I'd been too unsure to do until now. "Soon, I'm going to be too big to crawl all over you. You won't want me to anyway."

He slid his palm over my belly and rested it on the fullest part. "If you can't crawl, I'll move you. As long as you want to fuck, I'm going to want it too. I'm crazy attracted to you, and your getting bigger with our baby has only deepened that. You give me this body, I will fucking worship it, Shira. Got it?"

I nodded, my eyes clamped tight. "I got it."

He tipped his head down to put his lips close to my ear. "Don't forget it. Not even for a second."

I wouldn't be able to. No one had ever said anything like that to me before. No one had ever touched me reverently or cared for me the way Roman did. I wouldn't be able to forget any of that.

That was the problem.

Chapter Thirty-Three
Shira

Mary licked my hand with her little sandpaper tongue this morning. Is the world coming to an end? I hope not. Too many good things are yet to come. Mary was probably just celebrating me leaving town.

Is it sad to say I'll miss her? I fear we're in a toxic relationship and I've come to like her abuse.

I'm going to miss you the most. Send me regular updates on you and Beanie. If you think it's too much, it's not enough. I want pictures and videos. Everything.

Adrian will be by in the morning to take care of the litter. You can avoid him. He expects it. It won't hurt the few feelings he has.

I'll be back as soon as I can. Trying to channel you and do some good.

XX,
Rome

Despite what Roman had said in the note he'd left me the morning he'd flown to Chicago, avoiding his brother when he was in my house didn't feel right. So, Monday morning, I put on my robe and padded downstairs to greet Adrian when he showed up.

He was washing his hands when I made it into the kitchen.

"Good morning," I chirped, infusing all the cheerfulness I contained in my body. Adrian made me nervous, but I wouldn't allow it to show. This was my chance to truly enact my *kill-'em-with-kindness* game plan. I wasn't going to blow it.

Adrian whirled around, his hands dripping water on the floor. He looked at me, his jaw flexed, then he turned back to the sink, shutting it off.

"Litter's taken care of," he grunted. "Breakfast's on the counter. Everything good?"

He didn't look at me as he asked this, so I peeked in the bakery bag he'd left for me. A mango tart and a lemon bar waited for me inside.

I sucked in a breath and tried the cheerful thing again. "This looks delicious. Thanks so much, Adrian. Would you care to join me for breakfast? I don't need both—"

"If there's nothing else you need, I have to go." He dried his hands off on his pants. "I'll be back in the morning."

Before I could say another word, Adrian strode out of my house, leaving me flabbergasted.

Maybe he really was in a hurry. Maybe he had somewhere to be. Adrian was pretty curt in general. There was a chance it wasn't personal.

Yeah, right.

All I could do was keep trying. Tomorrow was another day.

Roman: *It's strange waking up and not heading to your house. I think I've gotten used to you, Shira.*

Me: *I don't know if that sounds like a good thing.*

Roman: *It's a good thing when I'm there. It's a fucking nuisance when I'm far away and cannot engage in my routine. I've been off-kilter all day.*

Me: *Who knew cleaning a litter box could be the thing that balances you?*

Roman: *You're cute, baby, but that's not it and you know it.*

Me: *I do? Then what is it?*

Roman: *The thing that balances me is starting my day doing something for you. That's what I'm missing.*

> **Me:** *I don't know what to say except that's sweet.*

> **Roman:** *Say you miss me.*

> **Me:** *I miss you a lot* ▢

***

This time, I was awake and dressed when Adrian arrived. He started when he spotted me at the counter in the kitchen. Despite feeling like I looked like a lunatic, I beamed as brightly as I could at him.

"Good morning," I singsonged as he dropped a bakery bag on my island. "I made coffee if you'd like some. I have tea as well if that's more your thing."

He scratched the side of his head and turned toward the utility room. "I'm going to go take care of the litter."

I stayed where I was, waiting for him to return. He had to walk by me to leave the house, and I'd be damned if he didn't at least speak to me for a minute or two. Surely Roman had told him to be nice to me. I couldn't imagine he'd appreciate Adrian blatantly ignoring me.

But that was what he did. He swung through the kitchen, Mary yowling at his heels, and washed his hands. When he finished, he turned around, glancing over me as he dried his hands.

"Do you need anything else?" he asked.

I took a page from his book and ignored his question by countering with one of my own. "Would you like coffee or tea? I'd love company for breakfast."

His gaze flitted to the coffee maker beside me then the bakery bag before he exhaled heavily, shaking his head. "Can't. Have somewhere to be. I'll be back in the morning unless you need something before then. Goodbye."

He walked out, and much like the day before, I was utterly confounded. How was I going to kill him with kindness if he didn't stick around long enough for me to even get one shot off?

To be honest, his brusque dismissal was hurting my feelings. I knew I didn't deserve it, but obviously Adrian thought so, and I couldn't brush that off as easily as I wished.

Mary wound around my ankles, meowing a story to me, probably about how much more she liked Roman than his gruff brother.

"What can I do to make Adrian Wells like me, Mary?" With great effort, I bent down and picked her up. My bump had become her perch lately. She nestled in, her head butting my chest. "Don't say 'nothing.' He's Roman's brother, so I know he can't be all bad. I've just got to figure out how to get under his shell."

"Reowwww," Mary replied.

"I know, sweet girl." I scratched the top of her head and sighed. "We'll try again tomorrow."

⚶

Roman: *We're getting somewhere in our negotiations.*

Me: *Somewhere good, I hope.*

Roman: *Somewhere good. Unfortunately, that means I'll most likely be here through the week so long as you're doing well. Are you?*

Me: *I'm doing great, Rome. Bea and Clara took me for ice cream tonight. Beanie kicked for ten minutes straight after that. He either loved it or the cold pissed him off.*

Roman: *Dammit, Shira. That doesn't make being away from you two any easier.*

Me: *I'm sorry. I thought it was cute and you'd like to know.*

Roman: *It's cute as hell, which is what makes it so damn hard to miss. I appreciate you telling me, though. Don't hold back.*

Me: *I won't.*

Roman: *Good. And since he's my boy, he loved the ice cream. He was dancing to show you how much.*

Adrian tried to repeat what he'd done the last two days, but I'd had enough. My trembling arms crossed above my belly as I stepped in front of him as he tried to make another swift exit.

"I don't understand, Adrian." There was no disguising the quiver in my voice. Confronting men was not in my wheelhouse. In fact, it went against every survival instinct that had been instilled in me at a very young age. But I was going to be a mother soon, and that made me brave. "Why are you being this way?"

He took a step back, eyeing me warily. "I'm in a hurry, Shira."

"As you said. But that doesn't explain why you won't even be polite to me. You're in my home, doing me a favor, and you won't even let me thank you. I know you don't think I'm good enough to be the mother of your nephew, but this is the hand we were all dealt."

His mouth opened and closed, then he scratched his head, something I'd noticed he'd do when he didn't want to make eye contact.

"I never said that."

"Not in so many words, no." I raised my shaking chin, trying my best to say what lay heavy on my heart. "I know you think it, though. I'm used to people thinking the worst of me. It's my own fault. It's...difficult for me to be in new situations, especially with men, and I come off as cold. I'm working on it, but it takes time to undo a lifetime of hiding inside myself. I'm trying, though, for my son. I want to be the best mother I can be."

Adrian shifted, stuffing his hands in his pockets. His mouth flattened into a hard line.

"I'm sure you will be," he stated.

"I will be, you're right. I had the best mother. She risked her life to keep me safe. And once we were safe, she never let a day go by without making me feel loved. She could sew any dress without a pattern and carry a perfect tune. My mother was all I had in the world. I don't want that for Jonah. I want him to know his uncles, to be supported and loved by you guys."

"He will," he promised.

"I think he will," I agreed. "I love that for him. So, so much. But that means we'll be around each other for a long time to come, and I don't want him to see his mother being ignored and set aside."

Adrian started to speak, but for once in my life, I didn't allow a man to interrupt me.

"I know you think I married Frank for money, and you're right, I did." He jerked back in surprise, but I was undeterred. "I was twenty when we got married, my mother was dead, I had next to nothing, and he promised to take care of me if I took care of him. My husband had been sick our entire marriage. I'd been his companion, best friend, and nurse. He was my protector, best friend, and benefactor. If that makes me a gold digger, I suppose that's what I am. If that's why you dislike me...well, I don't know how to change that, Adrian.

"But no matter what I did to get here, Joanne Saltzman was my mother, so I know I'll be a good one too. I will do everything in my power to be as good as she was. That means if my son's uncle isn't treating me right, as viscerally uncomfortable as it makes me, I have to say something. That means I am asking you to please find a way to get over your first impressions of me and take me for who I am standing in front of you."

I sucked in a shuddering breath and clenched my hands at my sides so I didn't tuck my hair like I desperately wanted.

"I care about Roman and Ben and Nate. I'm already madly in love with my son. I would like us to, at the very least, be civil around one another. For now, that's all I'm asking—that we be civil."

As I finished my speech, a sharp pain took the breath right out of my lungs. Doubling over, I clutched my belly and gasped.

Chapter Thirty-four
Shira

My son was tap dancing on my organs. Given who his father was, it shouldn't have surprised me he had the power to beat me up from within. His jabs kept coming, making it impossible for me to take a full breath.

Firm hands took me by the shoulders, and Adrian's urgent voice was next to my ear. "Christ, are you okay? Is it the baby?"

"I'm okay," I wheezed. "He's just going a little crazy right now."

"He is?" One hand let go of me to hover over my stomach. "Is it...can I...?"

At the doubt coloring his words, I looked up at him. His brow was ridged in consternation as he stared at my belly.

"Here." I took his hand and placed it where Beanie was kicking. The instant Adrian made contact, Beanie doubled his efforts, knocking the wind out of me again.

"Holy shit," Adrian breathed. "Holy shit, holy shit, holy shit. That's him. That's Jonah."

"Yeah," I quivered. "He's on fire this morning. He doesn't usually hit me quite so hard."

Adrian seemed like he was in a daze for a moment, feeling his nephew for the first time. When I gasped again at another painful jab, he unfroze and took me by the elbow.

"You need to sit down. Roman will have my head if anything happens to you on my watch." He escorted me over to my dining room table and gently pushed me down in a chair. Then he crouched in front of me, eyes like his brothers' sweeping over me before landing on mine, filled with concern. "What can I do to help?"

I shook my head. "I'm fine, I promise. He's just really active this morning. Probably telling me to chill out, which is a good idea."

His brow pinched. "Christ, Roman's going to kill me. The last thing I intended was to get you riled up."

I chuffed. "Did you think giving me the cold shoulder for three days straight wouldn't make me react?" Feeling my heart ramp up again, I took a deep breath and slowly exhaled. Then I started again, calmly. "Maybe you did. If you were someone less important to Roman and Beanie, I would have let it go like I have most of my life. But things have changed, and I can't allow that anymore. What would my son think if he saw his mother allowing herself to be treated that way? What if he internalizes it and allows it to happen to him? I'm sorry, Adrian, but I can't let this slide."

He grunted, almost falling back on his ass before catching himself on the table. "You're right. I was trying to follow Roman's orders, but I screwed up, and I'm sorry for that."

"Roman's orders?"

He turned his head and reached up to scratch the side of it. "He...uh, told me not to talk to you while I was here."

"What?" I cried. "He told you not to talk to me? Why would he do that?"

Before he could respond, his phone rang. He didn't even look at it before he said, "That's him calling for a report."

"Answer it."

Adrian slipped his phone out of his pocket and sat in the chair next to mine. Roman was requesting a video call, so Adrian answered, holding the phone close to his face so Roman wouldn't see his surroundings.

Roman skipped a greeting and any pleasantries, getting straight to the point. "How is she?"

Adrian glanced at me, the corner of his mouth hitching. "She seems well."

Roman groaned. "Give me more than that. Was she dressed? Still sleeping? Did she look in the bakery bag?"

"Dressed, yeah, but as far as I know, she hasn't looked in the bag yet. Remind me again why I'm not allowed to talk to her? It feels off to be in her house and not have a conversation with her."

"You know why," Roman intoned. "You can talk to her when I'm there. I don't trust you not to be an asshole on your own."

Adrian raised an eyebrow as if to say, *"See? Told ya."* And he had. I hadn't quite believed it. Now that it was confirmed, I didn't know what to think.

I leaned closer to Adrian so Roman would see me too. "Don't you think it's rude for Adrian to barely even say good morning to me? I have to say, it's given me a major complex."

Roman's face disappeared from the screen, and all we could see was the ceiling. The silence that descended went on so long it seemed the call had been dropped.

"Roman? You there?" Adrian asked.

Movement, then Roman's flushed face came into focus. "You're with her and still at her house."

"Yes," we replied in unison.

"*Fuck*." He yanked at the side of his hair, and I could practically hear the strands screaming for mercy. "What the hell, Ade? Couldn't you have told me she was there? And, Shira, never thought you had it in you to team up with my brother against me."

"We were having a conversation when you called," I informed him. "Do you know how crappy it's made me feel having Adrian ignore me every day?"

His sigh was so heavy, his head bowed. "I messed up. *Shit*, Shira. I thought he'd be in and out without interacting with you, and on the off chance you ran into each other, I didn't want him to hurt your feelings."

Adrian's throat rumbled. "You think very little of me."

"No, I just know you can be a dick, and you have a history of not being very fucking kind to the woman next to you. This was my misguided attempt at protecting you both so your relationship didn't get further sullied." Roman's gaze latched onto me, steady and intense. "I'm sorry. I didn't think this through. My mind has gone in several different directions lately when all I want is to be there, focused on you and the baby."

A wicked grin spread across Adrian's face. "Speaking of the baby, he just kicked the hell out of Shira. Your kid is going to be a brute. I'm pretty sure he bruised my hand."

"Your hand?" Roman's gaze darted between us. "He touched you?"

I had to laugh. "I put his hand on my belly when your son started going wild."

He nodded. "As long as it was your choice."

"Of course it was. Adrian might've hurt my feelings, but he wouldn't *hurt* me," I assured him.

Adrian had gone stiff beside me. "I hope that goes without saying."

"It does, it does," Roman rushed out. "I'm sorry. This is unexpected, and I'm being a dick. Being so far away is wearing on me."

"I get that," Adrian conceded. "If it's any consolation, Shira handed me my ass right before you called. I'd say she's doing just fine."

Roman's mouth twitched. "You did? What happened to killing him with kindness?"

"I tried that. It failed." I grinned at Adrian. "So I handed him his ass."

The three of us talked for a few more minutes until Roman had to head to a meeting. Once we hung up, I invited Adrian to join me for breakfast, and this time, he accepted. Though, when I tried to get up, he scowled at me and told me no fucking way.

So Adrian brought breakfast to me, splitting the pastries between us. He made me coffee too, but only after looking up online if I was allowed to have caffeine.

I could only laugh. The Wells brothers had their differences, but they were definitely cut from the same cloth.

We were eating for a few minutes before Adrian sipped his coffee then spoke. "We were abandoned by the people who were supposed to love us the most. Our mother was there one day, gone the next. I was a child at the time, but when I search my memories, I can't find any warning. She left without a goodbye and never came back."

He set his mug down beside his plate. "Our father never picked up the slack. He was addicted to his job, his focus always on getting the next fix. For him, that was making billion-dollar deals. I'm not sure he loved us at all, so I understand why my mother left him, but not why she left us." He shook his head. "Roman stepped in. He shouldn't have had to, but he decided taking care of us was his job. He made appointments for us, signed permission slips, set up carpools so we'd have rides to the activities he'd arranged for us. He started doing all this when he was twelve, and to be frank, he's never stopped."

"He's a caretaker," I whispered.

"He is," he agreed. "So, I wasn't surprised he jumped in with both feet when you told him you're pregnant. That's who he became after our parents abandoned us. Me, on the other hand...I grew wary. It takes time for me to trust anyone new in our lives—and that's when they arrive without baggage. He'd told me a lot about your background, what he'd thought was true at the time anyway, so when he gave us the news, my instinct was to protect *him* since I knew he wouldn't protect himself."

"That makes sense."

"I was wrong about you, Shira. I knew that before you told me everything you went through. I'm sorry I've treated you in such a way you felt you had to expose your past for it to stop. It's not fair for me to judge what your marriage was or wasn't from the outside."

He scoffed, brushing his hands together. "I run a sex club, so I know a thing or two about judgment. I'm disappointed in myself for being so close-minded. I know better. That isn't who I am. It won't happen again, and you can trust your son will never see me setting you aside or ignoring you. He'll be safe around me. You both will, I promise you."

"Thank you." I believed him, not because of what he was saying, as lovely as it was, but because he was here. Roman's order for him not to speak to me might've been wack, but he trusted Adrian to be here for me. That meant a lot to me, and it made it easy to forgive him and let go of how we began.

I stuck out my hand. "Hi. I'm Shira."

His brow crinkled as he looked at my hand, but he quickly understood what I was doing and slipped his palm against mine, squeezing.

"Nice to meet you. I'm Adrian."

"There. We started over. A clean slate."

He cocked his head. "That easy?"

"Why not? We've both said what we needed to. Now we can move on."

"Yeah." Something clouded his gaze, a thought or realization. "He chose well. He might not have meant to make the choice, but he did, and he did it right."

It took me a few beats to understand he meant me. He thought Roman had done well in choosing me as the mother of his child.

That was lovelier than anything I could have hoped for.

Chapter Thirty-Five
Roman

I HAD A FEW more days before I made it back to Denver, and I was climbing the walls. Adrian wasn't making it any better with the shit he was telling me.

"You should have seen it, Ro. The mother started bawling, then Shira was bawling, and all the kids joined them. It was a mess. It was…one of the most beautiful things I've ever witnessed."

Turned out, this was why I hadn't wanted Adrian to speak to Shira. Now that he'd gotten over himself, they were becoming friends, and she'd invited him to be there with her for the final walk-through of the house Building Dignity had rehabbed for a family in need. I'd been sent pictures and a video, but it wasn't the same. I didn't want to be jealous of my own brother, but I was, and there was nothing I could do to fight it.

"You're right, I should have seen it." I rubbed my jaw, exhausted from the days of never-ending meetings. Where I'd once lived for the thrill of negotiation, all of it felt tedious. "What the hell am I doing here again?"

"You're getting matters settled so you can take time off when your son arrives. That's what is important right now," he reminded me.

"Right." I squeezed my eyes shut. "And getting the best deal I can for the employees of GoldMed. Vantage is jerking us around, trying to get away with cutting corners. Nate and I have made it clear what we need for this deal to go through, but they keep coming up short."

He huffed. "It's funny. You've done deals like this multiple times, and I've never seen you so invested in anything but the bottom line."

"Right. You're right about that."

As much as it bothered me, there was something of my father within me. Investing in failing companies had become somewhat of a game to me, and taking care of the employees wasn't my top priority.

When I'd first started at GoldMed, I'd come in hot on Shira, throwing her own words in her face—though I'd thought they were Frank's—about not forgetting the human element behind the bottom line. While I'd never forgotten the human side, it had been far down on my list of considerations when I made business decisions—until now.

People were going to be out of jobs. There was no avoiding that, though I'd tried my hardest, and it bothered me more than I expected. I knew that was because of Shira.

"Shira?" Adrian asked.

"Yeah, Shira. She's good. Like, good down to her marrow. It's part of her genetic makeup. It doesn't come naturally to me, but when I'm with her, I want to be better. I want to be good." Puffing up my cheeks, I blew out a heavy breath. "What is that?"

He chuckled. "I mean, you love her, right? It's natural for a man to want to be good enough for his woman."

I wasn't a man who moved impetuously. My decisions were carefully thought out, along with my emotions. I sifted through them, untwisting them from external complications so I could better understand how I was feeling and why. I'd done the same when it'd come to Shira. I'd parsed my feelings for my son from my feelings for her, finding the place she'd claimed in my heart stood alone. It would have been there without the tie of our son binding us.

"I do love her," I admitted. "She hasn't had it easy, and I've been a part of making it harder."

"She told me some things about that."

"You two are regular ol' friends now, huh?"

He chuckled. "Are you actually jealous? That's insane, Rome. You know that, right?"

"I'm jealous that you're there and I'm here. I know you won't swoop in and steal her from me, but I'd rather be the one holding her when she's crying." I paused. "Tell me you held her when she cried."

"I did. I don't know if I was good at it, but it's hard to stand there when that woman is in tears. It does strange, painful things to my chest."

I grinned. "That's your heart, Ade."

"Heart? What's this nonsense you speak of?"

I could picture him grimacing. Adrian had a lot of good qualities, but being open with his emotions wasn't one of them.

"It's all right to care, you know."

"I thought we were talking about you," he intoned, done being the subject of discussion.

"We were."

"All right. You miss your girl. Finish what you need to get done and come back to her. It's pretty simple."

"It should be," I hedged.

"It is, so why do you sound doubtful?"

"I worry I started us off so wrong, she won't ever be able to fully trust me. I think—no, I know I'm not good enough for her. Those are things I'm working on, but it'll take time, and I'm not sure I'll have it."

"You can't be serious. In what realm are you not good enough for *anyone*? Shira's really great, and I finally get why you and our brothers are fully on her team. But, Christ, you're the best man I know."

"You know a lot of sexual deviants."

He laughed dryly. "Don't brush me off. Besides, sexual deviants aren't inherently bad. You can stuff it with your puritanical bull-shit."

"I'm kidding. As one of the sexual deviants who's visited your club, I would never cast true aspersions on the other members."

If Adrian was curious about what Shira and I had partaken in that night in room ten, he'd never ask. Discretion was his middle name, and he was very much a firm believer in "live and let live." My brothers and I chided him on his chosen profession, but he took it seriously, and I was proud of him for what he'd built.

"The point stands," Adrian stated. "You made mistakes, but that doesn't disqualify you from being good enough to be with Shira. Remove that from your thoughts and concentrate on moving for-ward. You have a lot of good coming to you. Why focus on the bad?"

I dragged my fingers through my hair, exhausted and homesick. "A lifetime of feeling like nothing I do is enough is hard to shake."

"That might be so, but it also isn't true. Look at Nate, Ben, and me. We're where we are because of you. You were a kid yourself, but you basically raised us. I can speak for myself, but probably Nate and

Ben too, when I say we still look to you as an example. Our parents were trash humans. That shaped how you see yourself, but it's a lie, Rome. The truth is how the people who know you best see you. You just have to make yourself believe that."

Me: *I'll be home tomorrow, baby.*

Shira: *Really?! It's been a week. I was convinced you'd moved to Chicago.*

Me: *You're not getting rid of me so easily.*

Shira: *I don't want to. Did you make a deal?*

Me: *It's not done yet. Nate's staying on. I'll sit in on meetings via video conference. I've been gone long enough. It's time for me to come home.*

Shira: *I'm looking forward to seeing you. Mary and Beanie are too. I'm working tomorrow, but I can cook dinner when I get home if your flight lands on time.*

Me: *I'll see you after work. And I'll do the cooking, baby.*

CHAPTER THIRTY-SIX
Shira

I WOULDN'T ALLOW MYSELF to feel giddy about Roman coming home today. Relieved, yes. My due date was swiftly approaching and having him so far away had been a constant point of worry in the back of my mind. I needed him to be here when Beanie came.

I'd missed him too, of course. We'd become close friends on top of being lovers, and I liked knowing he was right next door—though, lately, we'd ended up sleeping in the same bed more often than not.

Kit knocked on my open office door. She was still on maternity leave but had popped in to get a few things done. She'd brought Brooke with her, who was currently hanging out with Elliot in his office down the hall.

"I'm going to head home. Joey has a recital in her preschool dance class, so I have to tame her mop into a bun. I wish I could take you home with me. You always have the best buns."

That made me smile. Joey was absolutely adorable, but she really did have a whole lot of hair for being such a tiny little girl. "I would volunteer, but Roman's coming home today."

"Ah." She slinked into my office and perched on the chair across from mine. "How are things with Roman? I feel so out of the loop these days."

"I talk to you almost every day."

"I know, but we don't gossip. Chatting in the break room is the best part of having a job."

I tilted my head. "I thought it was the fulfillment of providing a permanent home to families?"

"That too. It's, like, fifty-fifty."

I laughed. "You know, I have to agree. When I left GoldMed, the thing I missed most was my lunch meetings that were really just scheduled socializing."

She waved me off. "You're avoiding my question. How's it going with Roman?"

"Great, actually. I think we'll work well as co-parents."

Her brow pinched. "Co-parents? I thought you were...I mean, from what I saw in Breckinridge, I assumed it was more. You're not together?"

"We're not. I'm sorry if that destroys some romantic notion you had. We're friends."

She cast a dubious glance at me. "You and I are friends. You and Roman are more than that. But if that's your story, stick to it for as long as you need to."

"We have nothing in common except the baby," I argued.

Kit shrugged. "And Elliot used to be so intolerable as a boss, I wrote snarky little notes about him and stuck them in my tampon box. I've found the most wonderful things in life are the ones you don't see coming. I let myself fall in love with Elliot, and now I have my Josephine, Theo, and Brookie. We built a whole little world."

"I'm happy for you—"

"Just don't close yourself off, Shir. I saw how Roman looked at you, and I recognized it very well."

A tiny cry sounded outside my door, and a moment later, Elliot appeared, holding Brooke with her little pink fists raised.

"I held her off as long as I could, but you know I can't take it when she cries."

Kit slipped out of her chair and took her fussing baby from her husband. "Are you hungry?" she cooed as her daughter slammed her head into her chest and rooted around. "I think you are. Let's feed you then go home to tame your sister's hair."

Elliot wound his arm around her shoulders and tucked her into his side, guiding her toward the luxe pumping room he'd designed for her when she'd had her first baby. At the last moment, Kit glanced back at me and waggled her eyebrows.

I imagined she was saying, *"See? You could have something just like this."*

And they were so beautiful together I let myself daydream what it would be like if Roman and I were like Elliot and Kit.

Only for a minute or two.

*

Roman: *Just got in. Come over when you're done with work.*

I wasn't giddy. That wasn't what this buzzing beneath my skin was. Nor the fluttering of my heart. Those were probably alarming pregnancy symptoms I should have reported to my doctor—not a side-effect of being on my way to see Roman for the first time in eight days.

I forced myself to go to my house before I went to his. Mary yowled at me the second I walked in the door, and I wondered if Roman had already been by to see her.

"Did you have a visitor, my love?"

My girl was sensitive to change. Lately, when I came home, she leaped onto the arm of the couch so I didn't have to bend down to pick her up. With Mary in my arms, I wandered into the kitchen, pouring a drink to kill some time.

"I'll just wait a few more minutes before I go over there. He just got off a plane. He probably needs to decompress. *I* need to decompress."

Mary pressed her paws into my chest and started making biscuits while purring. On top of the perch she now had to sit on, she seemed to love all the new padding my body had grown, and I didn't mind all the extra snuggles she'd been giving me lately.

"Maybe I should go change. Then again, all he sees me in is lounge clothes, and I like this dress."

"Reooowww," Mary replied.

"Exactly."

I lasted until Mary was finished making biscuits and squirmed out of my arms. Once she was off bathing in the last sliver of sunlight, I had no more reasons to stall.

With my heart jammed in my throat, I locked my door behind me and started down the sidewalk to Roman's house. I made it to his front gate when his door opened and a lithe brunette stepped out. Roman was right behind her, laughing at something she said.

When she wrapped her arms around his neck and he reciprocated, I had to grab hold of the gate so I didn't fall over. I must have made some kind of noise since they both swung around to face me.

"Shira," Roman called. "You're here."

I nodded, too flustered to say anything. Now that I saw her face, I recognized the woman from the auction. Had he been seeing her this whole time?

"Oh, wow, this is Shira." The brunette was down the porch steps and in front of me before I could react. She grinned at my belly, stopping just short of reaching for it. "I was just dropping off a baby present. I can't wait to see the little guy in person. I'm so excited."

"Oh." I swallowed hard. Roman was approaching us, but I couldn't look at him.

He stopped beside me, gently touching my shoulder. "Shira, this is Rosalie. I think you two might've met at the auction."

"We didn't formally meet," Rosalie supplied.

"Ah well, those functions are always a blur," Roman replied, which was funny because I remembered that night clearly. I remembered the two of them laughing together and sitting beside each other during the presentations. And what came after. Roman's mouth on me, his insatiable need to bring me pleasure. For me, that night had been marked something important. For him, it was a blur.

"It's nice to meet you, Rosalie." I tucked my hair behind my ear. "I'll let you guys have your privacy. See you later."

Then I spun around and raced back to my house as quickly as my legs would carry me. It wasn't fast enough. Roman caught my elbow before I could even put one foot on my porch.

"Where are you going?" He sounded bemused rather than guilty. But I supposed he had nothing to be guilty about since he hadn't done anything wrong.

I refused to turn my head to look at him. If I did, I would burst into tears, and that simply wasn't going to happen. "I'm sorry. I didn't mean to interrupt something. You can go back to her."

"Shira, look at me. What are you talking about? Why did you run away?"

"Like I said, I'm giving you privacy with your...with Rosalie. Enjoy your evening."

Somehow, I slipped free from him and made it to my door, but he was nipping at my heels when I let myself inside. I just wanted to drown in this wave of sadness on the verge of breaking over me, and I wanted to be alone when that happened. Roman seemed to have other plans.

"Shira, look at me," he demanded, though not angrily. I sensed he was being careful with me. It was so very Roman it made this all the worse.

I lifted my gaze, knowing he would see the sheen blurring my eyes. "Please, just go. We can talk about this later."

His brow dropped. "What do you think is happening? I'm trying to understand why you would think I need privacy with Rosalie."

I shook my head, unable to say the bitterly obvious words.

He cocked his head as he frowned at me. "Do you think I'm seeing her? And you're what—bowing out so I can be alone with her? Is that what's happening here?"

In order for this to end, I would have to speak. That much was obvious. "I don't want to get in the way. I'm fine. You can go back home and be with her. We'll have dinner and catch up another night."

He stared at me for several thrashing beats of my heart. Then, grunting, he stalked past me into my kitchen. I turned, stunned to find him with his hands braced on the island, his head bowed low.

What was going on? Why wouldn't he just go so I could begin to piece together how to survive and endure this?

Without warning, he straightened, pinning his gaze on me. "I'm not a cheater, Shira. The fact that you would accept that from me makes me unbearably sad."

"I don't think you're a cheater," I croaked. "We aren't together—"

"We're not together?" he barked harshly, making me jump. "How the fuck can you say that?"

"We aren't."

This, I knew for a fact. I might not have a ton of experience, but even I knew in order to be a couple with someone, a discussion had to come first. That had never happened. Roman and I had sex, but we weren't a couple.

He blinked at me as if he found me to be a puzzle he couldn't solve. "So us spending almost every night together means nothing. We eat breakfast and dinner together, spend our weekends together, fuck every chance we get—bare, might I add. We tell each other we miss each other when we're apart and have shared deeply personal parts of ourselves. All of that means nothing?"

"It means a lot," I replied. "But I understand you have a life outside of me and Beanie—"

"You *are* my life."

He wasn't yelling, but his anger was visceral, filling the room with thick, spiky air. I tried not to be afraid of him. Deep down, I knew he would never lay a violent hand on me. But my instincts told me to run, hide, and be quiet. That was my focus—not the words coming out of his mouth.

He started for me, slow, cautious. "Rosalie is Nate's ex-girlfriend and a family friend. Even if you didn't exist, I would never go there with her. But you do exist, and you have become everything to me. I'm in love with you, Shira. Don't you feel even a fraction of the same for me?"

I clutched my belly, panic activating my limbs to flee. It was all I could do to stay rooted to the spot. "If not for Beanie, you never would have looked twice at me. You didn't before you knew about him, and that's fine. I knew what this was from the start."

He stopped where he was, several feet from me. I could only bear to look at him in my periphery, but I didn't miss the way his entire body jerked like I'd struck him.

"What are you *doing*?" he hissed.

"Isn't it true? You're standing here because of the baby, not me."

His hands balled at his sides. "That's true, I am. We both know you never would have let me into your home if our baby didn't exist, so your accusation is a two-way street. But for you to think I'm in your bed every night because of our son insults everything we've shared. I've spent the last few months falling deeply in love with you, and you're ready to shove me out the door to be with another woman. What is that, Shira?"

Deeply in love? That couldn't be right. He might have thought he loved me, but he had to be mixing up his feelings for the baby with feelings for me. There was no way this beautiful man truly wanted *me*. A woman like me lived within certain parameters, and that would go well beyond that—so far, it was unimaginable.

"You don't love me. I think once the baby is here, you'll see that," I whispered.

He raked his fingers through his hair with vicious force. "Is it not good enough? Is that why you can't feel it? I thought I was showing you, but maybe I don't know what the hell I'm doing. This is new for me, but fuck, I thought I was doing a good job. Now, I don't know. I'm feeling a little lost here. I can't think of how to love you harder other than cutting my heart out and showing you your name carved in every chamber. But what if that's not enough?"

My ears were ringing with alarm bells. I shook my head to try to clear it, but a wave of dizziness struck me. Reaching out blindly, I braced myself on the wall beside me.

"Shira." Roman rushed to me and guided me to the couch. He sank down next to me, taking my face in his hands. "Are you okay? You're pale."

"I'm fine. Please don't worry. It's been a long day, and now this...I think I just needed to sit down." Tears slipped past my defenses, streaming down my cheeks. "I'm sorry, Roman."

"You don't need to be sorry. I'm the one who wasn't loving you well. If I had been, you wouldn't be sitting here crying. You'd be in my arms after eight goddamn days out of them. I just need to know what more I can do to keep you."

A sob racked through my body at his defeat. I hadn't meant to do this to him, but I couldn't let myself believe any of it was real. Roman Wells didn't happen to me. That wasn't my lot in life. That had always been okay. I'd never even considered wanting someone like him. But now that he was here, I couldn't reach out and grasp him, not even when his arms were outstretched, begging me to.

He was as gentle as could be, wiping my tears and stroking my hair, and it was too much. My mind rebelled against the idea that Roman could be mine, and if he wasn't mine, I had to get away from him until my defenses were fortified again.

"I need to be alone," I said softly.

"No," he croaked. "I need to fix this."

"There's nothing to fix. I have to think, all right? We can talk tomorrow."

His hands fell away. "I came back here for you."

My lids fluttered closed as I nodded. "Beanie's doing well. He's had the hiccups a lot lately. I read that's part of practice breathing, which is amazing."

"For *you*, Shira." His sigh was heavy. "I'll be back in the morning for Mary."

His exit was quiet, barely a whisper. Another sob ripped through me as his keys turned the locks from outside, taking care of me even after everything.

Beanie kicked me, reminding me he was there. I placed my palm where his foot was pressing against me, wishing Roman was beside me, feeling this along with me.

"What did I do? And how do I make it better?"

CHAPTER THIRTY-SEVEN
Shira

THE KNOCK ON MY door made my heart flutter, and it had only just calmed down. I tried not to show my disappointment when Bea was the one standing on my porch.

"Hey, you," I greeted.

Her eyes narrowed. "You look like shit. What gives?"

My laugh came out as more of a sob, but that was because I'd only just conquered my tears as well. It had taken two hours and a batch of muffins to make my chin stop quivering. The fact that I'd made them just how Roman liked them—overloaded with cinnamon—hadn't helped matters.

"I'm an absolute mess, Beatrice."

Her face crumpled. "Oh, honey." Then she was inside my house with her arms around me. "What's wrong? I hate seeing you cry. It physically pains me."

I sniffled into her hair, which magically smelled like blueberries. "Roman always says that."

That was all it took for me to fall apart. Bea walked me over to the couch and let me cry on her shoulder, all while she patted my arm and hummed a familiar song. My friend wasn't naturally touchy-feely, which meant I truly looked as hopeless as I felt.

My crying petered off into periodic hiccups and little gasps, allowing me to listen to the song Bea was humming.

"Are you humming 'Bohemian Rhapsody'?" I asked.

"Mmmhmm. I find it more soothing than 'Twinkle, Twinkle.' And look, you stopped crying. My girl is a Queen fan."

Laughing, I sat up and wiped my cheeks with the backs of my hands. Bea raked her eyes over me, concern crinkling her brow.

"I came over to ask if you wanted to grab dinner before I remembered Roman was coming back today." She glanced around. "Is his flight delayed? Is that what's got you down?"

"No, he's back."

Her eyes rounded. "Then why aren't you with him? You've been fiending for him all week."

I sucked in a breath, and it hurt. My throat felt like it was filled with broken glass while my chest was being squeezed in a vise. But I had to talk this out, and Bea would give it to me straight. She didn't know any other way.

"I went over to his house, but he was with another woman."

Bea went from zero to a hundred in two seconds flat. Her face flushed cherry-bomb red, and she sprung from the couch, her arms flinging outward.

"He *what*? Are you kidding me? Oh, that guy—that fucking guy. Where is he?" She marched toward my door then spun around. "I can't believe him. I fully trusted him—"

"Wait—why are you so mad?"

Her eyes looked close to falling out of her head. "Uh...are you kidding me, Shira? That handsome bastard is cheating on you when you're growing his giant son! How could I not be mad?"

I scooted forward. "Do you think Roman and I are together?"

She slapped her forehead. "Well, I hope not now. God, I'm going to throttle him."

"We were together?" I whispered.

Hands on her hips, Bea stared at me for a long time. "Okay, what is going on? Why do you look like you just saw a ghost?"

"The woman was a family friend. Nothing was happening, but I thought it was, and I told them I would leave to give them privacy. Roman was *not* happy with me."

Her jaw dropped, leaving her mouth hanging open. "Why in the world would you do that?"

"Because we never talked about any of this. We're together all the time, but I never thought we were a couple. The only thing we ever said was we would be friends—which we are."

"Shira," Bea breathed, her fingers flying to her mouth.

"I told him he's only with me because of Beanie."

"Oh, Shira." She shook her head like I'd said something tragic.

"He's Roman Wells." Bea just stared at me, waiting for me to elaborate. So, I did. "You've seen him. He's tall and so handsome, he takes my breath away, a former pro athlete with insanely thick thighs and glorious veins in his forearms, outrageously successful, and kind. Really, truly kind. That kindness is why he's with me. If not for Beanie, he'd have nothing to do with me."

"Wow. I've never heard one person be so incredibly wrong."

"Which part?"

She waved her hands in a wide circle. "All of it, babe. You named a lot of that man's good qualities as if they're reasons for the two of you not to be together, but to me, you just made a list of why he's approaching good enough for you."

Is it not good enough? Is that why you can't feel it?

"That isn't it at all."

She puffed her cheeks and blew out a powerful breath. "Let's get real. The bean was the catalyst, forcing you and Roman to get to know each other on a very raw, gritty level. From what I've seen, you more than liked what you found in him, and he obviously liked the hell out of what he found in you. After all, the man isn't dim."

"We like each other. We're friends."

"Okay, he isn't dim, but maybe you are."

I scrunched my nose at her. "That isn't nice. I'm sad. You're supposed to be comforting me."

"Why would I comfort you when you're screwing everything up?"

"Bea, come on," I whispered, exhausted from the war brewing within me.

"What else did he say? Just spill it."

Shaking my head, I got up from the couch and started for the kitchen. "He said a lot of really lovely things I can't let myself believe."

I started transferring the muffins from the tin I'd baked them in to a plate. I had no idea why I'd baked these since this recipe didn't taste good to me. Roman and his brothers loved it, but I doubted he'd accept anything from me now.

Bea stopped on the other side of the island. "Like what?"

"Like he's fallen in love with me. He hasn't, though. He loves the baby, and once he's here, he'll see that. He didn't like when I told him that, but I can't, Bea—if I let that in, I'll fall apart when he takes it away."

"Shira, god..." Bea shook her head. "What is wrong with you?"

My chin quivered as I looked at my friend across from me. Bea was something of a black cat, swatting at people who annoyed her, but she'd never been anything but sweet and gentle with me—except now.

Now, she seemed like she was pissed off.

"What?" I asked.

"You can't just tell someone they don't know their own feelings. It would be one thing if you didn't feel the same for him, but I've seen the two of you together. I know when two people are stupidly in love, and that's you and Roman."

"We're friends," I insisted, though my defense didn't ring true—even to me.

"I'm not going to ask why you think you're not worthy of a big, passionate love. You settled for a sexless marriage to a man you might have loved, but there's no denying he definitely took advantage of your age and position. But you're older, a shit ton richer, and you don't have to settle anymore. Why in the world are you not letting Roman love you?"

I can't think of how to love you harder other than cutting my heart out and showing you your name carved in every chamber. But what if that's not enough?

"He's beautiful," I replied weakly.

"And so are you. Not every kind of beauty has to scream." She stole a muffin from the plate and peeled the wrapper. "Your kind of beauty is a whisper. The closer you pay attention to it, the more you understand and become attuned to it. And once you are, you can't believe you didn't notice it in the first place."

My eyes burned so badly, I had to squeeze them shut for relief. "That is the sweetest thing anyone has ever said to me."

"I'm certain Roman's said sweeter things."

"It's strange waking up and not heading to your house. I think I've gotten used to you, Shira."

"You give me this body, I will fucking worship it."

"Have you seen how beautifully you're growing our son? You can handle anything."

"You can be a mess with us."

"...you have become everything to me."

A different kind of wave crashed into me, knocking down my flimsy barriers and flooding me with Roman's words, smiles, gentle caresses, and all the soft looks he'd given me. There was friendship behind all of it—and so much more. It had been that way for months and months, and I'd refused to see it. My brain had decided enough was enough and gave it all to me at once.

"He has," I agreed, leaning over the counter to catch my breath. "He's said so many lovely things to me."

"You've deserved every one of them. It's your time, Shira. If you don't really live, what was the point of everything you did to survive?"

I almost staggered from the weight of her question. What *was* the point of what my mom had endured and what I'd been through to get here if I didn't make the most of what I now had?

Bea took a big bite of her muffin. She chewed twice then her face morphed into a look of horror. Bright red eyes rounded, and her mouth puckered in disgust. Then she ran for the sink, spitting violently. I followed her, worried she was choking. When she stuck her mouth under the faucet, I realized that wasn't the case.

"Oh my god," she cried between huge gulps of water. "Something's wrong with those muffins. Don't eat them. Throw them away immediately."

"There's nothing wrong with them. Roman and his brothers love them."

Bea straightened, snatching a towel to wipe off her face. "No human being could love those muffins. They're vile."

I folded my arms over my bump. "The Wells brothers do. They all eat everything I cook."

She shook her head. "There's half a container of cinnamon in them. Did you make a mistake when you were mixing the ingredients?"

"No. Well, the first time I made them, I added too much, but Roman loved them. He seems to really love it when I add a lot of extra garlic and pepper to his dinner too. It doesn't taste good to me, but he always clears his plate. Even Adrian devoured my ginger cookies. And that time I ran out of sugar, I used extra ginger to make up for it..."

I trailed off, considering what I was saying. None of the food I'd made for Rome and his brothers had tasted right to me, but he'd insisted it was delicious. He'd also done most of the cooking lately.

"So, Roman eats your disgusting cooking and tells you it's delicious?" Bea snorted. "If that's not love, I don't know what is. He has it bad for you, Shira."

My hand flew to my mouth. "Oh my god. He hates my cooking and eats it anyway so he doesn't hurt my feelings because he despises when I cry!"

"He loves you."

"He loves me," I whispered.

She knocked on my forehead. "Glad it finally sank in. Now, get your butt in gear and get your man. Don't make him wait."

"You need to make the most of this life you've got, Shira. Grab it with both hands."

I picked up the plate of muffins. "Here goes nothing."

CHAPTER

THIRTY-EIGHT

Roman

I couldn't figure out how not to be angry. I really didn't want to be angry at Shira. Logically, I knew the shit she'd pulled was all about her and not me, but I wasn't succeeding. Deep down—maybe not even that deep—I still grappled with not feeling worthy of love. No matter how hard I pushed or how high my accomplishments stacked, I couldn't shake the feeling of being lacking. My brothers would tell me how wrong I was—they had, many times, in fact—yet here I was, rattling my chains in a big empty house because the woman I loved didn't believe it.

For a man with my baggage, her rejection was a knife to the gut. I could tell myself Shira was shutting me out to protect herself until I was blue in the face. It wasn't that she didn't trust me; it was that she'd come from the lesson she'd learned far too young—stay quiet and endure. But when it came to deep wounds that hadn't healed, logic had no place.

I should have eased her in. Called her my girlfriend months ago. Told her I loved her when I was holding her in bed weeks after that. Let her come to me with her own declarations in her own time. I'd made mistakes, thinking Shira would understand how things were.

But we were coming at this from two different directions, and today had been a blindside.

Still, I was pissed.

She was there, and I was here.

That wasn't right. My gut roiled, and my entire body protested being this close to her and not having her in my arms. She'd put that distance there, and maybe it was right and needed, but I didn't give a damn. If I was going to get her where I needed her to be, she was going to have to be within touching distance to do it.

Resolved, I headed to my front door. Before I could make it there, there was a light, timid knock that froze me in place. Only one set of knuckles made that sound on my door.

She'd come.

She'd fucking come.

I closed the rest of the distance and swung the door open. Taking her by the elbow, I pulled her into my house and locked the door behind her. For good measure, I planted myself in front of it so she couldn't escape. That might've been barbaric, but I was past reason. She wasn't leaving.

Parched, I drank every inch of her in. She was holding a plate of muffins, which was strange, but her face was what caught me. Cheeks ruddy, eyes bloodshot, nose pink, lips swollen—she'd clearly spent a lot of time crying, and that tore me up.

Her chin wobbled. "I'm so sorry, Roman."

I nodded once. We were in this place partially because I'd kept my mouth shut. There would be no more of that. It was time to lay it all on the line.

"You really hurt me." The plain, bare truth at the core of it all. She'd really fucking hurt me.

She took in a shuddering gasp. "I know that now, and I hate that I did. I baked your favorite muffins to make up for it."

Arms outstretched, she offered me the plate, and I didn't have it in me to turn her down. My body had become somewhat inoculated to her brand of cooking. I barely felt the burn when I swallowed anymore.

As soon as I took a muffin, she swatted it right out of my hand.

"You were going to eat that!" she cried, the plate slipping from her fingers.

"You made it for me," I stated matter-of-factly. It *was* a matter of fact. She'd gone through the trouble of making food for me, so I was going to eat it, even if it caused irreparable damage to my organs. Between that and seeing her upset, the choice was obvious.

"Roman." My name was a lament from her trembling lips. "Oh my god, Roman. I've been poisoning you—and you've let me!"

Glancing from the scattered muffins to Shira, who was more distraught than I'd ever seen her, all my residual anger fell away. Stepping over the muffins, I scooped her into my arms. She only wiggled for a moment before surrendering and melting into me, allowing me to cradle her.

I carried her through the living room, up the stairs, to my bedroom, and settled us on my bed. My legs were outstretched in front of me while Shira rested sideways on my lap, nestled against my chest. We had a lot to say, but right now, I needed this. A few minutes to ground myself in the feel of her, warm and solid. It'd been a few hours since she'd been here, and in that time, I'd convinced myself she was never coming back.

Her fingers curled into my shirt, gripping the material tight in her fist. Her other arm hooked around my neck, and those fingers slid into the back of my hair. I tucked my face into her crown and breathed her in.

"I thought my tastebuds were messed up," she whispered. "But it wasn't that. You were eating everything I made for you even though it was inedible because you didn't want me to be upset. You even made your brothers eat it."

I stiffened. "Who told you it was inedible?" If they'd upset her...

She tilted her head back to look up at me. "Bea. I think what she really said was they're vile. I kind of think she's telling the truth—which means you haven't been."

I'd have words with Bea. She cared about Shira, and she was a good friend, but I would not stand for—

"Roman." Shira's fingers lightly tapped my cheek. "I think you didn't tell me because you didn't want me to be upset. And you made your brothers eat my cooking for the same reason. Why else would you have done that other than caring about me and my feelings? You do love me, don't you?"

"Yeah, I do."

I could have left it at that—the most important, bare-bone fact. But I knew my Shira needed evidence to support my claim. She had to know I wasn't just telling her I loved her on some whim. Like any other major shift in my life, I'd thought it over until I was certain.

"I took my time getting there. As soon as you told me about our baby, my instinct was to be near you to protect you. *That* was all Beanie, but once I got near you and we had time to actually get to know one another outside of our assumptions, it became all about you. It's my fault for only verbalizing any of this now, but I guess in the back of my mind, I wasn't willing to hear you say you weren't there with me. I should've done it anyway, but that's history. The fact remains: I've examined my feelings. When I say I'm in love with you, I mean *you*, Shira—not the mother of my son, *you*." For once, she was giving me her eyes, and I searched them for what I needed from her. "Do you think maybe you could love me?"

Her lips rolled over her teeth, and I thought I wasn't going to hear it. For those few seconds, I decided to be okay with that. So long as she let me love her, we'd get there. She'd eventually feel safe enough with me to let herself fall.

But she swept away all my plans of winning her over with her sweet words.

"I love you too, Roman Wells."

"Christ," I breathed, my forehead falling to hers. "That's all I want from you. You loving me and letting me love you."

"You have it."

"Then I'm content. So damn content."

Her hand flattened on my jaw. "You're always so careful with my feelings, and I failed in reciprocating that. I'll be better about that. I want to take care of you the way you take care of me."

"It's okay. I don't need taken care of."

I never had. Even before our mother cut and ran, I'd always been the one to check in on my brothers. It came naturally to me in part, but even when I was a little kid, I thought I had recognized a void that needed filling—something our friends had that we'd been lacking. So, I'd filled it any way I could. These days, my brothers didn't need me like they had back then, but when push came to shove, I was the primary support person. It made me feel purposeful, and I'd never once resented them for my position.

But the idea of Shira taking care of me? Yeah, I liked that, and if she wanted to give that to me, I wouldn't turn her down. If we could get to a place where we leaned on each other, we'd be unshakable.

"No, it isn't okay, Rome. I let you go for three hours believing your love wasn't enough, and that's just wrong. I didn't identify the way you treat me as love because I've never had anything like this. Before I met you and knew you, I wouldn't have even dreamed of knocking on a man's door not knowing without question he would be happy to see me. I wouldn't have been able to climb into his lap, sure he'd welcome me with open arms. I wouldn't have fathomed a man would understand where my limitations came from and help me inch past them. Nor would I have imagined this man would be endlessly patient when I couldn't meet his eyes then find a way for me to make it my choice."

Her lips touched mine, a whisper of sweetness.

"Roman, you've been loving me, and I didn't even know it because it's brand new to me. I did know you treated me like I was something precious, but I thought it was because of Beanie. And that was all because of the limits I'd placed on myself. It had nothing to do with how well you've loved me."

I closed my eyes and inhaled, filling my lungs with her and the words she'd uttered. Releasing it with a shudder, my arms went tight around her.

"I threw that in your face, and I'm so sorry for that," she murmured, stroking my jaw. "We had a hard beginning, but since then, you've been nothing but good to me. I'm going to be good to you too, Roman. To start, I'm never cooking for you again."

A grin split my face as I let it fall against the top of her head. "We're just going to be good to each other, and I don't mind cooking for you and our family. Nights we're too busy, we'll get takeout."

Her lips pressed against my jaw. "I like the sound of 'our family.'"

"That's what we're doing here, Shira. When you fell asleep in the glider that day, I imagined getting you pregnant again and again. Part of that was because it turns me on to think about fucking you with that intention, but mostly, I think we're making something beautiful here."

"How many?" she asked.

"How many what?"

"Kids. How many do you want?"

"I'm open to negotiation, but I like having a lot of siblings, and I wouldn't mind giving that to our boy."

"So four?" She smoothed her hand over her belly. "I was an only. I know I want him to have at least one sibling. Can we see how that goes?"

Relief and something that felt a lot like optimism poured over me, warm and cozy. "Yes, baby. We can see how that goes. One, two, or seven, I'm going to fucking adore every child you give me like I adore you."

She let out a breathy laugh. "Not seven, Rome. Get that out of your head."

"Fine." I nuzzled her temple, rubbing my nose back and forth. "We can pretend we're making seven. I'll settle for a little playtime with you."

"We can do that." Her arms slid around my neck. "I adore you too, Roman. You are something special I didn't know existed. But

I found you, and now that I know you're mine and only mine, I'm going to work my butt off to keep you."

For a man who'd been abandoned by his mother and had never done enough to hold his father's attention, hearing those words from the woman who'd become the most important person in my life healed a rift in me. It made being disposable and unvalued by my mother and father into a scar instead of an open wound. Shira and I both had work to do; that much was clear, but if we were in this together, trusting the solidness of our relationship, we would get where we needed to be.

"Haven't you been paying attention? All I want is you and our family, baby. You've got me free and clear."

"And you have me," she promised.

Then we have all we need.

Chapter Thirty-Nine
Shira

Ben crossed his arms. "I don't like her."

Nate swatted the back of his head. "No one asked your opinion."

Adrian raised his eyes from his phone for the first time this evening. He wasn't big into basketball, unlike the rest of his brothers, but on a rare evening he wasn't at work, he chose to hang out after we all ate dinner anyway. I'd learned the Wells brothers simply liked to be around each other, no matter the activity.

"Her background check is pristine, and her references are glowing."

Ben narrowed his eyes. "See? That's suspicious. It's probably all fake."

Laughing, I let my head fall on Roman's shoulder. With five of us on the couch, it was a tight fit, so Roman had snuggled me into his lap. Though, truthfully, that was where I spent most of my time these days. It was just as well since that seemed to be the only place I could get comfortable. I was a week away from my due date, the baby was measuring almost nine pounds, and my belly was large and in charge. My back ached, my ankles and feet were swollen, my face looked like the moon...and I had never been happier.

"For what it's worth, I think she had a few parking tickets," I said.

Roman glared at Adrian, who was no longer paying attention. "You checked our nanny's references?"

"Naturally," he intoned.

The funny thing was, I wasn't even a little surprised all the Wells brothers were invested in our nanny choice. Roman and I had interviewed several candidates over the last few weeks and had finally settled on Louise. The kids she'd been nannying were heading off to school full time, and that was the only reason she was leaving her current position. We were lucky to find her.

"She's a gem," I said. "Besides, she's Elliot and Kit's nanny's sister, and she's watched their children several times. Do you think Elliot Levy would vouch for someone less than perfect?"

"See?" Nate rounded on Ben. "They have it covered. Relax."

Ben had not uncrossed his arms. "I'd like to meet this woman."

"You'll meet her when she comes to work for us," Roman barked.

I slid my palm over his jaw. "He's just being protective."

"I don't like him questioning our decision," he grumbled. "You love Louise."

"I do, and Ben will love her too. I'm not worried."

Lately, I hadn't been worried about much. Once Roman and I'd had our big talk, we hadn't stopped talking. It was as if we'd broken something within ourselves, and instead of internalizing every tiny thought, we shared it aloud.

I now understood Roman more than ever. He may have been this massive, powerful man, but he had wounds almost as old as he was and a center that needed tending to. I knew something about that.

We were careful with each other, mutually aware of the old hurts we both carried. I had to unlearn being quiet and enduring, and

Roman was making it easy. When it was just the two of us, we had a steady sense of peacefulness I'd never experienced before. His brothers always came along to shake things up so we didn't get bored, though I doubted that would ever be a problem.

When we weren't talking, we were going at it. Even with my giant belly, Roman got creative. We couldn't keep our hands off each other because right beside the love and peace we had uncovered was a fiery passion that burned brighter every day.

Like most nights, I fell asleep on the couch, and Roman carried me upstairs when the game was over. I could have walked, but he liked carrying me, and I didn't mind giving him that. Not one bit.

We got ready for bed together. Mary scampered off to her snoozing spot at the foot, giving us both the stink eye for daring to interrupt her sleep, then quickly settled down in the ultra-luxurious cat bed Roman had bought for her.

I hadn't moved in with Roman. Not officially, at least. Unofficially, I slept here every night, and Mary spent most of her time here too. Slowly but surely, all her accessories and necessities had migrated, and my belongings seemed to be piling up as well. Roman hadn't said a word, but I'd caught him running his hand over my dresses hanging in his closet and smiling to himself. So, I was pretty sure he was liking where we were going.

I sat in bed, my back against a pile of pillows, rubbing lotion on my arms. Roman took the bottle and went to work on my feet. His thumb dug deliciously into my arch. He did this nightly, massaging my feet and legs until I was boneless.

"I'm going to miss it when you don't do that anymore," I slurred.

"Who says I'm going to stop?" He kissed the tip of my toe. "These feet carry around the two loves of my life. They deserve to be treated with care."

"Well, that's sweet. Is there a part of you that needs massaging?"

He took my foot and placed it on top of the thick ridge of his cock. "Always."

I reached for him. "Then come here and let me take care of you too."

Beanie stretched, a foot or knee digging into me so hard, I hissed. Roman followed my hand on my belly, rubbing the spot where our son was trying to break free.

"You okay?" he murmured.

"He's running out of room."

"He'll be out soon enough, then he'll probably regret giving up his comfy spot."

I tipped my forehead into his jaw. "I think he'll be pretty comfy here too."

His hum reminded me of Mary's contented purrs. "You know I love you?"

"I do." I spread my fingers on his cheek. "You know I love you too?"

"Yeah, baby, I do." He rubbed his face against mine. "You and Beanie are going to live here with me, aren't you?"

My heart flipped inside my chest, which wasn't easy since my organs were pretty squished these days. Now that he'd asked—well, sort of asked—I realized I'd been waiting for this. Wanting it. Of course he was giving it to me. Roman always gave me what I wanted.

"Yes, Rome, we are."

"Then we better get all your stuff moved over here tomorrow so we don't have to deal with it after he comes."

"Tomorrow?"

"I'm not feeling much like wasting time." He turned his head to kiss my wrist. "You?"

"No more wasting time."

With a deep groan, he moved behind me, wrapping his body around mine. His hand roamed over my belly and the slope of my hip before spending a generous amount of time on my breasts.

When it was time, when we were breathless and needy and had shed our clothes so our skin slid together, I lifted my leg, and Roman thrust into me.

We made quiet, lazy love, rolling hips and greedy hands. He kissed my shoulder and throat, then turned my head to take my mouth. In my ear, he whispered his happiness to have me in his bed permanently. I wove my fingers between his and sighed my agreement.

There was a part of me that was afraid—we were facing the unknown, after all—but then I remembered all of this was unknown.

Except Roman.

We had been connected by a letter since I was nineteen years old. I *knew* him. Not every one of his stories, but who he was at his core.

He was mine.

He traced the curve of my belly and rocked into me, planting himself deep. Mouth beside my ear, he nibbled my lobe, then said, "This part I'm going to miss. Do you have any idea how sexy you are right now, Shira? You're in full bloom, baby."

My insides quivered, pulling him even deeper. "Then you'll have to work hard to get me this way again."

"It won't be hard work. It'll be my favorite pastime. Fucking you to get you pregnant and round with our baby. Dripping tits and pussy. God, you sure seven is off the table? Not sure I'm going to be able to stop at a reasonable number."

I tilted my head to nip the underside of his jaw. "Move, honey. Make me come, and you can probably convince me of anything."

With a growl, he snapped his hips, hitting a spot inside me that made my eyes roll back. And he kept hitting it until I was shaking all over and moisture dripped from the tips of my breasts. Once he felt that on his palms, Roman followed me over, then methodically cleaned every last drop of milk.

Then he took my face in his hands and traced the slopes with his fingers while studying my features. The part of me allergic to attention squirmed, but the sureness that Roman adored every bit of me, including my face, pounded my insecurities back.

He pressed a kiss on each of my eyelids and the tip of my nose. "I adore you, Shira."

"I feel that." I lifted my head to kiss his lips three times, then once more for good measure. "I adore you too, my Rome."

For once, Roman fell asleep before me, holding me snugly against his chest. It might've been the persistent ache in my back keeping me awake or the thoughts of all the things I had to get done before Beanie arrived.

The bright side? I had at least a week.

I smiled to myself. I hadn't done that in a while, searching for a bright side when it had once been a habit. Looking at the man sleeping beside me in the dark, I knew why. My days with him were all light. There was nothing to search for or sort through. I was living in the bright side.

The backache persisted all night. I slept off and on, the waves of pain waking me. The following morning, the ache spread around to my front, tightening my belly.

It wasn't consistent, so I decided to keep it to myself. I knew Roman. He would cart me off to the hospital before I even got the word "contraction" out of my mouth. Fortunately, he was distracted with the task of moving my things to his house. He'd recruited his brothers to carry what they could by hand, including my beloved dining room table.

Adrian scratched the side of his head. "Rome has a table. Why are we moving yours?"

I pointed at Roman's dining set. It was fine, but it had no personality. He'd probably had a designer choose it for him while I'd fallen in love with my table and chairs. "Because this one is going to my house."

Since the decision for me to move in with Roman had been officially made last night, we hadn't decided what to do with my house. I assumed his brothers would be around even more when Beanie was here, Ben especially, and they'd need a place to sleep if they wanted, so for now, I'd keep it.

Nate rolled his shoulders. "Is there any reason you couldn't hire movers?"

Roman patted his back. "Last minute decision. If there's anything too heavy for you, I'll hire professionals."

Nate scowled. "Nothing's too heavy for me."

Another wave of pain hit me, like a band tightening around my stomach. My hand shot out, bracing on the wall as I attempted to breathe through it. This one smarted far more than the others had, and it seemed endless.

Eventually, it eased, and I could breathe again. Straightening, I looked up, gasping when I found Ben right in front of me, a deep frown on his face.

He wagged his finger in a circle near my middle. "What was that?"

I rolled my lips together and shook my head. "Nothing."

He narrowed his eyes. "It was a contraction, wasn't it?"

"Maybe." I bit my bottom lip. "Probably."

Roman whipped around, alarm widening his eyes. "You're having contractions? How long?"

"They're not consistent yet," I replied.

He stalked over to me, taking me by the shoulders. "How long, Shira?"

"My back started hurting last night—"

"Last night?" he yelped. "What are we doing here? We need to get you to the hospital."

Ben ran for the door, waving his keys over his head. "I'll get the car!"

Adrian strode for the stairs. "I'll grab the bag."

Nate glanced around the room. "Uh...is there something I can do?"

I grabbed Roman's wrists. "It's too soon. They'll just send me home."

"Then they send you home." He cupped my jaw. "I'll give you almost anything, but not this. I need Dr. Sharma to check you out, make sure you and Beanie are doing well. All right? For me?"

He sounded so sweet, but beneath it was a sharp edge of panic. I knew he would be like this, which was why I'd kept my contractions to myself. But now, he was pleading for me to make him feel comfortable, and I couldn't deny him that.

"Okay. We'll go get checked out."

He exhaled, his forehead falling to the top of my head. "Thank you, Goldie. If she sends us home, we'll stop for donuts or cookies. Whatever you want."

I laughed. "Don't think I won't take you up on that."

A horn beeped frantically outside at the same time Adrian raced down the stairs with my hospital bag.

Roman's mouth hitched. "Looks like it's time to go."

I slipped my hand in his. "Let's go then."

I had no doubt we'd be back here in an hour or two. With cookies. Lots and lots of cookies.

Chapter Forty
Roman

Shira blinked up at me from her hospital bed. I folded my arms, glaring down at her.

"Seven centimeters."

Her lashes fluttered as she gave me a wobbly smile. "So maybe my back ache had been the start of labor."

"You think?" I shoved my fingers through my hair. "I'm not equipped to deliver a baby."

Reaching for me, she snagged my hand and brought it to her lips. "We're here, honey. Beanie looks great, I feel fine in between contractions, and Dr. Sharma is just down the hall. Don't be mad at me."

"No." I dropped into the chair next to her bed and gathered her hands in mine. "No, baby, I'm not mad. I'm freaking the hell out, which I did not expect, but I'm not mad at you. You're incredible, going through labor without saying a single word. I wish I could have been rubbing your back to ease your pain all night, but that doesn't matter now."

Dr. Sharma hadn't sent us home. By the time we'd gotten checked in, Shira's contractions had been coming every few minutes. She hadn't admitted it was real labor until the doctor checked and found she was already seven centimeters dilated, though.

"Oh." Her fingers tightened around mine. "Oh, it's coming."

She sat upright, a gust of breath exploding from her. Her head fell forward, and I stood, but there was nothing I could do other than breathe with her and let her hold my hand. It didn't sit well with me, being so helpless when she was suffering, but I had to set my feelings aside. Thinking about myself right now was useless. Shira needed my focus.

After an eternity, her body relaxed, and her hold on my hand loosened. "That was intense. Wow."

I brushed her hair out of her face. "You did so well, baby. So, *so* well."

It was on the tip of my tongue to ask if she wanted me to fetch the anesthesiologist, but I bit that down. Shira wanted to try this med-free, and I'd promised to support that. Offering her pain meds wasn't part of our plan, but the second she asked for them, I'd be hitting the call button.

"Can you pull my hair back?" she asked.

"Back? Me?"

Her chin wobbled, and her eyes shimmered. "I don't feel like I can do it. My arms...I just—I can't."

"I know, I know." I kissed the top of her head and scanned the room for her bag. "I'll do it. I have to let go of you for a minute to grab a hair tie. Is that okay?"

"Please. I'm going to rip it out if it touches my shoulders for another second."

Luckily, she'd packed plenty of hair ties. The downside, I wasn't well versed in styling women's hair, and Shira had a lot of it. I sensed I didn't have much time to mess around, though, so I did my best to gently gather it high on her head and wrap a soft scrunchie around it. Once it was up, Shira released a long breath and rubbed her legs over the sheet covering them.

I touched my lips to her forehead. "Better?"

"Yes." Her legs shifted restlessly. "I think—no, I need to stand. Can you help me stand up?"

I hesitated, my gut churning. But Shira knew her body, and I wasn't about to argue. Together, we eased her to her feet, her hands clinging to the bed rail. She swayed, and I swayed with her, holding her hips until another contraction struck. I did as she asked, putting pressure on her hips and keeping quiet through it. We went on like that for a while, the breaks between her contractions becoming shorter and shorter.

There was a rhythm to it. Breathing, swaying, pressure, the steady beep indicating our son's heart was beating as it should. Time stretched and snapped around us, but we were in this bubble together, moving to the song we'd composed ourselves. My panic abated, giving way to a certainty Shira could handle this, which meant I would have to as well. For her. For our son.

We rocked, swayed, breathed, and in between, Shira asked me to kiss her neck or cheek or tell her something about rugby or a funny brother story. Impossibly, I was able to make her laugh.

"I think...I think maybe Dr. Sharma should come check me," she said after a contraction nearly knocked her over. "That felt different."

Minutes after I hit the call button, the doctor bustled in. Gloves on, she checked Shira's progress. With a warm, reassuring smile, she declared, "All right, Shira. You're fully dilated. If you're feeling the urge, I want you to push with the next contraction. Let's see what happens."

Just like that, we were here, the final stretch.

With her hands locked in mine, Shira pushed. Silent but fierce, she channeled every ounce of her strength into bringing our son into the world. The doctor's voice was a hum in the background, but my focus was on Shira—on her flushed, determined face, the sheen of sweat on her brow, the tremor in her arms.

When the doctor urged her to reach down and touch our baby's head, her lips parted in wonder.

"Oh my god." Her voice cracked with awe. "I just touched his head, Roman. I touched his hair. He has hair."

I bent down and rolled my forehead along hers, my own breath hitching. "That's amazing, baby. Soon, you're going to be able to touch all of him. He's going to be in your arms. You just have to push a little longer."

Her brow furrowed with resolve. "I can do it."

"I know you can. You're unstoppable, Goldie."

Shira pushed and pushed, even more determined now that she'd felt the promise of our boy. He was real, and he was coming.

I watched her flushed face, beautiful in the power behind it. God, she was so small, but she contained the ferocity of a lion. If I hadn't been completely in love with her before we'd walked into this room, this would have done it. There was nothing like seeing her gather her strength and use it as a weapon to fight through what I imagined was unbearable pain. And she did it with grace. Pure, beautiful grace.

"Okay, one more big push and his head will be out," Dr. Sharma announced. "Can you give me a big push, Shira?"

"Yes," she declared, her chin digging into her chest.

Holding her leg and her hand, I leaned forward, watching as my son's head magically, miraculously emerged from Shira's body.

Rivers swelled within me, climbing up my throat until I had to let out a choking sob.

"That's it." I kissed Shira's knuckles. "He's almost here. You're doing amazing, baby."

"Give me one more," the doctor said.

Shira did. She gave one more hard push, her fingers squeezing the life out of mine, and then he was out. The doctor lifted him and placed him on Shira's chest. A nurse rubbed him with a blanket while another suctioned his nose and mouth. I stood stock-still, the reality of my son being in the world striking me dumb and useless.

His angry, indignant wail rocked me out of my stupor, and everything changed. I bent down, putting my head beside Shira's to meet our son together.

"Look at him, Rome," she sobbed, running her fingertips along his back. "He's really here."

"You did that." Thick emotion coated my throat, and my vision blurred from the well of tears threatening to spill. "You brought our boy to us. He's gorgeous."

"Isn't he?" she choked out. "He's massive too."

A laugh blended with a sob broke free, and my lips fell on her wet cheek. I tasted salt from her tears and sweat. And underneath, the sweetness of her skin. She turned to me, taking her eyes off our squalling boy for a moment to kiss my lips.

"I love you so much," I murmured against her mouth.

"I love you too," she cried softly. "You can touch him, Rome. He's yours, you know."

I jerked with the realization I hadn't given myself permission to reach for him. It hadn't really hit me that he was real and actually here with us.

"He's mine," I whispered, laying my hand on his back, right below Shira's. "God, he's so warm."

It was surreal to finally touch the body I'd been feeling inside Shira's belly the last few months.

Her giggle crackled with tears. "That's exactly what I was thinking. Warm and perfect."

"So perfect," I agreed, since there was no other word for this tiny human we'd created together. No matter what he did or who he became, I'd always clutch his first moments close. My perfect boy, given to me by his magnificent mother.

I'd known it before, but it was cemented then. This woman and the family we created were my whole world. More than I'd ever thought I'd have. I would do everything in my power to be their pillar to lean on, their cushion to fall on, and the open arms for them to run into. It didn't matter if she gave me one baby or seven; my arms would be big enough for all of them.

CHAPTER FORTY-ONE
Shira

I STROKED THE SOFT curve of my son's cheek as he suckled at my breast. Dimly, I was aware my entire body was one giant ache, but the one I felt most acutely was in my chest. A sweet, unbearable pressure, as if my heart had grown too large to be contained, pressing against its bony cage.

Breathlessly in love, I surveyed his miniature features.

"I don't know who he looks like," I whispered to Roman, who was attached to my side, an anchor in the new world we'd been launched into together.

"Maybe some of both of us," he said, his voice rough with emotion. He dragged a blunt fingertip along Jonah's cheek, ending at the cleft in his chin. "This is all me, though."

Hearing his father, Jonah's mouth stilled, and he unlatched with a small, wet pop. His heavy-lidded eyes rolled around a bit before fluttering closed. Drops of colostrum dotted his pink rosebud lips. After he'd been cleaned up and examined, a nurse had brought him to me, and he'd latched on hungrily, nursing for nearly an hour. That meant Roman hadn't gotten to hold him yet.

"It's your turn." I offered Jonah to his father. "Take him, honey."

Jonah was a big baby, even bigger than predicted at nine and a half pounds and twenty-two inches, but when Roman took him and tucked him against his chest, he looked tiny.

Roman's watery eyes met mine as he grinned from ear to ear. "My boy." He rubbed his cheek against Jonah's head, covered in a blue-striped cap, and sighed the kind of sigh only a man meeting his child for the first time could make. "He feels so fucking good."

His raw, unfiltered awe knocked the breath from my lungs. Fumbling for my phone, I took a picture of the two of them together, needing to capture this moment, though I knew I'd never forget it.

Roman eased into the chair next to my bed and held Jonah in front of him, scanning his swaddled body and little round face with reverence. Then, with a low chuckle, he lifted Jonah higher and rubbed noses with him, his tears finally breaking free.

"Heeyyy, Jonah," he whispered, his voice thick and shaky.

I didn't think I could possibly cry more, but seeing Roman look at the son I'd given him with unrestrained devotion sent me over the edge. These tears were mixed with laughter though, a release of joy the likes I'd never known. Unbound by the past, happiness that was free and clear and mine. Like Terry had told me, I grasped it with both hands and claimed it as my own.

"You look good together," I managed to say around the lump in my throat.

Roman's eyes found mine again, the same adoration he'd given Jonah now aimed squarely at me. "How is this possible?"

I pressed my lips together to hold back another sob. "I don't know, but it is. He's ours, honey."

He brought Jonah to his chest again, then his head fell back against the chair, his breath hitching. "How could anyone ever walk away from this?"

"You and I will *never* understand," I vowed with conviction. Just as we would never understand how a parent could hurt their child. We didn't have that in us, and I was glad we couldn't wrap our minds around it. No matter what, Jonah would be safe with his parents.

"I love you, Roman."

He gave me a watery smile. "Love you the most, Goldie."

I took another picture of them and sent it to his brothers, Bea, and Clara, who were waiting with bated breath to hear news. Their replies were immediate—excited, overjoyed, flipping out—but they didn't ask to come to the hospital, and I loved them for that. This time was ours to adjust to becoming a family of three.

For the next twenty-four hours, Jonah rotated between sleeping, nursing, and pooping, while Roman and I drifted through an exhausted haze of love and disbelief. Our smiles were constant, goofy things that appeared without warning for no reason other than we were deliriously happy.

Sooner than I expected, but not *too* soon, we were sent home.

Ben was waiting for us when we arrived, sweeping the door open to let us in. He planted a kiss on my cheek first, then gave me a big bear hug.

Pulling back, he ruffled my hair and grinned. "You're a mom!"

I laughed, giving his solid arm a shove. "You're an uncle!"

Ben rocked back on his heels, a pleased flush rising on his cheeks. "Wow. That's right. Cool as hell, huh?"

I returned his grin. "I'm pretty happy about it."

Roman put down Jonah's car seat, and the brothers embraced, slapping each other's backs and holding on tight. Ben murmured something in Roman's ear, and Roman nodded, swiping at his watery eyes. "Hell yes, I am."

Mary swirled around my ankles, drawing my attention. "Rrreowww," she greeted.

"Hello, my little love." I was finally able to bend down to pick her up. "You have a new brother, Mary. He doesn't do much yet, but soon, he'll be your best friend."

She placed her paws on my chest, tilted her head as she examined me, then settled in. My stomach had shrunk a lot already, but there was still a perch for her to sit on for now.

Once Jonah was out of his car seat and Ben had scrubbed his hands under Roman's supervision, he let him hold his nephew. Ben stared down at the little sleeping bundle, his look of wonder echoing the ones Roman and I had been wearing since yesterday.

"Hey, buddy. It's your favorite uncle, Benny." Ben sniffed, squeezing his eyes tight. "You might get confused because your daddy and I have the same face, but here's a hint, I'm the more handsome one. Plus, I'm a lot cooler."

Roman groaned, but his smile matched mine. Ben was just the first in a long list of people who were going to love this boy simply because he was ours. How lucky was he? He would never know anything else.

Ben continued his conversation with Jonah. "But you're going to love your daddy the most anyway. Take it from me; he'll love you no matter what you do. You might make some dumb mistakes, but he's gonna have your back, little man. And your mom, don't even get me started. That woman carried you around in her body. Do you know how small she is? But she never complained because she loved you from the very start. What a great life you're going to have, pal. I can't wait to be a part of it."

Roman put his hand on his brother's shoulder. "Love you," he said gruffly.

Ben grinned at Roman then me, his eyes glassy and bright. "I thought newborns were supposed to be small. This baby feels like a brick house."

Weightless laughter floated out of me. "Well, he's a Wells boy."

"I thought maybe you'd balance his genes out." Ben shook his head, snuggling Jonah closer. "This combination of the two of you works just right, though. I like this kid a lot already, and he hasn't even bothered to open his eyes to greet me."

"We like him too," I agreed.

More Wells brothers arrived soon after, all equally enamored with their new nephew. Even Adrian, who was always so contained, shed a tear. Just one, and he wiped it away quickly, giving me a sheepish little smile when he saw me noticing.

Bea and Clara stopped by too. They didn't stay long, bringing us food, giving us both hugs and holding our son for a minute or two. Bea promised she was just a call away if we needed time off, even if it was the middle of the night, and on her way out, Clara took my hand.

"You're in the bliss stage now, but if you get the blues and need someone to talk to, I know what it's like. Don't hold it in, okay?"

I promised her I wouldn't, and I truly meant it. Clara had been my friend for years, cracking through my ice queen reputation and finding the real me. If I needed her, I would go to her, no questions asked.

Finally, we were down to the three of us again. Exhausted, we trudged upstairs. Mary wandered into our bedroom for a moment, heard Jonah crying, and took off for a quieter spot. Fortunately, Roman had bought her multiple beds. He'd claimed he didn't want her on his furniture, but we both knew he liked spoiling her. Mary had her choice of places to sleep in this house, and as long as my girl was comfortable, I didn't mind.

After nursing Jonah, Roman changed and swaddled him and carefully laid him in the bassinet beside our bed. The two of us lay together, my head on Roman's chest, his heartbeat steady under my cheek.

"Two days down," he murmured.

"A million more to go," I finished.

"Thank god. Don't think I'll ever get enough of these days."

"Even with no sleep?"

He kissed my crown and sighed. "Even then. I think we're going to have to renegotiate about seven."

I smiled into his chest. "Seven isn't happening."

His arms tightened around me. "A man can dream, can't he?"

"Why not? You've made my dreams come true, after all."

He pulled his head back, his lips ending up on my forehead. "You're saying I have a chance?"

That made me laugh. "Not seven, but probably more than two." I trailed my fingers over his collarbone. "How about you give me a little time to recover before asking me for more children?"

He paused. "What if I ask you something else?"

I yawned. "Ask away, honey. Though, I warn you, I'm seconds from nodding off, so you'll have to be quick."

"I had other plans for this, but—" From nowhere, he produced a small, navy-blue box and placed it on his chest. "The thing I want most is to have a life with you."

Heart in my throat, I propped myself up on my elbow. "Roman, I—"

He tapped my lips, his gaze soft on mine. "I will love our family no matter how big it grows, and you'll always be at the center of it—the very heart of everything. Will you marry me, Shira?"

"What? I...uh, I didn't expect this." My eyes dropped to the box. He'd clearly been planning this since before Jonah was born. "You really want to marry me?"

"Yes, I do. Never been more sure of anything." He flipped the box open, revealing an elegant sapphire surrounded by small, round diamonds. It was pretty, but right now, I only had eyes for Roman. "I love you, Shira. I think we're at the start of building something beautiful together, and the one thing that would make it better is if you would agree to be my wife."

I'd been proposed to before, but the sole commonality between these two instances was the question that was asked. The first had been for convenience and companionship—a need on both our parts. There'd been lots of love there, but not the right kind. Not the kind that made my heart skip a beat at the prospect of spending a lifetime together.

In stark contrast, neither Roman nor I *needed* to be married. The only thing we would be getting out of a marriage was a legally binding agreement. Yet, he wanted to marry me so badly, he couldn't wait for flowers or candlelight—and knowing him, that had been his original plan.

When I searched inside myself, I didn't have to go deep to find I was bubbling with excitement at the prospect of becoming Roman Wells' wife. It would be different this time. It would be real, and he was right; it would be beautiful.

"Yes!" I flung myself at him, which was a mistake given how tender I was, but I didn't let the pain stop me from wrapping my arms around his neck. "Yes, my answer is yes. I love you so much."

The ring forgotten, he wrapped me in his arms and rolled us to our sides. He ran his nose down mine and gently kissed me.

"I'm going to be a good husband, Goldie. We're going to have the best life," he promised.

"I don't doubt you at all, Rome. Look how good we already have it." I kissed him again, slow and deep, the kind of kiss that needed to happen in times like these. "By the way, what did Ben whisper to you when we first got home?"

"Ah." The corner of his mouth hitched. "My brother asked if I was going to marry you."

My breath caught in my throat. And he hadn't just said yes, but "hell yes," because he loved me and couldn't wait to marry me.

I kissed him again, harder, deeper. His fingers tangled in the sides of my hair, and he rolled his forehead along mine.

"You're happy?"

I nodded.

"Feel good?"

Another nod.

"Love me?"

"Love you."

His exhale gusted across my lips. "Ready to start down this new path with me?"'

I immediately knew he was referencing what I'd written to him long ago, back when we were little more than strangers yet connected on a level we hadn't understood.

You can walk a hundred paths in your lifetime. If this one is coming to an end, that doesn't mean it's the end of your dreams. You'll get up, walk down a new path, and find the next dream.

I was more than ready to walk this path beside Roman, Jonah in our arms, to seek our next dream together.

I answered him the only way I could.

"Hell yes, I am."

EPILOGUE
Roman

Two years later

Jonah squealed with laughter and made a run for it. Fortunately, he was in our fenced-in yard and couldn't escape, but Ben was hot on his heels.

"Come on, buddy. Don't you want to sit down, maybe for a minute?" Ben called.

That only made Jonah run faster, following the edge of the yard like it was his personal racetrack.

Shira crawled onto the bed behind me and leaned over, her chin on my shoulder, the curve of her belly pressing into my back, peering at the tablet in my hands. "Is Ben chasing Jonah again?"

"Yep."

She snickered. "Doesn't he know if he stopped chasing him, Jonah would stop running?"

"I've told him, but as much as he complains, I think my brother enjoys the chase."

It was true. Jonah was tall for his age, but Ben was an adult, not to mention a professional athlete. He could have overtaken Jonah in two steps if he'd really wanted to. Instead, he spent his days letting my son run him ragged. Ben liked it, and Jonah couldn't get enough.

Jonah loved all his uncles, but it was no surprise Uncle Benny was his favorite. They shared the same head of curls—though Jonah's were black and glossy, like his mother's—and a similar sense of humor. Jonah cackled at funny faces and fart sounds, which coincidentally stirred Ben's funny bone too.

I trusted Ben implicitly, including with my son, which was why I felt comfortable whisking my wife away on a babymoon for five nights and leaving Ben in charge—with the help of Louise, Jonah's beloved nanny. That didn't mean I could stop myself from watching the security cameras around our house. Seeing Jonah happy and not missing us made it easier to enjoy the time away,

Plus, my kid was really fucking cute.

Shira nuzzled her nose into the side of my neck. "Do you think we could press pause on the Ben and Jonah show for a while?"

Tossing the tablet aside, I shifted so I could grab her and pull her into my lap, right where I wanted her. She smelled like sunshine and chlorine from her dip in the private lap pool outside our villa, and miles of her skin were on display in the white bikini I'd bought her for this trip.

Shira wasn't a bikini girl on a normal basis, but she didn't mind wearing one when it was just the two of us, which was exactly why I'd booked this resort. Five solid days of my wife walking around in next to nothing, showing off her pregnant belly. I was feeling pretty damn good about this decision.

I spread my hand on her bump and dipped to pull her bottom lip between my teeth. "You have my full attention, baby. What are you going to do with it?"

"I was thinking of a walk on the beach, but now I'm wondering if you have a better idea."

"We can do that...later." I dragged the cup of her top sideways until her nipple popped out. "There's no way I can see you in this bikini and not need to be inside you."

"Then it's a good thing I'll only wear it on vacation. Otherwise, we'd never get anything done."

Lifting her nipple to my mouth, I swirled my tongue around the tight point. "You're damn right, baby."

It wasn't just the bikini that had me salivating over her. Shira turned me on like no other on a regular basis, but pregnant with my baby? I went hard just looking at her swollen tits and rounded belly blooming with life. Luckily for me, my insatiable desire aligned with her increased need to be fucked.

Even with a toddler at home, we managed to make time, but since we'd arrived at the resort two days ago, we'd been going at each other like rabid animals.

It wasn't hard to believe we matched in this area, given how we met. Shira still liked for me to take her without asking, to move her into positions I wanted and give her what I thought she needed. Knowing and loving each other on a soul-deep level hadn't changed the fire between us. What had changed was my wife now being able to voice her desires. She told me when she wanted to play, and if she wanted to try something different, she wasn't shy about communicating that.

I loved that I got that part of her. Shira would always be reserved and nervous in social settings, but my steadfast love for her had gotten her to a place of comfort with me. She knew she was safe, adored, and important.

That meant Shira had become free with her voice, confident enough to tell me she loved me for no reason other than she did. She asked me questions about my work and was transparent in her admiration for my accomplishments. Over time, I'd stopped waiting for her to tire of me and leave. There wasn't another shoe waiting to drop. We were for life.

Before we went to dinner, we video-called Jonah and Ben. Jonah was only two, but he was adding to his vocabulary every day. He'd spent the last few minutes showing his mom and me each of his toys and naming them.

Shira was rapt, encouraging him to continue, praising him each time he put a toy in front of the screen. I knew my wife, and she meant it. She thought every little thing Jonah did was amazing, and she always let him know.

"What's that one called?" she asked.

Jonah's brow furrowed as he considered the stuffed animal in his clutches. "That's a effant!"

"That's right," she cooed. "It's an elephant. What's an elephant say?"

Jonah turned his arm into a trunk and trumpeted for his mother and me before running off to gather more toys.

Ben's face filled the screen. "Your kid is a maniac. He's going to bed at seven—I'll be going to bed at seven oh five."

Shira snorted a laugh. "Considering you live next door and we see you almost every day, I'm pretty certain you were well aware of what a busy bee he is, yet you volunteered to watch him anyway."

We'd never sold Shira's house after she moved in with me, and Ben had started spending more and more nights there. Eventually, he'd moved all his things there and hadn't left. I was lucky to have a wife who understood my bond with my twin, and luckier still that Ben could read the room for the most part and gave us privacy when we needed it. He might not live next door to us forever, but for now, it worked well for all of us.

Ben palmed the top of Jonah's head when he returned and flashed us a wide grin. "Did I say I didn't like it? As a maniac myself, we get along swimmingly."

We talked for a few more minutes until Jonah waved, said, "Bye-bye," then scampered away. He liked us well enough, but when Uncle Benny was around, he was happy as a clam.

After the call, we strolled through the resort toward our dinner location by the beach. A Caribbean breeze lifted Shira's hair, strands floating around her face and neck. I brought our joined hands to my mouth and kissed the back of hers.

"How does this babymoon compare to your first?" I asked her.

"Two very different experiences, honey. Having a girls' weekend was what my soul needed then. Having time alone with you is exactly what I need now. No phones, no work, no brothers popping in. This is perfect, don't you think?"

"I do think." I brushed her shoulder with my arm. "Do the brothers pop in too often?"

"No. I would have told you if it was too much. I love that we have a family that pops in. I never thought I'd have that. It's kind of the best."

"They're going to be all over us when Ruby's here."

Shira laughed, her hand moving to rest on her belly. "I can't believe how mystified all four of you are that there's going to be a girl Wells."

"What can I tell you? We were convinced we only produce boys. I don't know what to do with a little girl."

I hadn't believed the blood test telling us Shira was carrying a girl. Then, weeks later, I'd asked the ultrasound tech to triple-check. When she showed us the girl parts, I finally accepted.

It wasn't that I didn't want a little girl; it had just taken some time to wrap my head around it since I'd been expecting a brood of boys. Now, I couldn't wait to see what being a girl dad was all about.

Since Shira said we had a theme, we'd chosen the name Ruby, after the New Zealand rugby player Ruby Tui. Whether my girl liked rugby or not, it was a pretty name from a strong namesake.

"I have a feeling you'll do much the same as you do with a little boy—chase her around the yard, make her laugh, listen to everything she has to say." Shira's fingers squeezed mine. "You can do it."

"You're with me, I can do anything."

I believed that deep down in my gut. We made each other better, stronger, and we damn sure made each other happier. So long as we stuck, we'd have all we needed.

We already had so much. One wild little boy. Soon, a little girl. Close bonds with my brothers. Strong ties to our friends, who were essentially family now. Countless memories and healing wounds we'd previously given up trying to fix. We'd built a life together with intention, the kind made brick by brick to withstand any storm that came our way.

We had given each other more than we'd ever hoped for.

All because a lost boy had written a letter, and a girl with a heart a hard life couldn't break had taken the time to write him back. She'd told me way back then I'd have a beautiful life—and she couldn't have been more right.

Stay In Touch

Author's Note

Shira came to me in a little throw away scene in Sincerely, Your Inconvenient wife. Luca told Saoirse that Frank Goldman's wife was a cold fish. Once the idea of a misunderstood society wife was planted in my mind, I couldn't let it go. Sweet, shy Shira needed a true happily ever after!

Shira will always be shy and uncomfortable in new situations. Her beauty will always whisper. But she is understood and loved for exactly who she is. Isn't that the happy ending we all want?

Okay, that's definitely what I want!

I have to thank my beautiful author friends for being a steadfast sounding board and source of support. I always feel understood and loved with you guys.

My PA, Amber, basically reads my mind. Never leave me, okay?

My cover designer, Kate, isn't allowed to leave me either!

Actually, none of you are. Stay right there, buddy. You're in this with me for the long haul.

About Julia

Julia Wolf is a bestselling contemporary romance author. She writes bad boys with big hearts and strong, independent heroines. Julia enjoys reading romance just as much as she loves writing it. Whether reading or writing, she likes the emotions to run high and the heat to be scorching.

Julia lives in Maryland with her three crazy, beautiful kids and her patient husband who she's slowly converting to a romance reader, one book at a time.

Visit my website:
http://www.juliawolfwrites.com